The author was born in Scotland, and after serving in the Army, embarked on a career in industry.

He has worked in several different sectors in senior roles and was latterly CEO of a large international data capture company.

He retired for the first time in 1995 to take on a consultancy designed to help new businesses become established.

In 2018, he finally retired from business life to become a full-time author.

John lives in Scotland and Portugal with his wife, and they have two grown-up sons.

The Revenge

John Reid

The Revenge

Vanguard Press

VANGUARD PAPERBACK

© Copyright 2023
John Reid

The right of John Reid to be identified as author of
this work has been asserted by him in accordance with the
Copyright, Designs and Patents Act 1988.

All Rights Reserved

No reproduction, copy or transmission of this publication
may be made without written permission.
No paragraph of this publication may be reproduced,
copied or transmitted save with the written permission of the publisher, or in
accordance with the provisions
of the Copyright Act 1956 (as amended).

Any person who commits any unauthorised act in relation to
this publication may be liable to criminal
prosecution and civil claims for damages.

A CIP catalogue record for this title is
available from the British Library.

ISBN 978 1 80016 905 0

This is a work of fiction. Names, characters, businesses, places, events and incidents are
either the product of the author's imagination or used in a fictitious manner. Any
resemblance to actual persons, living or dead, or actual events is purely coincidental

*Vanguard Pres
s is an imprint of*
Pegasus Elliot Mackenzie Publishers Ltd.
www.pegasuspublishers.com

First Published in 2023

**Vanguard Press
Sheraton House Castle Park
Cambridge England**

Printed & Bound in Great Britain

To my dear friend, Bert Harvey, who celebrated his one hundredth birthday on the 5th October 2022.

To my wife for her ongoing and constant support. To Kaya Consulting for their innovative and sometimes unusual marketing proposals and my friend, Jimbo, who is also a source of encouragement and amusement.

Chapter One

Charles Robb sat in his prison cell, dressed in his own clothes. Unsurprisingly, they didn't fit as well as they had before he started his sixteen-year prison sentence for fraud, corruption and money laundering. He smiled as he thought of the little man in Savile Row who had fussed over every stitch in an effort to produce the perfectly fitted suit. If only he could see his work now.

Robb had served just under eight years of his sixteen-year sentence and was being paroled due to his status as a well-behaved prisoner. He'd been a model prisoner, and apart from a few run-ins with one or two of his fellow guests, his time behind bars hadn't been too bad. He had had time to think, especially about the people who had put him here.

He remembered the false promises, the easy words telling him not to worry, his so-called friends leaving him take the fall so they could carry on with their comfortable lives. He had tried to tell everyone he wasn't guilty, that he knew who was responsible for the deaths of his wife and son. He hadn't realised that easy money and easy friendships came with dangerous and frightening consequences and ruthless people.

Charlie Robb had spent the last seven years plotting revenge on the people who had ruined his life; the people who were responsible for the murder of his family. The one thing that had kept him going and kept him sane was the thought of revenge.

A prison warder opened Charlie's cell door. "Right my lad, let's go, time to see the governor." The prisoner and prison warder walked amiably together up and over the various metal walkways before exiting 'B' wing to the rear and taking the well-manicured path that led to the administration building and the office of the governor.

While Charles Robb waited in the outer office he looked at himself in the full-length mirror on the far wall. What looked back at him was, to his mind, a shadow of the man he would have seen seven years and four months ago. He was still just under six foot tall and still had a full head of salt and pepper hair. His once beautifully fitted suit looked to be at least one size too big, perhaps two. His white shirt was too large; he noted the gap between the collar and his neck had grown and now he could place his fingers in it. Overall, Charlie thought he looked OK, but only just.

He was called into the governor's office and subjected to what he guessed was the usual speech given to all prisoners. The governor, who appeared to be a kindly man, delivered his well-rehearsed words with a boredom that told Charlie everything. The dos and don'ts of the outside world, keep only good company, do not mix with known ex-offenders and most importantly, keep all appointments with the probation service.

The governor took eight minutes to deliver his prose after which prisoner Robb was free to go. Charlie collected the brown paper parcel containing his worldly wealth from the security hut beside the main entrance, signed out as prisoner C. Robb and left HMP Whitby behind him. Now Charlie Robb was free to live his life, but it wouldn't be the life he had known, but a life that had only one goal. REVENGE.

Chapter Two

Charlie took the bus from outside the prison gates, known as 'the Ferry', because it ferried ex-prisoners away from prison. Arriving convicts came in a different form of transport. The bus journey to Whitby railway station took twenty minutes.

Charlie was surprised by how euphoric he felt at being able to look at the passing scenery, and how much he had missed the sight of open fields and trees. There were four other passengers on the bus all of whom had just been released.

At the station the London train was running late. He visited the station café and ordered a coffee. Sitting by the window he took out the envelope he'd been given by the governor. In it was fifty pounds in five-pound notes, the address of the halfway house he was to live at for the next six months as part of his parole conditions, a railway warrant to cover his train fare to London and an address and phone number for his parole officer. The note told him he was expected at his parole officer's office at eleven a.m. on Monday. The distorted voice of the station tannoy announced that the London train was arriving at platform one. Charlie finished his cold coffee and made his way to the train.

Sitting in his window seat, he looked out at the rapidly passing countryside. The effect of the blurred images had a soothing effect, and he closed his eyes. He wondered why prisoners were released on Saturday mornings. The motion of the train lulled him into a dream-like state. In his mind he could see his wife Joan and their son Trevor as they were on a summer's day nine years ago, her blonde hair moving over her face as she pushed Trevor on a swing. Trevor had been four- years old and was as bright as a button. Charlie had been doing well as a financial advisor and was earning enough to have purchased a large house in Henley. The family had only been in the house for three months, but it was already perfect. Joan had had an easy commute to her London office and Trevor had made friends with a neighbour's son who was the same age. Both boys were set to start at the same school and were already firm friends. Charlie had set up his home office and had attracted new clients. His business was busy and successful.

As the train rocked and swayed Charlie was aware of someone gently shaking him awake. It was the ticket collector. He saw the brown paper parcel on Charlie's lap and knew he was an HMP Whitby old boy. Charlie handed over his travel warrant to be told by the collector he should have exchanged the paper for a real ticket at the station. "Don't worry, sir, this happens all the time with your lot."

The collector produced a ticket and explained to Charlie it was good for use on the underground in London. As the ticket collector moved on, Charlie sat staring out of the window. This small incident alerted him to his new status. He was an ex-convict on parole. Even in the eight years or so he had been behind bars the world had moved on. He knew he would have to adjust.

When the train arrived in London Charlie navigated his way to his accommodation. It was an old Victorian terrace building in Stratford. It looked rundown and unwelcoming from the outside. As Charlie pushed the dark green painted door, he realised the inside was even worse than the outside. He stood, taking in the dilapidated appearance of his new home, when a scruffy individual appeared from one of the several doors that led off the inner hall.

"You, Robb?"

Charlie was immediately intimidated by this large unkept man with his dirty vest and large beer belly. He stood as tall as Charlie at just under six foot tall, but he was at least fifty pounds heavier than Charlie, although the extra weight was all around his middle.

"Yes, I'm Robb."

"You're late. New residents is supposed to be here before one." The voice was rough from smoking too many cigarettes and was definitely uncultured. He obviously hadn't shaved in a few days and his breath was foul. "I'm Mr Collins, the superintendent here. You're in room twelve on the first floor. There's a notice on the back of the door giving you the rules and regulations. If you have any questions, don't ask, just get on with things. I don't like being disturbed." Mr Collins handed Charlie a large key that had a paper tab attached to it by string. The tab said 'twelve'. Without another word, Mr Collins returned to his room leaving Charlie standing in the middle of his new and downmarket world.

Room twelve wasn't a disappointment, but it was worse than Charlie expected based on the evidence of the building and Mr Collins. There was an old bed with some fresh linen and a couple of folded blankets. A cracked sink stood in one corner and a free-standing brown wooden wardrobe with a mirror built into the door stood against the far wall. The floor was covered in a threadbare carpet that seemed to hold Charlie's shoes to it. There was a smell of cats although Charlie noted the rules of the establishment pinned to the back of the door said, 'NO PETS'.

Charlie sat on the bed that seemed to sag as he put his weight on the old springs, looking around his room for a few minutes. He pulled himself together and unwrapped his parcel. It contained the few items he'd been allowed to keep in prison. He stood up and lifted a blue shirt from the parcel, a sponge bag that contained his washing items, two pairs of boxer shorts and two pairs of socks. He put his haul of clothes inside the wardrobe and his sponge bag beside the sink. He looked at his watch. It was 4.15 p.m. on Saturday. Charlie sat down on the bed thinking this wasn't how he planned to live, but it would do for now.

Prison had been an eye-opener for Charlie. He'd started his sentence with fear and trepidation but soon realised most inmates were scared at first, even the career criminals. He'd met most types and had received an education. He knew where to get guns, drugs and criminal associates should he need them. One convict had even explained how to crack a safe and where to fence stolen property, and where and how to obtain documents to create a new life with a false identity. Charlie had no intention of pursuing a life of crime and once he'd used his newly acquired contacts to help with his revenge, he would leave the country and settle somewhere warm. He intended to become a mass murderer and serial killer as himself, but then he would become a law-abiding citizen with his new identity. He removed his jacket and stretched out on his uncomfortable bed, intending to plan his next step, but after only a few seconds he fell asleep.

***

Major Simon Havers was seated at his desk in his headquarters. Its front was an upholstery repair business on Brompton Road. It wasn't normal for the major to work at the weekend, but he'd had an urgent assignment handed to him by a secret government committee. He'd read the document over several times and was unhappy with its contents. The major was responsible for a clandestine group that operated below the radar and undertook work that could never be admitted to by the government. It was two years since the major's group had been formed and their record of success was one hundred percent. Simon Havers was proud of his record.

His operation had been started from nothing, the first step being the recruitment of technicians, trainers and operatives. He'd established a training school in Scotland and the headquarters he was sitting in this Saturday afternoon. The calendar on the wall showed it was Saturday February 5. The headquarters also acted as a research and development function and supplied his agents with any ordinance they might require to complete their tasks.

He once more studied the brief he had been given. It appeared an RAF test pilot was thought to be on the verge of trying to steal the latest vertical take-off jet, classed as highly secret, and fly it to a foreign power. The brief said that under no circumstances could the jet be allowed to fall into unfriendly hands. The pilot in question had recently appeared on television and was becoming a regular on talk shows. He was a bit of a star with a large social media following. The Ministry of Defence were happy to have this poster test pilot in the public eye. They thought it made for good publicity.

However, the brief explained that as this pilot had become more famous for his media work, a civil servant at the MOD decided to do a deeper background check on him and discovered he had political leanings towards North Korea. Despite his highly skilled and classified job he'd only been vetted by the security services up to level three. His Korean ancestry wasn't originally considered significant, but this new check rang alarm bells.

The brief on the major's desk was unusual. He normally received specific and non-ambiguous instructions. However, this time he had been instructed to discover the test pilot's intentions, and at his sole discretion, was to decide on a course of action that would protect the good name of the RAF, save the government any potential embarrassment, and ensure the new aircraft remained safe. He was instructed to eliminate the test pilot if, in his opinion, the rumours of his impending treachery were true. He was to arrange for Squadron Leader Max Ho to disappear.

Major Simon Havers needed help. His brief called for swift action especially if the squadron leader were assessed as a risk. He knew that swift action meant he had less than forty-eight hours to come up with a plan. For the first time since his unit had been established, he broke protocol and lifted his phone. He knew where to get help.

***

Charlie Robb had spent some of his fifty pounds allowance on a burger and a pint of beer at a local and not very inviting pub. Sunday morning saw him up and dressed by nine. During his fitful sleep he had started to plot and try to formulate a plan for his revenge. He told himself to take things slowly, and he intended to leave the biggest offender to the end.

With a heavy sigh he thought back to how he and his family had been living in their dream house in Henley, and how good things had been. They had been happy and Charlie was building a successful business. Then, one day Charlie received a phone call from a financial adviser called Geoffrey Lockwood. Lockwood told Charlie he'd heard good reports about him, and he had several high-net-worth clients who were keen to use Charlie's services. Charlie was delighted and Geoffrey Lockwood sounded a straight-up guy on the phone. They arranged to meet the following week in town.

"Come to my office, Charles, we're in the Shard building, sixth floor. See you Monday at eleven. We'll get things cracking and go to lunch." And so it all started. Charles Robb and Geoffrey Lockwood became friends, colleagues and unofficial partners.

On this dull Sunday morning in February Charlie decided to familiarise himself with his old stamping grounds. He was happy to leave the sordid environment of his room behind and get out in the fresh air. With funds limited he took several buses to arrive in Henley at 11.15 a.m. He alighted at the main bus station, and picking up his bearings, walked the three miles to his old house. As he approached it, he wondered who was living in it now, and if any of his old neighbours would recognise him.

He walked down the tree-lined avenue, realising he was over-dressed, still wearing his eight-year-old Savile Row suit that appeared to be hanging from him. Charlie smiled to himself. If any of his old neighbours did see him, they wouldn't recognise him.

There was a convenient bench on the grass verge separating the road from the pavement with a plaque on the back in memory of someone's dog that had been run down by a car. From this bench, Charlie had a decent view of his old house. The red brick still looked sharp, and the paintwork looked fresh. There was a Porsche 911 sitting outside the double garage. The new owners obviously had children as there was a pink bike sitting beside the car and a two-wheeled scooter abandoned just inside the drive.

A tear appeared in Charlie's eyes as he thought what might have been. If he hadn't trusted Geoffrey Lockwood nor his so-called clients; if he hadn't become carried away with the easy money; or if he'd stuck to his principles and walked away sooner. He wondered what Joan would have looked like now and if Trevor would have gone to the grammar school.

Self-pity wasn't part of Charlie's make up, but he couldn't help thinking what might have been. He recalled the night he'd returned home to find Joan and Trevor dead on the living room floor. They'd been shot. He had been frantic, out of his mind with shock and wondering who could have killed them. The police hadn't been much help and even now the case was open and unsolved.

Charlie sat in the cold, watching the property and scanning the neighbourhood. It was as he remembered it, suburbia, well-maintained houses and gardens belonging to middle-class people who only wanted to be left in peace to pursue their ordinary and successful lives. Charlie walked back to the bus depot. The idyllic life he'd planned all those years ago would never again be for him. He'd decided on another path that would make living in this street impossible.

***

Major Havers knew he would have to think carefully about which operative he would assign to this new case. He was back in his office on Brompton Road on Sunday having spent most of Saturday night going through the files of his now large number of operatives. Each had their own skill set but this was a difficult task.

He opened a file marked Eric Stokes and saw a photograph of a reasonably handsome man he knew was forty-six years old. It described him as above average intelligence and someone who used his initiative. He had successfully carried out nine assignments however it was recorded that on several occasions he had deviated from the agreed plan. Eric Stokes was clever and resourceful, got the job done but had a tendency to ignore orders.

Eric had been the third recruit onto his team of agents and had proven to be the best. Now known as Dominic Barns, he hadn't had an assignment for a few weeks. With a flourish, the major closed the file. He'd chosen his man. Dominic Barns would settle any scores with Squadron Leader Max Ho.

***

Charlie Robb, having walked the three miles back into Henley, decided to have a pub lunch. He knew The Four Feathers served a decent Sunday lunch. He and Joan had often gone there as a treat and enjoyed their traditional roast beef and Yorkshire pudding. Charlie found a table beside the fireplace and ordered the full works, just as Major Havers was deciding to give his assignment to Dominic Barns.

It was 2.43 p.m. by the time he had finished, and the place was emptying out. The fire that had been roaring was dying down and sitting in his comfortable chair still enjoying the heat from the fire, Charlie's mind drifted back to the second of his targets — Sebastian De Roy.

Charlie had met Sebastian, who preferred to be called Seb, about a week after his first meeting with Geoffrey Lockwood. Sebastian was an old Etonian and said he was an investor. The meeting took place in Geoffrey Lockwood's offices. Seb told Charlie he'd heard good things about him and looked forward to working with him.

As Charlie reminisced, he recalled he had taken an instant dislike to Seb. He seemed too smooth and slightly arrogant. He said he was investing his family's money and expected exceptional returns. Despite Charlie explaining his role as an intermediary, Seb insisted he would only invest if Charlie became more hands on. The sum of five million pounds was mentioned. Charlie now realised it was this sum that turned his head. He had agreed with Sebastian that he would do as he had requested. This was Charlie's first mistake and one he now regretted.

Charlie left The Four Feathers and headed for the bus station and his long journey back to his Stratford halfway house. He told himself tomorrow he'd start to put his temporary life back in order. He had a mission and four people to kill.

Chapter Three

Monday, February 7 started dark and grey. There was rain on its way and as Detective Chief Inspector Steve Burt walked to his office in New Scotland Yard he wondered if he should have taken his car. He arrived at his office at 8.40 a.m. to find Detective Inspector Matt Conway at his desk, drinking coffee and reading a crime report.

"You're early, Matt, couldn't sleep?"

"No problem with sleeping but my neighbour has just taken in a stray dog and the bloody thing barks from about three in the morning." He smiled at his senior officer. "I got you a coffee. It's on your desk."

"Thanks. Anything come in over the weekend?"

"Nothing for us. It's all very quiet. I'm just wrapping up the smash and grab jewellery raid case. Bob is doing a good job of tidying up the other stuff; you know, reports for the CPS, etc. How long do you think we'll keep him?"

Matt was referring to the other staff member of Steve's Special Resolutions Unit. Detective Constable Robert Class had been transferred to Steve as his administration assistant. Robert was a graduate entry and was expected to be moved on as part of his training. He had been with Steve longer than he would have expected and no one would be surprised when he was transferred. "Who knows? You know how graduate entry works, always onwards and upwards." Steve gave a shrug and entered his inner office.

There was the usual mountain of paperwork that the DCI did his best to avoid. He scanned most of it and placed the majority in his pending tray. He saw a folded note from his boss, Commander Perry Hargreaves. Steve stared at the note remembering Perry's predecessor, Commander Daphne Bloom.

Daphne Bloom had tried to have Steve's unit disbanded because it didn't fit into any organisational chart that she could understand. With help from other senior officers, Steve had successfully foiled the commander's plans. Luckily, she wasn't well regarded and had been transferred out over a year ago. Perry Hargreaves had been appointed to replace her and had immediately reinstated Special Resolutions to its former status.

Steve unfolded the note. It simply said to be in Perry's office at ten a.m. Steve started to deal with the other items that looked more urgent when Bob knocked on the door frame of his open office door.

"Got a minute, sir?"

He waved his admin assistant in and indicated he should take a seat. Bob was still young looking although Steve knew he was twenty-seven and older than most graduate entrants. He was, as usual, dressed in jeans, shirt and round neck sweater. "I've just been up to personnel. They wanted to discuss my next posting."

Bob looked sheepish as he gave a shy smile. "They suggested a spell in uniform on general duties would help my career." Bob paused for effect. "Thing is, sir, I told them to stuff it. I hope you don't mind but I said I'd rather stay where I am for another year."

Steve sat up. "It's your career, Bob. I'll happily sign you on for another year. You're a good fit for the unit and after losing Poppy last year you've become invaluable."

An obviously embarrassed Robert Class stood up and shyly thanked the DCI. As he was leaving, he turned to Steve. "Any word on a replacement for Poppy?"

"No. To be honest, Bob, I don't think anyone could replace Poppy. We do have a vacancy, but I haven't pushed personnel to fill the post. I'm not sure we're ready."

"Yeah, I know what you mean, sir. It's been a bit quiet since we lost her. Maybe a juicy case will lift our spirits instead of all this routine stuff we've been getting."

Steve smiled and shrugged; he knew Bob was right. Special Resolutions had been set up to solve cases other department heads couldn't solve. It was unique within New Scotland Yard. Steve could take cases from any department and second officers to his unit as he needed them. His core of permanent Special Resources officers had never exceeded four including himself. Over the years Steve's unit had solved some of the most baffling cases the Met had ever handled. Some senior officers saw Special Resolutions as a dumping ground for cases they didn't want. Each case they had taken on had been solved. Steve was proud of his team.

The reference to Poppy took Steve back to a previous case. Detective Constable Amelia Cooper, known as Poppy, had been Steve's admin assistant before Steve had pulled a few strings to have her appointed to frontline duties in his team. Steve sat back still feeling guilty over her death. She had been killed in the line of duty trying to save two criminals. The case centred on a secret technology that was being stolen. Poppy had been convinced she knew who was involved but Steve had dismissed her views. He constantly told himself that if he'd listened to her, she might still be alive. He knew he was being hard on himself, but he carried the guilt. He also wondered who had been the mysterious hooded man who almost saved Poppy. The after-incident report of Poppy's killing told of a masked gunman who had shot Poppy's killer a few milliseconds after Poppy's death. He'd never been identified but the DCI was still trying to find this man.

Steve arrived at Commander Hargreaves office for his ten a.m. appointment. Sally, the commander's secretary told him to go straight in. Seated at his conference table Perry Hargreaves was talking to a man in army uniform. Steve noted he was a lieutenant colonel in army intelligence.

"Ah, Steve. Come in and meet Colonel Richard Walters." Perry Hargreaves using his arm, gestured to the army officer. Steve noticed the lieutenant colonel was fairly small at only around five foot eight inches tall. His lack of medal ribbons indicated his career had been spent commanding a desk. As he shook hands Steve felt the officer's grip was vice-like and his eyes were very penetrating.

As the three men sat, Sally arrived with coffee and biscuits. Steve drank his coffee and smiled inwardly as he compared Colonel Walters to Commander Hargreaves. Both men were probably in their early fifties, but the army man looked older. The policeman looked younger and fitter.

"Now Steve, Richard has approached us with a problem. I've explained you are one of the few officers who have been thoroughly vetted by the security services and you have signed the Official Secrets

Act. What you are going to be told must remain secret. I know I don't have to say it but to be certain, nothing must leave this room."

Steve liked Perry Hargreaves. He was a no-nonsense policeman whose only goal was to catch and lock up bad people. Steve acknowledged he understood as he helped himself to another ginger snap.

Richard Walters' accent wasn't easily identifiable, but the DCI thought he may have originated from the northeast, possibly Newcastle.

"May I call you Steve?"

"Please do, sir."

"Steve, we have a slight problem concerning a possible spy and a highly secret aircraft." The lieutenant colonel reached down and withdrew a file from his briefcase. "The main test pilot on the development programme is an officer called Squadron Leader Max Ho. As you might expect from his name, his origins are in the far east, North Korea to be exact. He came to this country as a five-year old child, did well at school, his family became citizens and Max joined the air force more or less straight from school. He showed great promise as a single seat jet pilot and was rated well above average."

The colonel paused and sipped his coffee. He looked directly at Steve. "I'm telling you this as background for what's to come. He was so good he was sent to the USA test pilot school where he graduated top of his intake. Naturally when our new VTOL jet was in development, Max was the obvious person to lead the test flying programme. He had been vetted as all military personnel are up to level three. During his career there had never been any suggestions that he was not totally loyal."

The colonel paused to allow Steve to absorb what he was hearing. Satisfied his narrative was making sense, Richard Walters carried on. "One of the mandarins at the MOD took it upon himself to bring Max's security clearance up to level one. After all, he was privy to highly classified secret information. MI6 and MI5 together with military intelligence took on the task and discovered he had links to a group of North Korean supporters based here in London. He was followed a few times and it seems he meets this group regularly. Background checks on members of the group show they are a bunch of fanatics, supporting the North Korean government. If they were only sounding off, we'd not be too concerned, but given Max Ho seems to be part of their group, you can imagine we are now very concerned."

Steve had listened to the colonel's story so far. "I hear what you say, sir, but I'm not sure where we fit in?"

"I'm coming to that, Steve. You see Max Ho has become something of a celebrity here in the UK. You may have seen him on some of those quiz shows or being interviewed on BBC News about something or other. At first the authorities thought it was a good idea to have a dashing fighter pilot out there promoting the military, especially given his ethnic background. It was thought to be good for recruitment." The colonel looked between the commander and Steve. "Now the difficult bit and the answer to your question."

Richard Walters paused to draw breath before sighing and continuing. "I received a phone call from an old army acquaintance of mine, Major Simon Havers. We were at Sandhurst together and have kept in touch over the years. He is heading up an unofficial unit sponsored by the government to undertake tasks the government need doing but cannot be seen to be involved in."

Steve sat up and leant forward. "You mean like an unofficial police force?"

"Not exactly. There are things going on all the time that the government don't want in the public domain. Simon's unit takes care of embarrassing problems. He makes them go away."

The colonel was for the first time looking embarrassed. Steve asked, "What do you mean he makes problems go away?"

"He has the scope to undertake any actions he sees fit if it is deemed to be in the national interest. In short he has people who are an embarrassment to the government eliminated."

Steve had heard rumours of such a clandestine operation, but never expected to find himself face to face with it. "OK, colonel, forgetting for one minute the legality of this, where do we come in?"

"When we learnt of Max Ho's politics someone in the Ministry of Defence panicked. A secret committee was called together, and a brief was sent to Simon Havers to investigate the squadron leader. The brief instructed him to take all steps to protect the project, meaning the aircraft, and do whatever he saw fit to avoid a government scandal.

Someone thinks that Max Ho is preparing to steal the aircraft and fly it to North Korea and our boffins say it is possible. The jet flies at three times the speed of sound and is completely invisible to radar. If Ho did steal it the chances are he'd get away with it and a rogue state would have access to western aviation technology."

"Yes, OK. So, a top-secret plane may or may not about to be stolen. But why us?" Steve couldn't see why he was being given this information.

"As I said Simon phoned me. He asked if I could get police surveillance on Max Ho. He wanted to know if you could gather evidence of Max's treachery before he authorised his assassination. Obviously, I was not to divulge Simon's identity or purpose, just ask for the surveillance."

"What!" Steve stood up not believing what he was hearing. "Are you serious? You are asking the Metropolitan police to investigate a man in order he can be killed? With the greatest of respect, colonel — you're mad."

Commander Hargreaves placed a hand on Steve's sleeve and asked him to sit down. The DCI did but his blood pressure was up. Perry Hargreaves took a more conciliatory tone. "Richard, based on what you've told us, I'm surprised you're here just because an old acquaintance asked you to help in an illegal enterprise."

The colonel sat back and stared at the DCI while answering the commander's question. "You're right, Perry, but you see I hadn't any input into the decision to activate Havers' unit. He phoned me out of the blue. Of course, I knew such units existed but had no idea Simon Havers was involved. When he asked for my help, I tried to have his orders cancelled. Unfortunately, a secret committee issues such notices and protocol states once issued they cannot be cancelled."

Continuing to look at Steve, the colonel said in a deferential tone, "I don't want you to help him, Steve, I want you to stop him. These units only do one thing and that means terminating targets. I saw his brief this morning and Simon doesn't have the manpower to carry out such a surveillance. He's supposed to verify and quantify the risk posed by Max Ho and take action but with a lack of resource he'll never have time to prove Ho is innocent. Max Ho is as good as dead unless you can show Simon Havers Max Ho is no threat."

The three men sat in silence before Commander Hargreaves spoke. "You're telling us this Havers fellow is instructed to get evidence of Max Ho's guilt and if he's satisfied the pilot is guilty, he has been ordered to kill him?"

"Yes, but as I said he doesn't have the number of people nor the correct skills. That's why he called me and asked for the police to keep Ho under surveillance. If I go back and say you won't help, then I'm sure he'll have Max Ho killed even if he's innocent. In the espionage business if you kill first, you can't be wrong."

Steve was still puzzling things out. "What if I went and arrested your major now?"

"Nothing. He's an unaccountable asset. If he talked someone would take him out before he went to trial and another group would be given the job of taking care of Max Ho. Believe me, Steve, if you can prove Max Ho is innocent, I'll make sure he lives. If you prove he's guilty, you'll be doing your country a great service and Major Havers will save the country a heap of embarrassment and a fortune on a spy trial."

Once more the three men sat in silence considering the colonel's last statement. Eventually Perry Hargreaves stood up. "Richard, you've given us a lot to think about. Can you leave that file with us?" Perry was pointing to the file the colonel had brought. "Give us the rest of the day to think things through. I'll call you later."

Lieutenant Colonel Richard Walters stood and shook hands with Perry and Steve. Before walking towards the door of Perry's office he turned to face the policemen. "Technically, I'm in breach of the Official Secrets Act. You could arrest me for what I have just disclosed. We all have to do things and live with their consequences. I'm asking you to help me and do something you don't agree with but is for the national good."

Once the colonel had gone, Perry Hargreaves resumed his seat. Both policemen sat in silence. Each man lost in his own thoughts. "What do you think, sir?" Steve was in a state of mild shock.

"He's got some nerve; I'll give him that. But look, Steve, I'm thinking we have to assist him. I don't like the cloak and dagger stuff any more than you do. If this Max Ho is guilty, we should prove it and get him off the street before the murder squad moves in on him. If, as the colonel says, we can't stop it then at least we'll know a guilty man has been taken out."

Perry Hargreaves stood once more and paced his office. As he paced, Steve sat in silence. Perry spoke once more.

"Let's look at this, Steve. Richard Walters is correct when he says we have the surveillance skills and the manpower this Major Havers doesn't have. If we prove Ho is innocent, then this hit squad run by the major will take no action."

It was obvious to the DCI that his boss had arrived at a decision. "Let's give the colonel what he wants. You haven't much on just now so you can work on it. Let me know what extra resources you need. Take the file and keep me posted. I'll talk with Colonel Walters and ask him to hold back on any action against Ho until you give your report. Remember he told us Ho isn't flying, and they've grounded the aircraft for supposed additional maintenance, so we have time."

Steve stood up, lifted the file and shook his head. He was clearly unhappy with his assignment. "OK, sir, I'll get on to it."

The DCI left to brief his team. As he was leaving Perry Hargreaves called to him. "Oh, by the way, Steve, I've filled your vacancy for a permanent member of staff. I know you're reluctant to replace DC Cooper, but time moves on. His name is Detective Sergeant Simon Griffiths. He's come over from one of the outlying stations that have been closed. He's an experienced officer so it'll be a change for you not to have to break someone in, and who isn't a graduate entrant." Perry gave a soft smile. "Take him under your wing. Things will be a bit strange for him at first. He'll be with you this afternoon. Personnel have sent you his file."

Steve knew Poppy had to be replaced and thought now was as good a time although it didn't sit comfortably with him.

Chapter Four

As Steve was leaving Commander Hargreaves office, Charlie Robb was entering the Probation Service offices located in Hackney. It had taken Charlie over an hour by public transport to journey from his accommodation in Stratford to these offices. When he entered, he was greeted by a small, crowded waiting room full of odd-looking characters. Charlie counted eight people waiting. He knew it was easy to stereotype these obviously ex-cons, but considering his own situation, he found he had sympathy for most of these rough-looking individuals.

There was a window built into a partition that separated the office from the waiting room. Within the window was a sliding glass panel that was opaque and reinforced with thin wire. A small shelf protruded into the waiting room and Charlie noticed an electric bell on top of the shelf. Charlie walked to the window and pressed the bell.

He waited a few minutes and pressed it again. This got an almost instant response. An elderly lady with grey hair stuck on top of her head and wearing bright orange spectacles with old fashioned wings, banged open the sliding glass window.

"Yes. Name and time?"

Charlie realised this wasn't going to be a pleasant experience. "Robb. I was told to be here at eleven."

The woman clicked a few keys on her computer keyboard before looking up and seeing Charlie for the first time. She seemed to examine him before pointing out into the waiting area. "Take a seat. Mrs O'Sullivan's running late. You'll have to wait."

Before Charlie could thank the woman, she'd closed the glass and was gone. Charlie found a seat next to an older man who looked reasonably dressed in a suit, collar and tie. Charlie was wearing his only suit but had put on his clean blue shirt with an open collar. He hadn't ventured into the only bathroom on the first floor of his halfway house accommodation, choosing to use the sink in his bedroom. Washing his hair and shaving with a disposable razor hadn't been easy but he had managed. Overall, he was pleased with his appearance for today's interview with his probation officer.

Charlie looked around and began to realise how far he had fallen. He thought about the third person who was responsible for his downfall. He remembered Anthony Maple well. He'd visited Charlie at his home office the day after Charlie had been introduced to Sebastian De Roy. Anthony or Tony as he told Charlie to call him, said he'd been recommended by both Geoffrey Lockwood and Sebastian De Roy as an advisor who could be trusted. Charlie recalled Tony as a small overweight man who appeared permanently flushed. He couldn't sit still and was constantly fidgeting. He told Charlie he understood he was more than a financial advisor and that he represented clients who were seeking better returns on their investments than legitimate sources could offer. Charlie had asked Tony what 'legitimate sources' meant. The little man had pushed the question to one side and instead told Charlie he had three million pounds to invest. As Charlie sat on his uncomfortable red plastic chair, he realised how foolish he had been. The lure of such sums being invested through his firm and the commissions had turned his head. He knew with hindsight he had been slowly sucked into a world of greed and corruption.

Charlie had been so wrapped up in his thoughts he had failed to notice the room was almost empty. The man sitting next to him was gone and there was only one other ex-con waiting. The glass window slid open, and his name was called out. He approached the window.

"Room six." The woman pointed to a door at the far side of the waiting room. "I'll buzz you through, third on the right." Without further comment the glass was closed and a buzzer sounded followed by the click of the door being released from its catch.

Charlie found room six, knocked and entered. Sitting behind the desk was a pretty woman in her mid-thirties. She was dressed conservatively in a two-piece trouser suit and a white blouse. Charlie noted she was not wearing any makeup.

"Have a seat, Mr Robb. I'm Connie O'Sullivan, your probation officer. I'm sorry to have kept you waiting." She looked up as she was halfway through her opening statement.

"No problem. My appointment was for eleven and it's only 11.45 a.m. but it's nice to meet you, Mrs O'Sullivan." Charlie regretted his sarcastic remark as he was instantly taken by this beautiful and cool woman. In an attempt to salvage the situation, he blurted out what he hoped was a light-hearted remark. "I suppose you'll give me the dos and don'ts in the life of an innocent ex-con on parole."

Connie O'Sullivan sighed gently and placed her pen on top of Charlie's file. "Mr. Robb, almost all of my clients start of by claiming their innocence. Some genuinely believe it but it's not my job to listen to them rerunning their trial. A court of law found you guilty, that's why you are here. The sooner you accept that the sooner your rehabilitation into society can begin. Are we clear?"

Charlie took to this woman even more. She had character and was clearly no fool. "Yes, I'm sorry." Charlie tried to look contrite but finished up with a smirk on his face just like a schoolboy who has been given a dressing down by a teacher he didn't respect.

Connie O'Sullivan obviously recognised the situation and the severity of her statement. Looking at Charlie she gave a slight smile and her face lit up. "Sorry, perhaps that was a bit severe for our first meeting. Now, I'm very busy so no more distractions." Connie took her pen and opened Charlie's file. From the way she read it, it was obvious that this was the first time she had heard of Charles Robb.

It took a few minutes of silent reading before the probation officer looked up from the file. "Right, that all seems straightforward. Are you happy at your halfway house?"

Charlie grinned. "Well, no, it's dirty, damp and unhygienic but I suppose I'm stuck with it. The manager is a lazy sod who doesn't want to be disturbed and I'm not too keen on my neighbours."

Connie O'Sullivan smiled once more at Charlie's description of his digs. "I'll see if I can get you better accommodation." Connie made a note in Charlie's file. "Now, what about work? Do you have any prospects?"

Charlie had rehearsed the lie he was about to give, in anticipation of this question. He'd been well taught in prison. "Yes. Some of my old contacts who know I was set up have offered me work. I can't practise as a financial advisor any more, but I can be useful to them in the back office." The prepared speech was to ensure Charlie didn't finish up working in a heel bar and having to report for work every day. He had other plans.

"Well, that's good. I'll need the details of your employer for my records."

Once more, Charlie was prepared. He produced a piece of paper from his inside jacket pocket and handed it to Connie. She noted it said, GEOFFREY LOCKWOOD ASSOCIATES, Floor Six, The SHARD, LONDON. His prison teachers had told him the probation service never check the information you give them. If they didn't need to find you a job, then your life would be easier.

Satisfied, Connie placed the paper in Charlie's file. "This is very good. Now Charles…"

Charlie interrupted her. "Please. My friends call me Charlie."

"Right. Now… Charlie, this is my card." Connie handed over her business card. It gave her name as Mrs. Constance O'Sullivan, the office address and phone number and an emergency mobile for out of hours use. "During the first three months you will report here once a week. Shall we say four p.m. every Monday?"

Charlie shrugged. He knew he wouldn't keep many of these appointments, but the time sounded fine. He thought if he stretched their meeting out till after five, he might take Connie for a drink. He came to, as he realised she was still talking.

"Good, now you are not to get involved in any criminal activity, nor meet any of your previous associates. Your National Insurance records have been updated and your driving licence is of course still valid. If you have any questions or run into any difficulties call me. Otherwise, I'll see you next Monday at four p.m. February 14."

Connie stood up from behind her desk. As she did so Charlie noted she only stood an inch shorter than him. Her business suit did nothing to disguise her figure nor her inbuilt grace. She noticed Charlie's slight leer. She was used to it and knew how to brush it off. "Mr. Robb, I know you have been locked up for the past seven years and four months and that you won't have seen many women but please close your mouth."

Charlie flushed and stammered, "I'm sorry, I didn't mean to…"

"It's all right, Charlie, I'm used to it. For your information I title myself 'Mrs' to keep the wolves away. I'm not married, and I like my job. See you next Monday."

As Charlie left, Connie O'Sullivan wondered why she had told Charlie Robb she wasn't married. She'd never admitted that to any other client. She felt her face redden as she sat down, retrieved another file for another client and pressed the buzzer to let the orange-haired lady on reception know she was ready for her next client. It was 12.34 p.m.

***

Just as Charles Robb was sitting down in front of his probation officer, Steve arrived back in his office, carrying three coffees as a result of a diversion to the canteen. He called Matt Conway and Bob Glass into his office.

Once everyone was settled and enjoying their coffee, Steve opened the file on Squadron Leader Max Ho. "We have an unusual case handed down from the top. Unfortunately, I can't give you the whole story. If I did, we'd all be shot." The attempt to lighten his message only got a mild response from his team.

Standing up and taking an enlarged photograph of Squadron Leader's Ho's security picture, Steve walked towards his white board, and using magnets, stuck the picture to the board. He then wrote Max Ho's name underneath. "This is our subject of interest. His name is Squadron Leader Max Ho. He's a serving RAF test pilot and I'm told something of a celebrity on daytime television and social media."

He returned to his seat and his coffee. "Our job is to put him under surveillance. Like I said I can't give you specifics but our boy there," Steve pointed to the board, "might be up to no good. It's our job to find out without letting him know."

Matt Conway spoke up. "If he's military I'd guess it's something to do with the MOD. Why don't they get MI5 or MI6 onto this?"

"Like I said, Matt, you can speculate but I can't confirm or deny anything. What I can tell you is that the powers that be don't think the security services have the skills or manpower to keep this guy under surveillance." Steve used the security services as a cover for Major Havers' unit. "That's our job. Now the question is, how the hell do we do it?"

Matt puffed out his cheeks. "I presume it's a twenty-four/seven job, so we'll need more bodies."

"Agreed. We'll get whatever we ask for."

Bob Class was sitting studying the photograph. He was looking at it with an intensity that worried the DCI. "Are you all right, Bob?"

The admin assistant realised he hadn't been listening. He heard his boss and shook himself. "Oh, er, yes, sorry, Steve. I was just thinking, I'm assuming despite the obvious secrecy that this is a sanctioned operation?"

Steve hadn't thought of it in those terms. "If you mean, did we receive an order from Commander Hargreaves, then yes. But it's best if we keep things under the radar. Why do you ask?"

Bob leant forward. "Rather than have eyes on him each hour of each day, couldn't we use electronic monitoring, or use a combination? If this guy's such a media star he could be difficult to keep tabs on, you know, if he's at an all-ticket function, that sort of thing. If we could bug him, we'd know where he was even if we couldn't see him."

Steve skimmed through the remainder of Max Ho's file. It gave his London address, his car make, model and registration and his telephone numbers. It showed he was a member of the Military Club in Pall Mall, and he had a girlfriend who lived in Oxford. Steve passed this information onto his two team members. He sat considering Bob's suggestion. "I like the idea, Bob, but part of our brief is to monitor anyone he meets and confirm they're clean, however, I take your point. You see when I said we have to prove he's clean I should have said we have to prove he's not plotting anything with undesirables, like foreign agents, for example." Steve knew he'd gone too far in passing on this detail, but he knew his two detectives needed this data to better understand what was being asked of them.

Matt spoke up. "Steve? If this surveillance is kosher and approved but we need to keep it quiet, can't we use, let's say, some irregular techniques along the lines Bob's talking about?"

A sly grin appeared simultaneously on Matt and Bob's faces. Matt carried on. "Nothing too illegal and of course nothing that could be traced back to us. I'm sure Terry Harvey will have a few ideas."

Terry Harvey was a good friend of Steve's and was head of Technical Support. He'd gone the extra mile for the team on several occasions. Steve hadn't seen much of Terry since Poppy's murder as Steve's caseload had been light. Terry had been Poppy's uncle and although Steve knew Terry and his wife didn't blame him for Poppy's death, he was embarrassed to meet Terry in case questions about Poppy came up. There was also the masked man who had shot Poppy's killer and how he might have saved Poppy if he'd fired a split second earlier. Terry knew about this and had referred to it at their last meeting. Because Terry had a point, Steve was keeping a copy of the coroner's report on his desk as a reminder to do his best to discover the identity of the mysterious killer.

"You may have a point, Matt. I'll talk to Terry. Meantime, here's the file on our man. Bob, make sure it stays in the office. No one sees it and don't put anything on the computer system. Got it?"

"Sure thing, boss."

"Now, I want a full workup on our target. I want everything we can find. Finances, sexual orientation, friends, girlfriends, even his inside leg measurement if we can get it. Bob, ask Mrs Harvey to help if you need to, tell her I asked you. Matt, work up an outline plan. Figure out how we can keep tabs on Mr Ho in case we finish up doing it the hard way."

The two detectives left to have a canteen lunch and pursue their assignments while Steve returned to his desk and tried to understand what was going on. He took his mobile and dialled a number. He knew someone who might help if he was prepared to talk.

***

Eric Stokes, now known as Dominic Barns, had just returned from a midday run around the back streets of Chelsea and its parks. As usual he had pushed himself hard and was covered in sweat. As he was about to enter the shower, his mobile rang. He knew very few people had the number so it must be work. He hit the reply button.

"Hello, darling, remember me?"

Dominic almost dropped the phone. It was Samantha Cowley, the beauty who carried out tasks for Major Havers. Dom had enjoyed a few nights of horizontal athletics with Samantha and had hoped for more before she disappeared from his life.

"Samantha. How could I forget you?"

"Oh! Quite easily. I hear you have been doing well. You never know I might visit you one lonely night if you keep getting rave reviews."

"I'd like that, but what do you want?"

"The major has a job for you. I'm to collect you at three o'clock and take you to him. He's not at the Brompton Road HQ. He's somewhere else. No need to get dressed up, it's purely informal. Bye bye, darling, see you at two." The line went dead.

Dom found the sound of Samantha's silky voice was enough to arouse him. Instead of a hot shower he opted for a cold one. He gradually increased the temperature and stood with water cascading over him remembering how beautiful Samantha was and how athletic she had been between the sheets. He dressed casually and examined himself in the long mirror attached in his bedroom. He wanted to look good for her and hoped a few more nights of fun might be coming soon.

Samantha arrived at exactly two. After a quick peck on the cheek, Dom got into the passenger seat of her classic MG and the pair set off to meet Major Simon Havers. Samantha drove towards the M25 before slipping onto the M3 and Guildford.

"Where are we going?"

Dom struggled to get Samantha to hear over the roar of the wind. The collapsible roof of the MG was down. Samantha either didn't hear or ignored Dom's question. Leaving the M3 at the Guildford exit, Samantha navigated a few country roads until they arrived at a country inn just outside Guildford centre. It was 2.49 p.m. and the inn was closed. There was only one other car in the car park as Samantha pulled in and parked.

"Come on, darling, he's waiting."

Dom got out of the low car admiring his driver's movements as she walked towards the back door of the inn. She was dressed in white tight-fitting jeans that exaggerated her every movement, a white low-cut blouse that was at least one size too small, revealing her magnificent figure.

Major Havers was seated in the empty bar. The table in front of him was empty. Not even a bottle of water was obvious. "Good, you made it. Take a seat, Dom. Samantha, dear, go into the kitchen and make us a nice pot of tea, there's a good girl."

Samantha pranced off leaving the major and Dom sitting in silence. Major Havers spoke first. "Right, Dom. You've had a few weeks to relax after your last assignment. It's time to put you back to work." He leant down and produced a file from his briefcase. He pushed it in Dom's direction. "Read that! We wouldn't normally meet to discuss an individual assignment, but this is different. I need your input."

Dom opened the file and read about Squadron Leader Ho and his suspected treachery. "So, I'm to tail him, see if he's meeting undesirables that may pose a threat before eliminating him? If he's innocent I leave him alone and I do all this by myself." Dom sat back and pushed the file on the table towards the major.

Simon Havers looked at the file and then at Dom. "Of course not, but we must determine if this pilot is a threat before we take action. You'll see he has a high public profile and if we get it wrong, all hell will break out, especially as he's a darling of the media."

"If the security services think he's dirty, let's just remove him." As he said this, Dom thought he was becoming overly blasé about murder.

"I agree but you've read the brief. If we think he's innocent, we leave him alone. If he's not, we take him out, but it's my decision."

Samantha arrived with the tea. Having poured two cups, she wiggled her way back to the kitchen without saying anything to either man.

Once Samantha had gone back to the kitchen, the major picked up the file and returned it to his briefcase. Dom, realising an uncomfortable silence had descended, broke it by asking, "So what do you want me to do?"

"I've asked the police to put our target under surveillance…" The major saw the surprised look on Dom's face. "Yes, I know, it's a bit unusual but you couldn't possibly keep our man under surveillance all the time. I've used a contact I have in military intelligence to ask the police to provide this service. They have no idea we exist nor of our ultimate sanction if they show our target is guilty. They'll watch him for a few days, report on his movements and who he meets. We'll get the report and if action is needed you can carry out the assignment. In the meantime, I'll issue the usual briefing. I want you to get to know the squadron leader's habits, and plan to remove him but because of his media profile, he'll have to disappear without trace. No body. Understand?"

Dom finished his tea. "Yes, sir. No body. When will you declare this active?"

"When I get the police surveillance report. They haven't said they'll do it yet so if they say they won't, you'll go active tomorrow morning and take him out as soon as. We can't take the risk he may be clean."

"Got it."

"Good. Now Samantha will return you to your accommodation and probably provide a few hours of distraction."

Major Havers left as Samantha returned. "Come on, darling, time to go."

Dom followed the convent-educated beauty to her car. He had a big smile on his face in anticipation of what was to come. It was 3.36 p.m.

Chapter Five

Steve finished the phone call to his contact. He was uncomfortable with his latest orders and wanted clarification and guidance. He had worked with Sir Patrick Bond, the now retired head of MI6, during previous cases. Sir Patrick and Steve had known each other for several years and had a mutual respect for each other. Sir Patrick had once tried to recruit Steve into MI6. However, Steve's need to use Sir Patrick's knowledge had created difficulties and the two men, although civil to each other, were no longer friends.

Steve's initial approach to Sir Patrick had been awkward but after a few difficult moments and a hurried explanation from Steve, the pair had agreed to meet for a drink at five, at Sir Patrick's club in central London.

The DCI was about to leave and visit Technical Support when a man appeared in his doorway carrying a suitcase. Looking up, Steve saw a badly dressed man of about five foot eight inches tall, with a full head of unruly greying hair that looked as though it had never been combed. He was wearing an old badly-fitting sports jacket and dark grey trousers. Under his sports jacket he wore a multi-coloured sweater with an off-white shirt and no tie. Steve noticed his florid complexion and his oversized stomach. The man stood looking at Steve before saying, "I'm looking for the boss, a DCI Burt. I suppose that's you?"

Steve said nothing for a few seconds. "Yes, and who are you?"

"I'm Simon Griffiths, posted to your unit. Call me Si, everybody does."

Steve thought this was not how he had envisaged Poppy's replacement. He didn't look like a police officer and didn't appear to behave like one. Steve felt this experienced officer who appeared to be in his late forties needed a lesson in manners. "So, you're Detective Sergeant Simon Griffiths. Do you understand the word 'sir', Detective Sergeant, because since you arrived, I haven't heard it once?"

The newcomer dropped his suitcase with a bang and without being invited took the chair in front of Steve's desk. "Sir, I've been transferred to your unit under protest. They closed my old nick and I applied for early retirement, but my old station commander didn't like me and refused my application. Maybe if I put my papers in again, you'll sign them off."

The DCI noticed his new DS hadn't shaved for a few days and his breath smelt of alcohol. He moved a few files around his desk until he found the internal envelope from personnel that contained DS Griffiths' record. He also saw the file on Poppy's inquest. It reminded him he had another, personal agenda on his desk. Steve left the new man sitting while he took his time and examined his file.

Simon Griffiths had been a police officer for twenty-two years. He'd been in CID for most of his career and had been a sergeant for twelve years. His appraisals were fairly neutral. After initial promise it appeared he was stuck in a rut. His arrest rate had always been high and there were a few disciplinary notes concerning his methods when seeking confessions and securing convictions. He was rated at his rank and not recommended for further promotion. Steve recalled Commander Hargreaves' comment that the new man came with experience. He wondered if he needed this DS's experience.

Si had sat quietly while Steve read his file. "Right, sergeant, I don't know how you did things before but here, for a start, we have a dress code. You'll present yourself in a tidy condition wearing a tie. Unless you are growing a beard you will shave regularly. Next, you'll observe the courtesies of rank, I'm sir or boss. You'll show respect to the other officers of this unit and more importantly, you'll pull your weight. Is that understood?"

Si sat and stared. He was quiet for what seemed a long time. He gave a deep sigh. "Listen, boss, I've heard it all before from my various station commanders. I know how to do my job. I catch villains and put them away. I'm good at it. I've told my previous masters if they don't like me, or what I do, then get rid of me. I'm ready to take retirement. I'll make you the same offer, all you have to do is sign the papers."

For a reason he didn't understand, Steve liked this insubordinate, little police officer, but he didn't show it. His northern accent had been rounded indicating a long time in London, but a trace of the north was still there. Leaning forward and placing the palms of his hands face down on his desk, Steve looked directly at Simon. "The officer you are replacing was killed in the line of duty. She was trying to save the lives of a couple of nasty and corrupt individuals. You've been posted here as her replacement, and you'll honour her memory by doing your best work or I'll arrange to have you down the road handing out parking tickets before you can say pension. You're here to work and you'll get no easy route to retirement from me. Is that clear?"

Simon sat listening to what the DCI had said. "Well…SIR, I hear you and I'm all yours but don't expect too much. That suitcase contains my worldly possessions. My fourth wife threw me out and I'm now billeted in the section house until I can find more permanent digs. That's four marriages I've given to the job. I've told myself number five won't be sacrificed in the same way. I want to be a civilian, but she won't hang around waiting for you to push me out, sir!"

Steve had heard of similar domestic upheavals caused by the job but never four broken marriages, although it sounded as though Si had number five lined up. Steve smiled inwardly. He didn't look like a ladies' man. "OK, Si, you get settled in and report back here tomorrow at eight. But Si, no drinking on the job. Your breath smells like a brewery."

Poppy's replacement smiled and stood. He nodded his head, lifted his suitcase and marched out without a word of goodbye. Steve wondered how he would get on with his new sergeant. Time would tell.

***

At the same time as Poppy's replacement was walking with his suitcase towards the Metropolitan Police's temporary accommodation block for single officers, Charles Robb, having left the probation office, was entering the Nat West Bank branch just up from Holborn tube station in London. He was immediately approached by a girl holding an electronic notebook. "Good afternoon, sir, can I help you?"

Charlie looked around and was surprised to see there were no counter nor tellers. "Er, yes, I'd like to see someone about access to my safety deposit box."

The girl looked surprised and asked Charlie to have a seat on a single chair that hadn't been designed for comfort. As he waited Charlie noticed people arriving through the front door were all greeted by similar girls each holding an electronic notebook. Each customer was directed to a bank of cash dispensers where, apparently, they could conduct all their banking business. Charlie overheard a conversation between a customer and her greeter. The girl said the bank was cashless and directed the customer to another branch. "At this branch you can only withdraw up to five hundred pounds a day from our ATMs."

Charlie was amazed at how the world of banking had changed since he had been on holiday at Her Majesty's pleasure. After about ten minutes the girl arrived and asked Charlie for identification. Using his still valid driver's licence, the girl seemed satisfied and asked Charlie to follow her. He was taken to a back office where a man who looked like an eighteen-year old boy sat behind a desk. After introductions, and Charlie being informed he was talking to the area controller, he was asked to complete a form giving details that only the owner of the safety deposit box could possibly know. The eighteen-year-old entered the information into a computer and eventually smiled, stood and asked Charlie to follow him.

The pair entered a vault below the bank. The room comprised only four walls of metal flaps and a table in the centre of the room. There were no windows, and the fluorescent overhead light gave the room a strange feeling. The area controller opened a metal flap that was one of the many secured to the walls and extracted a sizable metal box. He placed it on the table.

"There you are, Mr Robb. I presume you remember your security number. I'll leave you here. Please take as long as you like. When you're ready to leave, push the bell by the door and it will open. If you close and relock your box, you can leave it on the table. We'll replace it." The area controller left without another word.

Charlie entered a six-digit number that corresponded to his date of birth into a keypad positioned on top of the box. It sprung open immediately he keyed the last number. Inside was Charlie's security. During his time working with the rogue, Geoffrey Lockwood, Charlie had come to realise things weren't above board and that too many transactions were being carried out in cash. He had been naïve in the beginning but quickly wised up. He'd started diverting cash to protect himself never thinking he'd end up as the fall guy and going to prison. As he stared down at all the cash, he told himself this was his revenge money. He knew the box contained exactly five hundred thousand pounds. To himself he whispered, "This is only the beginning. You will all pay with your lives and your fortunes."

Charlie took several wads of notes and stuffed them into the inside pockets of his jacket. He stuffed more into his trouser pockets and the side pockets of his jacket. He estimated he had removed about one hundred thousand. Smiling, he closed the box lid, relocked it using his code and rang the bell by the door. On cue the locked door clicked open and Charlie Robb, late of Her Majesty's Prison Whitby, left the bank and hailed a taxi. It was 2.55 p.m.

The taxi took Charlie to the Marks and Spencer store on Oxford Street. He bought two suits that seemed to fit him well, six shirts that came with ties, several packs of underwear, socks and three pairs of shoes. As he was trying on his suits, he transferred his cash into a green M&S plastic bag he'd been given by an assistant. He had the girl who took the money for his purchases put them in several plastic bags. He next went to the upper floor where he bought a large suitcase. He put the rest of his new wardrobe inside it, added the bag containing the cash and closed the suitcase.

Charles Robb, exited onto Oxford Street and hailed a cab. "Mayflower Hotel, please." Charlie's new, if temporary, life had begun. He'd never see the halfway house in Stratford again.

***

Having sent his new sergeant off to get settled in, Steve made his way to the Technical Support Unit run by Inspector Terry Harvey. No matter how hard he tried, Steve couldn't shift the guilt he felt about the killing of Terry's niece, DC Amelia Cooper, known as Poppy to everyone she met. Despite Terry explaining to Steve that he understood he couldn't have prevented the killing, Steve continued to feel responsible. Poppy had been headstrong and had had a theory about a previous case. Her theory had finally been proved correct, but Steve had initially dismissed it. Poppy had followed it up without proper backup knowing if she admitted what she was doing, Steve would have stopped her, with disastrous consequences.

As he entered Terry's domain, he saw his friend deep in conversation with one of his technicians. Terry stood away from his seated colleague and indicated Steve should follow him to his office. Terry's office was small and usually looked untidy. Today was no exception. "OK, what do you need?" Terry grinned as he moved a pile of computer printouts onto the floor.

"Nothing much. I need to pick your brains and see if you can help."

"Fire away, I'm all ears."

For the next twenty minutes Steve told Terry everything he could about his brief to put Max Ho under surveillance. "You see Bob Class thinks we can save a lot of manpower if we could track him electronically. The problem is the powers-that-be want to know who he's meeting. Given his media profile Bob reckons there will be times we won't be able to follow him."

"Mm. Interesting, and you want to know if we can help?"

"Yes."

"How legal do you need this to be? Will it finish as evidence in court? You know how the judiciary are these days about illegal surveillance."

Steve thought back to his meeting with Lieutenant Colonel Walters and the existence of Major Havers' unit of assassins. "It's very unlikely anything we do or discover will make a courtroom if that helps." The DCI knew what his friend was thinking but remained silent, preferring Terry to make his decisions.

"If we're talking off the books, then yes, we can do something." Terry sat back and played with a paperclip. He had a broad smile on his face. "We've just received new kit that would be ideal for this. We can call it field trials. Can you get me five minutes with this guy's mobile?"

"We can try."

"Right. If you can, I've got a bug that will activate our recorders every time he receives or makes a call. We'll also be able to tell you where he is every minute of the day even if his phone is switched off, always assuming he carries his phone. This implant transmits all the time, and we'll pick up the GPS locators. It can also use the camera on the phone to transmit pictures in real time. His battery life will go down, but the chances are he won't notice."

Steve was amazed. "So, we can hear all his calls, know where his phone is at least and if the phone isn't in his pocket, we'll see whatever the phone's camera is seeing?"

"Yes, but I'll need his phone."

Steve sat back thinking. "I get the listening to his calls bit and knowing where his phone is at least. I even get the camera, but we need to know who he's meeting."

"Mm. Not so easy. Hold on!" Terry left his office and through the glass panel in one wall of the office Steve saw Terry talking to a tall man with long black hair tied in a knot on top of his head. After about five minutes Terry was back. As he entered, he closed the door.

"Right. I've spoken to Andrew, my senior tech. He's the one who's developed this gadget with an outside agency. Depending on the circuitry in the phone we may be able to hear what your target is saying even though he's not using his phone and it's switched off. It's not certain but Andrew thinks it's possible."

Steve's jaw dropped. "You're a bloody miracle worker, Terry. So, if we can get Max Ho's mobile and if it's the correct type, we'll be able to hear all his calls, know where he and his phone are at all times, see what the phone's camera is seeing and now, we might be able to hear his conversations. Is that about it?"

Terry had a satisfied smug grin on his face. "Yes, don't you love technology?" Terry stopped grinning and sat forward. "But we'll need his phone."

"Do you need it here or can you stick this bug in anywhere?"

"We'll need it here. Andrew will have to play with the circuit board. And he told me to forget five minutes, he'll need at least an hour. Oh! And he suggested putting a tracker on your man's car just to be sure."

"Right. Getting his phone away from him for all that time won't be easy. We might manage five minutes but now you're talking an hour here so that's at least four hours he'll be without his phone. Leave it with me, we'll see what we can do."

As Steve was leaving, Terry stood up. "Remember, Steve, all of this is highly illegal and anything you learn can never be admitted to. If word got out, we'd both be in handcuffs."

The DCI smiled and waved a farewell to his friend.

When he got back to his office via the canteen to collect three coffees, he called Matt and Bob into his inner office. Seated around his conference table he told the two detectives everything Terry had explained to him. "Now, we need two things." Steve stood beside his whiteboard that was fixed to the wall. He wrote as he spoke. "First, we need a surveillance plan to show how many men we need to keep watch on Max Ho assuming Terry's gadget works. Second, and this is the hard one, how the hell do we get Max Ho's phone away from him?"

Matt and Bob looked at each other. Neither man spoke for several minutes until Matt leant. "Well, if this is legal, I'm a Dutchman. I presume it's all under the radar, so the obvious time to relieve him of his phone is when he's sleeping. No one sleeps with their phone, and they certainly don't use it when they're in bed. That could be the time to nick it and get it back before he realises it's gone."

Steve admired Matt's criminally active mind. "Not bad." Steve looked at his watch. Remembering his appointment with Sir Patrick he wound the meeting up. "Bob, try to figure out a manpower plan. Matt, think more about your idea and how we can get the phone. I'm off to meet a man who might let me in on a few secrets."

Before he could leave Bob Class spoke up. "Boss, we know bugging like this without a warrant is illegal. I'm not sure we should condone breaking the law like this. Can we at least get a warrant?"

Steve conceded Bob had a point. If they were caught none of them would have jobs and would probably serve time. "According to Terry this bug thing is experimental, so we'd be unlikely to get a warrant. Plus, we'd have to show all our cards and I can't do that. Even you two don't have the full picture. I think we'll have to rely on Terry's view that as the bug hasn't been approved, we're just carrying out field trials. And remember, anything we find out about this Ho character will never see the inside of a courtroom. Sorry, Bob, but there it is. We just have to do our jobs and not get caught."

Bob Class nodded but didn't look happy.

The DCI left for his meeting.

***

Max Ho had been stood down from flying duties due to his test aircraft having additional safety checks. He loved flying and was never happier than when he was around aircraft or on an RAF base. Due to the highly secret nature of his flying and the aircraft, Max had been stationed at a disused military airbase in East Anglia, near Lavenham. He enjoyed the countryside but found the lack of nightlife frustrating. There were few fellow officers on the base and the mostly civilian technicians had rented property and moved their families into the area.

Max was now in his London flat looking forward to a week's rest. He had a busy schedule of television recordings and had several parties lined up. At six-foot, with Asian good looks, Max was in demand especially by the ladies. His casual attitude to life and his athletic body had proven to be a winning combination and he had never been short of female companionship.

He'd bought his flat in Greenwich a few years ago. He'd regarded it as an investment but now he had committed himself to the cause of his country of birth, he knew his time in this luxury fourth-floor apartment was limited. The thought of life in North Korea didn't really appeal to Max but he was committed to the leader of the rogue state and had been promised a good life courtesy of the state when he defected with the new aircraft.

Plans had been made to fly over Russian and Chinese territory. Because of the stealth capabilities of the plane no one would even know he was overflying their airspace, but this was an international joint treaty event and protocols had to be followed. All three countries would benefit from having access to the aircraft.

Max was now thirty-three and had enjoyed his time in the UK and the Air Force. He sat looking over the millennium dome through his large sliding patio doors and wondered how he would be remembered. He knew his parents would disown him but wondered how his social media followers would react. No date had been set for the hijacking, but it would be soon. The trials were almost over. Sitting in his comfortable rocking chair he closed his eyes. It was 4.37 p.m. He had time for a snooze before hitting the town.

***

Steve arrived at the In and Out Military Club before five p.m. for his meeting with Sir Patrick Head. The doorman ushered him inside the grand detached Victorian building where he was greeted by the front of house manager. "Sir Patrick hasn't arrived yet, sir, but you are expected. Perhaps I can escort you to our members' lounge and offer you some refreshments." The DCI was amazed at how the other half lived. This was like something out of a movie set. Everything shouted privilege and money. The house manager with practised grace pushed open a set of heavy looking mahogany doors and ushered Steve to a club chair situated beside a roaring fire.

"I'm sure Sir Patrick won't be long, sir." Steve was once again asked, "May I offer you some refreshments?"

"Yes, a coffee would be nice, just black, no sugar."

The house manager nodded and silently disappeared. A quick glance around told Steve he was the only one in this gigantic room that smelt of old leather, lavender and wealth. There were leather chairs of various designs grouped around the room. Each group had a coffee table at its centre. A larger table sat against one wall and seemed to contain every daily newspaper produced. A quick glance showed Steve there were magazines next to the newspapers. Everything looked well-ordered and tidy.

The coffee arrived at the same time as Sir Patrick. Steve stood and shook hands with this retired but still influential spymaster. As Head of MI6 for over ten years, there were few things Sir Patrick didn't know about how the country and its governments worked. Although he had been retired for a few years Steve noted this ex-spy chief still looked as he did when Steve had first met him. He was a tall, imposing character whose presence seemed to fill a room. He had gained a few pounds since their last meeting, but Steve thought the extra weight suited him. His figure was still muscular and there was only the beginning of a bulge around his stomach.

Both men sat opposite each other, eyeing each other up. Sir Patrick had ordered himself a brandy and settled himself comfortably in his leather chair. The first five minutes of their meeting was spent sparring like two boxers, feeling each other out. They chatted amiably about nothing in particular until Sir Patrick, now sipping his brandy broke the spell by asking, "OK, Steve, what do you want?"

"I've been given an unusual assignment. It's not a proper case but I want to pick your brain. I can't say too much but it involves national security."

"Sounds intriguing. Go on."

"What do you know about secret government killings?"

Sir Patrick didn't like the question but his years as Head of MI6 had taught him not to overreact. "I'm sorry, Steve, but I'm not following."

Steve knew he had to box clever with Sir Patrick if he were to learn anything. "It's a simple question, Patrick. Are there groups who work for the government who are sanctioned to assassinate people?"

Sir Patrick leant forward and placed his brandy on the coffee table. He scanned the room and saw it was empty. "Steve, if you're asking that question you must be mixed up in something dangerous. My advice is to get out of it as soon as you can."

The DCI had known this interview would be difficult. "But such organisations do exist?"

Sir Patrick gave a sigh and looked at Steve as a teacher would look at a naughty schoolboy. He stared at Steve and appeared to come to a decision. "You know there are events that governments would rather not have revealed in the public domain. Usually anything that needs to be kept secret can be dealt with by D notices and the like, but every so often an event will occur where the problem isn't the tabloid press but something else. Sometimes actual proof is the issue."

Sir Patrick sipped his brandy. "Say for example it is suspected a government minister is about to defect to say Russia. Even if he didn't steal classified documents, he'd have a head full of secrets the government would not want in Soviet hands. The security services would investigate but we don't always get the type of evidence you'd need in a court of law. Under normal circumstances we couldn't pursue the individual in the courts and anyway, what would the charge be? The minister hasn't done anything. So, we have a dilemma. We think he might be going off to Ruskie land, but we can't prove it and the government would be hugely embarrassed if he went. So, what to do?" Sir Patrick finished his brandy. "The answer is to quietly remove the offending problem. In my example a simple road accident or a drowning would be arranged. The government would mourn the loss of a dedicated minister and there'd be no scandal or embarrassment." Sir Patrick sat back and allowed Steve time to absorb what he had said.

"I see that, it's all very neat. You're saying such hit squads exist."

"I couldn't possibly comment but I believe so." Sir Patrick gave a sly grin.

"And these squads are government approved?"

"Ah, well now." Sir Patrick Head felt he was being drawn into saying too much. However, he carried on. "If such an organisation exists it would carry out jobs for the government in such a way that the government would never be seen to sanction or condone their activities. Any funding would be through various untraceable channels. If your lot ever investigated any of their activities, you'd be warned off, even though you know you're dealing with murder."

Steve finished his now cold coffee. "So how does it work? Who sanctions these teams?"

"I'm not sure I can answer that. All I can tell you is that there is a committee, run by the MOD, made up of the security services, military intelligence and a senior but invisible civil servant. Anything that might be embarrassing to the government is discussed by this committee, and unless a more legal solution can be arrived at a decision to issue a notice for elimination is issued. This of course is all done in the name of national security and the public good."

"You're telling me, people are being knocked off without proper evidence against them?"

Sir Patrick stood without answering Steve and pushed a wall-mounted bell, summoning a waiter. He ordered another brandy. Steve declined the offer of a drink. Sir Patrick resumed his seat. "Now. Are you going to tell me what this is all about? Remember I am security cleared."

Reluctantly, Steve decided to expand on his project. "There's a person of interest that is suspected of, in your words, something that might embarrass the government. Apparently, the order has been given to one of these hit squads to eliminate him, but they need to gather evidence of his guilt first. It seems this is a bit unusual. We've been approached because we have the manpower and the skills to put this person under surveillance to prove his guilt or innocence. The logic is, if we prove he's innocent, he won't be bumped off."

"It's a classic cop out. There's no way the Metropolitan Police should be anywhere near this. All I can tell you, Steve, is that whoever the target is, he's a dead man walking. These secret assassination squads only exist for one reason. They eliminate people for the government. Shoot first, ask questions later. As I said in the beginning get out of this now and forget everything you've learnt. These people are dangerous." Sir Patrick's second brandy arrived.

The two men sat in silence. Steve was analysing what he'd learnt while Sir Patrick wondered how deeply the DCI had entered the world of national security.

After a few more minutes of awkward silence, Steve stood up, thanked Sir Patrick and left.

Sir Patrick removed his mobile phone from his jacket and made a call. He needed to discover what the DCI was involved in.

Chapter Six

Steve arrived at his office early on a damp and miserable Tuesday morning at 7.33 a.m. His wife, Alison, had cooked him his breakfast and told him she was worried he wasn't eating properly. This was a common theme within the household. Rosie, their six-year-old daughter, had announced last night that she was going to become vegetarian. Steve had laughed while Alison pretended to take the comment seriously before placing a bowl of beef stew in front of their daughter. "That's good, dear, you can start tomorrow." Steve remembered Alison's sly grin as they ate their meal.

His wall calendar told him today was February 8. He sat down behind his desk with his door closed. He needed to think. He took an A4 pad from his desk drawer and started to doodle. This way of analysing problems had become his preferred method of clarifying things in his mind.

His meeting with Sir Patrick had only confirmed what he knew. Such assassination squads operated in the UK with the blessing of the government but what he now knew was that authority for such actions was given by a secret committee who appeared to be judge and jury. Although Sir Patrick hadn't stated it, Steve thought this might be a set up. Why would the assassination orders suddenly put the decision to kill or not to kill onto a functionary? And why involve the police?

Steve doodled and made graphs and charts. None of them meant anything. All he'd achieved was to confirm what he knew. Despite Sir Patrick's warning, he was determined to see his instructions through and possibly save an innocent life, if Max Ho was deemed to be clean. On his pad he wrote in large block letters, '*FIRST TIME WE SOLVE A MURDER BEFORE IT HAPPENS.*'

Bob and Matt Conway arrived, Steve called them in and started to debrief them on their tasks set to them yesterday. Just as Bob Class was setting up his laptop, a figure appeared at the office door. It was DS Simon Griffiths. To Steve's eyes he looked exactly as he had yesterday except he wore a tie that wasn't tied at his throat but hung a good four inches below the collar of his none too clean shirt.

"Si, welcome, come in." Steve wasn't impressed by his new detective but decided to give him enough rope. Maybe after a few days, he'd sort himself out. Si grunted and took a seat at the table. Steve made the introductions. He could tell by Matt Conway's expression that he didn't think much of Si as Poppy's replacement.

"Right, Si, you'll have to catch up." Steve outlined the project and as he got to the part where he explained the project was secret and not strictly legal, plus they needed to have the target's phone for half a day without him realising it was missing, he noticed Si Griffiths suddenly perk up. He seemed alert and interested. "Now, Bob first, what about the target's finances? Anything there look dodgy?"

Bob hit a few keys on his laptop. "Nothing stands out. He gets his RAF salary plus his flying pay and test pilot allowance. As a single man I'd say he was doing OK. His bank balance is always in four figures, his salary covers all his outgoings including his mortgage on an apartment in Greenwich and there's enough left for him to have invested through a brokerage firm. He seems to have built up quite a portfolio of investments. Overall, financially, he's doing OK. I asked Mrs Harvey to have a look, but she couldn't find anything to suggest he had other unknown sources of income. He seems clean, boss."

Steve wasn't surprised but at least they knew Max Ho wasn't on the take. "OK, Matt, you next." He glanced at Si Griffiths who was still showing a lot of interest.

"First, I took a drive over to Greenwich last night and found the apartment block he lives in. It's very modern and security seems tight. CCTV cameras everywhere, keypad door entry system and a concierge on duty twenty-four seven. Seems our Max is on the fourth floor."

Matt paused as he gathered his thoughts. "You asked if I could think of a way to get hold of his phone for Terry Harvey. The only thing I could come up with is that when he's sleeping, he's not using his phone and wouldn't miss it. I thought about breaking into his flat but security's too tight. The only other thought was a woman."

Steve held up a hand. "If you're suggesting we set him up with a tart who nicks his phone when he's asleep, drops it to us from the fourth floor and we somehow get it back inside his flat before he wakes up, forget it. Upstairs wouldn't go for it."

"That's all I've got Steve. I can't see another way."

When Si Griffiths spoke, his unique accent filled the room. He was seated with his elbows on the table. "If you don't tell upstairs, they'll never know."

Steve took a deep breath. "They'll know, sergeant, because I'm duty bound to tell them. Plus, we'd have to find a girl willing to do it. Also, we don't have time to set up such a honeytrap." Steve hoped his new sergeant had got the message that he wasn't pleased with him.

Undaunted, Si carried on. "Well, if it's so important why not just lift his phone?"

Matt sat forward. "Go on, what do you mean?"

With a theatrical sigh, Si stood and approached the white board. With a black marker pen he drew a matchstick man. "This is your target. Do you know where he'll be at say one o'clock this afternoon?"

Steve looked at Bob, who rapidly hit some keys on his laptop. "Because he's still on active service and not on leave he has to report his whereabouts in case he's needed. I got a copy of his movements from the MOD although," Bob blushed slightly, "they don't know we have them."

Steve wondered if he commanded a unit of police officers or crooks. Si Griffiths smirked an approving grin.

Bob continued, keying as he spoke. "He's at the BBC centre from one thirty this afternoon. The notes don't say what he's doing but he'll be there till six tonight, then back at his flat. There are no details of his plans after six p.m."

Si wrote beside his stickman the time, one thirty p.m. followed by BBC. "That's it. I can have someone stake out the BBC Centre. When our guy arrives, he'll dip him and give the phone to me."

Si drew more stickmen showing the thief and himself running back to Scotland Yard. "I'll get it back to your technical blokes and they can put the bug inside. If your man is at the BBC, chances are he won't be using his phone. He'll never miss it."

Steve was impressed but voiced an obvious flaw. "How do we get the phone back to him without him realising it's been missing?"

Si drew another stick figure but this one had an old-style policeman's helmet drawn on its head. "We don't. We send it back with a uniform. He tells this Ho that his phone was found outside the BBC and handed in to the police. From the information on the phone, they'd know it was Ho's phone and as it was found outside the BBC they'd know where to find him." Si stood triumphant in front of his audience. He continued. "Believe me. He'll be so grateful to get his phone back he won't give anything else a second thought."

The room descended into silence as Si retook his seat. Matt looked at Steve. "It could just work and there's no downside I can see."

Bob Class nodded. "Having a police officer return the phone gives this whole thing credibility. I agree with the sergeant, but where do we get a pickpocket?"

Steve smiled. "I think he is about to tell us."

"I've worked the streets all of my career. I know a guy, very reliable when he's sober, who'll do this for fifty quid, no questions asked."

Steve liked the plan. "OK, Si, I'll inform Terry Harvey. Bob, give Si a copy of Max Ho's picture. His pickpocket friend will need it." The DCI took out his wallet and handed Si fifty pounds. His mind briefly went back to his first case as head of Special Resolutions. All he ever did then was hand out money. "Go off now and try to set it up." Steve looked at his watch. "It's 10.44 a.m. I'll have a motorcycle cop stationed outside the BBC from one p.m.. When you get the phone, give it to him. He'll get it here faster than you can."

Si stood, smiled and gave a mock salute. "Sure thing, sir." He turned and disappeared, leaving the room wondering what had just been agreed.

After a few minutes of comments and character analysis of their new colleague, Bob reported that if Terry's gadget worked as advised, then three teams of two officers should be enough to keep tabs on Max Ho. Steve felt the mood in the office had improved since an apparent solution to their problem had been found but ended the meeting wondering what he'd set in motion. He went to find Terry Harvey and then report to Commander Perry Hargreaves although he wasn't sure how he would explain their plan.

***

Charlie Robb, now resident of hotel suite 1001 of the Mayflower Hotel, had risen slowly on this Tuesday morning. He'd had room service with a full English breakfast, coffee and toast. After a hot bath, Charlie had shaved, dressed and made his way downstairs for his appointment with the hotel's barber. He wanted to look his best. He'd placed most of his cash in the hotel safe, and looking resplendent in his new clothes and haircut, he set out to meet a man. A man who could sell him a gun.

His prison education had extended to who on the outside could get whatever. A man called Keith, who would be found every day in a William Hill betting shop just off Mile End Road was the go-to man for weapons. In prison it was said Keith would get you a tank if the price was right. Charlie had more modest ambitions. He took public transport and during the uncomfortable bus ride told himself he should hire a car. The betting shop was like all William Hill outlets, corporately branded and soulless, with badly dressed men, some of whom were drinking beer from cans. Charlie had been well schooled on how to handle this initial contact with Keith. He approached the counter and asked the slim youth with bad acne if Keith was in. Despite the youth's lack of years, he was suspicious and initially ignored Charlie's question. A twenty-pound note slipped over the counter changed this and the youth nodded in the direction of a large, solidly built man dressed in a grey sweater, jeans and trainers. Keith looked as though he had once been a weightlifter, but his muscle tone was gone, and his large waist measurement was testament to his lack of training.

Charlie walked slowly towards Keith. He'd been warned Keith was difficult and temperamental probably due to the drugs he'd been taking since his weightlifting days. Charlie stood beside the big man but said nothing. Eventually Keith who was engrossed in a race from Epsom that was being shown live on television, turned to his right. "What do you want?"

His voice was full of menace. Keith continued to look at the race but constantly glanced at Charlie. "Big Jimbo sent me, he said you were the man." Charlie felt ridiculous. This form of contact wasn't realistic in films, never mind real life.

"Oh yeah! Is that right." The big man was obviously London born and bred. "What else did he tell you?"

"He said you would help an old friend."

Keith clearly knew this form of introduction but was suspicious of strangers. "Meet me round the corner at the Five Bells in about half an hour. Now leave, you're not dressed for here."

Despite his time in prison, Charlie felt uncomfortable around professional criminals, especially those with a tendency towards violence and was glad to leave. He went in search of the pub and found the lounge bar. It was empty and the seating looked more comfortable than the dirty and damaged chairs in the public bar. Despite the early hour, he noted there were eight regulars all drinking beer in the public bar. He ordered a sparkling water, found a seat as far away from the entrance as he could, and waited.

As he sat drinking his water, he thought about what he would do if Keith did provide him with a gun and bullets. In his mind he saw himself shooting the four men who had ruined his life starting with the fourth and the one who had done him least damage. He had thought at one point he might reprieve Colin Clark but his time in prison had hardened him.

Colin Clark had been the last of the four to appear in Charlie's life. He remembered Colin had phoned saying Geoffrey Lockwood had suggested he contact him. They had arranged to meet in a pub close to Colin's house in Queens Park in London. Charlie was now very busy and was spending more and more time networking on behalf of his new and wealthy investors. He seemed to be their full-time advisor. Charlie hadn't signed any new clients apart from those recommended by Geoffrey Lockwood since Geoffrey had entered his life. Meeting Colin on his own turf hadn't been too much of a problem.

The mild-mannered little man in his mid-forties had been conventionally dressed and looked ordinary, not someone to stand out in a crowd. Colin had told Charlie he understood he could achieve higher returns on investments because he took risks other advisors didn't. Charlie tried to explain this was not true, but Colin retorted by saying Geoffrey Lockwood had told him with Charlie his invested money would be safe. As he sat in the empty bar, Charlie agreed with himself that this was the beginning of the end. He'd slowly allowed himself to be manipulated by his then three main investors to be more proactive in seeking out investment opportunities. He knew in the beginning such activity was against the rules but the amounts he was earning in commissions had turned his head and he had thought no one would ever find out.

Colin Clark wanted to invest one million pounds with Charlie on the same terms as Geoffrey Lockwood and the others. He'd emphasised he had accrued the money over several years and planned to retire once Charlie had doubled his money. Mysteriously, he told Charlie he couldn't get any more cash to invest. Unknown to Charlie, Colin Clark was an assistant bank manager who had been embezzling clients' funds for years. Colin was a timid man but had a passion for the high life especially pretty ladies. He told Charlie when he'd doubled his money, he'd leave his wife and would whisk his latest girlfriend away to the Far East and a life of luxury. Charlie recalled that at his trial Colin had offered to speak up for him but instead remained silent. Despite glowing promises of support, not one of the four investors helped him. With a sly grin, Charlie said to himself, *'well, your turn is coming'*. He downed his water and ordered a pint of best.

***

As Charlie Robb was entering the Five Bells, Steve entered the Technical Services unit. Inspector Terry Harvey was as usual on the main floor area without his jacket and his sleeves rolled up. Steve waved and headed directly to Terry's office.

"Well, can you get the phone?"

Terry looked and sounded excited. "This new device is a game changer if it works. All the lads want to work on it, but I'll keep it to myself and Andrew."

Steve was impressed that Terry was still so enthusiastic about his job despite the number of years he'd been doing it. "We don't have the phone yet, Terry, but we have a plan." He went on to explain the plan and the need to get it back to Max Ho before say five thirty, at the latest.

Terry was grinning. "Which criminal mind thought that up? It's so outrageous it might work."

"It had better work, Terry, it's all we have." Reluctantly, Steve explained that DS Simon Griffiths was Poppy's replacement, and it was his plan. Steve was reluctant to talk about Poppy to Terry but saw this opportunity when answering Terry's question.

Steve saw Terry take a pace back. The mention of Poppy's replacement must have come as a shock. Quietly, Terry spoke up. "She'd have been proud of this plan. It has Poppy all over it. It sounds like your new DS should be a good fit."

Steve saw Terry wipe a small tear from his eyes. "Now, if you get the phone here by motorbike by two, I'll have Andrew on standby to get started the moment it gets here. We'll try and get everything sorted by four but remember it'll take longer to test than to fit."

He was grateful that Terry had taken Si Griffiths' appointment so well. "I'll have the motorbike on standby from twelve ready to get it back to Broadcasting House. I'll set up a uniform to be outside the BBC wearing an overcoat over his uniform from four. When the bike rider gets there, he'll hand over his coat and go into the BBC carrying the phone. I'll get someone from here and have him briefed." The DCI looked at his friend. "What could go wrong?"

Both men laughed as Steve waved to Terry and left to brief Commander Perry Hargreaves.

Chapter Seven

Detective Sergeant Simon Griffiths found the person he was looking for in a bar on a housing estate in Tower Hamlets. His name was Alfred Bunny, but everyone called him Cakes after Alfred the Great and the story of him burning the cakes. Alfred had at one point in his criminal career been imprisoned for setting a fire in a cake shop. No one was injured and he got two years. His nickname seemed appropriate.

Cakes was a career criminal who had been in and out of prison most of his adult life. He wasn't intelligent and was easily led into trouble by smarter criminals than him. He did however have a unique skill. He could lift anything from anyone, and they'd never know. His fingers were delicate and sensitive. He often told people that if he could read, he might have been a concert pianist. No one believed him.

Cakes saw Si enter the pub and immediately made to leave via the back door. The DS was wise to this move and angled his approach to Cakes cutting off his retreat. "Come on, Cakes, I have a nice little earner for you, no need to run." Si placed his hand on the little man's shoulder and guided him back to the seat he'd just left.

Si was pleased to find Cakes outwardly sober and pleasantly dressed in jeans, shirt and dark sweater. Given the weather he also had an ex-army combat jacket. Cakes stood around five foot six and weighed about one hundred and twenty pounds. His hair was thinning, and he'd taken to wearing glasses that gave him a false air of competence.

Si sat down. "Now Cakes, I've got a little job for you, a simple dip. Nothing you can't do in your sleep. There's a fifty in it for you but you have to come with me now. I'll explain in the car."

"Mr Griffiths, you've got me confused with someone else. This is the new me, I don't do pickpocketing now.. I'm what you call a businessman, I buy and sell things."

The DS gave an exaggerated sigh. "Listen, Cakes, the only thing you sell is stuff that's been knocked off and the only stuff you buy is what other people steal, so don't muck me about. You come with me and dip this individual relieving him of his phone. There'll be no comeback, you won't be in trouble, and you'll make fifty quid." The DS looked Cakes directly in the eye. "If you don't, we could suddenly find a bit of coke or blow on you and that could get you a few more years inside." Si stood and looked down at the little man. "Shall we go, time's pressing?"

Cakes, seeing no way out, stood, put on his ex-army jacket and accompanied Si out of the pub. He would be fully briefed on the journey to Broadcasting House.

***

Max Ho scanned the view from his lounge window as he contemplated what the day ahead might bring. He had an appointment at the BBC to be interviewed on today's topical events and what role people from ethnic backgrounds played in today's society. Max considered his likely responses and concluded he'd take his lead from the programme presenter. He looked at his watch which showed it was 11.21 a.m. Time to leave. He had to be at Broadcasting House by twelve thirty and knew the journey should take just under an hour.

Max exited Oxford Circus tube station and made his way to the BBC's oldest centre at Broadcasting House. He found the large open square that was formed by the building itself imposing. He had often wondered during his various visits what the real estate value of this square would be if it were ever sold. It was after all, located in central London where land prices were huge.

He had his mobile in the left pocket of his jacket. The weather was cold, and rain threatened but he wasn't wearing a raincoat. He knew the makeup department within the BBC would sort out his looks before the programme was recorded.

Max was about one hundred yards from the main entrance when a small badly dressed individual approached him offering to sell him a series of brushes. "Everything for the home, guv."

He had a clothes brush as a sample of his wares and before Max could object, he started brushing down Max's jacket. "Look at that. You'd be amazed how much muck comes off your clothes with our selection of brushes." The man continued to hold Max's jacket in various positions whilst he brushed away imaginary pieces of grime. Max continued to walk as the little man brushed and chased him. Max saw a motorcycle cop parked just up from the entrance to the BBC and considered reporting the brush salesman. In the end he pushed him away. "Look. I'm not interested, now get out of my way."

Max entered the revolving doors of the building leaving the little man outside. Unseen by Max, Si Griffiths received an object from the little brush salesman and handed it to the motorcycle cop who had apparently been taking a break. As the motor bike sped off at exactly 12.24 p.m. Si slipped the DCI's fifty pounds into Cakes' hand. "Good job, Cakes, I'll see you around."

***

Charlie was halfway through his beer when the big man he knew as Keith entered. Unknown to either man Cakes had just stolen Max's mobile phone. Keith looked around and walked towards Charlie. He lowered his large frame into a seat opposite Charlie.

"Right. What does Big Jimbo look like?"

Charlie had been told his outside contacts would be suspicious and he should expect to be questioned before he would be accepted for what he claimed to be. "He's about five foot six, in his fifties, weighs about one hundred and thirty pounds and is doing life for killing his wife's fancy man."

Keith who was clearly no candidate for Mensa scratched his stomach while he searched for another question. "What colour's his hair?"

"I don't know, he's bald."

"Mm. And he said he was an old friend?"

"Yes. He said you'd help out an old friend."

"Get me a pint and we'll talk."

Charlie did as requested, and after a visit to the bar, returned with two pints of warm beer. Keith lifted his and in one swallow drained half the contents of his glass. He gave a strange burping sound as he wiped his mouth with the back of his hand. "Right, what do you want."

"Big Jimbo said you're the go to man if you need a gun. I need a gun."

"What kind of a gun?"

"I don't know." Charlie felt embarrassed he'd not researched the different types of guns. "I thought you could advise me?"

"Did you?" Keith drained the remaining half of his beer. "What are you going to use it for?"

This seemed an odd question and Charlie didn't feel comfortable answering it. "I'm not sure that's any of your business."

Charlie thought he'd offended the big man as without warning he stood and looked down at his potential customer. "I'm off for a slash. You get another round in." Without looking back, Keith left for the toilet and Charlie bought him another pint.

When Keith had returned and resumed his seat, he once more took a large swallow of his warm beer. He noted Charlie was nursing his beer. This told Keith Charlie probably wasn't much of a drinker. Once Keith had settled in, he answered Charlie's question. "It is my business, Sonny Jim. I need to know what you want a weapon for so I can sell you something that'll do the job, and by the way, if things go wrong, we've never met." Keith stared at Charlie who understood the implied threat. "So! What's it about. What do you need a gun for?"

Charlie thought it would do no harm to explain to this stranger what his plans were. "I've a score to settle with four ex-business colleagues who set me up. I've been inside for over seven years for something I didn't do." Charlie, having started his tale, knew he'd carry on. He felt he was in the confessional. "They caused the death of my wife and son. I'm going to kill each of them, that's why I need the gun."

The big man was surprisingly sympathetic and understanding. "Are you sure? It's one thing to have done a stretch but multiple murder is something else. For that they throw away the key. Do you have a plan on how you'll do it?"

"Not really but I want them to know it's me pulling the trigger."

Keith swallowed the rest of his beer. "And you're sure about this? Killing up front and personal isn't easy. A lot of hardened villains have bottled out of it. Why not let me get you a rifle? Easier to shoot from a distance and more clinical."

Charlie felt he was once more talking to a counsellor similar to the ones he'd met in prison. He shook his head. "Look Keith, I'm no marksman. I couldn't aim a rifle and hit anything. At least with a gun close up I can't miss."

Keith sat back examining his customer. "OK. You'll want a small calibre pistol, say a point two-two. I've got some Eastern bloc jobs that'll do you. It's five hundred quid. The gun and forty rounds of ammunition. Meet me here tomorrow at the same time and bring cash. All the identification numbers have been filed off the pistol. It'll be a chamber type, and I'll deliver it loaded. It takes six rounds and it'll be sanitised, no prints, no DNA. If you wear gloves it'll stay that way. Just one point. If you reload it make sure you wear gloves. People have been caught leaving a thumb print on the end of a bullet.

"After tomorrow we won't meet again, and the handover will be quick. I'll not hang around. If you're not here, I'll be off. I don't know who you are, and I don't want to. Understand? If Big Jimbo vouches for you, that's good enough."

Charlie nodded. Keith stood and left Charlie contemplating what he'd just set in motion. Charlie ordered another small beer and sat thinking and dreaming of how he would take his revenge.

***

The stolen phone arrived in Terry Harvey's technical section at 12.51 p.m. Terry and Andrew, his senior technician, immediately set to work inserting the small, miniscule device that would allow Steve full access to Max Ho's life for the next few days. Andrew had reported to Terry that the mobile was the model that would allow him to at least attempt to turn it into a full visual and twenty-four hour, voice transmittable device.

Max Ho would be under constant surveillance from the time he left the BBC based on Bob Class's plan. Matt Conway would oversee this and work with the three teams of watchers. Steve walked into Technical Support and was surprised by how calm and orderly it seemed. Given the arrival of the stolen phone he expected the place to be buzzing. He walked up to Terry who was hovering over a technician Steve took to be Andrew. Andrew had a large, illuminated magnifier positioned over the phone. Steve noticed the back was off the phone and the complicated looking circuitry that made it work was exposed. Andrew looked totally focused on his task. Terry turned to greet him with a beaming smile on his face. "It looks good, Steve. It's the right type of phone, so we should be able to deliver everything we said." Terry was like a young child. He could hardly stand still as he moved from foot to foot. It was clear to Steve his friend was excited.

"How long will you need, Terry?"

"Depends. Andrew here thinks to reconfigure the circuitry won't take more than an hour. We'll need another hour to test it and put a new fully charged battery in so there's no obvious extra battery drain, at least for the first twenty-four hours." Terry excitedly glanced over Andrew's shoulder as the senior technician completed another task on the intricate electronics of Max Ho's phone. As he looked up back at Steve, he smiled. "Looks like it's going well." Terry looked at his watch. "It's now 1.35 p.m. Andrew will need another say forty minutes, add an hour for testing and another half hour for any fault finding. Round it up to say four to be safe."

Steve considered this and nodded. "It's a bit tight but it'll work as long as you don't need more time. I've already got a motorbike on standby from three pm. I'll update traffic but I'll leave it at three in case you finish early."

His mind was spinning. "Let me know as soon as you think you're ready." Steve walked away and over his shoulder said, "Thanks Terry, if this works, I owe you a beer."

***

With nothing particular to do, Charlie Robb took the train to Gatwick Airport. He'd decided he needed a car and had calculated Gatwick Airport was the best place to get one. He'd be just another traveller in need of wheels. The shortest queue was at the Avis desk, but it still took thirty minutes to get to the head of the queue and another fifteen to complete the paperwork. Charlie paid cash for a fourteen day hire of a new Mini. It wasn't cheap despite being low season and the young, serious looking man who served him told him that if he'd pre-booked the price would have been thirty percent less.

Charlie had paid extra to have a car with sat nav built in. After inspecting the car for damage and finding none, Charlie sat in the car deciding what to do. He knew his first victim would be Colin Clark. He suddenly realised he knew nothing about his victim's current circumstances. A lot could have changed while he'd been away. He told himself the first thing to do was to confirm they still lived at the same addresses. With a smile, based on having a part of a plan and a purpose, Charlie keyed Queens Park into his sat nav, turned the ignition key and left the Avis rental carpark at Gatwick Airport. It was 4.11 p.m. He told himself he'd probably get caught up in rush hour traffic but decided it didn't matter. He had time and he needed to feel comfortable driving again after almost eight years including his time in pretrial custody. He followed the sat nav instructions and as he drove tried to remember Colin Clark's address. He had a dossier on all four men in a notebook that was resting in the inside pocket of his jacket. He smiled at the mental exercise he was enjoying trying to remember when all he had to do was look at his small notebook. He drove on telling himself, when he got to Queens Park, he'd stop and reset the sat nav once he'd looked up Colin's address.

With the aid of his sat nav, Charlie found the house of Colin Clark. It was a Victorian terrace that had rocketed in value during the London property boom. The whole street looked affluent and what Charlie remembered of Colin, he thought the little man might be out of place in this now affluent suburb of London. He found number 17 Blossom Avenue and parked a few doors past. He wasn't sure how to approach this. He only wanted to confirm if Colin Clark still lived at number 17.

As he walked past the neatly tended lawns and the houses that had turned their front gardens into off street parking, Charlie saw a man in the garden of number 15 who was trimming his hedge using a pair of hand operated shears. "Good afternoon, not a bad day for February." Charlie was jovial as he tried making polite conversation as he passed by the man.

"I suppose, but this hedge seems to keep growing. The more I trim it, the more it grows."

"Sorry, I can't help, I'm no gardener." As Charlie appeared to be ready to carry on past, he stopped and with what he hoped looked as though he had just had a sudden thought. "I don't suppose you know a Colin Clark that used to live here?"

The gardener stopped trimming his hedge and smiled. "Old Colin, he used to live next door." Stroking his chin, the man in number 15 seemed to be thinking. "He moved out about two years ago. He got involved in a messy divorce. He's moved to Kent, Bromley I think." Once more the gardener stood silently thinking. "Yes! Bromley. We got a Christmas card with his address. Why. are you looking for him?"

"Yes, we're old buddies. I've been working in the Far East for a few years. We always said we'd meet up once I got back but I've lost his new address. I don't suppose you could give me his Bromley address?"

"No problem, just a minute." The man entered his house and a few minutes later reappeared with a piece of paper. "There you are, I've added his phone number just in case you need it."

Charlie thanked the man and slowly wandered back to his car. Outwardly he was calm but inwardly he was elated. His first kill was in sight if Keith could produce the gun.

***

As Charlie Robb was leaving the rental carpark, an excited Inspector Terry Harvey appeared in Steve's office holding Max Ho's phone. "It's done, we've tested it, and everything works. I've taken a dump of his call history in case you ever need to see who he's been calling."

Si Griffiths had returned earlier and was sitting at his desk in the outer office. He overheard Terry's comments and entered Steve's office. "It's coming up for four. Do you want me to get that thing down to traffic and the motorbike lad?"

"Yes Si, it's for a PC Wheeler. He's been briefed on what to tell Max Ho about finding his phone. Remind him to call in as soon as he's handed it over."

He took the phone and disappeared. Terry took a seat in front of Steve's desk. "Now we wait. I hope the hell he doesn't question the personal service." Terry looked anxious.

"You look like an expectant father, Terry. Relax, let's just wait. Ho should have his phone before say five o'clock even if our PC Wheeler has to wait to hand it to him. Let's go grab a coffee." On the way past Bob Class's desk, Steve stopped. "Bob, Terry has a dump of calls made by our target. Terry, can you give it to Bob? Bob, have a look and see if anything pops up."

Terry reached for his mobile and hit a few keys before announcing, "There, you should have it, Bob." The two detectives left for the canteen and a nervous wait whilst Bob started interrogating the numbers called by Squadron Leader Max Ho over the past month.

***

PC Wheeler arrived outside the BBC at 4.53 p.m. He parked his large BMW motorbike, removed his helmet and his dayglo jacket before entering Broadcasting House. He immediately spotted a reception desk and a uniformed security guard sitting behind it. As PC Wheeler approached the guard finished a phone call and looked expectantly at the policeman.

"Can I leave my helmet and jacket with you?" Without waiting for confirmation, PC Wheeler placed his items on top of the high counter. Seeing nothing wrong, the guard took them and placed them on the floor on his side of the desk.

"I understand you have a Squadron Leader Max Ho in the building?" PC Wheeler was a large intimidating man, standing over six foot tall.

Without asking questions the guard looked up and started keying into his computer. After a few minutes he eventually looked at the policeman. "Yes, that's right, he's in studio seven, recording a radio programme. He should be almost finished."

"Can you call him please? I need to talk to him."

"Oh! I can't do that. I can call the studio and see when he's likely to be finished."

"Fine. Can you make the call?" PC Wheeler stood and while the guard spoke quietly into his phone the policeman took in his surroundings and as he did so, recognised several faces he'd seen on television coming and going. He thought his twelve-year old daughter would love to be with him now.

The guard eventually replaced the receiver. "He's just left. The producer is on her way down with him now. If you wait over by the security gate, you can't miss him."

PC Wheeler did as he was instructed and a few minutes later a smiling man of Oriental origins appeared talking to a middle-aged lady who only came up to his shoulder. The pair shook hands, and the tall Oriental man passed through the revolving security turnstile.

"Excuse me, sir. Are you Squadron Leader Max Ho?"

A surprised Max took a pace back and answered suspiciously, "Yes."

"We found an item earlier today, sir, that we believe belongs to you." PC Wheeler produced Max's phone and held it so Max could see it." Max started tapping his pockets to see if it could be his phone. He fully expected to find it in his jacket pocket.

After a frantic few seconds, he looked at the PC in amazement. "Where did you find it?"

"Is it yours, sir?"

Max took the phone and examined it. He switched it on and started to scroll through various data bases only he had. "Yes. It's definitely mine, but how did you know?"

"It was handed to a beat officer just outside the main door here, sir. The officer took it to our lost property office and the sergeant in charge switched it on and was able to see your name on some of your e-mails. It seems you're a bit of a favourite of his wife's, so he recognised your name. Given it was found outside the BBC and knowing you're a bit of a personality, he sent me here on the off chance, to see if you were here and if it was yours." PC Wheeler warmed to his story. "Seems he was right."

Max Ho stood, relieved, as he realised how important this phone was to him. "Constable, please tell your sergeant I am very grateful, and I shall take every opportunity to praise the police. This is magnificent service."

Not wishing to overplay his role, PC Wheeler simply said, "I'm glad we could be of service, sir."

The constable walked towards the guard to retrieve his helmet and jacket, just as a relieved Max Ho left the BBC building and headed for Oxford Circus tube station. He didn't see two ordinary looking men in cheap nondescript suits take up position behind him.

The surveillance of Max Ho had begun.

Chapter Eight

There was an air of excitement as Steve arrived at his office on Wednesday, February 9. Bob Class was typing furiously on his keyboard, while Matt Conway was on his mobile. He noted his latest member of staff, Simon Griffiths, wasn't at his desk. Both officers nodded an acknowledgement to their boss but carried on with their tasks. Before Steve could enter his inner office, Bob had stopped typing and said, "Inspector Harvey wants to see you, sir. He said it was urgent. Seems the phone's working."

Bob sat back and smiled as he saw the look of relief on Steve's face. "Right, I'd better get over there. Any joy with the phone log from Max Ho's phone?"

"Not so far, but I'm working on it."

Steve nodded and carried on into his office where he left his briefcase before setting out to the area of Technical Support. As he was leaving, Matt Conway said, "Before you go Steve, our surveillance teams reported nothing unusual in our boy's movements last night although the late team said he finished up in a strip club and took one of the girls home. If the phone's working it might be interesting to listen to what they talked about, that is if they talked at all." Both Steve and Bob grinned.

"You keep your mind on the job, Matt, I'll do the jokes." Still smiling, Steve finally set out to meet Terry Harvey.

Terry Harvey was as usual standing in the midst of a bank of computer screens talking to two very young-looking technicians. He wasn't wearing his jacket and had already loosened his tie and undone the top button of his shirt. Seeing Steve, he waved him over. "This is Pete and Brian; they've been monitoring Max Ho's phone."

Steve looked bewildered.

Terry carried on seeing the confused look on Steve's face. "OK, this is how it works. Andrew put the chip in the phone and redid some of the electronics so it's now voice and sound activated. So we don't miss anything. Pete and Brian here have rigged up a recorder that kicks into action every time Ho's phone goes live."

Steve saw where Terry was coming from. "You mean each time he uses the phone?"

"Yes. But remember, we were able to rig it so we could hear any speech or noise. Ho doesn't have to be using his phone for us to hear what's he's saying. If he closes a door, we'll hear it."

"And all this is being recorded?"

"Exactly. I've arranged with a mate of mine to transcribe each twenty-four hour recordings, so you'll have a paper record, and then there's the camera."

"Ah, yes, did it work? Did you get any pictures?"

"We got some but when he has his phone in his pocket, we get nothing. But interestingly, he charges his phone on a nightstand beside his bed. It must be one of those latest horizontal chargers where you don't plug the phone in. All you do is lay it on a wireless charger."

Steve could see Terry had something more to say. "And?"

With a smile the inspector switched on a monitor. "There! You're looking at Max Ho's bedroom as seen through the camera in his mobile phone. The picture quality isn't great, but we can enhance any images that become important. Looks like the squadron leader is a bit of an athlete." Terry smiled as the pair watched Max Ho and the girl from the strip club enjoying each other.

"We're recording the video link separately. All in all, I'd say Andrew's done a great job. I just hope we don't get caught."

"Thanks, Terry. This is great work." Steve became serious. "I've got teams following Ho on the ground. I'll try and get this operation over and done with before the weekend. The less time we're using this spyware the better."

"Good, because I confess, I'm feeling a bit exposed. Have you told Commander Hargreaves about this?"

Steve thought back to his meeting with Perry Hargreaves yesterday. The commander had been very clear. Steve was to get this surveillance wrapped up and get back to proper policing. He was already getting questions from Colonel Walters. "Er! No. He wasn't in a very receptive mood. I got an impression he wouldn't approve if he knew."

Terry gave a deep sigh. "I hope you know what you're doing, Steve. If we're caught, we'll be hung out to dry."

"Yes, I know. I'll take all the heat if it comes out and keep you out of it."

Terry Harvey laughed. "And how will you explain the technology? Thanks for the thought, my friend, but I'm in this with you up to my neck." Still smiling, Terry touched the side of his nose. "Just don't get caught. I'll keep these two on monitoring duties and if anything that sounds important comes up, you'll be the first to know."

Steve admired Terry's courage and loyalty. He knew both their careers would be over if word got out as to what they were doing. Steve left Technical Support determined not to drop his friend in any sort of trouble.

Back in his office Steve picked up the coroner's report into the death of DC Amelia Cooper or Poppy as she was known. Steve's meeting with her uncle Terry Harvey had brought back the memory of the pain he knew Terry had felt when Poppy was shot by a spymaster while following up her own theory of a kidnapping case the team had been working on. Steve had kept the file on his desk to remind him he had vowed to discover the identity of the masked man. No one knew who he was, but it was a loose end the DCI was determined to tie up.

Steve looked at his watch. It was 10.15 a.m. He wandered into the outer office. He knew Matt would be out chasing up the teams who were keeping tabs on Max Ho. Bob Class was still typing into his computer and DS Simon Griffiths' desk was still empty.

Bob looked up and stopped keying. "I don't know if it's significant boss, but our boy has been calling the same mobile number twice a day for over a week. I've tracked it down but it's an unregistered phone." Bob looked expectantly at his DCI. "What do you want me to do?"

Steve stood thinking and was about to give Bob an instruction when DS Si Griffiths arrived munching into a bacon roll. Steve made an exaggerated motion with his left hand as he looked at his watch. He made no effort to disguise his angry tone. "My office NOW, sergeant!"

As Si Griffiths shrugged and walked past his senior officer, Steve turned to Bob. "Good work, Bob. Keep going through his phone records. When you're done, make a list of calls we should take a closer look at. Terry Harvey may have a few ideas."

Seated behind his desk, Steve instructed Si Griffiths to remain standing. "Sergeant, I don't know who the hell you think you are, but in my unit, you have to have a bloody good reason for turning up after eight a.m." Steve deliberately calmed himself down. "Let's hear it. Why have you only now arrived?"

Si finished his roll and wiped the grease from around his mouth using the back of his hand. He was about to pull over a chair from the conference table. "Don't sit down. I'm waiting for your answer."

"Well, like I told you, SIR, I'm all about retiring. I'm staying in that crappy section house with all those young, keen coppers most of whom haven't even started shaving. My world's in a suitcase along with all my possessions, so if you'll forgive me, I'm not too bothered about your rules or your unit, SIR."

Steve felt for this untidy looking policeman and to a point regretted his anger. Si was wearing the same jacket and trousers as yesterday, the same stained tie hanging loosely around his neck but a different shirt. Steve noticed the collar of the shirt was frayed. This was not someone who would be selected for a police recruitment poster.

"OK, sit down!" Whilst Si did as instructed Steve had an idea. "Look Si, you have been posted to my team and you'll knuckle down and at least act like a detective sergeant. Your attitude is disrespectful to your fellow officers." Steve stared at his errant colleague trying to gauge how much of what he was saying was getting home. He carried on. "Now, listen. You've explained about your domestic situation, about your broken marriages and frankly I believe you think the whole world is against you. You think your solution is to take early retirement. Well, if you help me out, I'll see what I can do to get you what you want."

Si's jaw dropped in surprise. "Well, keep talking sir, anything to get out of this mob." He was smiling and showing off his yellowed and crooked teeth.

Steve sat back reconsidering his decision but eventually agreeing with himself it was the only plan he had. He picked up the coroner's report on Poppy. "This is a coroner's report on the killing of your predecessor. You'll see the circumstances of how she was killed. The actual killer was himself shot a split second after Poppy." The DCI went on to explain the context of Poppy's involvement and how he still felt guilty that he hadn't given her more support. He explained the case they were working on and why Poppy had been where she was.

"The guy who killed Poppy's murderer seems to have shot from outside, entered through the French windows, lifted a briefcase and disappeared. He was dressed in black and wore a balaclava so he wouldn't be recognised. If you can find this man, your retirement is guaranteed. What do you say?"

Si sat staring at the DCI's desk and the file. "You said there were two witnesses and they're doing time. Can I speak with them?"

"No reason not to but remember they are on espionage charges so you may find it more difficult to get in to see them. Special Branch took over the case. If you need my help, just ask."

"Right. And if I find this gunman, you'll sign my papers?"

"Yes."

"And this is the only case you want me to work on?"

"Yes."

"Right sir, I'm your man. With my contacts finding this bloke shouldn't be hard. There can't be too many shooters who could have pulled of that shot."

"I hope you're right, sergeant." Steve handed Si the file. "Get Bob to get you a copy of the original case file. It'll help you see the bigger picture. When you find this bloke, you're to tell me and no one else. This is between you and me. Understand?"

"Yes, sir." With a flourish Si Griffiths, now looking much happier than when he arrived, stood, replaced his chair and with the file under his arm made to leave.

"One other thing, sergeant, I'll authorise a five hundred quid grant from the Met's hardship fund. Use it to smarten yourself up. Buy some new gear, Primark do some cheap bargains. Draw the money from treasury this afternoon." As an afterthought, Steve said, "And keep me informed. I don't want you totally off the grid. I need to hear from you every day. Is that clear?"

A happy detective sergeant saluted with his free hand. "Loud and clear."

As Steve's office door closed behind Si he wondered again if he had made the right decision. "Too late now, Steve my boy, let's see how it works out." The DCI often spoke out loud to himself when he felt under stress.

***

Charles Robb was sitting in the foyer of the Mayflower Hotel, consulting his London A to Z. His meeting this Wednesday morning with Keith in the Five Bells Public House was scheduled for around eleven thirty. Charlie had asked the concierge to get him the full address of the Five Bells just off the Mile End Road. He now had this information and would key it into the sat nav of his new hire car. It was 10.36 am. Unknown to Charlie this was exactly the same time DS Simon Griffiths was leaving his boss's office to seek a killer and earn his retirement.

Charlie walked into the Five Bells pub at 11.22 a.m. As before, he ordered a sparkling water and took the same seat he had used yesterday. He allowed himself to daydream how he might kill Colin Clark. For the first time since he was sentenced the reality of what he was planning, hit him. He'd never fired a gun before and had certainly never killed anyone before. He came out in a light sweat as he realised he was not prepared and despite his overwhelming desire for revenge, he questioned whether he could carry out the killings he had fantasized about for years. In a near panic Charlie decided he couldn't go through with his plan for revenge and decided to leave. Just then the door of the lounge bar opened and Keith walked in.

Charlie, on seeing the big man, sat down. He quickly told himself even if he bought the gun, he didn't have to use it. Keith took the same seat as yesterday. Without speaking he laid a cardboard box slightly smaller than the average shoe box on the table. "Everything you need is in there. It's a .22 like I said and twenty-four bullets. That should be enough. The gun and ammunition are sanitised, no prints and no DNA. The gun is untraceable so there's no comeback on me." Keith leant forward towards Charlie. "If you cock it up, you're on your own.

Remember to wear rubber gloves at all times especially when you're loading the thing. Now, I'll have my five hundred quid."

The now reluctant assassin pulled an envelope from the inside pocket of his jacket and slid it across the table. Keith ripped it open and quickly confirmed the amount was correct. Satisfied, Keith stood, and without another word, left leaving Charlie with a glass of fizzy water and a cardboard box. Charlie didn't know what to do. He didn't want to open the box in this public place. He decided a trip to Bromley to see where Colin Clark lived wouldn't do any harm. He told himself he could park up in a layby and examine his purchase although he told himself he wouldn't use it.

With this sketchy plan in his head, Charlie Robb left the Five Bells and headed for Bromley in Kent. It was 11.32 a.m.

***

Max Ho enjoyed his slow starts in the morning. When he was flying, he'd never get to lie in bed beyond six a.m. It was eleven thirty and he was only now deciding to leave his bed. He recalled the girl he had brought back last night and smiled as he remembered how her body was covered in tattoos and some of them were in hard-to-reach places. He'd called her a taxi just before three a.m., paid her the fee they'd agreed, and ushered her out of the door of his flat. He didn't care what happened to her after she left. She'd served her purpose.

Max stretched over and grabbed his phone. He checked it was fully charged and he hadn't any unanswered calls. With a shudder he thought back to yesterday and the policeman who returned his phone. His whole life was in this phone and its loss would be devastating. He secretly thanked the police as he replaced his phone on the nightstand and headed for his bathroom and a shower. He told himself he'd have to be more careful in future.

Dressed and scrubbed, Max Ho left his flat in Greenwich. He was travelling by public transport to his only appointment of the day. He was meeting three gentlemen from the country of his birth to learn when his mission on their behalf should be completed. He had the address of a café in Haringey and directions on how to find it.

The two plain clothes police officers who saw Max leave his building had no idea where he was going but were relieved he had chosen public transport. Following someone by car in London was difficult. One officer scurried to get closer to his target whilst the other stayed with their car. He would receive messages from his colleague as Max's journey unfolded and manoeuvre the car, so he was always able to provide back up if it were needed.

As Max made his way towards Haringey, not only was he being followed but his phone was constantly confirming his location.

The trip to Haringey was long and tedious. Max had been told to look out for people following him, and to be aware he may be under surveillance. Max largely ignored the advice. He wasn't aware anyone was interested in him and knew his role in the RAF gave him a certain status. He was cautious but not overly concerned. Using a collection of underground trains and buses, Max Ho arrived at the café that said it specialised in Far Eastern food. The building was located in a narrow lane off Haringey High Street and looked as though it were ready to fall down. The café looked as rundown as the building.

Had Max taken more care he might have spotted a man standing at the end of the lane innocently talking on his mobile phone. This was his police shadow contacting his partner in the car. The shadow having told his partner where he was then made a second call to DI Matt Conway.

The red paint on its door was flaking, and the only window hadn't had the attention of a window cleaner in years. Max entered the dark and dingy space that had at one time been a café. The room still contained a few tables and a few chairs as testimony to its heritage, but everything was covered in dust and cobwebs; this café was not a going concern. From what Max assumed was a back room a small Oriental man appeared. He was carrying a pistol and pointing it at Max. "Who are you?"

Max wasn't afraid but was nervous. The other North Koreans he'd met previously were cultured and educated. They'd taken tea and discussed how he could help his native land and how he would be treated as a hero if he succeeded in hijacking the aircraft.

This reception and the premises were completely different. "My name is Max Ho. I'm supposed to meet someone called Sky here at two." Max's watch told him it was 1.51 p.m.

The little man with the gun continued to point it at Max. He made his way past Max to the door and using all his strength banged it shut and bolted it at the top. He lowered his gun and jammed it into the waistband of his trousers. "Come. You are most welcome, Ho." The man bowed to Max and using his arms indicated that Max should follow him. The man entered the back room and held back the old heavy and dirty curtain that separated the back room from the main floor. On entry, Max saw two other Oriental men sitting at a round table. Both were smoking and the atmosphere was heavy with cigarette smoke and not helped by the use of a paraffin-powered lamp that allowed black smoke to rise into the closed atmosphere of the room.

Max estimated the room was about twelve-foot square and had no windows. The only source of light was the paraffin lamp. The floor was covered in an old threadbare multicoloured carpet that Max could just see. One of the men stood and gave a small bow. "Welcome, Ho, I am Sky. It is from me you will receive your instructions. You must be honoured to know your instructions come directly from our glorious leader who sends you his personal good wishes."

Max knew the culture in North Korea was different and knew how things worked. This formal introduction was all part of a ritual designed to put everyone in their place and signify their importance to the cause. The man called Sky indicated Max should sit. "Can we offer you tea, squadron leader?"

Max realised he hadn't eaten. "Yes, thank you." As he sat his mobile phone rang. Max extracted it from his jacket pocket and seeing it was from a withheld number decided not to answer it.

The man calling himself Sky looked at the phone. "May I ask that you switch your phone off, squadron leader. We find they can be an unknown and often unwelcome source of information." Max obeyed and switched his phone off but left it by his right hand on the table.

The withheld number call from Matt Conway had worked. Having received the call from Max Ho's watcher, the team at the Yard realised the phone wasn't picking anything up from the conversation the pilot must be having inside the derelict café. With the phone now in the open the technicians were able to record the conversations and see inside the café.

Sky didn't introduce either of his colleagues. Max wondered how good the other's English was and how much they would understand of his upcoming discussion with Sky.

Making polite conversation as he waited for his tea, Max asked how Sky had got to the UK. "Our glorious leader ordered teachers from the university to infiltrate ourselves into European countries. I was a professor of English, so it was natural that I was assigned to London. My journey was not easy. I was smuggled into the land to the south by fellow patriots. I hid for several months whilst I acquired the necessary forged papers that made me appear to be a South Korean citizen. With these papers I flew to London and now because of our glorious leader's forward thinking, I am here to assist you in your daring adventure that will mean our country will be in its rightful place on the world stage. With your aircraft as the prototype, we can have a world class air force better than all of the Western worlds."

Max hadn't heard this speech before and was impressed. He was however grateful that Sky stopped his narrative and turned his attention to pouring the tea.

The recorders within the technical support area of New Scotland Yard were now recording and seeing everything that was going on in the dingy little café. They even saw the tea being poured from a cracked teapot. Terry Harvey was amazed by the photographic resolution considering how dark the café was.

The next hour could determine Max Ho's fate depending on what was said.

Chapter Nine

Detective Sergeant Simon Griffiths was happiest when he was on the streets meeting criminals he'd known for years, many of whom he'd arrested, usually more than once.

The promise of early retirement had put a spring in his step, and he was determined to discover the identity of the hooded gunman the boss wanted found. He had an idea where to find the informant he thought was most probably able to help, but like most of his snouts who didn't want to be found, the trail was cold. As Si walked between cafes, betting shops and pubs looking for his man he thought about the DCI. He realised Steve Burt was an OK guy. Si knew he'd pushed the boundaries with his attitude and insubordination, yet the DCI had arranged the five hundred pounds grant realising Si was down on his luck. He told himself, "Not many bosses would have done that." He suddenly had a warm feeling about working for this boss.

Si found the downmarket brothel he was looking for. It supposedly traded as a night club, and Si knew the vice squad visited it regularly. It was owned by an ex-con called Pete Hathaway. Pete was a career criminal who had spent half his fifty years inside one prison or another. The last time Si arrested him was for pimping and having drugs with intent to supply. Pete had been given an eight-year sentence, but a kindly parole board had released him after just under four. Pete was harmless. He wasn't big and not known to be violent. Si thought of him as a slob in a five foot eight-inch-tall body. He had a tendency to wear vests instead of shirts and his greying hair always looked like it needed washing. He had always been slim, weighing no more than one hundred and forty pounds dripping wet, but to his credit he knew his place and had never tried to muscle in on the bigger crooks' territory.

Pete had bought the club on his release and for the past few years had stayed out of trouble. Si knew an old lag like Pete would never be completely clean and would still have underworld contacts that might be of use to him in his present search. Pete owed Si a favour or two for turning a blind eye to some of Pete's less serious but still illegal activities over the past few years. It was time for Si to collect.

He entered the club through a side door. The gaudily painted purple main door was locked. Inside, the place smelt of bad body odour and cheap furniture polish. Si knew the layout having been a guest of Pete a few times. He recalled the girls were all past their sell by dates and the clientele were mainly older men all too drunk to realise they were buying fizzy lemonade thinking it was champagne at ten pounds a glass.

Si looked around the dark space. There were a few lights on behind the bar and a red emergency exit light illuminated the door Si had just entered through. A scantily dressed girl who might have been fifteen but looked like thirty was sitting at one of the tables seemingly playing a game on her mobile phone.

"I'm looking for Pete."

"Yeah. So what?"

"I want to talk to him. Is he in?"

"Couldn't say."

Si approached the girl. On inspection it was obvious she was high probably on cocaine. "Listen, dear." Si bent down to look her squarely in the eyes. "I'm police and you're high. So put a civil tongue in your head or I'll have you up on drug charges. Now, is Pete in?"

It took the girl a few seconds to understand. Once she did, she nodded weakly. "Yeah. He's in his office but I think he's sleeping."

Si knew where the office was, but the girl helpfully pointed to a curtain that hung in the far left-hand corner. Si knew Pete often lived in his office for days at a time. It was against all the regulations, but Si wasn't bothered. Compliance with local planning laws wasn't his thing.

To Si's surprise the office door was ajar. He pushed it fully opened to see Pete sitting at his desk. "Well, well, if it isn't my favourite detective. What the hell do you want?" Pete's words were slurred, and the reason was obvious. He had a half empty bottle of single malt whisky on his desk and a glass containing the amber liquid in his hand.

"Bit early to be on the booze Pete. Drowning your sorrows?"

"None of your business but I suppose you'll want one?" Pete reached for another glass from the shelf behind his desk. Si nodded and sat on the unmade bed that was against one wall of the room. Pete poured a large measure and topped up his own glass. Si stretched across and picked up the glass.

The detective sergeant sipped the liquid surprised by the ferocity of the burn as the liquid slid down his throat and hit his stomach. "Good stuff, Pete, your taste's improving."

Si looked round the room. Apart from the desk and the chair Pete was sitting on plus the bed Si was using, there was no other furniture in the room. The air was thick with cigarette smoke and the floor had been left uncarpeted to show the floorboards. The walls had once been white but were now a muddy grey colour. "Still not had the decorators in then, Pete?"

Pete looked suspiciously at the detective. "Never mind the small talk, Mr Griffiths. Just tell me what you want?"

"I'm looking for Tom Thumb, but nobody seems to know where he is. I thought as you owe me, you might like to help me find him?"

"Why do you want Tom?"

"My business, Pete. You know how it works. Now do you know where he is?"

. Instead of thinking how he might help Si, Pete was looking for an angle that might benefit him. "No, Mr Griffiths, I haven't seen Tom in months."

Si's pool of informants consisted of low life characters like Pete who maybe washed three times a week, to higher end individuals like Thomas Clearwater known to the criminal fraternity as Tom Thumb due to his liking of the small cigars of that name. Tom showered every day, wore expensive clothes and used aftershave by the gallon. He was a Mr Fixit within the London underworld but was also an informant. Si felt Tom would be a good bet to shed light on the identity of the hooded man.

"Pete, don't lie to me. I know Tom comes to this club once a week to meet with certain high rollers for a bit of illegal gambling. If you keep lying, I'll have to get a bunch of bobbies down here with their size ten boots. Now, be sensible, just tell me where I can find him?"

As Si sipped his whisky a sly grin came over Pete's face. "If I did know how you might find him, what's in it for me?"

Si tilted his glass to his lips and drained it. He stood and slowly walked towards Pete who sat back in his chair trying to increase the distance between him and the policeman. Si wasn't big but he was bigger than Pete. Without warning, Si pulled Pete's dirty vest towards him, ripping the material. He let go a punch that winded the night club owner and allowed him to sag back into his chair. Si took the whisky bottle and poured himself a small measure before emptying the contents onto the floor.

"Now Pete, remember it's me you're lying to. You know I can be good, or I can be very, very bad." The detective allowed a tone to enter his voice. The tone was full of malice. "Don't try and negotiate with me. Understand?"

Pete still feeling the effects of the punch, nodded. Si continued to stand and finished his whisky. "Good, now where will I find Tom Thumb?"

Si left the club at two p.m. exactly, as Max Ho was being served tea, and Charlie Robb arrived in Bromley.

***

Charlie wasn't sure how he would proceed. He had scared himself by just thinking about how he could ever consider taking a human life. As he drove following his sat nav he glanced at the cardboard box on the passenger seat. In the distance he saw a pub with a large and busy car park. He decided to have something to eat and consider what he would do next.

Despite the number of cars in the car park he had no difficulty finding a table in a corner well away from the other customers. He nervously placed his box on the chair opposite him and ensured the chair was fully under the table. He ordered the gammon steak and a small beer from the pretty waitress who arrived at his table within minutes of him sitting down. The beer arrived quickly, and Charlie noticed the pub was emptying. The lunchtime trade was over.

With his beer in his hand, he sat back and allowed his mind to wander. He worked out various scenarios in his head hoping to find a solution and a plan. He reminded himself that his present circumstances were caused by the greed of the four individuals who in Charlie's mind, had deliberately set him up to take the fall when their criminal enterprise was discovered. He remembered arriving home to find his wife and son lying on the kitchen floor and a monster of a man standing over them. He had still held the kitchen knife he'd used to kill them in his hand, the pools of blood surrounding his wife and the small figure of his son lying with staring eyes still holding his mother's hand.

He heard the big man tell him not to squeal to the cops or he would get the same as his family, and saw himself collapsed beside the bodies, holding his wife and son, their blood seeping into his clothes. Then the big man had left, saying the words that had driven Charlie on towards his revenge.

"Mr Lockwood is not a man to be crossed. Keep your mouth shut and do the time that's coming to you." Charlie couldn't remember the big man's face now, nor recall any of his features, but he did recall the message. He also remembered his overwhelming desire for revenge against the killer and those who had hired him, although at the time, racked with grief, he had no idea what the message meant.

That was nine years ago, and his memory had faded. He now found it difficult to remember images of his wife and son. Had he not had photographs of them from happier times it would almost be as if they had never existed. He knew finding the big killer would be impossible, but he did know the four people responsible for his family's deaths.

His thoughts were interrupted by the arrival of the pretty waitress with his lunch. Charlie wiped his eyes with his napkin and began to pick at his meal, but he wasn't hungry. He hadn't planned to think about the night of his family's murder, but the details had come flooding back. The scene in the kitchen when he walked in on that Tuesday evening was engrained in his memory. All Charlie Robb wanted was revenge, starting with Colin Clark.

After paying for his meal, Charlie set off to find a pharmacy where he bought a pack of disposable gloves as advised by Keith. With the cardboard box on the front seat of the mini, Charlie followed his sat nav to the home of Colin Clark. He'd hoped to have a plan, but now the need for revenge was stronger than ever. He couldn't get caught until all four investors were dead. Once that had been achieved, it didn't matter what happened to him.

As he drove, a rough plan formed in his mind. He knew he wanted each of his investors to know they were going to die, and Keith had supplied a weapon for that purpose. In the case of Colin Clark, Charlie decided a frontal approach would be best. He'd simply knock on his door and see how things developed from there.

With the aid of his sat nav, Charlie found Colin Clark's home. It was a Victorian terrace in a less than fashionable part of Bromley. The small front garden was overgrown, and the windows were dirty. Each house in the row looked the same. Sitting in his car and wearing a pair of disposable gloves, Charlie loaded the small black pistol. It took six bullets. Placing the cardboard box containing the rest of the bullets in the car's boot and with the pistol in his jacket pocket, Charlie approached the front door of number 77.

He rang the bell and waited. He nervously realised he hadn't thought of a cover story. Before he could start to think the door opened and a woman in her early fifties, dressed casually, stood in front of him. "Yes. Can I help you?"

"Does a Mr Clark live here?"

"Yes. Who are you?"

Ignoring the question, Charlie rushed on. "Is he at home?"

"No. Who are you and what do you want?"

"I'm an old friend and I need to talk to him. Are you Mrs Clark?"

"No. I'm his partner if you must know. Now who are you? Colin doesn't get any visitors."

Still ignoring the woman's question, Charlie asked, "When will he be back?"

The woman looked suspiciously at Charlie.

"He won't be back till late. He works part time in the office and then in a pub. It's in the City, The Cock and Squirrel, just off Fleet Street. If you want to talk to him that's where he'll be from four till eight. City pubs close early." The woman was about to close the door but stopped to ask, "What's your name?"

"It doesn't matter, I'll catch Colin another time." Charlie turned and left the woman with the door halfway closed.

***

At three p.m. Terry Harvey called Steve Burt. "We've got something. Care to pop over and have a listen?"

"You bet, I'm on my way."

Steve walked over with Matt Conway and Bob Class to the viewing area of the Met's Technical Support team. Terry was as usual leaning over one of his technicians examining a computer monitor as the three detectives walked in. All three knew the procedure and each took a seat awaiting Terry's attention. Terry acknowledged their arrival with a wave but continued his conversation with the technician. Steve recognised the seated man as Andrew, Terry's senior man and the person who had fixed Max Ho's phone.

After about five minutes a smiling Terry took a seat located to one side of the large television screen that dominated the room. He could see all three detectives from his position. "Right then. First, we have the audio of the meeting your man had with someone called Sky. From his accent we knew he was probably from the Far East but during the discussion he tells us he's from North Korea. I'll play the audio first. We've enhanced it but we lost the initial part because the phone must have been in the target's pocket. Matt called him and we have everything after that."

Matt interrupted. "I've had his shadow confirm he left the so-called café at 2.49 p.m. Looks like he's on his way home."

"Good." Terry turned to his senior technician. "Andy, start the audio please?"

Everyone sat in silence as they listened to Sky explain how he had been ordered to arrive in the UK and be available to serve his glorious leader. Terry, using a remote controller, stopped the recording. "I don't think there's any doubt your man is talking to someone from North Korea."

Terry restarted the recording. The audience heard tea being served and more talk about how Max Ho would be treated back in the land of his birth. Max was heard describing his career in the RAF and how much he enjoyed flying. The man called Sky was heard to say that with Max's skills and service to the great and glorious leader, he would be given a senior post in the country's soon to be new Air Force.

At the mention of Air Force, Steve sat forward, concentrating.

The recording continued and Sky was talking. "We have arranged for you to give us your flight plan. Our Russian allies want you to carry this small device." A faint noise was heard as Steve looked quizzically at Terry and Matt. The conversation carried on. "You are to switch it on when you enter Russian airspace. It will send out a coded message our allies can interpret, and they will be able to track you even though their radar systems cannot see you. Is that clear?"

A voice everyone assumed belonged to Max said it understood. Sky's voice was once more heard coming from the speakers. "Our Russian allies will assist you with refuelling and in order you can talk to them, here is the radio frequency you should switch to when you activate the transponder. They will guide you to a suitable airbase."

The faint sound of paper being folded was heard before Max spoke. "I understand all that but is it wise to trust the Russians? What do I do if they simply impound the aircraft and keep it for themselves?"

Sky appeared not to have thought of this possibility as it took him several seconds to answer. "A good but unworthy question, squadron leader. Our Russian allies know how important this venture is to our people and indeed theirs and our Chinese friends. We have a three-way alliance to use your aircraft as a model for our future Air Forces. Our glorious leader has had personal assurances from the leaders of both Russia and China that we will share in this glorious weapon that you are bringing to us. We have already arranged to have Chinese and Russian engineers available to welcome you. They are the best aviation brains in the world. Production arrangements in all three countries have already been started, so please, squadron leader, do not entertain such negative thoughts."

Max was heard speaking again. "I understand and I apologise. After I take off from Russia what are my instructions?"

Sky was heard responding. "You will continue to fly east, and I believe you have indicated you will require a second fuel stop in Russia.

You will leave the transponder switched on and remain on the same radio frequency. As before you will be guided to an airfield and refuelled. At this second stop you will be given a different radio frequency, but you will continue to leave the transponder switched on. Our Chinese friends will monitor your progress and afford you the right to overfly their airspace and be refuelled. Once you leave the Chinese airfield your next stop will be in our glorious People's Republic. We will speak to you on the same frequency as the one the Chinese give you. Once you have safely landed your first job is done."

The recording was silent for a few minutes. The police officers listening could only imagine what was going on. Eventually the voice of Max Ho came through the speakers. "My aircraft will be unarmed. The UK authorities won't just let me lift off and disappear. They'll try and stop me. Remember they have connections with other European Air Forces. What do I do if I'm intercepted?"

The man known as Sky was apparently ready for this question. His voice immediately thundered from the speaker. "My dear Max, your aircraft cannot be seen on radar. You have told us it is faster than any other fighter in the world and it can fly higher than the Americans U2 spy plane. Our experts say it is impossible for you to be intercepted and this is why you will only activate your transponder once you are over Russia. The West would never dare violate such airspace and if they did such is the importance of your mission that Russian fighters would be sent to intercept any Western incursion."

The speakers fell silent, then Sky continued. "We have everything ready for the seventeenth of this month. That is in just over one week. You have said the aircraft is grounded for additional servicing, but you must be ready for the seventeenth. Here is a phone number you are to call one hour before you steal the aircraft. The person who answers will put everything into motion. Do not steal the aircraft without phoning that number as instructed."

Once more the speakers fell silent. The sound of chairs being pushed back was heard before Sky was back. "Squadron leader, our glorious leader and our entire country are counting on your success. Your courage will shine far into the future as you help us become equal partners in the tri-alliance with our neighbours, a glorious beginning for all of us. Good luck, we shall not meet again but I will be kept informed of your successful exploits."

Max was heard saying his goodbyes before the recording started spitting out static. Max must have put his phone back in his pocket.

Everyone in the viewing room sat back, each thinking their own thoughts. The DCI spoke first. "Well, there's no doubt our man, Max, is guilty. He's clearly tied up with the North Koreans and he's planning to give them this secret fighter. Question is what do we do? This is an unofficial inquiry. My orders are to write a report and submit it proving if Max Ho is innocent or guilty." Steve saw a warning look on Matt Conway's face. Neither Terry nor Andrew the technician had been read into the case. The DCI was in danger of saying too much. He nodded his appreciation to his DI.

"We have the video if you want to see it. It was very grainy, but we've managed to clean it up. There's not much to see because the phone was static once it was placed on the table."

Steve was keen to learn as much as he could. Serious decisions would have to be made. "Let's see it, Terry. We might learn a bit more."

Andrew, sitting in front of his bank of monitors, typed a few instructions into his keyboard and the large TV screen jumped into life. Terry was correct. Apart from the teapot and a teacup being placed on the table, the image was static. The speakers were still switched on, so everyone heard once more the conversation between Max Ho and Sky. As they watched, Max had obviously touched his phone and it moved a few degrees to the right before he returned it to its original position.

"Stop it there!" Steve was on his feet and sprang towards the oversized TV screen. "Play it back a few seconds to when the phone is moved and stop it." Andrew did as requested. "Now can you forward it frame by frame and freeze each one until I ask you to move to the next one?"

The room could see Steve was excited, but no one knew why or what he was looking for. Andrew moved the first four frames on Steve's instructions. There was nothing to see. When the fifth frame was shown, the DCI stepped closer to the screen. Almost talking to himself he was heard to say "Yes," before asking Andrew to show frame six. As soon as it appeared Steve jumped back. "Yes! Yes! Yes." The image on the screen was faint but it was clearly showing an Oriental man sitting at the table. "Unless I'm mistaken, that's our man Sky." Turning to Terry, he said, "Can you enhance that shot?"

Terry looked across to Andrew who nodded and started keying into his bank of computers. While he was doing this Bob Class spoke up. "Why do you want to know what this Sky looks like, sir?" Matt and Terry had been wondering the same thing.

"If we can get a clear image, we might discover who this Sky is. If he's a North Korean spy he's better behind bars than out there running around stealing our secrets. Besides, I have a plan. We'll discuss it later."

Everyone knew better than to further question the DCI. Once Andrew had finished massaging the image it reappeared on the screen but this time brighter and clearer. It showed what appeared to be a small Oriental man with a full head of black hair and a distinctive cherry birth mark on his left cheek. The image was crystal clear and anyone meeting this man would instantly recognise him from this picture.

"Well done, Terry, and you, Andrew. Can you get me copies of that image as soon as, please? Also, Terry, keep the phone live for another twenty-four hours and Matt keep the watchers on our Max Ho. I've a hunch we've more to learn." The DCI signalled his troops to return to the office leaving Terry and Andrew to wonder what exactly was going on.

Chapter Ten

Steve and his team returned to their offices as Sir Patrick Bond entered his old MI6 building to be greeted by the receptionist who knew him when he was head of the service.

"Good afternoon, Sir Patrick, no need to sign in, sir. Mr Russell is waiting for you in conference room ten. You know where it is of course."

The receptionist had been sitting at her desk for what appeared to Sir Patrick to have been forever. He knew she had served MI6 for over thirty years as its receptionist and showed no sign of retiring.

"Thank you, Audrey, I'll just make my way up."

Sir Patrick arrived on the tenth floor and entered room ten. It was one of the smaller conference rooms within the imposing structure that housed MI6, but Sir Patrick thought it was one of the most comfortable. A small cabinet sat in one corner housing the room's alcohol store. Despite it only being a little after four, Mike Russell, the current head of the service, sat at the table holding a small glass of whisky and appeared to be reading a file. He stood to greet his guest. "A drink, Patrick?"

"No, thank you Mike, despite being retired it's a little early for me."

"Fine, have a seat. I gather you're seeking out information on hit squads?" The present head of MI6 seemed to regard the subject as a bit of a joke. His attitude suggested there were no such things.

"Yes, I understand a contract has been placed on a member of our armed forces but gather there may be some uncertainty. Care to comment?" Sir Patrick didn't like his replacement and felt he wasn't up to the job. He was enjoying this encounter.

"Well, Patrick, you know I couldn't possibly confirm or deny anything."

"Mike." Sir Patrick let out a theatrical sigh. "I know what goes on. I want to know if you have any active cases at the moment involving a military man?"

Mike Russell sat back and looked Sir Patrick straight in the eyes. "Not that I know of."

"Fine. Can you ask for an up to date position now and confirm to me that is indeed the case."

Russell stood and using the internal phone dialled a three-digit number and spoke briefly to someone on the other end. Sir Patrick couldn't hear what was said. Mike Russell replaced the receiver and being on his feet beside the cabinet, took the opportunity to refill his glass.

Seated again at the table, Mike Russell asked, "Why do you want to know if we have any active elimination cases?" He was clearly suspicious of his predecessor's motives.

Sir Patrick had no intention of answering until he had more information. "Just something that's come up." Patrick Bond shrugged and sat back.

Silence filled the room until a sharp knock at the door announced the arrival of a woman Sir Patrick knew well. She used to be his personal assistant, now a function she performed for Mike Russell. After the usual greetings and 'not seen you for ages' talk, the woman called Hillary sat opposite her old boss. She had brought a thin file.

Mike Russell smiled before asking, "Sir Patrick here is asking if we have any active elimination cases on the go at the moment. I've told him we don't, but he seems to want confirmation."

Hillary opened the file and pushed it towards Sir Patrick. "That's a summary of all our elimination cases for the past twelve months. You'll see everyone has been crossed through, meaning it has been dealt with."

Patrick picked up the file. The single sheet of A4 paper contained four lines, each neatly typed giving a name, a reference as to the unit assigned to carry out the task and a date that indicated when the assassination had been carried out. The last entry was dated six months earlier. Sir Patrick pushed the file back across to Hillary. "And that's it, you're certain you have no elimination cases ongoing?"

Mike Russell looked to be getting angry and was trying not to show it. "Look, Patrick, we've told you, no. Now that's an end of it."

Patrick was disappointed. He knew Steve Burt was working on an active case and knew MI6 would be aware of it. However, it appeared either MI6 were covering something up, or Steve's information was wrong. Sir Patrick needed time to think. "I'll have that drink now, Mike, a small brandy."

With a badly disguised show of annoyance, Mike Russell poured the brandy. As it was after five p.m., Hillary had a gin and tonic. Patrick sipped his brandy and wondered what to ask next. "Do you have any ongoing military related operations?" The question was posed to the two MI6 officers.

Mike glanced at Hillary who saw the look of apprehension on his face. She answered. "Well, Sir Patrick, as you know there are always ongoing operations. Some include the military, but can I ask what you are looking for? I have an awful lot of files."

Patrick had noticed the look that passed between Mike Russell and his personal assistant. He decided to try a shock tactic. "Yes, Hillary, I understand." He paused for effect to gauge the reaction of his next comment. "Does the name Squadron Leader Max Ho mean anything to you?"

Mike Russell's jaw immediately dropped. "What! How! When!" He was taken completely by surprise. Eventually the head of MI6 regained his composure while his assistant who had remained calm at the announcement of Max's name, tried to interrogate her old boss. "Where did you get that name, Sir Patrick?"

It was obvious something was going on and Sir Patrick needed to know what. "Hillary, I asked about assassination squads, and you have shown me the list and given me an assurance that you have no active cases, but one last time. Are you sure?"

"Absolutely. Unless someone is running their own private operation, but that's not possible."

Sir Patrick had a sudden thought. "Who's heading up the go or no-go committee now? It used to be Toby Grove, but I know he retired."

"As you well know, Patrick, the committee that oversees the decisions as to whether an individual is a threat to the government of the day or not is not called the go or no-go committee." Mike Russell had taken on his pompous persona. "The committee is now chaired by Lord Patrick Scotland. They make the decisions on such matters."

"In my day we had a liaison group with the go no go committee." Sir Patrick was being deliberately provocative. "Does that still exist?"

"Well, of course we have inter-departmental meetings from time to time but not on a regular basis." Mike Russell was still being pompous.

"What if you found someone who needed eliminating? Do you still go to the committee?"

"Of course not. MI6 answers only to the Prime Minister and his Cabinet. We do not go cap in hand seeking permission to do our job. If someone is a perceived danger, then we deal with it ourselves." He was still being pompous, but Sir Patrick thought this was to cover his lack of knowledge of this topic.

Sir Patrick was getting concerned and pressed on. "If you decide that a target has to be eliminated, do you still go directly to one of the assassination squads?"

Mike Russell looked pleadingly at Hillary who, seeing his uncertainty, replied. "Yes, Sir Patrick, but as I told you, we have no active cases."

"Why did the name Max Ho spook the pair of you?"

Once again Sir Patrick saw a look pass between Mike Russell and his assistant. No one answered and Sir Patrick allowed the silence to do his work. Eventually Hillary once again spoke. "Sir Patrick, you will appreciate that for certain secret reasons we cannot go into details of any ongoing operations. With Mr Russell's permission I can tell you that Squadron Leader Ho is assisting the department on a very delicate case. We are dealing with the need to identify certain enemies of this country. Beyond that I cannot say."

It was Sir Patrick's turn to be shocked. "Max Ho is working for MI6?"

Mike Russell appeared to come to life realising his assistant was stealing the show. "We cannot comment of course but such a thing is not beyond the realms of possibility."

Sir Patrick suddenly realised he needed to talk to Steve. If MI6 were using Max Ho as some kind of operative, why was he on a 'to be killed' order that supposedly came from within the Ministry of Defence. "I don't suppose you can tell me what he's working on?"

"Alas, no, but rest assured it is important."

Sir Patrick knew he would learn no more. He stood, thanked Hillary and Mike Russell and left. He looked at his watch. It was 4.49 p.m. If he were quick, he might find Steve Burt still in his office.

***

Since leaving Terry Harvey's unit, Steve, Matt and Bob had been debating what they had learnt.

"It's obvious Max Ho is intending to nick this plane. We heard it for ourselves."

"And it's going to be soon." Bob Class was looking serious. "How do we tell anybody what we know without telling them we broke the law to get it?"

The DCI had been surprisingly quiet, allowing his junior officers to debate among themselves. He had listened to their concerns and theories about how to proceed but eventually had arrived at a decision. "Listen, it's my problem, OK? I was sworn to secrecy, but I told you to help you understand what we were doing. Now it's down to me and only me." Holding his coffee cup, Steve walked to his desk, lifted the internal phone and spoke to his boss, Commander Perry Hargreaves. He made an appointment to see the commander at five p.m..

As a final thought, the DCI had asked Bob to open an electronic encrypted file and transpose the text of the conversation they had heard. Terry Harvey had already had it typed up. Bob was also instructed to scan the picture of the man with the strawberry birthmark onto the file.

At exactly five Steve walked into Perry Hargreaves's office. Both men sat down at the commander's conference table. Perry was dressed in uniform but had removed his jacket which hung over the back of the chair behind his desk. "Right, Steve, I presume it's about the shadowing job for that Colonel Walters?"

Steve agreed it was.

"Well, let's hear it. Have you found out if he's dirty or not?"

"Er, yes, sir. I'll give you a written report, but it looks like he's dirty. We have evidence of him meeting some North Koreans and of them discussing how the aircraft would be flown to North Korea."

"Good work. I'll call the colonel now. If I have your report first thing tomorrow, I'll set up a meeting and you can debrief him yourself." Perry saw his DCI wasn't looking happy.

"What is it, Steve? Your evidence is sound, isn't it? And you're satisfied that this Ho character is dirty. If we've proven it and the government decide they don't want a court case, then there's nothing we can do. We have to turn a blind eye." Perry saw his words weren't getting through. "You do agree, don't you?"

"Yes, sir. I see the bigger picture but there are a few things you should know."

Perry Hargreaves leant forward listening.

"The way we got the information was a bit irregular. You did say if he were dirty then how we acquired our evidence wouldn't be heard in court. Well, that's good because we bent all the rules."

The DCI went on to explain how Max Ho's phone had been lifted and how Terry's boffins had adapted it. The commander was fascinated by the tale and when Steve had finished, Perry beamed. "I've never heard anything like it in my life. I knew you had a reputation for sailing close to the wind, but this takes the biscuit." Commander Hargreaves was laughing. "Well done, all of you. You were given a brief and you've fulfilled it and in record time. I must say I thought it would be impossible to prove Ho's guilt or innocence and he'd just disappear. But you have evidence of his guilt so a guilty man will be dealt with, even if not by conventional means."

"That's not the point, sir. With respect, we are police officers. We uphold the law. Surely we cannot condone the illegal killing of an individual even if they are acting against the public interest?"

"I agree, Steve." Perry Hargreaves sighed. "And you're right but you heard Colonel Walters, the government cannot be seen to be embarrassed. A public trial would achieve nothing. Look, if you're unhappy, I'll take this over now. Just give me your report."

The DCI shrugged. "No, it's OK, sir. I just feel we're acting as judge and jury..." Before Steve could finish, there was a light tap on the commander's office door. His secretary stood with the door open. "Sorry to disturb you, sir but a Sir Patrick Bond is in reception asking to speak to DCI Burt, urgently."

Perry Hargreaves looked quizzically at his more junior officer. Steve blushed. "He's the ex-head of MI6. I asked for his help in understanding how these rogue units operate. I'm afraid I may have given away more information than I should have."

Perry nodded. "You'd better sign him in and have him shown up." The door closed and the two men sat in silence before the commander spoke. "I didn't know you had such friends in high places, Steve?"

"He's not really a friend, sir. It's complicated but I know I can trust him. I felt I needed to know more about these assassination squads, and he was the obvious man to ask."

"And you gave him information on your operation?"

An embarrassed DCI sat like a schoolboy. "Yes, sir, I'm afraid I did."

The tap at the door was heard again and Perry's secretary ushered Sir Patrick into the room. "I suppose we'd better have some tea and coffee." Perry stood to greet his guest. Steve nodded to Sir Patrick but remained seated.

All three men sat at one end of the table. Perry and Steve looked expectantly at Sir Patrick. "First of all, commander, DCI Burt has read me into an operation that you are conducting on behalf of military intelligence. I believe his intention was to learn from me what my previous job entailed with regard to silent eliminations."

Sir Patrick was talking with an air of authority and looked to be completely in charge. As he usually did when talking with implied authority, he spoke with a crisp tone. "Before I continue can I ask that you invite Lieutenant Colonel Walters to join us. I believe he can be found in the MOD building five minutes from here. It is only 5.16 p.m. he will still be in his office."

Commander Hargreaves looked surprised at this sudden request. "Sir Patrick, I understand you have retired. I am aware of your previous relationship with DCI Burt." Perry Hargreaves lied but was determined to learn what it was from Steve when Sir Patrick had gone. "I'm afraid I need a reason to summon a senior officer at short notice."

Smoothly, Sir Patrick replied. "Simply tell him his career is about to go up in smoke and you wish to discuss the Max Ho affair."

Perry wasn't easily intimidated. "You are joking, Sir Patrick?"

"No, Commander, I am deadly serious and deadly is the correct word. Please make the call before we have to summon the colonel from his home. He leaves the office in a few minutes. Please believe me when I say this is very serious."

Perry looked at Steve who nodded. "I think I'd make the call, sir."

Commander Perry Hargreaves made the call and nine minutes later at exactly 5.29 p.m. four men sat round the commander's table. Perry's secretary had provided tea, coffee and biscuits.

After the usual and not unexpected questions as to why everyone was present, Sir Patrick, without referring to any notes, asked for silence and opened the impromptu meeting.

"A few days ago, DCI Burt asked me to look into the existence of hit squads sponsored by, but denied by, the government. As the previous head of MI6, I of course knew such squads existed and had in the course of my duties, employed their services as the need arose."

Sir Patrick paused for effect. "This afternoon I visited the present head of MI6, a less than impressive chap called Michael Russell. My purpose was to discover who had authorised the operation against a man called Max Ho. I understood from Mr Burt that this Max Ho was on an assassination list authorised by the MOD committee that considers such things, but the authorisation was caveated allowing the officer in charge more discretionary powers than is normal. In short, he was to satisfy himself that Squadron Leader Max Ho is indeed guilty. This is, in my experience, most unusual. It was for this reason I decided to enquire further from my successor."

Sir Patrick looked at Colonel Walters. "Colonel, I understand it was you who involved the police in this matter?"

Colonel Walters looked confused and had no idea why the ex-head of MI6 was seeking answers involving such highly classified information. He decided to play along in order to learn what was going on. "Yes, an old colleague of mine is head of an elimination unit. I'm not sure how much I should divulge, Sir Patrick, but I can tell you his orders required him to satisfy himself of Max Ho's guilt before issuing the kill order. He called me because he has neither the investigative skills nor the manpower to carry out such an order. I concluded the Metropolitan

Police, having the skills and the manpower, were the obvious organisation to help. After all, a man's life is at stake."

Sir Patrick studied those around the table. "Quite so, colonel." Silence descended before Sir Patrick carried on. "You see, gentlemen, as a result of my meeting earlier I have unearthed a problem." Patrick Bond stood and began to pace the room circling the table. "It appears the left hand does not know the right one exists. MI6 are using Max Ho as an agent. He is not on their kill list, in fact quite the reverse. He is being asked to discover the identities of North Korean spies. The story about stealing a top-secret aircraft was dreamt up by MI6 as was the squadron leader's willingness to betray his country."

This was like a bomb going off in the room. Steve was the first to find his voice. "But Sir Patrick, we have him on tape. He's clearly working with the North Koreans."

"That's his brief, Steve. It has to look real otherwise he'd not be taken seriously. He is in fact a very brave man."

The colonel was next to speak. "If what you're saying is true, then why have the MOD committee issued the eliminate order?"

"I don't know, Colonel, that's why I asked that you be here now. You are the one with connections to the committee. Is there something we don't know? The fact that the commanding officer of the assassination team has been told to ensure Ho's guilt before carrying out his orders, is a little suspicious don't you think?"

Perry Hargreaves had been listening intently. "If DCI Burt hadn't disobeyed his orders by asking for your help Sir Patrick, we would be signing this Max Ho's death warrant now, having proven his guilt when in fact he is working for the Secret Service?"

"Yes, Commander."

"How could this happen? It's unbelievable."

Sir Patrick shrugged. "I agree." He looked at Colonel Walters.

The colonel stood. "Excuse me, I have to make a call." He headed towards the office door opening his flip top mobile phone as he went.

Steve had been thinking. "Sir Patrick, do you know exactly what Max Ho's mission is?"

"No, not really. This Mike Russell wouldn't give too much away, but from experience I'd say his brief is to identify the ringleader and discover what other connections they have in this country."

"We have a recording of a meeting Ho had with some North Koreans. There's a reference to someone called Sky. From the recording it sounds as though Sky is the main man. There's also reference to the Russians and the Chinese."

Commander Hargreaves interrupted Steve. "Yes, well, DCI Burt, I'm sure at the appropriate time the recordings will be called for. As a retired head of MI6, I'm sure Sir Patrick doesn't need to have chapter and verse as to what is on the recordings."

Sir Patrick was about to reply that he certainly wanted to know what the recordings said when Colonel Walters re-entered the room. He looked flushed. He walked towards the table but didn't sit. "There's to be a meeting tomorrow at nine a.m. in Whitehall. You are all instructed to attend. If you have any questions, you can call this number."

Colonel Walters placed a piece of paper on the table. "The meeting is in room 2003 in the main annex. The Minister for Internal Security will be present together with everyone involved in this mess. I fear a few heads might roll."

Colonel Walters wished everyone a good evening and left. Sir Patrick did likewise, saying, "It's been a long time since I was summoned by a government minister. See you all tomorrow, just like old times." A jovial retired head of MI6 got to the office door and turned around. "Oh, I'd bring everything you have with you tomorrow. I have a feeling a few awkward questions could be asked, and you may need all your ammunition." With a wave, Sir Patrick was gone.

Perry Hargreaves picked up the paper with the phone number. "I'll have this checked and I'll have to see the commissioner. We'll need approval to attend this meeting tomorrow. Get everything together as that jumped up spy said, Steve. If I don't call you tonight then we are cleared to attend, but remember, say as little as possible. We don't want to get caught up in their dirty little games."

The DCI left to write his report but thought better of it. If he put down on paper everything that had happened, he could be giving out too much information, plus he was tired. As he arrived in his office despite the late hour, Bob Class was still working.

"Bob, can you pull together everything we got from Terry earlier on? Electronic copies and hard copies if you can manage it and include that photograph of the Oriental guy from the meeting with Max Ho. No need to do it now. I'll be in early tomorrow and we can sort it out then." Steve knew Bob would work late and complete the task. Everything would be on his desk when he arrived tomorrow.

***

Charlie Robb lay on his bed in his room at the Mayflower Hotel. As DCI Burt was leaving New Scotland Yard, Charlie was planning his first killing. He thought back to the advice he'd received from his fellow inmates in Whitby prison. He knew where his intended victim would be and when. He remembered being told to do a thorough reconnaissance of any area where a crime was to be committed. He'd been told about CCTV cameras, about wearing clothing that could be discarded after any job. His education had included details of DNA, of powder transfer if a weapon were involved, and how important it was not to leave any forensic evidence behind and to always wear gloves. One old timer had gone into great lengths explaining how to blend into a crowd and remain invisible.

Charlie smiled. He had a lot of information that could turn him into a master criminal, but it was all wasted. He had only one task on which to use his newfound knowledge: The killing of four individuals, starting tonight.

After leaving Colin Clark's female friend, Charlie had shopped in a cheap, out of town store that appeared to sell everything. He bought a pair of jeans, a tee shirt, a pair of black trainers, a cap and a lightweight overcoat. Now wearing these items, he stood admiring himself in front of a long wall-mounted mirror. With a pair of disposable gloves covering his hands, he placed the gun in the right-hand pocket of his new overcoat and headed for the hotel's underground garage.

At 6.26 p.m. Charlie carefully exited the garage, having keyed the name of the pub into his sat nav. He followed the instructions and realised the Cock and Squirrel was located up a pedestrian-only lane. The traffic in Fleet Street was light so he was able to slow down and caught a glimpse of the pub standing at the head of the pedestrian cul-de-sac. Remembering his prison education, he was careful not to drive too slowly past the end of the lane.

From his A to Z of London, Charlie knew there was a twenty-four hour multi car park less than a mile away. Using his newfound criminal knowledge, he parked his car on the first floor making sure his cap was pulled well over his face and ensuring he didn't look directly into the obvious CCTV cameras. He even wore his disposable gloves to press the buttons to receive a ticket. He placed the ticket in the back pocket of his jeans.

On leaving the car park Charlie took a direct route back to the pub. As he reached the lane, he glanced in the direction of the pub but kept walking. He saw a few hardened smokers standing outside with their beer. There were no streetlights in the lane except for four wall mounted lamps that gave off a very faint light. The main illumination came from the pub. Light flowed through the large, frosted glass window that ran almost the full width of the lane. Charlie walked on for another hundred yards before crossing the road and reversing his direction back towards the pub. He noted two CCTV cameras neither of which were a concern. There was a traffic camera zeroed onto the road. He had been told such cameras also captured people but decided this traffic camera and the two CCTV cameras were not a problem.

Charlie carried on past the end of the lane still walking on the pavement on the other side of Fleet Street. This vantage point gave a wider angle and Charlie was able to confirm his original findings. He also spotted, on the left side of the lane heading towards the pub, another small opening that looked as though it were an alleyway. He made a note to check this out. He recrossed Fleet Street and headed for the pub. As he approached the pub entrance he slowed and glanced to his left when he was opposite the alley. It was dark but one of the wall lights was directly opposite so the small amount of light this lamp gave off was enough to see by. It seemed to be a bin store of some sort and only extended about six feet off the lane.

Pulling his cap over his face, Charlie entered the pub. It was a traditional looking drinking house with a large bar that was still surprisingly busy. Charlie casually walked towards a back wall where there was a bit of space. He stood taking in his surroundings and trying not to be too obvious, and scanned the room looking for Colin Clark. He spotted him at the far end of the bar pouring a pint and talking to another barman. Charlie deliberately squeezed into a corner of the bar at the opposite end and ordered a small beer. He didn't want Clark to know he was in the bar. Charlie found a spot beside a pillar and tried to look as though he were just another office worker having a beer on his way home.

The bar started to empty, and Charlie used the pillar to hide himself from Colin Clark. "Come along, please. It's almost eight. Drink up, please. We're closing." A large man who could easily be the manager was shouting from behind the bar. From his vantage point, Charlie made a show of finishing his beer. He counted four people still in the bar and finishing off their drinks in compliance with the manager's orders. With his back to the bar, Charlie left behind the last drinker to leave. As he approached the door, he heard over his shoulder the manager say, "You get off home Colin. I'll tidy up. See you tomorrow."

Charlie heard a reply of, "If you're sure, then I'm off. I'll just grab my coat."

The would-be killer waited outside the pub and pulled on two pairs of disposable gloves just as Keith, the gun seller had recommended. Standing there he realised he looked too conspicuous even if there was no one about. Charlie moved to the alley where the bins were kept and waited just inside the entrance. He was shaking. His whole body wasn't under control. As he heard the pub door open and footsteps approaching, he took a deep breath. Now he was committed, a sense of calm came over him and Charlie found he was no longer shaking. The desire for revenge had taken over.

Standing directly in front of his target Charlie spoke with an assured calm he hadn't felt a minute ago. "Hello, Colin, remember me?"

The little man stopped, not recognising Charlie. "If it's money you're after the pub's closed and I only have my bus fare."

Charlie tried to adopt the tone of a real gangster. After all he had lived with a lot of them for about eight years. "I don't want your money, Colin, I'm here to take your life."

Colin Clark suddenly realised who this man standing in his way was. "Oh Christ, you're out." Stumbling to get his words out Colin started to apologise saying he was the junior member of the four. "I only went along with them because they said I'd make money. Look at me Charlie, I'm down on my luck, my money's gone. I'm working two jobs just to make ends meet."

It was obvious to Charlie that this little greedy man didn't realise the seriousness of his position. Charlie pulled his gun. On seeing the weapon Colin sobbed. "Charlie don't kill me, I did nothing. It was the other three. You're an honest man, I know that now. I wanted to come to court to…"

Charlie held his forefinger to his lips indicating that Colin should stop talking. This frightened Colin more than the sight of the gun. He made to turn and run back to the pub, but Charlie saw this move coming. "Don't even think about it, Colin. I'll shoot you in the back if I have to." Moving towards the pub Charlie signalled with the gun that Colin should move in front of him into the alley. Once there, Colin appeared to break down. "Please, Charlie, I didn't do anything. You can't shoot me."

"I've spent eight years in prison because of you. I've lost my family, my reputation, for what? So, you greedy cowards could get rich at my expense." Charlie was reliving his past. "Why did you have to kill my wife and son? Just tell me that?" Tears were welling up in Charlie's eyes.

Colin Clark was equally emotional, now realising he was about to die. "Christ, Charlie, please don't kill me. I can help you. I know where Lockwood keeps the records. They'll show you were innocent. Maybe get your conviction…" BANG.

Charlie closed his eyes and pulled the trigger. In the confined space of the alley the bang seemed like a bomb going off. Charlie opened his eyes to see Colin Clark slumped on the ground. The .22 bullet had made a neat hole in the centre of his forehead. Standing over the body, Charlie thought he would be sick. He leant against the wall and breathed deeply. His initial reaction was to run and keep on running. Looking at the body of Colin Clark gave him no satisfaction. There was no elation, no joy, no unbridled rush of euphoria. Charlie was, if anything, sad, but knew he had to leave this scene. Placing the gun back into his coat pocket, he walked quickly back to the end of the lane and turned right. His mind wasn't working. All he could think about was the killing. He'd taken a human life. There was no going back.

Slowly the mist that clouded his brain lifted. He decided to leave his car in the car park and walk back to his hotel. He reasoned if the body were discovered quickly, the police wouldn't be looking for a man out for a walk. All the way back to his hotel, Charlie listened out for sirens and expected to see blue flashing lights driving in the opposite direction to that he was walking in. To his surprise and relief and after an hour of walking he arrived at the Mayflower Hotel without being stopped or seeing any evidence that the body had been discovered. Feeling calmer but in need of a stiff drink, Charlie entered the bar area of the foyer and ordered a large whisky. He carried his overcoat with him, not daring to let it out of his sight. The gun was still in the pocket of the coat.

Chapter Eleven

Steve arrived in his office just before eight a.m. on a wet and miserable Thursday. It was February 10th. The temperature overnight had dropped below zero and hadn't risen much since. The strong cold wind had held the temperature down and overall, it wasn't a very welcoming morning.

Bob was at his desk as Steve walked in. "All the stuff from yesterday is on your desk. I've given you a memory stick and a hard copy file of the conversations we heard. I've cut a disk, so you have the video from the phone on a CD and that picture you wanted is in a separate file."

Steve knew Bob was on the ball but was nonetheless impressed by his admin assistant. "Good job, Bob, thanks." Steve walked to his desk and saw the information Bob had just summarized neatly stacked. Steve opened the file to read and refresh his memory before attending the nine a.m. meeting in Whitehall, but quickly realised he remembered everything that had been said, so closed the file.

"Anything from Matt Conway?"

Bob put his head round the door. "Yes, sir. He says the watchers are still on Ho, but they have nothing to report. Apparently, he stayed in once they followed him home. I don't know about the phone. It's possible Inspector Harvey has something now, but I went over to Tech Services earlier and they didn't have much."

"Thanks, Bob. Look, I've to go to a meeting this morning. When Matt gets in ask him to hold the fort and keep Terry Harvey in the loop."

"Will do, boss."

***

Looking at his watch, Steve realised he had to get going. Gathering the files Bob had prepared he left to walk to Whitehall. He had no idea where he was going so allowed himself sufficient time in case he got lost.

The DCI found room 2003 in the annex behind the grand building that was simply referred to as Whitehall. He was glad he had allowed enough time as he took a few wrong turns before finding the correct room.

As he entered, he was surprised to see so many people. He counted at least ten. Steve spotted Commander Hargreaves dressed in his best uniform, standing holding a cup of coffee and talking to a woman he didn't recognise. As Steve approached, the commander broke off his conversation with the lady, and ushered his DCI towards the long table covered in a white sheet on which was an urn of coffee and tea together with enough cups and saucers to serve twice the number in the room.

Perry Hargreaves looked serious. "I spoke with most of the top brass last night Steve. They want this thing over with. It was made clear to me that I should never have sanctioned the operation and you have exceeded your authority in bugging Max Ho's phone."

Perry placed his cup and saucer on the long table. "Don't worry, no one's coming after us. I got a *don't do it again* and I'm supposed to tear a strip off you, so don't do it again." Perry Hargreaves smiled. "We'll keep our powder dry and make sure we're not involved after this meeting. Understood?"

"Yes, sir." Steve scanned the room. "Who are all these people?"

"I've no idea. I think most of them are civil servants or advisors. No doubt we'll find out."

Steve saw a long table at the far side of the room. He counted twelve chairs and wondered if there would be twelve people in attendance. As the clock moved towards nine, people began to take their seats. There was a seating plan and in front of each chair a triangular shaped piece of white cardboard stood displaying the name of the person allocated to each seat. Perry and Steve found their names and were surprised to see they had been placed more or less in the middle of the table.

Everyone seemed to be talking at once. Most people had large files in front of them. Steve withdrew his slimmer files from his briefcase and explained to the commander that Bob Class had done an outstanding job pulling everything together in a short space of time.

As nine exactly, the door opened, and three men walked in. The room instantly fell silent. Steve recognised Sir Patrick Bond who was leading the way, and another man as the Minister for National Security, Edwin Pinter, although the third man was unknown to Steve. All three men took their seats more or less directly opposite Perry Hargreaves and the DCI. Steve wasn't sure if this was good or bad.

After a few minutes of informal greetings, the minister opened the meeting.

"It appears we were about to commit murder. An operation sanctioned by MI6 without prior consultation with MI5 or the security services was put at risk because of overzealous officials, most of whom are sitting around this table. I have been made aware of most of the facts, but I have asked Sir Patrick Bond who recently retired as head of MI6 to head up an inquiry into what actually happened."

"It seems Mr Russell, the present head of MI6, was made aware of a North Korean cell operating in London. In order to discover the identities of these people his department set up a legend that a serving officer, Squadron Leader Maxwell Ho, was sympathetic to the North Korean cause and was prepared to deliver our latest secret aircraft into the hands of these North Koreans."

The minister turned to Mike Russell for confirmation. He simply nodded. Edwin Pinter carried on. He carried a presence that immediately singled him out as someone of authority.

"Because correct consultation procedures were not carried out word leaked out that an RAF officer was about to steal a secret aircraft. This fiction caused an official at the Ministry of Defence to alert a committee headed by Lord Patrick Scotland who acts independently in times of national crisis." The minister nodded to a large red-faced man with thinning grey hair and dressed in the Whitehall uniform of dark suit, white shirt and old school tie who was sitting two down from Steve but on the other side of the table.

"That is correct, minister."

Edwin Pinter was reading from notes clearly prepared for him. Steve wondered if Patrick Bond had supplied the narrative.

The minister continued. "Now, it seems the committee, having received various reports from individuals seated around this table, decided to place a kill order on this officer, Maxwell Ho. The justification was that to arrest and prosecute a serving officer as a spy would damage the government's reputation and give our enemies information, we'd rather keep secret. However, there was obviously a degree of nervousness within the committee and the order issued to Major Simon Havers to eliminate Mr Ho was caveated as to ask the major to satisfy himself of Mr Ho's guilt before giving the kill order."

The minister turned to his right. A military looking man dressed in an expensive looking light grey suit, nodded and said, "That is correct, minister. I have an operative on standby but to date I have still to give the final order."

The minister looked perturbed. "Just so, major." Edwin Pinter returned to his notes. "I understand, major, you were not satisfied with these orders and sought assistance from Colonel Walters." Once more the minister turned in the same direction as he had when addressing Major Havers. Colonel Walters was sitting one chair down from the major.

"That is correct, sir. Major Havers explained his order and the caveat it contained. He asked me to help prove Mr Ho's guilt or innocence."

Edwin Pinter once more referred to his notes. "Not having the resources or the skills you contacted the Metropolitan Police for assistance?"

The colonel nodded.

"I understand Commander Hargreaves became involved at the behest of Colonel Walters and the commander subsequently delegated the task of following Mr Ho to DCI Burt." The minister's eyes settled on both policemen. There was a quizzical look on his face.

Commander Hargreaves nodded and Steve took his cue from his boss and also nodded.

The minister, still referring to his notes, continued. "I understand, DCI Burt, that you were successful in your task. I believe you used some unorthodox methods, but you have proven, based on the story fabricated by MI6, that Squadron Leader Ho is in fact working with the North Koreans?"

"Yes, sir. We have recordings of a meeting that took place yesterday afternoon. Without knowledge of his acting for MI6 the recordings seem to confirm his guilt as a traitor."

"And your report to Commander Hargreaves and subsequently to Colonel Walters would have declared him guilty."

"Yes, sir."

"And Colonel Walters," the minister once more turned in his chair to look directly down the table, "you would have passed this information onto Major Havers, and you Major Havers would have ordered the elimination of Mr Ho?"

Both the colonel and the major nodded, although Colonel Walters added. "Yes, minister, that's about it."

Edwin Pinter sat back and puffed his cheeks. He was a fit looking man in his early forties. Steve knew from TV interviews that the minister was a lawyer by profession. His questioning made that obvious.

"I trust everyone present is aware how close we have come to committing murder and what a complete cock-up this whole affair has been. Had it not been for DCI Burt disobeying his orders, based on his unwillingness to see any human being killed without due process, and Sir Patrick having the gumption to look into the DCI's concerns, a grave situation resulting in the murder of a patriot would have occurred. I hope everyone present sees that."

The people present nodded, and a few uttered a "Yes."

The minister wasn't finished. "Now, I want Sir Patrick, Mr. Russell, Lord Patrick, DCI Burt and Commander Hargreaves to remain. Everyone else can leave but please prepare a report detailing your total involvement in this affair. Remember, this meeting never happened. Each of you will be called to give evidence to Sir Patrick's inquiry and you will be required to explain your part in this affair." The minister turned to a sombre looking man dressed in the standard Whitehall uniform who was sitting next to him. "I don't think we need involve MI5 from here, Charles, I'm sure MI6 and Sir Patrick will keep you updated going forward."

The head of MI5, stood, nodded and left with the others.

Suddenly the room was less crowded, and the minister called for tea and biscuits. Steve continued to sit but his brain was in gear and racing. Something about this whole affair seemed wrong. He couldn't work out what it was but knew it was important. He decided to say nothing and allow what was to come, simply happen.

With the room emptier, those remaining moved seats to gather around the minister. Commander Hargreaves and the DCI remained in their original chairs.

"Well, gentlemen." The minister appeared more relaxed. "It would appear we have dodged a bullet, but we need to know how such a thing could happen. Lord Patrick, your committee authorised the order to eliminate this Max Ho. Sir Patrick's investigation will unearth the reasons, so we do not have to go into detail now. However, I am disbanding your committee with immediate effect. It is clear there is too cavalier an approach to unlawful killings. We need more checks and balances."

The tall, well-built man now sitting beside the minister looked shocked but resigned. He nodded and said nothing. Lord Patrick Scotland knew how to play the political game. Steve concluded correctly that this must be Lord Scotland and noted he was not asked to leave. The DCI wondered why if his murder committee was now a thing of the past. He had no answer.

Looking at Colonel Walters, the minister sighed. "Richard, I realise you are military intelligence and as such are not part of this. It is all about catching these North Korean spies. I believe you acted correctly in involving the police. They after all are the experts at tracking people and gathering information. You are excused with the thanks of Her Majesty's Government."

The colonel mumbled a thank you to the table in general and left the room.

Steve counted. There were now only six men left in the room. He wondered what was coming next.

"Major Havers," the minister continued as he looked at the major, "yours is one of two units set up to handle delicate operations on behalf of the government. Of course, the work you do can never be admitted to and will always be denied. Nonetheless, you perform an invaluable service, and your unit will remain in being although, subject to Sir Patrick's findings, your command structure may change."

"Thank you, sir." Major Havers smiled as he acknowledged the compliment. "My unit will always be prepared to take hard actions."

"Yes. Just as a matter of curiosity, you said you had an operative ready and primed to take care of Ho once you gave the order?"

"That is correct, sir."

"What will this agent do now he is to be stood down?"

"He will await a new assignment. This particular chap has been on standby since his last job. I don't know if you remember minister, but we were involved in the Judge Plough-Henderson affair about ten months ago. We don't kill that many people each year, so my chaps have a lot of down time. They spend a lot of time training." The major grinned and gave out a small chuckle.

Steve who had been sitting trying to work out what was worrying him suddenly sat up. He had given DS Si Griffiths the task of tracking down the masked man who had expertly shot the killer of his colleague and Terry Harvey's niece, Poppy. Steve wanted to question the major immediately, but with great self-control decided to say nothing. He wondered if this major held the key as to the identity of the man dressed in black, but he knew this was neither the time nor the place.

As Steve put the major to one side he continued to worry, realising that he still felt something was not quite right. The minister was dealing with each person present in a different way. Lord Scotland's committee had been disbanded, Sir Patrick was to head up an inquiry and Major Havers was to have a new reporting structure. The DCI was impressed by the minister. He was talked of as a future prime minister and Steve could see why. The man was decisive and clear. His six-foot frame and broad shoulders gave him an immediate presence and he was obviously no one's fool. Steve wondered what lay in store for himself and Perry Hargreaves.

"Now, Mr Russell, as head of MI6 you must shoulder the responsibility for this failure in communication. It is clear to me that you and your department lacked focus and that nearly resulted in an innocent man being killed. I advise you to consider your own position and that of your senior people who were involved. I leave future actions to you. I hope I make myself clear."

Mike Russell turned red and looked as though he were about to argue. Instead, he simply nodded and stared at the table.

"Now commander, the Metropolitan Police's role in this is commendable. DCI Burt deliberately disobeyed an order by involving Sir Patrick. He is to be commended for his courage and you for your leadership in this matter." The minister studied the two policemen. "I do not want police resources squandered looking for a killer if the killing has been officially sanctioned."

The minister turned over a page from the notes he was reading from. "Subject to Sir Patrick's final report, I propose each time an elimination is sanctioned, you Commander Hargreaves will be notified.

Perry Hargreaves went to interrupt the minister who held up his hand to silence him. "I am aware of your objections to any kind of killing without due process, but as you know, such things occur. You have the necessary security clearances and Sir Patrick has spoken of the Metropolitan Police in glowing terms. I intend to speak with the commissioner after this meeting and arrange such an exchange of information. It will be strictly on a need-to-know basis."

Steve was intrigued by this turn of events. He knew Perry was, like himself, set against anything that was unlawful, but saw the sense in knowing if a particular murder had been government sanctioned, then that meant the killer was untouchable. He saw the waste in investigating such a killing, as the killer would never stand trial.

Something was disturbing him, but whatever it was just wouldn't surface. Steve sat back saying nothing, struggling with his thoughts. The minister finished speaking to Perry Hargreaves. Steve hardly heard anything of what he had to say.

"I think that concludes our business, gentlemen. Sir Patrick will receive a copy of DCI Burt's report and he in turn will report to me in two weeks with his report on this sorry affair."

The minister rose as did the others except Steve who remained seated and was obviously thinking hard and had turned very pale. He was lost in his thoughts. "Are you all right, Mr Burt?" The minister looked down on Steve.

The DCI hardly heard the question. "Yes, minister, I think so." The problem that was concerning him had slowly crystallized. "Can everyone please sit down for a moment? I have a few questions that I think are relevant to our situation." Steve still looked slightly lost.

The minister looked at his watch. It was 10.37 a.m. and he had another meeting at eleven. He wasn't used to having his schedule disrupted but seeing the intensity of Steve's expression, sat down and the others followed. "Go on, DCI Burt, I can give you fifteen minutes."

Steve drew breath, rapidly rearranging his scrambled thoughts into some form of logic. "Mr Russell, what were Squadron Leader Ho's instructions exactly?"

Mike Russell, who was shocked by the minister's poorly veiled suggestion that he should resign, was reluctant to answer. In truth he was not up on his brief but didn't want to admit it. "Well, he was to get close to the North Korean spy ring on the pretext he would steal the new stealth fighter."

"Yes. I understand that, but what was his mission?"

"To identify the leader of the spy ring."

"And how does he communicate with you?"

"Well, by ordinary phone. He knew he wasn't under suspicion."

Steve leant forward. "Mr Russell, was he instructed to inform you on a regular basis as to his progress?"

Mike Russell didn't know but assumed this would be the case as it was one of his officials who was the case officer on the project.

"Before you came here today, did you get any report that Ho had been in touch?"

The remaining people seated around the table were fascinated by Steve's questions but had no idea what they were leading to.

"I receive a morning briefing report in summary and there was no reference to Max Ho having been in contact."

Steve sighed; he knew his next question was critical. "If Max Ho's primary task was to identify the ringleader, would you expect him to notify you as soon as he knew who this person was?"

"Of course. I know he was instructed to call in day or night with any relevant data. The identity of the spy ringleader is critical to Ho's mission."

Steve paused and opened the file he had brought with him. The minister looked at his watch. He decided to stay and be late for his next meeting. He was intrigued by the DCI's line of questioning. Steve pulled the image of Sky from his file and slid it across the table towards Mike Russell.

"I believe that is the man you are looking for, Mr Russell. He calls himself Sky and Max Ho spent almost two hours with him yesterday discussing the plans to steal the aircraft."

Everyone round the table sucked in air. Steve's statement seemed to create a vacuum in the room.

Looking at the minister, Steve continued. "Minister, we have an audio recording of their meeting, and it is clear the project to steal the aircraft is being taken seriously. From what Mr Russell has said, Ho should have informed his case officer of that meeting and the identity of Sky. He also should have called in the cavalry to arrest the men he met, but he failed to do so."

Steve paused for effect. "Minister, I believe despite the events described here today, that Max Ho is in fact a traitor and is intent on stealing the aircraft."

Everyone including Perry Hargreaves stared at Steve. Silence descended on the room.

Eventually Major Havers spoke. "Excuse me, but are you saying the execution of Max Ho should be on again?"

The minister looked perturbed. He ignored the major's question. "You are sure of this, Mr Burt?"

"As sure as I can be, sir. The fact he didn't report the meeting nor disclose he had met this Sky I personally find suspicious."

Sir Patrick who had been listening quietly and was impressed by Steve's logic spoke. "There is one way to prove this. Ho is unaware that we have both the photograph and an audio recording of his meeting. Mike, get on the phone and have the case officer call him and ask if he has anything to report. If he says no, then Steve is correct."

The minister nodded. "Good idea, Patrick. Mr Russell, please do as Sir Patrick has suggested."

Mike Russell left the room holding his mobile. The minister was impressed by Steve. "How did you get the picture and the audio recording Mr Burt?"

Steve looked at Perry Hargreaves who answered for Steve. "Minister, there are some things best not referred to. I'm afraid our source of this information is one of them."

"Come, come commander, I'm the Minister for National Security. We must have no secrets from each other. This whole meeting is off the grid. We have been discussing something that is ultra-secret, and we do not expect anything that has been said in this room to be repeated outside. So again, Mr Burt, how did you get the information?"

Perry turned to Steve and shrugged. "You'd better tell him."

Steve outlined how Max Ho's phone had been lifted and how Terry Harvey's technician had inserted software and reconfigured the memory board within the phone to allow both audio and visual recordings from the phone. He went on to further explain there were officers following Ho and his every movement was being monitored.

As Steve finished, Mike Russell re-entered but before he sat down the minister looked at Steve in disbelief. "Mr Burt, I'm glad you are on our side. What you have described is nothing short of brilliant even though in your more controlled world it was probably illegal. Well done!"

"Thank you, sir, but Inspector Harvey deserves the credit."

As Mike Russell sat down the minister finished his conversation with Steve. "Quite so, but you were the one to authorise it and take the responsibility."

Everyone now turned to the present head of MI6. Mike Russell looked crestfallen. "Ho's case officer spoke to him as requested. He told him he had no new information and was having difficulty tracking down the leader."

Once more silence filled the room and once more Major Havers asked if he had the green light to carry out the execution order. Lord Scotland who had remained silent throughout the meeting, also ignored the major and asked, "Commander, what do you recommend?"

Perry Hargreaves considered the question and not having sufficient detailed knowledge of events turned to the DCI. "Steve, you know more about this than I do."

Steve's mind was racing ahead. He addressed the meeting as a whole. "If the object is to capture this Sky person, then we need Max Ho to lead us to him. I think it is most unlikely we will discover his whereabouts on our own. We have twenty-four hour surveillance on Ho so he's not going anywhere. I presume security surrounding the aircraft is tight so again, there should be no issues." Steve sat back. "I think we need to create a situation where Ho has to contact Sky. From the recordings Sky says Ho will not meet him again, but if we could create a situation that required another meeting, we could follow Ho and lift the whole group."

Lord Scotland leant forward. "I presume you will continue with the illegal tap on his phone?"

"Yes, sir. It gives us full details of what Ho is up to. This, plus our physical surveillance, means we can monitor his every move."

Edwin Pinner once more checked his watch. It was 11.39 a.m, and he was very late for his next meeting. "I must go, gentlemen. It sounds as though collectively you are capable of working this out. Please liaise with Sir Patrick before taking any action. Mr Russell, please give every assistance to DCI Burt and the police. Commander Hargreaves, Mr Burt, I look to you to help resolve this mess and ensure this aircraft is not hijacked." The minister stood up. "That's it, please keep me informed." He turned to Sir Patrick Bond. "Patrick, we'll talk later."

As the meeting broke up Perry turned to Steve. "So much for a low profile and getting us out of this." He smiled at the DCI. "I wonder what the commissioner will say?"

Both men walked back to the Yard. Perry to report and Steve to think. It was 11.46 a.m.

As they walked Steve suggested to Perry that the photograph they had of Sky should be distributed to all officers on an 'if seen, report but do not apprehend basis'. "Good idea. Get it to me and I'll arrange for distribution at shift changes," Perry said as they walked into the Yard.

Chapter Twelve

Charlie Robb had had a restless night's sleep. He had dreamt about the murder of Colin Clark. His dream was more of a nightmare as he saw his victim lying in the alley with the bullet hole in his forehead. He couldn't remember pulling the trigger, but knew he had. As he sat in his bed, he felt depressed and angry with himself for carrying out the act of revenge. No matter how much he told himself Colin Clark was one of those responsible for ruining his life, he didn't find any pleasure in the killing.

Charlie rose, showered and dressed in one of his suits. He had no appetite and decided to walk to the car park where he had left his hire car. He had neatly folded what he regarded as his killing clothes in the bottom of the fitted wardrobe in his room. Remembering the advice he'd received when in prison, he intended to collect his car and return it to the hire company at Gatwick Airport. He had been told to regularly change cars as CCTV might pick up the same car at different times and be able to trace him. Regularly changing cars would avoid this.

As he walked, he allowed his mind to wander and could picture his wife and son more clearly. He recalled Sunday lunches in the garden of the local pub, the golf club he had been a member of, together with the friends he had played with regularly on Saturday mornings. That had been his life before he had got involved with Geoffrey Lockwood and his corrupt practices.

Revenge was once more front and centre of his thoughts. He now knew that he would carry on and kill the remaining three men who were responsible for his current situation. His second victim, Anthony Maple would be next. Like Colin Clark, Maple hadn't been the main instigator, but he had been involved and would pay the price.

Charlie considered visiting the alley where he had shot Colin Clark, but the advice from fellow prisoners was never to return to your crime scene, so Charlie walked on.

After paying his parking fee, he set out for Gatwick Airport. Traffic was initially slow, but he didn't mind. Today was Thursday. He'd have the afternoon to plan the killing of Anthony Maple.

The Avis car hire desk at Heathrow didn't question why Charlie was returning his car early. With the paperwork completed he visited the main terminal and had a cup of coffee. He then returned and hired a car from Hertz. The car he was given was a black Honda CRV automatic model with sat nav. Charlie sat in his new car and looked up his small book to confirm Anthony Maple's address. He keyed in the address in Bushy Park and set off to survey the area.

As he exited onto the M23, Charlie noticed the clock on the Honda said it was 11.46 a.m. Had Charlie known it or been remotely interested, this was exactly the time Perry Hargreaves and Steve were making their way back to New Scotland Yard.

Charlie hadn't wanted any breakfast but the rumbling in his stomach told him he was over his earlier concerns about the killing and that he was hungry. He ignored his hunger and focused on following the lady from the sat nav speaker system who was directing him to his next target in Bushy Park.

***

Detective Sergeant Simon Griffiths was standing in a doorway opposite a block of cheaply built council flats.

Si had been tracking down Tom Thumb for two days now. The man was slippery and knew how to hide. Si had called in all the favours he could and had on a few occasions been told Tom had just left, but he had learnt Tom had a woman friend who lived in these flats in Peckham and that he often spent the night with her. He also knew that Tom was not an early riser and very rarely was seen outside before noon. Si looked at his watch. It read 11.46 a.m.

No one Si had spoken to or threatened knew the apartment number of Tom Thumb's lady friend, so Si was committed to keeping watch in the hope he would appear. He had also been told that Tom had moved up in the world and no longer frequented his previous haunts, such as the seedy night club, to play cards. No one Si spoke to knew why this had happened, but the rumour was that Tom had discovered something about a certain individual and was blackmailing them. Suddenly, Tom had a decent and regular income. Si had stored this information up for future use.

The February weather wasn't designed to make standing in doorways a pleasant experience. Si's feet were feeling cold and despite wearing a cap and scarf his nose felt like a block of ice and his gloved hands were numb.

Several people came and went from the flats but at 12.18 p.m. a small dapper-looking man wearing a black fur-trimmed overcoat and a black trilby hat appeared. It was Tom Thumb. Si knew from his past association with Tom, that he didn't drive. As Tom left the flats he turned right, and Si followed.

Tom Thumb walked at a brisk pace and didn't appear to be taking any precautions to avoid being followed. With Si about fifty yards behind, Tom crossed a series of main roads, and ten minutes later, entered an upmarket looking pub. Si held back allowing Tom time to settle down. After a few minutes he followed his target inside. The pub wasn't busy with only two tables occupied. It didn't look like anything Si normally associated with this part of London. It appeared to be more of a wine and tapas bar than a solid working man's drinking place. The interior was chrome and glass and very minimalist. The bar was small, and everything appeared geared to waiter service.

Si spotted Tom at one of the white tables beside an alcove that seemed to house a larger round table set for ten people. Tom's table was well away from the other patrons.

"Afternoon, Tom, you're a hard man to find."

Tom who was reading a complimentary newspaper looked up and almost choked. This was the last person he expected to see and instantly knew what was to follow would not be good. "What do you want, Mr Griffiths? I'm waiting for my morning coffee, and I don't want to be disturbed."

When Si noted Tom had folded his newspaper he sat down. "I'll join you." Si called over to a waiter and ordered a black coffee.

Both men studied each other before Tom once more asked, "What do you want?"

Si knew how to deal with criminals like Tom Thumb. Men who survived on the edge of organised crime, who would undertake any illegal act if it enhanced their status within a gang. Men who held a lot of information but had no reason to share what they knew with the police.

"Well, Tom, I don't want much, just a few pieces of information. You see I'm on a case for my new boss and if I give him what he wants I'll be allowed to retire. If you help me, I'll be out of your hair for good."

Tom smiled. "Not before bloody time, Mr Griffiths."

The coffees arrived. Si had intended to pay the bill but when he saw the amount, he passed the metal tray containing the printout of the bill over to Tom. Tom Thumb got the message but said nothing.

Both men sipped their coffees. Si admitted he'd tasted worse. "I need to know who's working for government hit squads these days?"

Si looked sternly at the detective. "Hang on, Mr Griffiths, I don't know anything about hit squads."

"Of course you don't, Tom, but I know you know a man who knows a man who does. I only want a name of someone further up the pecking order than you who might know."

Tom placed his cup in its saucer. "I don't know anything, Mr Griffiths. The people who might know about these things aren't criminals, they're civil servants and I don't mix with that lot."

Si ploughed on. "But you do know a few people who have been killed by these squads?"

"No. I've no idea. They don't go broadcasting it from the rooftops you know!"

"Agreed. But I know you were involved a few years back with a European gang and one of their number was fished out of the Thames. No one was convicted of it and the word at the time was that a government hitman had carried out the killing." Si stared at Tom who was now looking flushed.

"Yeah well, that was then. Sure, I heard the rumours but I'd nothing to do with it."

"I'm not looking to pin blame. Who were you working for when this guy was found dead?"

Tom lifted his coffee cup and drank. "Mr Griffiths, you know it's more than my life's worth to tell you that, if I did, I'd be a dead man walking." Tom replaced his now empty cup. "Sorry, I can't help you."

Si sat back in what he thought was a very uncomfortable chair. Tom appeared to be getting ready to leave as Si put his hand on his arm. "That's a pity, Tom, you see I'm also investigating a case of blackmail and you're in the frame." Si lied but with a sincerity born of years dealing with people like Tom Thumb.

Tom didn't move but slouched back in his chair. "Mr Griffiths, I don't know where you get your information but believe me, I'm clean." This was said without conviction.

Si knew he had nothing but having spent years on the streets knew how to bluff. "Fair enough, Tom, we'll just go down to the local nick and get you processed and charged. Your bank account will tell us everything we need to know. Your victim has their own records, so it'll be easy to prove."

Tom Thumb could see he was not going to escape despite his denials. He sat thinking and Si allowed the silence to linger.

"OK. If I give you a name, you promise not to look into anything else that I might be involved in?"

Si smiled. At last, he was about to get what he came for. "Tom, like I said, I only want a name. I'm retiring so you won't see me again." Si paused as he leant forward to become closer to Tom's face. "But if you lie to me and give me a dud name, I'll have a squad all over you." Si put on his most intimidating expression learnt over the years. He could see Tom Thumb was nervous.

Tom leant back. His top lip was moist from sweat. "All I can tell you is I was working for Benny Stockton. He got involved with that Eastern lot and he said one day he had arranged for their leader to be taken out. He boasted no one would be charged because the killing was government approved." Tom stood and was now in a hurry to leave. Si grabbed his arm.

"Where will I find this Benny Stockton?"

"He has a second-hand car lot in New Cross. It's a front for his other businesses. He's usually there." Tom pulled his arm from Si's grasp.

"Please don't tell him you got his name from me. Like I said, I'm dead if he finds out."

Tom left the bar leaving the bill unpaid. Si took five pounds from his pocket and left it on the metal tray. He didn't leave a tip.

***

Steve returned to his office and sat thinking about the events of the past two and a half hours. He shut his door and sat back with his eyes closed trying to understand what had just happened. After about half an hour he only had a vague idea of his way forward and asked Matt, Bob and Terry Harvey to join him. It was 12.17 p.m. and Detective Sergeant Simon Griffiths was still drinking coffee with Tom Thumb.

"Right. The operation regarding Max Ho is still on. We have been instructed to continue surveillance." Steve realised he was putting his own spin on events. "Terry, will the phone continue to give us the audio and visual links?"

"No reason why not provided the battery holds up. We noticed he was recharging earlier last night and there's no evidence he suspects anything." Terry Harvey knew Steve and was aware something was bothering his friend but said nothing.

"Good. Matt, can you keep the watchers going?"

Matt Conway studied the rota he'd prepared for the officers seconded to Steve's unit for the purposes of shadowing Max Ho. "The six I have been using are due rest days, Steve. I can keep them going till tomorrow, but if the operation goes into Saturday, I'll have to bring in fresh replacements."

This wasn't good news. The officers watching Max Ho would have begun to understand his movements and how he did things. New men would take time to settle into their task.

Steve thought for a few seconds. "Are they due some time off?"

"When they came over, I told them it was only for a few days." Matt looked quizzically at his boss, and with a sly smile, asked, "What are you thinking? Overtime to keep the same six?"

"Not a bad idea." The DCI had an equally sly grin on his face as he looked at Matt.

"I'm sure if you have the budget, they'll jump at it."

"Right. Never mind the budget, set it up Matt. I'll worry about the money."

Matt Conway shrugged and made a few additions to his handwritten rota. "Any idea how long this will go on for?"

"Ah!" Steve knew he would have to brief his team including Terry Harvey but still wasn't sure how much he could divulge.

Sitting back, he scanned the expectant faces. "I was called to a meeting this morning to discuss the Max Ho case. Thanks to Terry and Bob I had a report that established Ho had met with some North Koreans." Steve paused. "I think everyone here knows that."

Agreement all round. "Unfortunately, I can't tell you any more other than it's complicated. We are instructed to maintain surveillance but be ready to arrest Ho and whoever he is meeting when the powers that be order it." Steve felt uncomfortable lying to his team, but felt he had no choice. "That means Terry, I'll need hourly reports sent to Bob and instant reports as soon as Ho meets or speaks to anyone."

Looking at Terry, he added softly, "This is important, Terry, national security is at stake. We have to act on a minute's notice when we have any information. Sorry but I think you'll need a technician on this full time from now on."

Terry Harvey looked around the table and once more saw a concerned expression on his friend's face. "No problem, Steve, I can do that but just to be clear, you want hourly reports to Bob, but also instant reports to Bob if Ho meets anyone or talks to anyone any time of the day or night?"

"That's about it. I'll brief Bob and get him help out of hours but essentially this whole operation depends on you getting information out in good time for us to arrest Ho together with the people he is meeting." Steve realised he couldn't explain about Sky but hoped his cover story would be believed.

Terry Harvey made a note but asked in a slightly incredulous tone. "You mean you want to know everyone he meets or talks to?"

"Yes. We can screen out those of no interest, as the powers-that-be know exactly who they want and believe Ho can lead them to them. As soon as you make the correct connection, we'll pounce."

"OK. You're the boss. I'll get on to it, but you'll have to cover the overtime bill." Terry stood up knowing his part in this meeting was over. As he left, he turned. "I'll set up a comms link to Bob, both verbal and e-mail."

He looked at Bob. "I've got a new toy. You speak into a microphone, and it instantly connects to you and at the same time, converts any speech into an e-mail." Grinning as he left, he was heard to say. "You'll love it."

The three remaining detectives smiled as the head of Technical Services departed. They all agreed Terry was one of a kind.

Steve was once more looking solemn. "Matt, stick with your watchers. I don't think they'll add anything other than a physical presence on the ground. We'll get this one using technology."

"Understand, Steve. Will the watchers be in on the arrests?"

"I don't know but probably, it will depend upon which branch of the law makes the arrests but Met muscle never goes wrong."

Matt was about to pick up on Steve's reference to 'which branch' but decided to leave it. It was obvious there were things going on that Steve was not divulging.

Turning to Bob, he said, "Right, young Robert, your part is vital. I think we can rely on Terry to give you the reports. I suspect most of the meetings and conversations won't mean anything and you won't have to react to many of them."

The DCI examined his admin assistant closely. "But if you hear any reference to someone or something called SKY, you need to act. Every time Max Ho uses the word SKY especially if he is talking to him, I need to know no matter what time, day or night. Have you got that Bob?"

Bob Class wasn't sure he did have it. "You said this was a twenty-four -hour operation and we will be actively monitoring Ho's phone throughout." Bob looked at his boss. "I get that, sir. Inspector Harvey is going to send me hourly reports showing Ho's general activity?"

"Yes."

"What do I do with those reports?"

"I want you to scan them for anything that might be incriminating for Ho. Also look out for any references to upcoming meetings. Anything that might give us an early warning of what he's planning. There should be no reports when he's sleeping for obvious reasons so you can arrange with Terry each night when the hourly reports can stop."

"OK, sir. I've got that and you'll arrange some cover although I don't think I'll need it."

Steve smiled inwardly. He knew Bob would want to do everything himself and that he was keen and able. "Bob, no one can do everything. I'll arrange for an assistant you can use as you see fit. Fair enough?"

Bob's face lit up in a wide beaming smile. "Fair enough, sir. Now what about these instant reports? You say anything verbal has to be reported by Inspector Harvey immediately, whether it's on his phone or if he's meeting someone. Can you explain what I'm to do with this?"

Steve realised not being able to give Bob all the facts was a problem. "Bob, there are things going on I can't tell you, but yes, anything Max Ho says, Terry will immediately pass on to you." Steve sat forward to emphasise the importance of his next statement. "If you hear any reference to North Korea, a fighter jet, someone called Sky or any reference to any meeting, I need to know the instant you do. As I said, anytime, day or night."

"Right, but if there's none of these references, I just ignore them."

Steve realised he was placing a lot of responsibility on his junior officer's shoulders and for a second considered cancelling his plan. "Yes, Bob, if he's ordering a takeaway, that's something Terry would report as an urgent message, but you can discount it as not involving any of the items I've described."

"Got it. And similarly, if he's talking to his tailor, you don't need to know?"

"That's it. As with the hourly reports it's unlikely there'll be any voice traffic once he's in bed, so you'll be able to work something out with Terry regarding the stopping of instant reports." Steve's brain was running forward as he added, "Of course, if Terry's technician picks something up after you've stood down, he'll still call you and if it's one of our names then you'll call me."

"Yes, sir, I've got it. It's actually quite an ingenious way of filtering down to what we really want." Bob Class seemed happy with his new role and responsibility. "Do I call you at home?"

"Anywhere, my mobile will be on."

Steve brought the meeting to an end. "Matt, overtime for your watchers and Bob, you liaise with Terry. I'm off to see the commander."

It was 2.13 p.m. when the DCI entered the office of Commander Perry Hargreaves. Perry was at his desk with his jacket hung over the back of his chair. Steve had stopped at the canteen for a coffee and bite to eat before venturing to the twelfth floor of New Scotland Yard.

Perry was busy writing something and looked up when he saw Steve. "Have a seat, Steve. Give me a minute."

As Steve sat and waited, he thought about Major Havers and the hooded gunman. He wasn't sure why he felt he had to know the man's identity. After all, he wasn't the one who killed Poppy but had almost saved her life. The more he concentrated on finding this man the more he realised he needed closure. The hooded man had been there and knew what had happened. Steve knew witness statements and reports only told so much. To hear the whole story from someone who was there was the most satisfying way of understanding exactly what had happened.

Steve was still daydreaming when he realised Perry Hargreaves was talking to him.

"I've had a meeting with the top brass, Steve. They're not happy. It seems they thought we could just walk away, then the commissioner got the call from the minister. She's not happy and wants to see both of us at four today."

"She must know there was nothing we could have done."

"Yes, but she thinks we should have tried harder. Also, she's not happy about your involvement with the assassination team. She'll tell you herself but under no circumstances can you be seen to be fulfilling that role." Perry stood from behind his desk and joined Steve in one of the two leatherbound armchairs that had been part of the office ever since Steve could remember.

Perry continued. "I've had a call from a Timothy Shand. Seems he's Max Ho's handler at MI6. Michael Russell told him to call. He wants a meeting at six tonight and he's coming here. Seems Russell has thrown in the towel and gone off on indefinite sick leave, so this Timothy Shand is in charge of the Ho thing until Sir Patrick gets things sorted. I think he's back in charge at MI6 temporarily."

Steve listened and smiled. "The sly old fox, I bet that's what he's been angling for ever since he retired. You know, a recall to the colours."

Both policemen laughed and agreed.

Steve spent twenty minutes outlining what he'd arranged with his team and Terry Harvey. He explained his reasoning and Perry agreed it was a sound strategy.

"We still need to create something that'll force Max Ho to contact Sky, but I don't have a clue what it might be." Perry was almost talking to himself.

The DCI understood. "Maybe we should arrest him now, that might force Sky into the open."

"Mm. I wish we could, but I think that would be too simple for our security colleagues." The commander stood. "See you at four. Don't be late."

Steve left to see how Terry was doing and to find Major Havers.

Chapter Thirteen

Charlie, with the help of the satnav, found the street that Anthony Maple had lived in when he had last seen him. As he entered the avenue, he saw a pub on the corner of the street and the main Bushy Road. A quick glance at his car's clock confirmed it was approaching 2.25 p.m. Without any plan and still feeling hungry, Charlie parked in the pub's vast but almost empty car park and entered.

The pub was deadly quiet. Charlie didn't see any customers in the open plan restaurant and bar. The waitresses were wiping down tables and generally clearing up after the lunchtime trade. A large jovial looking man dressed in a white shirt and spotted bow tie was standing behind the bar polishing glasses. On seeing Charlie enter he stopped polishing and smiled warmly at his newest customer.

"I don't suppose the kitchen's still open, is it?" Charlie asked as he walked towards the barman.

"Oh! We normally finish serving food at two. Was there anything you fancied?"

"Nothing in particular, just food." Charlie smiled hoping it would help him be fed.

The barman was obviously an experienced landlord who didn't want to disappoint a customer if he could help. "Just a minute, sir. The kitchen staff are just sitting down to their lunch." He winked at Charlie. "They usually do themselves proud. I'll see if there is anything to spare." The barman left through a swing door positioned behind the bar.

Charlie stood looking around the pub. It was modern but decorated as though it were an old coaching inn. Fake wooden beams, clearly made of fibreglass, gave an olde world feeling to the room. Charlie thought the place warm and comfortable but clearly not original.

The large man from behind the bar reappeared. "How about lamb with mint sauce, boiled potatoes and vegetables?"

Charlie's mouth immediately watered at the thought of the food. "Yes, please, and can I have a small beer?"

The landlord poured the beer and disappeared again to order the food.

Charlie took his beer and walked towards a window table that was in the faint February sunshine. As he approached this table, he looked at the various framed photographs that were hung around the walls. Almost all were of teams of men and some women in groups of four. Charlie noticed the pub's golf team, both men and women, had pride of place. The photographs were bigger than the others. He also noticed the pub's darts team, skittle team and the quiz team. The quiz team photograph stood out because it was the only one that showed a trophy. Clearly the quiz team had won a large cup that was placed on the ground between the two members who stood in the middle of the line of four.

Charlie read the caption on the photograph — QUIZ TEAM REGIONAL WINNERS.

This was obviously a very friendly pub and the centre of the community. Charlie took his beer and sat at his table. The landlord appeared bearing a large plate of delicious smelling lamb. Charlie thought it looked and smelt like the best he had ever seen.

"There you are sir, tuck in."

The barman started wiping tables close to Charlie as a means of maintaining conversation. While Charlie ate, he was peppered with questions.

 Was he passing through? What brought him to the area? Did he have friends locally?

Charlie answered mostly with his mouth full. The landlord was a friendly type and offered a cup of coffee on the house once Charlie had finished his meal. He told the landlord it was the best lamb he had ever had.

Charlie accepted the offer of a coffee and was surprised when the landlord appeared in front of him with two cups. He pulled out a chair and joined Charlie. To make conversation Charlie pointed to the array of photographs. "You have a very active social side to the pub."

"Oh! Yes. I took this place over ten years ago now. It was a good pub but had no character." The landlord drifted into the past. "A few regulars said they'd start a quiz night. Then we had customers wanting to do a dominoes league, then darts, then golf. The latest is a car treasure hunt once a month." The large man was warming to his topic. "Yes. We have a great bunch of regulars, but it all started with our quiz team. They won the regional finals you know. It was a few years ago but still, it was a great honour, and you know the founding members still make up the team."

The landlord rose, removed the photograph of the quiz team from the wall and returned to give Charlie a closer look. Laying it on the table so Charlie could see it clearly, he said, "There you are, the original instigators of our social calendar."

The landlord carried on talking, but Charlie's brain was in a fog. He realised that the man standing on the right-hand side of the four was his next victim. Anthony Maple stood proudly having his photograph taken with the trophy. Charlie almost fainted as the large barman carried on talking. Charlie grabbed for his coffee cup and with an unsteady hand managed to get the cup to his lips and drink some of the strong, dark liquid.

The landlord hadn't noticed and hadn't stopped talking. Charlie had no idea what the man was saying. He sat composing himself from the shock and nodded from time to time. When the big man stopped for breath, Charlie jumped in. "You said these original members of the quiz team are still involved?" Charlie made it sound as though he were generally interested in such an unusual group.

"Oh! Yes. They're the four musketeers, have been as long as I've known them." The landlord drained his coffee cup. "They get the same train into town each morning, they all work in the city but at different jobs and they all come home on the same train. I can set my watch by them every weekday. They get off the train and come straight here for a pint or two before they go home. In truth, Tony's getting a bit of a belly on him. His wife has told me not to sell him any more beer." The landlord let out a real belly laugh.

The large man lifted the photograph and pointed to each face in turn. He started at the left. "That's Peter, he's an accountant. That's Freddy, he's a solicitor. That's Harry, he works in a bank and that's Tony, he's something in investments." Charlie didn't really listen, until the man's finger settled on the last face standing on the right.

"You're a very lucky man to have such loyal customers." Charlie needed to escape but didn't want to draw attention to himself by leaving too abruptly. He stood slowly, made a comment about 'better get going' and thanked the landlord for his meal. A bill was produced, and Charlie paid it leaving a reasonable tip for the staff.

Outside in his car Charlie drew deep breaths. His next target was within striking distance, and he knew enough about his movements to make a plan. He couldn't believe his luck.

He drove from the car park and found 44 Seymour Avenue. It was only a few hundred yards from the pub. Charlie parked his Honda opposite and admired the classical architecture of the detached Victorian house. There was evidence of a large extension to one side and a new double garage to the other. An additional room had been constructed above the garage. Charlie noticed the builder had made a very good job. The gardens were well tended, and a set of gates enclosed the foot of the drive. Charlie assumed they were electrically operated.

As he sat, Charlie once more drifted back to his former life. This large and beautiful house occupied by Anthony Maple reminded him of his losses and his need for revenge. He drove off, once again full of anger. He was determined to see his self-imposed task through. He told himself not to rush. His mentors in prison had preached the need for slow, meticulous planning whenever possible. Charlie would take their advice.

What he did know regardless of his final plan, was that Anthony Maple's days as a pub quizzer were now very limited.

***

Steve met Perry Hargreaves outside the offices of the Metropolitan Police Commissioner at 3.53 p.m. The commissioner's office area consisted of a large outer office occupied only by her secretary. There were various comfortable looking chairs and sofas for her guests to use while waiting for their audience with who many thought of as God.

The secretary asked both Perry and Steve to wait. "You're a few minutes early gentlemen. Please take a seat. The commissioner will see you shortly."

The two officers did as instructed by this rather snooty individual. She fitted the profile of a gate guard too well. No one would argue with her.

At 4.03 p.m. she answered an internal phone and instructed the officers to enter the inner sanctum of God.

"Gentlemen, thank you for being on time, I won't keep you." The commissioner was a career cop, well-liked by the rank and file but not by her senior officers. She had a reputation of not suffering fools and was as demanding of herself as she was of her senior aides. Sitting behind her large desk she initially didn't ask the pair to sit. She finished studying a report and then looked up. "I asked you, commander, to kill off this spy nonsense. DCI Burt should never have been encouraged to run with it. Now I hear that you, DCI Burt, have compromised our Technical Services by having them place an illegal tap on the suspect's phone. I understand the surveillance on this would-be traitor has been extended and is now running indefinitely, never mind the budget or the illegal nature of the surveillance!"

The commissioner closed the file with a thump. She sat back in her large executive chair. After an awkward silence lasting a few seconds longer than it should, she waved her arms at her two colleagues. "Oh! Sit down! You look like a couple of book ends."

This was the first touch of humour the pair had witnessed from the commissioner. Steve and Perry diplomatically ignored the comfortable leather chairs and instead took a pair of high-backed chairs from the conference table set.

Still sitting at her desk, the commissioner carried on but in a calmer tone. "I had a call from Edwin Pinter." She narrowed her eyes peering at the pair. "Someone I believe you met this morning. I know I authorised your attendance at the Whitehall meeting commander, but I didn't for one second expect the Minister for National Security to be there."

The commissioner looked at Perry expecting an answer. "No, Ma'am, we had no idea what to expect at that meeting."

"Yes. This was the meeting when you were supposed to get the Met out of the spy business." This comment was said with a heavy degree of sarcasm. "However, the minister has explained things and I now have a better feel for what was asked of you both. I realise you had little choice but to continue what had been started. He was wholesome in his praise of you both, especially you, DCI Burt. He told me that your initiative in taking responsibility for authorising the illegal phone tap and the way you executed the job was exceptional. He also said it was an endorsement of your management ability, commander, that the DCI felt he could take such actions."

She was smiling, obviously pleased by the comments of the minister. Both men started to feel easier, but without warning she slapped the palm of her right hand on her desk. Her previous light-hearted demeanour was instantly gone to be replaced by that of an angry woman. Almost snarling, she rose from her chair but remained behind her desk. "You are officers of the law. You do not enter into illegal acts no matter the justification. You, DCI Burt, report to Commander Hargreaves. You will obey his orders without question, and you will certainly not use your well-known cavalier approach to authority to circumvent them."

It was obvious this was no theatrical performance. The commissioner was angry. "And you, commander, for a government minister to tell me how pleased he is that I allow my officers a high degree of autonomy and how well you act as a manager was quite frankly an insult. We are a uniformed force with structures. We retain the support of the public only because we are trusted." The commissioner retook her seat.

"Now." She continued in a calmer tone. "We have this mess, and we must deal with it. All this about government sponsored assassinations is unfortunately real and we have to work with it. Despite my earlier comments I concede that on occasions and in the national interest we have to take, let's say, unorthodox routes to achieve our goals."

The commissioner was now calm and gave a slight smile. "Edwin Pinter has explained everything. Commander, each time you are notified of a state sponsored killing, I want to know. Clear?"

"Yes, Ma'am."

"And I do not want valuable resources wasted on investigating such cases. Clear?"

"Yes, Ma'am."

"DCI Burt, in different circumstances you would receive our congratulations on the initiative you have shown, and I suppose I am telling you now as the Commissioner of the Metropolitan Police that you have performed admirably." The commissioner waited, expecting a response.

"Thank you, Ma'am."

"But of course, you will not receive our official congratulations. Instead, you have been reprimanded for disobeying orders and creating an illegal situation the Met cannot be seen to have had any part in."

A deflated Steve Burt sat upright taking his medicine. "Yes, Ma'am."

She rose and walked towards her officers who stood to meet her. The interview was over. "Steve, being commissioner isn't easy and I have to do and say things for the sake of the force. Off the record I applaud your actions and know you only organised the phone tap thinking it would never be disclosed and never be referred to in court, but I hope you understand my position."

She extended her hand for Steve to shake. "Yes, Ma'am, thank you."

After shaking hands with Steve, the commissioner addressed both officers. "Carry on as you would but keep me informed." She looked intensely at Perry Hargreaves leaving him in no doubt it was his responsibility to maintain the channels of communication.

"I believe you already know Sir Patrick Head, but DCI Burt, don't let the old devil manipulate you over the coming days. Remember what I said about our service and our responsibilities."

"Yes, Ma'am."

"Good. Now off you go and remember Perry, I need to know what's going on."

Both officers left and headed for the canteen. The felt they had been well and truly taken down a peg and felt exhausted by the experience. They needed a coffee.

Over coffee they both agreed that despite the dressing down they had just had, they both felt somehow elated. Their path forward was now as officially sanctioned as it could be, and the commissioner had delivered her message loud and clear.

"I suppose that's why she's in charge, Steve. She's bloody good at what she does."

***

Si Griffiths had tracked down the car business run by Benny Stockton from his New Cross premises. He'd parked his car in a side street as Steve and the commander were entering the grand offices of the Metropolitan Police Commissioner. It was four p.m. Si placed a 'POLICE ON DUTY' card in the window of his pool car. He knew from experience that traffic wardens often paid no attention to such signs but regardless, Si took comfort from the fact he wouldn't pay the fine.

Benny Stockton's garage was larger than Si had imagined. There was a large, paved area outside a smart 1970s-styled flat roofed showroom. Standing on the opposite side of the road, Si counted eighteen modern and clean looking second-hand cars. From his vantage point he could see a further six cars inside the showroom.

Si decided to venture inside, so crossed the road and pretended to be interested in the cars on display, then wandered inside the showroom and was met by a man in his thirties, wearing a cheap suit and tie who introduced himself as Stanley, the sales manager. He was an imposing six- footer but had already gone to seed. His large belly and general pale complexion were evidence that he didn't use a gym. His size however suggested he had at one time been a very fit man.

"What kind of car are you interested in, sir?"

Stanley was all sales. Si wasn't interested and decided to get rid of this salesman.

"I'm not, sonny, I'm here to see Benny Stockton. Tell him Detective Sergeant Griffiths is here to see him."

The sales manager gave a dismissive grunt. "Mr Stockton isn't in."

Si let out a deep breath. "Don't play games with me, I'm told he's always here. Now either you go get him or I'll go find him. Somehow, I don't think you'd be very popular if I walked in on him. Do you?"

Stanley wasn't flustered by Si's threat. "What I should have said was, Mr Stockton isn't in for coppers." Stanley started to put his hand on Si's shoulder in an attempt to escort him off the premises.

Si pulled away. "One more touch, laddie and I'll arrest you for assault."

Stanley persisted. He was obviously Benny Stockton's minder, and as he tried once more to place a hand on Si's shoulder the smaller policeman turned ninety degrees and lifted his knee into Stanley's sensitive region. The lift was accompanied by a force that belied Si's stature. The bigger man collapsed holding the area between the top of his legs. With some satisfaction Si stood over the poleaxed salesman. "I'll just find Benny by myself then."

As a street fighter and a copper, Si knew most of the dirty moves. As he walked over Stanley, he allowed his trailing foot to accidentally smash into the sales manager's face with some force. "Oh! Sorry about that, Stanley." The salesman was out cold.

Si looked around and saw a door marked 'OFFICE PRIVATE.' He surmised this was probably where Benny Stockton was to be found. Without knocking he turned the handle and pushed at the door. As he entered, he saw a large television mounted on one wall. It was switched on and was tuned to a station showing horse racing. A man of medium build was sprawled out on a sofa gazing at the large screen. He was dressed in a black vest and long training pants as though he was dressed for a visit to a gym. The room had a seedy feel and smelt of sweat and heroin. Apart from the sofa there was a desk in one corner, a few metal filing cabinets and a small cupboard on which was placed several bottles of spirits. The walls had at one time been white and the grey carpet had last been cleaned in the previous century.

Si slowly closed the door as the man swung himself off his sofa. "Who the hell are you?"

"Ah! A good question. I'm either your new best friend or your worst nightmare. I take it you are Benny Stockton, proprietor of this establishment?" Si was using what he thought was his most polite and annoying tone. He spoke slowly and deliberately.

"It's none of your business. Get out of here." Benny now stood and shouted, "Stanley? Come and throw this idiot out. Break his bloody neck if you have to."

Without being invited, Si sat down on one of the chairs by the desk. "Stanley can't hear you, Benny. He's having a sleep or maybe he's in a coma. All I know is he's not coming."

Like some gangland bosses Si had come across in his career Benny wasn't a brave man without his minders. Such men were big in their minds when they had their supporters with them. Without backup, they tended to be less intimidating. In Si's opinion Benny fell into this category. His stature was such he would be no good in a fist fight and unless he had a concealed weapon that would give him strength, he was Si's to question. Given his dress, Si thought it unlikely this gang boss was armed.

Benny realising he was on his own, sat on his sofa and switched off the television. "OK. I can tell you're a copper, I'm clean, I've nothing to hide. This is a respectable business."

"I'm sure it is, Benny," Si continued in his friendly pleasant manner. "All I want is a name. Nothing too hard, one name and I'm gone. Then you can call an ambulance for your sales manager."

"What kind of a name? I'm no grass."

"I know that, Benny, but let me ask you." Si paused and pulled his chair closer to the car dealer. He leant forward placing his elbows on his knees. "Some time ago you were involved with an Eastern European gang that was operating here in London. Do you remember?"

Benny eyed Si suspiciously but said nothing.

"The leader of that gang was murdered. Remember?"

"Now listen, copper, whoever you are. I had nothing to do with that. You're not pinning that murder on me."

"Don't worry Benny." Si was still sounding reasonable. "I could fit you up for all sorts of things especially if you don't help me. Understand?"

Once more Benny stared at the detective and said nothing. Si continued. "You see, Benny, I think you asked someone to do you a favour and get rid of this European gangster. All I want to know is who you went to and why him?"

Benny flushed and grew red as though his blood pressure had spiked. "You must be joking. I don't know nothing about any murder and if I did, I don't know anybody I could call. Now bugger off, copper, you don't know what you're talking about."

Si sat back in his chair looking at Benny. "Oh, dear, Benny. You don't get it do you?" Si allowed an element of menace to enter his voice. What Benny heard was pure London with menaces. "You see I know you were involved and if you force me, I'll arrest you right now for murder." Si's voice was rasping and angry as he once more leant forward and allowed his spit to splash on Benny's face. "Don't give me a hard time here, Benny. Help yourself and give me the name."

Benny leant back, away from Si. He was frightened of this older policeman. Si thought he heard a faint cry from the gangster. Pressing home his advantage, Si stood and pulled the second-hand car dealer to his feet. Holding Benny with his left hand he smacked him across the face with the back of his right hand. Benny fell back onto his sofa. The force of the blow split his lip and he felt blood in his mouth.

"I'm not messing about here, Benny. I want that name. Now!"

Benny, crouched in the foetal position on his sofa, held up an arm in surrender. Si pulled him to a vertical position before allowing him to sink back onto his sofa. Benny clearly needed a few minutes to recover his thoughts. Eventually, after spitting blood from his mouth, he pointed to the tray of drinks on his cabinet and asked Si if he could have a drink. Si poured two large, neat vodkas and handed one to Benny. As he put the glass to his damaged lip the burning vodka stung, and he made an involuntary sound suggesting to Si that the alcohol was closing up his wound.

After a few minutes allowing Benny to settle down, Si began. "Right, Benny. Now I want the whole story, not just a name." Si's policeman's instincts were well tuned after so many years on the streets. He had a gut instinct there was more than just a killing involved here.

Benny was clearly resigned but put up one last show of defiance. "Look, copper, if I grass these people up, I'm dead. Will you guarantee my safety?"

Si smiled and took pleasure in his answer. "No." He saw the look of shock on Benny's face. "You've made your bed over all these years, so sleep in it. What I will tell you is that no one will ever trace what you tell me back to you. Once I leave here, you'll never see me again."

Benny sipped his drink and winced as the alcohol stung the open wound on his lip. He wasn't going to give in without a display of defiance. "Look, copper. I don't even know your name and you haven't shown me your warrant card." Benny became more righteous as though he were the innocent victim. "Maybe you're not a copper. Maybe I don't have to talk to you?"

Si stood over Benny. "You'd better believe I'm a cop. Like I said, give me what I want, and you'll never see me again. It's better for you that you don't know my name. People who know me sometimes get hurt." Si acted out his fantasy as a Chicago gangster. Once more and without warning, he smacked Benny across the face causing his vodka glass to smash against the wall. The force of the blow sent Benny back against the sofa. A large red bruise appeared on his cheek. He was crying from the pain and felt a few teeth work loose.

Si filled a replacement glass with vodka and handed it to Benny.

Neither man spoke as Benny once more regained his composure and tried to clear the ringing coming from inside his head.

Benny was a career criminal and knew there was no easy way out of this. He was confused as to how he was in this situation. Even through the pain coming from his lip and cheek, he vowed to discover who had grassed him up to this copper. He knew he would have to cooperate and that this was about as good a deal as he'd get in the circumstances. He decided to be helpful and started his tale slowly.

"OK. About a year ago this guy came to see me. I didn't know him, but he said he represented a gang that was operating in London in drugs and tarts. He said they were from Romania and were having problems getting established in London. He told me to take them under my wing and bring them into my business and we'd all flourish. He said it was a win, win."

Si interrupted. "You'd never met this person before?"

"No. He just appeared." Benny stopped to think and seemed to drift away. "It was funny. He was a proper gent, you know. Dressed well and spoke with a posh accent. He said he found the Romanians when he was working on something else." Benny realised he'd drifted. He shrugged and continued. "Anyway, he arranged for a meeting. I didn't like the people, especially their head man, but they could get some good stuff and their whores were a cut above, so we started doing business together. They were horrible people and didn't know much. Me, and some of my associates, finished up running their operation, and after a few months we didn't need them. We had access to their drugs and their women, but we kept a few on to help out with the language. Their boss man wasn't happy and threatened everyone involved. He even knifed one of my pimps, slashed his face." Benny was feeling his lip as he carefully sipped his vodka. He paused for a few minutes. Si sat sipping his drink waiting for Benny to resume.

"It became clear this Romanian head man was getting out of control. The guy who set the deal up was taking ten percent of the money every week so I told him, if he didn't sort this headcase out, his ten percent would be in danger. I told him this bloke was dangerous and he needed getting rid of." Benny looked pleadingly at Si. "Honest, copper, I didn't mean for him to be killed, just to be sent back to Romania."

"Go on." Si wasn't interested in Benny's finer feelings.

"It turns out this guy who set us up, works for the government. He let it slip one time. I don't know what he does, but he said he'd take care of it. Next thing I know the Romanian is found in a field in Suffolk with a bullet through his head. I got a call from the guy. He said he'd taken care of the problem and he now wanted fifteen percent of the take." Benny's lip had started to bleed again, and he wiped it with the back of his hand. "That's it, that's all I know, honest, copper."

"How do you pay this bloke?"

"He comes here every Saturday morning. He has a black briefcase and stuffs the cash into it and leaves."

"What's his name?"

"I don't know. He calls himself Mr Smith but that's not his real name. He told me if I ever got into trouble he could take care of things."

"What do you think he meant by that?"

Benny became very solemn. "He has people killed."

"And that's everything?"

"Yes."

Si's policeman's brain was still connected. "How do you contact him. Say you wanted me removed. What would you do?"

Benny looked exhausted and ready to capitulate. His inner strength was gone. Without thinking he said, "I place an advert in the *Evening Standard*, in the Situations Vacant." Benny pointed to his desk. "The advert's in the top drawer."

Si stood and retrieved the copy pf the advert.

'TYPIST WANTED. TOP SALARY. APPLY BOX 1160'

Si read it twice. "What happens after you place the advert?"

"He calls. I tell him the problem and he says he'll discuss it on Saturday."

"What if it's urgent?"

"He says nothing is so that urgent it can't wait a few days."

Si absorbed Benny's tale taking his time and ran several scenarios in his mind. After a long silence, Si spoke. His voice was full of menace. "Now, Benny, I've never been here! You don't know me. Right?"

Benny nodded as Si once more gently slapped his cheek.

"This Saturday man. You meet him as normal and don't contact him before Saturday. Understand?"

Again, the instruction was followed by a slap on Benny's cheek.

Si felt he had as much from Benny as he was going to get. He stood, slipped the advert into his jacket pocket, and once more patted Benny on the cheek hitting him harder than was necessary, and silently opened the door. He heard the sales manager groaning. "I think your boy needs some medical attention, but his next singing role will be with the sopranos."

Si left to return to his car. To his relief he had avoided the attention of the local traffic warden. He sat in his car scheming. He had the information the DCI needed but wondered how he could gain from it. Si was a devious copper who knew the value of information. He'd think long and hard and see the DCI in the morning.

***

Steve entered Commander Perry Hargreaves office at 5.51 p.m. in time for their meeting with Timothy Shand, Max Ho's handler at MI6. Perry hadn't laid on any refreshments. He was all business.

"Any word from Terry Harvey's crew?"

"Not really." Steve had visited the area of Technical Support before coming to meet the commander. "Terry has forwarded the hourly updates to DC Childs but it's all routine stuff. The voice traffic has also been sent to Bob, and he filtered out the rubbish. All we know is that Max has a heavy date tonight with a lady called Gloria who charges a grand a night." Steve smiled as Perry's jaw dropped.

"Bloody hell, for that kind of money I'd go on the game myself." Both policemen laughed.

They were still smiling when a serious looking man aged about thirty-five knocked on the door frame of Perry's office. He was dressed in the Whitehall uniform of dark suit, white shirt and college or regimental tie. He was of medium build with a full head of unruly black hair.

"Excuse me, I'm looking for Commander Hargreaves, the lady on reception gave me a pass." The newcomer held his plastic-coated security pass up for inspection.

Perry stood up and walked towards the stranger with his hand held out. "You must be Timothy Shand, we're expecting you. This is DCI Burt. Come in and have a seat."

Timothy Shand was not an imposing character. He seemed weak and unsure of himself. He shuffled rather than strode to the conference table not looking Steve or Perry directly in the eyes. His head was bowed towards the floor. He accepted a chair and without looking up, opened his briefcase and removed a file. He didn't say anything but sat, staring at his file. Steve thought this civil servant looked exactly like he should, a nerdy graduate probably with a first-class honours degree in something like Greek mythology from either Oxford or Cambridge.

Perry glanced at Steve who shrugged. "Mr Shand, you called this meeting. Perhaps you can explain why we are here?"

Timothy Shand seemed to suddenly realise he was being spoken to. "Oh! Yes."

Timothy seemed somehow disjointed. As he sat his body appeared to move independently from his brain. Steve had never met anyone with less presence in his life. He surmised Timothy Shand must have hidden talents.

Timothy began. "Well, you see, it appears Max Ho has turned rogue." The case handler suddenly seemed more alert. "I understand you gentlemen have identified this and are charged with assisting MI6 in uncovering his North Korean handler?"

Timothy looked at Steve and Perry for confirmation. Neither confirmed this was the case, so Timothy carried on. "Originally he was recruited to uncover the North Korean ring operating in London, but as you know, it appears he has been turned. In a phone call earlier today, he denied having met the North Korean called Sky, but we know from DCI Burt's surveillance he did in fact meet this Sky but has failed to report it."

Timothy opened the file he'd brought and studied it for a few seconds before continuing. "Our top priority is to find the leader of the ring and dismantle it before it can do any damage. It is unlikely the cover story we originally put out about Squadron Leader Ho being willing to steal the research aircraft will ever come to pass. The aircraft is too well protected but of course the squadron leader is unaware we are on to him. He may still believe that it is possible for him to hijack the plane. We feel he should be encouraged to think the plan is still feasible. In this way we hope he will lead us to the spymaster, this Sky."

Steve and Perry sat listening. Steve changed his opinion of Timothy Shand. The more he spoke the more impressive he became. He was clearly nobody's fool.

"The problem we have, gentlemen, is that according to the recordings secured by DCI Burt, Sky will not contact Max Ho again until after the hijacking. We have to devise a plan so the squadron leader will make contact with Sky, who will then feel it necessary to meet him again to discuss the new situation."

Steve and Perry nodded. They both understood but didn't follow their role.

"You asked what this meeting is about gentlemen? That's it. How do we contrive a set of circumstances that will see Max Ho and this Sky having to meet? I understand Ho is still under surveillance so that when they meet, we can immediately move in and arrest the entire ring."

Steve sat back. "How much of this comes from Sir Patrick Bond?"

"Almost all of it although I have merely repeated extracts of a report filed following this morning's meeting." Timothy smiled as he peered through his thick glasses and looked at Steve. "Sir Patrick said you would have a plan."

Steve laughed. "Did he indeed. Well, Mr Shand, I fear he's wrong, I don't have a clue."

The room was silent. Perry Hargreaves stood and paced between his desk and the conference table. Eventually he spoke. "I can see the need but I'm not sure devising a set of circumstances to achieve your goal, Mr Shand, is a police matter."

Timothy returned his file to his briefcase. "I'm afraid Sir Patrick disagrees. As you are running the surveillance operation, he believes you know more about Max Ho than anyone else and as such are in control of all the information you need to devise a plan."

Perry looked at the civil servant. He saw the logic but not the practicality. He looked at Steve who had remained silent and appeared to be thinking. On seeing the commander look in his direction, the DCI answered. "Mr Shand, if I can read my colleagues into this, we may be able to brainstorm a solution, but it will require some off the wall logic."

"Sir Patrick has told me to say he has complete confidence in you both. You have a free hand to engineer whatever is required and Sir Patrick would like a briefing at noon tomorrow at MI6 headquarters."

Steve's expression became one of incredulity. "What? He wants a plan in less than twelve hours?"

Timothy smiled. He stood having fulfilled his role as messenger. "I'm afraid so, Mr Burt, we'll see you tomorrow at noon."

With a wave and a general goodbye, Timothy Shand left.

Perry Hargreaves, still standing, looked at Steve. "You'd better get on with it. Remember the commissioner is counting on you."

With a sarcastic "Thank you" the DCI left to worry and think. He decided to leave everything until tomorrow morning and get Matt and Bob's ideas fresh. He also thought he might need Terry Harvey.

***

Major Simon Havers restlessly walked about his office located on Brompton Road. He preferred clear, unambiguous orders. His attendance at the meeting in Whitehall with the minister had unsettled him. The lack of a decision concerning the elimination of Max Ho wasn't sitting well with him.

The major had a secret that could end his military career in disgrace, but he knew it wasn't this secret that was responsible for his mood. He'd lived with his secret for a while now. He told himself he was soldier and would obey his orders no matter what. However, he had a kill order. He had a statement from the police confirming Max Ho was a problem. Under normal circumstances he would already have ordered Max Ho's death.

Like all good professional soldiers, the major went over events in his head, looking for the issues his orders had thrown up. Firstly, he told himself his original order had not been rescinded. It was all well and good for the minister to instruct Lord Scotland to stand down his committee and to say Max Ho was off limits until further notice, but the fact remained that he had a written order to eliminate the squadron leader.

As he sat agonising, Major Havers began to summarise the likely outcome of events yet to unfold. He knew it was inevitable that the order to kill Max Ho would be reinstated, but what if in the meantime, he slipped his followers and succeeded in stealing the jet? This thought worried the major.

After a few more minutes he arrived at a decision. He took an envelope from the top drawer of his desk and inserted four different coloured envelopes into the large brown self-sealed one. He wrote the name Dominic Barns followed by an address in Chelsea. He sat back remembering when he had recruited Dominic or Staff Sergeant Eric Stokes as he had been. Dominic was one of the major's most efficient assets. When the major had received his kill order for Max Ho, he had immediately thought of Dominic Barns as the instrument.

Major Simon Havers sat looking at the addressed, sealed and stamped envelope. It sat on his desk, almost daring him to post it. He knew the act of posting it would most certainly lead to Max Ho's death. He once more agonised with himself but came to the same conclusion. Whilst the politicians and the police played, there was a real possibility

Max Ho might succeed. He had a kill order from Lord Scotland that had not been rescinded and according to the police, the conditions attached to executing the order had been met. Max Ho was a traitor.

Without further thought, Major Havers left his office and pushed the envelope into a bright red pillar box located less than one hundred yards from his office.

Max Ho was a dead man walking.

***

Steve arrived home at 7.17 p.m. His wife, Alison, was in the bathroom, bathing their daughter Rosie before she put her to bed. Steve was exhausted both physically and mentally. He poured himself a large glass of Merlot that Alison had only recently opened. He sat in what had become 'daddy's chair' and tried to relax. His mind was in turmoil following the events of the day. The rich red liquid slid easily down his throat, and he began to feel it soothing him. He drank it quickly looking for an alcohol-induced escape. He rose and poured another. He heard his wife and daughter laughing in the bathroom and he smiled. Sitting with his wine he recalled how lucky he was to have found Alison and what a pleasure his daughter was. He loved them both and would do anything to protect them.

It was during these melancholy moments that his mind drifted to his job and his career. He loved his family and knew being a police detective wasn't conducive to a normal family life especially a police detective running an independent unit within the Metropolitan Police. He and Alison had often discussed life after the police. As a doctor running her own private practice, she was sympathetic to Steve's dilemma of wanting a more settled family life whilst enjoying the job he did.

As he sat daydreaming and trying to relax, Rosie suddenly appeared and launched herself at Steve. Only quick reflexes on his part avoided his wine being spilt. He put his glass down on a side table and lifted his daughter onto his knee. She was as usual excited to see him and kissed him wildly on both cheeks. She smelt of soap and bath salts. Her hair was damp and her pink dressing gown, covered in horses, was new.

"Daddy, I got a star at school today for my writing." As always when she had Steve to herself, she wanted to tell him everything. In thirty seconds, he knew all about her day, her triumphs and her disasters.

Alison appeared drying her hands on a large bath towel and looked at the clock. It was late for Rosie to still be up, but she decided to leave her snuggling up to Steve for a few more minutes. As a doctor, Alison saw the strain that was now a constant in Steve's appearance.

"Right young lady, school tomorrow, it's past your bedtime. Five more minutes with daddy and then bed." Alison smiled at Steve and added, "Dinner will be another half an hour."

Alison went to work in their open plan kitchen while Steve continued to listen to his daughter's experiences at school.

After their evening meal and with Rosie safely asleep, Steve and Alison settled down beside each other on their sofa. Steve enjoyed these evenings snuggling up to his wife and feeling her body close to his. "I'm sorry, darling but I'm on call for the foreseeable future. I'll have my mobile switched on permanently. Do you want me to sleep in the spare room so as not to disturb you if I get a call?"

Alison pulled sharply away from her husband, staring at him. "Certainly not." Her voice contained an element of shock. "You've never slept in the spare room, and you won't start now."

Steve pulled his wife back towards him and kissed her. He went on to explain what he could of the Max Ho case and of his meeting with the commissioner. He made no reference to the minister or MI6.

Steve and Alison had long ago decided to keep each other informed about their work, or at least as much as ethics would allow. Steve often used Alison as a sounding board for some of his cases whilst Alison told her husband about the few patients she felt an extra empathy with and often took under her wing.

The couple sat enjoying each other's company. Neither had switched on the television. Both were content to sip their wine in silence.

Alison edged away from her husband in order to see his face as she spoke to him. "Steve, I've been thinking. You've been working hard and to be honest I'm a bit worried about you. You haven't had a decent break for months."

Steve knew Alison was building up to something. He'd seen the signs before and knew to stay quiet.

"Well, it's your fiftieth birthday in a few months and Rosie has a half term break. I was wondering if we should book a boat on the Norfolk Broads for a week. Get right away, no phones, no TV, just us and the boat. What do you say?"

Steve was already visualising the boat, the water and the peace. "Won't it be a bit cold at the end of April?"

Alison gave her husband a gentle thump. "Don't spoil it, I'm sure it will be great. If it's a bit cold, we can wear thicker clothes. Come on!" Dr Mills was obviously enthusiastic about the break. "Let's book it."

Steve, with a great smile, hugged his wife. "OK, let's do it. If you organise it and give me the dates, I'll book the time off."

Satisfied, husband and wife settled down to discuss what they might do on their upcoming holiday and how Steve might celebrate his fiftieth birthday.

Chapter Fourteen

Friday, February 11 dawned like most mornings during the past week. It was cold, wet and miserable. The DCI hadn't been disturbed during the night and after discussing their holiday plans, he felt refreshed. He had something to look forward to.

As Steve walked into the shower at 6.23 a.m. Charlie Robb was on his way to Bushy Park. During the evening he'd devised a plan using the advice he'd been given in prison. He'd take his time and learn more about his victim. His plan was to wait at Bushy Park Station and follow his victim to his office in London. His fellow inmates had emphasised the need to know your victim and to plan where to bump him off. Charlie intended to wait until next Monday and today was an exercise in gathering information. He already knew from the pub landlord that Anthony Maple always had a beer on his way home in the evening. Charlie had a good understanding of the layout of the pub and Anthony Maple's home, at least from the outside. He had decided by following him to his office this morning, he'd have a more complete picture.

He arrived in the half full car park that serviced Bushy Station at 7.14 a.m. Wearing his killing gear and carrying his gun, he tried to avoid the CCTV cameras as he made his way to the ticket machine, paid for a whole day's parking, and with his cap pulled firmly over his head, he got back into his car. As it was dark, he was sure the CCTV cameras wouldn't be a problem. He'd decided to carry the gun just in case an opportunity arose that he couldn't ignore.

He knew not to stand on the platform for longer than was necessary. If he were spotted and seen to allow several trains to leave without him whilst he awaited his victim, this would look suspicious and possibly make him a person of interest in any subsequent investigation. He would wait in the car park and look out for Anthony Maple as he entered the only entrance to the small station. Charlie had already purchased a return ticket to London online, so as soon as he saw his victim, he could follow him onto the train.

At 7.53 a.m. Charlie spotted a figure dressed as a city gent should with a dark overcoat against the cold. The figure carried a brown soft leather briefcase and as it battled against the weather, Charlie saw it was Anthony Maple. There was a large powerful light above the entrance to the station and a newspaper vendor had his kiosk just inside. Anthony Maple stopped to buy a paper and as he did so, his head was fully illuminated by the light.

Charlie walked briskly towards the station. There was no doubt this was his next victim, Anthony Maple. Charlie followed at a distance dressed in his nondescript but deadly raincoat that held the .22 revolver that would end Anthony Maple's life.

The train arrived and Charlie watched his target enter a first-class carriage accompanied by similarly grey looking individuals all dressed in the same City uniform. Charlie had bought a first-class ticket so was able to sit a few rows back. He was near enough to listen to the conversation that took place between the group of men who clearly always travelled together.

The train pulled into Waterloo Station at 8.47 a.m. Charlie followed his target as Anthony exited the station and walked with purpose towards the office complexes that had sprung up just outside the station in York Road. Charlie got within five yards of his quarry before easing back a little.

Anthony Maple surprised Charlie by stopping at a coffee shop and sitting down and ordering a coffee and something to eat. He laid his briefcase on the chair opposite and took out his *Financial Times* to read. Charlie realised there were CCTV cameras all around and it was not good to be viewed hanging around without any apparent purpose. He made a split-second decision and entered the café. Careful not to look directly at Maple, he took a table at the rear of the café. From the comings and goings at the front of the café, Charlie thought this early morning must be their busy time with takeaway coffee and filled rolls.

The surly waitress took Charlie's order for a black coffee. He looked around and saw no CCTV. He removed his cap but kept his raincoat on. As he sat looking at the back of his target's head, he saw himself taking his pistol from his pocket and shooting Anthony Maple in the back of the head. He had heard various tales of how inmates had escaped the scene because there was utter confusion immediately after a criminal act, including murder.

Charlie dismissed this notion. He needed to speak with his target. He had to let him know why he had to die. He had to feel his revenge. Rage and frustration began to take hold of Charlie. Seeing the well-groomed individual who was responsible for his imprisonment and the murder of his family, Charlie fought hard to control his emotions. His coffee arrived and having something simple to drink like his coffee, helped calm Charlie down. He remembered his prison advice. Never kill anyone when you're angry. It's a sure way to get caught.

Charlie Robb was on a fact-finding mission. He had his pistol but had no intention of using it, until his target rose from his table and visited the toilet. The door was adjacent to Charlie's table. Anthony Maple walked by without glancing at the scruffily dressed man in a raincoat.

Charlie jumped from his seat and followed Maple into the toilet. He didn't know why and didn't bother to question himself. He had reacted on pure instinct. The toilet was small, and Anthony Maple was the only one using the facilities. He stood facing the wall. Charlie noticed there was a key in the lock on the inside of the main door into the toilet. Without thinking, he turned the key locking himself and his quarry inside the small toilet. Now Charlie was running on pure adrenaline and the need for revenge.

Anthony Maple became aware someone had entered the toilet but stared ahead ignoring the newcomer. "Hello, Anthony, long time." Charlie stood with his back to the now locked entrance door.

All Maple saw initially was a scruffy looking man wearing an old raincoat that was buttoned up to his neck and suddenly staring at the stranger who knew his name. Maple's jaw dropped. "Charles Robb!"

"That's right Tony. I'm glad you remember me."

Maple zipped himself up as he stood back from the urinal. Charlie noted he still retained the arrogant sneer he'd experienced the first time they'd met. For some reason the pub landlord's comments on Tony Maple's girth came to mind. Anthony Maple always thought himself better than anyone else. He made to walk past Charlie who held up his left hand and pushed Maple gently backwards. "Not so fast, Tony. We have business to attend to."

"Listen, Charles," said a sneering Maple. "We do not. Any business we had finished when you tried to give us up to the police to save your own skin. Now please move. I have a meeting to attend."

Once more Maple sought to get past Charlie. The space in the toilet was limited and unless Charlie stood ninety degrees on, Maple would not get past.

"You killed my family, Maple."

Arrogantly, Maple once more sneered. "Don't be ridiculous. Do I look like a murderer, now please stand aside!"

"Oh, you're a murderer all right and a crook. You and your pals have cost me eight years of my life. That's eight years I'll never get back." Charlie was warming to his topic. Anger was beginning to flow through his brain. He took a step closer to Maple. "Why did you pick on me? What had I ever done to you and your mates? Why ruin my life?"

Maple, still sneering, pushed Charlie back. "Because you were a greedy little man. We came to you with a proposal, and you jumped at it. All you saw was money. I agree it was unfortunate about your wife and son but as I recall, you reneged on our agreement and tried to turn us in to the police. Something had to be done. Now, will you get out of my way?"

Once more with an unbelievable arrogance, Maple tried to push past Charlie.

Charlie stood his ground and with a calmness he had not felt before, he withdrew his pistol. His voice was flat as he said, "Unfortunate! You think killing my wife and son was UNFORTUNATE!" Inside Charlie remained calm but he allowed his voice to express his anger. He pointed the .22 pistol at Anthony Maple's head. "You're an excuse for a human being. I'm doing society a favour by killing you. Look at you. You've grown fat while I suffered. All four of you are scum. You took everything from me, and you say it was UNFORTUNATE!"

Anthony Maple on seeing the gun and listening to Charlie held up his hands as in surrender and tried to back further into the small toilet. "Now hold on, Charles, if that is loaded, I'd rather you put it away. I apologise for my use of the word, of course it was tragic." Maple was now hard against the white-tiled rear wall.

Charlie took a pace closer. "I've already killed Colin Clark." It was Charlie's turn to sneer. "I felt sorry for him. Of all of you he was the least guilty, but he had to pay the price."

Maple was now sweating. His upper lip was wet, and his face was flushed. He still had his arms raised in surrender. "It wasn't me, Charles, I wanted to testify at your trial. I pleaded with Geoffrey Lockwood not to send that thug to frighten your family." Maple was desperate as he realised Charlie would pull the trigger. His mind was in turmoil. "I have money, you can have it all." The sound of Maple pleading was music to Charlie's ears. Maple continued to plead hoping that he might say something that would save his life. "Please, Charles. I have a family. My older son is sick. He…"

Charlie took another pace forward. His right arm was outstretched, holding the gun. "You have a family! You have a family! What about my family? You piece of scum. I had a family until you took them away." Charlie was almost shouting. He saw a red mist as he pulled the trigger.

The sound of the gun going off inside this small, enclosed space was like a bomb going off. The explosion served to make Charlie immediately aware of what he had just done. Anthony Maple was slumped on the floor. Blood was seeping slowly from a hole where his left eye used to be.

Charlie stood in shock for a few seconds before pulling himself together. Relying on instinct and his conversations with his fellow prisoners, Charlie looked around. He stood listening. Despite the blast no one had come to see what had caused the blast. He looked at his hands and realised he wasn't wearing disposable gloves. This would mean he would have gunshot residue on his hands. He told himself this was not good. He tried to remember if he had touched anything and concluded he had only touched the door handle and the key.

Slipping the gun into the pocket of his raincoat, Charlie unlocked the main door and removed the key. With his handkerchief he quickly wiped the handle and opened the door keeping the handkerchief in place. Outside he hunched over the handle hoping no one was looking as he locked the door and wiped the handle. He put the key in the other pocket of his raincoat and walked to his table. The old lags in prison had told him that if he ever did anything on the spur of the moment, he should get as far away from the incident as quickly as possible.

Charlie approached the till that was used for sitting-in clients to pay at. Anyone ordering takeaway items stood by the door and paid at a separate till. Although the queue for takeaways was busy, Charlie paid without waiting and exited the café. He tried not to run but on turning left, walked briskly back towards Waterloo Station. His journey was swift, and his mind was blank. He was in a state of shock. On entering the station, he immediately went to the toilets. Locking himself into a cubicle he sat with his elbows on his knees and shivered slightly. Still dressed in his raincoat and cap he replayed what had just happened. He'd killed Anthony Maple, the quiz player and one of the men responsible for his imprisonment and the murder of his family. His mind was in turmoil as he justified the killing to himself. It was a shock to realise he felt no remorse, no guilt and no feelings of euphoria at having killed his second victim.

Charlie sat and slowly became more aware of his surroundings, and he began to analyse his situation. He told himself he hadn't touched any of the surfaces inside the toilet so that was good. He had touched the main door handle, but he'd wiped both sides clean. He took the key from his pocket and began to clean it using his handkerchief. He told himself there were now no fingerprints on the key and he'd dump it far away from the café. He remembered the gunshot residue and his advice that to get rid of it he should wash his hands several times in hot soapy water. To be absolutely sure he was told additionally to wash his hands in a mixture of washing up liquid and scouring powder. To be safe, he should carry out this washing procedure four times a day religiously for three days. Charlie smiled recalling the conversation with old Stan. Stan was in for life for killing two bookmakers he said didn't honour a bet.

Charlie left the safety of the toilet cubicle and washed his hands vigorously before walking back onto the station concourse. His brain told him to heed the advice from prison and get as far away as fast as he could. Another part of his brain told him to go back to the café and see if there was anything happening. Looking at his watch, Charlie realised only thirty-two minutes had elapsed since he first entered the café. Wondering if the body had been discovered he decided to walk back but to stay as far away from the café as possible.

Charlie saw the flashing blue lights as he walked along York Road. He was on the opposite side of the road from the café. He walked slowly. He saw several police cars, two small white vans, two civilian looking cars and a black panel van. None of the vehicles was neatly parked. A uniformed policeman was tying blue and white plastic police tape between lampposts in an effort to mark out the no-go area for the public.

Charlie didn't stop although a small crowd had gathered looking on. He knew better than to join them, in case he was interviewed by the police, so he turned and returned to Waterloo Station. He caught the 10.22 a.m. train back to Bushy Park. He slept in his first-class seat most of the way exhausted due to the nervous energy that yet another one of the people responsible for his current plight had paid the penalty. He also dreamt about his meeting later in the day with his parole officer, Connie O'Sullivan. He wondered if she would go for a drink with him. A smile appeared on his sleeping features.

***

As Charlie Robb was pulling the trigger of the .22 pistol that killed Anthony Maple, Steve was talking with Terry Harvey. Terry was explaining what the electronic eyes on Max Ho had revealed over the past twelve hours. "It's all been very ordinary." Terry was talking while looking at a computer monitor. There was a lot of data that he couldn't simply summarise from handwritten notes. "We've put out the hourly bulletins and the more or less instant audio stuff. Bob Class has had it all and we've arranged between us that if any of his buzz words is mentioned then he'll get an instant alert."

"Max Ho hasn't revealed anything?"

"No, other than he's a bit of a sexual athlete." Terry sniggered like an adolescent schoolboy.

The DCI was disappointed at the lack of incriminating data, but accepted Terry and his team could do no more. "Terry? Can you come over in about five minutes? We have a problem to solve, and your input could be invaluable."

Terry Harvey looked sideways at his friend. "Sounds serious, I'll be there."

At ten a.m. Steve, Matt, Bob and Terry sat around Steve's conference table, silently sipping their coffee.

Steve hadn't worked anything out in advance. He started by swearing the group to secrecy and told them he was breaching the Official Secrets Act simply by briefing them. Each officer in turned vowed to remain silent as they heard the entire Max Ho story ending with the meeting yesterday with Commander Hargreaves and Timothy Shand.

"This Timothy Shand is Max Ho's handler. Like I said, we are now certain Max Ho is actually planning to nick this aircraft. We can continue to follow him as we are or bring things to a head. Remember MI6 want this North Korean who calls himself Sky. Sir Patrick Bond wants a plan from us to force Max Ho into another meeting with Sky. We'll be following him and hopefully if our plan works, we'll nab the lot including Sky and his other agents."

Steve sat back, as Matt spoke. "Fine, what's the plan?"

The DCI gave a sly smile. "That's why we're here, Matt. We don't have a plan, but we need one by midday."

Bob Class stood up and walked towards the white board that was fixed to one wall of Steve's office. He picked up a red marker pen and started to doodle. "So, our task is to bring this Sky into the open. Correct?" Bob wrote this on the board.

"Yes." Steve was intrigued, not knowing where Bob was going with this, but glad he had the initiative to do something.

Bob continued, "We know from the recording of the meeting Ho had with Sky that Ho was told he wouldn't see Sky again. Correct?"

"Yes."

"We now believe Ho is going to steal the aircraft. Correct?" Bob was writing these questions as he spoke.

"Yes." Steve knew better than disturb his DC's thought process.

"And we need a circumstance that will force Ho to ask for a meeting with Sky? Correct?"

"Yes, but where are you going Bob?"

"I'm trying to break the problem down into its constituent parts. Whatever we come up with both Ho and Sky will have to believe it. We need an event that is earth shattering and reported by the media. Anything less and they won't buy it."

Terry chipped in. "How earth-shattering, Bob?"

"That's it, sir. I don't know but I believe we need an event that the BBC will report that will affect the stealing of the aircraft without actually saying so. We have to be devious."

Bob returned to his seat and switched on his laptop. Everyone was silent, thinking hard but after a few minutes Steve spoke up. "I'm not too sure about earth shattering, Bob. You're right it has to be believable but I'd rather we came up with something a bit more low-key?" Steve glanced around the table. "Well, any ideas?"

He was disappointed to see the row of blank faces.

Matt put up his hand. "What about something weather related. We know Ho was given flight information and a transponder for his trip to North Korea. Suppose a freak storm was reported that meant the timetable had to be brought forward. Would he not have to meet Sky to receive new information?"

Steve stroked his chin. "Possible, but it doesn't sound right. I don't think from what I heard on the recording that the information Ho was given was weather sensitive."

Bob had his ear buds stuck in his ears as he scrolled through his laptop. He removed his earphones and switched on the sound. He replayed that part of the meeting between Ho and Sky where Sky handed over the transponder and coordinates for refuelling. No one around the table heard any reference to weather. Terry looked at Matt. "It's not bad, Matt, but the Russians have weather forecasters. If we said a tropical storm was about to hit southern England, I suspect they might know it was a fib."

All four officers laughed.

Steve sat back lost in his own thoughts. As had become normal when he was fighting a problem, he started talking out loud to himself. "We need something that'll bring Sky out into the open. But what?" The DCI was looking far into the distance and not seeing anything. "Suppose Ho became ill and couldn't nick the plane. Would Sky need to understand when he'd be fit enough to steal the thing and break cover?" Steve continued to wrestle with the problem. "What if Ho was dismissed from the RAF? He wouldn't have access to the aircraft. Would Sky and his band need to devise a plan to break into the airbase and have Ho fly the aircraft out."

As Steve spoke to himself and he discussed these options with himself, Matt, Bob and Terry made notes. The DCI sighed and sat up in his chair.

Terry Harvey who had been listening and thinking, stood and walked to the white board. As he picked up the red marker a knock was heard at the office door. Before Steve could invite whoever had knocked to come in, the door opened with a flourish and standing in the doorway was Detective Sergeant Simon Griffiths.

"Holding a meeting without me then?" Si closed the door behind him and spotting an empty chair, took a seat at the table. With an arrogance that was uncommon in junior officers he sat back. "Please carry on. Pretend I'm not here. I have some information for the boss." He looked at Steve who was trying to remain calm in the face of this obvious insubordination. "I've got a lead on your man, boss, I thought you'd like to know."

Steve was more than angry. "DS Griffiths, this is a closed meeting. If you have something to discuss this is neither the time nor the place." Steve knew better than to give a junior officer a real dressing down in front of other officers.

Si held up his hands. He clearly wasn't troubled by Steve's admonishment. "Just trying to help, sir. After all, you did say I was part of the team." He continued to sit and smile at those around him. Cheekily, he leant forward and in a conspiratorial way, suggested, "Maybe I can help if you tell me what's going on?"

The DCI couldn't believe how insolent his sergeant was. He was about to blow a fuse when Terry Harvey intervened. "Steve, if this is the DS who arranged to lift Max Ho's phone, he might have something to contribute."

Matt Conway was astonished at Si's nerve but remained silent. As his senior officer, Matt made a note to tear a strip off Si even if the DCI did.

Steve understood where Terry was coming from. Si had proven his street credentials already and the topic under discussion might need a few dirty underhand streetwise tricks. The DCI conceded Si might be useful. "OK, DS Griffiths, I suppose you might have something to contribute." Steve reminded Si of the sensitivity of what was under discussion and outlined the Max Ho dilemma they now found themselves in.

While Terry stood by the white board, Si looked serious. "You need to find a way of getting this Ho character to meet this Sky character, so you can arrest Sky? Is that about it?"

"Yes, sergeant, that's about it."

"Bloody hell. I didn't know police work could be like this." Si was genuinely interested and excited. "I might stay on if it's going to be like this."

The DCI noted that his DS was dressed more appropriately for the job. His hair had been cut and was neatly combed. He seemed to be wearing a new white shirt and his plain blue tie didn't show any signs of staining.

Terry Harvey spoke. "I've been thinking." He made a few notations on the board and drew a few interconnecting lines before speaking again. Turning to his audience, he continued. "Maybe we don't have to get Max Ho and Sky to meet. What if we gave Ho a reason to phone Sky?"

Terry's audience looked on, obviously mystified.

"If we knew Ho was phoning Sky, we might be able to do a form of reverse triangulation. If we could identify the mast that routed the call from Ho to Sky, we would know to within a small area where Sky was. From his picture, that birthmark makes him stand out. He'd be easily spotted."

Terry was about to carry on when Bob Class interrupted. "And if the area was small enough, we could swamp it with officers and like you say, he'd be easy to spot. We should be able to pick him up if we give it long enough." Bob sat back as Terry pointed towards him.

"Exactly. We'd have to leave the swamp team in place for as long as it would take. This Sky bloke must go out occasionally, and with the troops on the ground we should be able to nab him." Terry sat down.

The room was quiet. Everyone was lost in their own thoughts.

Suddenly Si spoke, breaking the spell. "No, it's a good plan, inspector, but a bit long-winded. What happens if this Sky never leaves his flat or house? Maybe he knows we're looking for him and he uses his followers to do his shopping and so on?" Si leant forward. "Surely we need something more direct?"

Steve agreed with Si but liked Terry's proposal. He was about to speak when Si took centre stage again. "Besides, surely this Sky bloke is holed up in one of the embassies. From what the DCI said he's probably North Korean secret service. From the few political cases I've worked, guys like Sky get themselves affiliated to a friendly country's embassy in order to claim immunity. If what you told me is true, it's either Russia or China." Si looked at the faces surrounding him. "Maybe all we have to do is stake out these embassies. If he doesn't know we're on to him, he'll surely come out and go about his business. Maybe we already know where to find him?"

Steve looked at Si in astonishment. "You may have something, Si. We're looking for a plan to smoke Sky out because we don't know where he is." The DCI stroked his chin. "But if you're right, we know he's in one of two locations." Steve sat back with a satisfactory smile on his face.

Matt Conway spoke next. His face was one of concentration. "If Si is correct, and I think he is, maybe we need two plans?"

"Go on, Matt." Steve knew Matt was a clear thinker.

"Well, with Terry's reverse triangulation system and assuming we can convince Ho to call Sky, we'd know the receiving mast and that would confirm he's likely to be in either the Chinese embassy or the Russian. They're far enough apart not to use the same mast."

Terry interrupted. His face suggested the penny had dropped. "And whichever mast pings, that's the embassy he's in. Brilliant, Matt."

Matt blushed slightly and shrugged.

Steve had listened and felt they were arriving at a workable plan. However, he needed to be sure. "Bob, can you please organise five coffees please? We'll take a five-minute break to gather our thoughts."

Bob Class went off to get the coffee and everyone except Steve filed out into the outer office. Steve wiped the white board clean and wrote using the red marker pen.

PROPOSALS.
1- BBC — BIG EVENT
2- WEATHER
3- ILLNESS
4- DISMISSAL
5- PHONE-TERRY
6- EMBASSY
7- REASON FOR HO TO CALL SKY
8- MIXTURE

When everyone had returned to their seats with their coffee, he stood up and walked to the whiteboard. He was conscious that it was getting near to noon, and he would have to close the meeting and go and see Sir Patrick Bond.

"Right. Thanks for all your input and insights. As usual we work better as a team." Steve had given a similar speech several months ago and thought this morning's meeting justified the praise he was giving his team. Even Si!

"Now, I've listed your proposals. I think we can quickly narrow our collective thoughts down but just to be sure we don't miss anything, let's look at them one at a time." Steve pointed to number one. "Some form of unspecified big event. Anyone think this is realistic?"

Everyone shook their head.

"Number two: Suggest bad weather might interfere with the flight." Everyone shook their heads.

"Three: Ho gets sick and Sky comes to visit him. Any thoughts?"

Then Si piped up. "I like that. If this Ho is sick, he can't nick the plane. They'd have to rearrange their plans. I'd bet if this Sky is the main man from North Korea and if he's promised his masters the aircraft will be delivered, any delay and he'd be a very nervous man. I've come across these Orientals before and believe me, they cannot lose face. I'd bet Sky would come running."

Steve considered Si's remarks. He looked at the rest of his team. Matt and Bob nodded. "It makes sense, boss." Bob Class looked excited.

"OK. Number three is possible."

Everyone nodded. Steve thought Si was proving useful despite his upcoming reaming out for his earlier insubordination.

"Number four: Dismissal. I personally think it's too way out. To make it look good would take weeks of planning."

Matt Conway nodded. "I agree, it's too cumbersome."

"Number five and number six combined: Terry's reverse triangulation or whatever that is and Si's certainty that Sky has been accredited to a friendly embassy such as China or Russia. If we somehow get Ho to call Sky, we'll know from the nearest mast which embassy he is in. We then swamp the area around the embassy and wait for Sky to appear. Any thoughts?"

Terry spoke first. "If Si is right about the embassy, and given he's flying the thing over both Russian and Chinese airspace, plus we heard on the recording the three nations are contributing to building the jet once it's delivered, he probably is in one or other. All I need is a five- second ping and I can tell you which one he's in."

"We know what Sky looks like so a swamp operation should catch him when he's spotted." Bob Class was still enthusiastic.

Matt Conway was looking less impressed. "I agree it could work but we still don't have anything to cause Ho to make the call."

The DCI thought Matt was right. It was a sound plan, but it was missing the vital ingredient. Terry spoke again. "When Si arranged for Ho's phone to be lifted, we downloaded all his contacts. There aren't many. You remember we decided not to call any of them for fear of spooking both Ho and Sky but now Si has suggested we're looking at the embassies maybe we could call each number on some pretext that wouldn't make them suspicious. If we get a ping on an embassy mast, we'll have Sky's number and be able to track it."

Steve's admiration for Terry knew no bounds. "You can do that without having Sky's phone?"

"We have a new experimental piece of software I need to try out. With it we should be able to track the number with the help of the provider. All we'll get is a GPS locator, not what he talks about, but we'll know where Sky is all the time his phone is switched on."

"Bloody hell, Terry, more experimental kit." Over the years Terry and Steve had been friends it was more common than not for Terry to help Steve solve his cases by trying out new experimental software. This was no exception.

Terry sat grinning while Steve worked out the implications of Terry's suggestion.

"So, you're going to call all the numbers on Ho's mobile on some pretext and when the other party answers, check out the receiving mobile phone mast. If one is serving the Chinese or Russian embassies, we'll assume that's Sky's number and you can track his movements…" Steve paused and smiled. "Using an experimental piece of software."

"That's it. If it works you can pick him up anytime you like without alerting your pilot."

Steve sat down and looked around the table. "What's the reason for calling all Ho's contacts?"

Silence descended until Si spoke up. "Well, if you don't tell them they've won the lottery, the next best is to say you're from the phone supplier and there's a problem with their account. If the inspector needs five seconds to verify the mast, all you do is hang up after five seconds and move on. People get these scam calls all the time. They don't think twice about it. They'll just assume the connection's been lost."

"DS Griffiths, you are without doubt, the most devious police officer I have ever come across." Steve was smiling.

Si smiled back. "I do my best… SIR."

Steve leant forward and recapped the plan. "Are we all agreed that Terry's and Si's plan is what I take to Sir Patrick?"

Everyone nodded a yes.

"Right. Terry, can you set things up? Si, you work with Matt on a script, and Matt, I want you to be the voice that calls the numbers. Bob, write up what we've just agreed, only the outline. I need it in fifteen minutes. I'll add the detail during the presentation."

Steve stood now full of action. "Good job, everyone. Let's get this elephant off our backs. I'm going to see the commander and brief him. Any questions?"

Everyone said no except Si who, smiling, said, "I need to see you about that other matter and your signature on my early retirement on full pension request."

Steve walked past the cheeky DS, shaking his head. "Later Si, I have things to do and so do you."

The DCI left to brief the commander before visiting MI6 headquarters and a meeting with Sir Patrick Bond. It was 11.34 a.m.

Chapter Fifteen

Squadron Leader Max Ho sat in his flat gazing at the view from the large sliding glass doors that led onto his terrace. Being February, the weather wasn't suitable for sitting outside.

As he sat daydreaming, he thought about the aircraft he was test flying. It was a thing of beauty, not just deadly but beautiful. Its long flowing lines gave it its stealth capability, the rubber tiles gave it an aggressive posture and overall design was well ahead of its time. Max considered himself fortunate to be part of the flight development programme.

He allowed his mind to wander back to his recent meeting with Sky. He'd never met Sky before but knew he was the senior spymaster for the North Korean government. Max knew Sky would remain in the UK until the mission was completed. He thought he might meet Sky once he'd stolen the aircraft, and everyone was safely in North Korea.

Max was anxious to get going and thought next Monday might be a good day to initiate the theft. He struggled with the logistics of the operation. He was back on duty on Monday. The aircraft would have been thoroughly serviced and anything that needed fixing would have been attended to. He was due to do some low-level sub sonic tests on Monday afternoon. Max considered that if the aircraft were perfect, then with enough fuel, he could simply crank up the speed to Mach Four and be on his way. He would be invisible to radar and only when he switched on the transponder Sky had given him would anyone know where he was. Max closed his eyes and thought about his flight plan. He'd put down in Russia for refuelling less than an hour after heading East. He wondered what the government would send after him. As Max thought about it he knew there was no way of capturing him or the aircraft.

He reached for his phone, not knowing that Terry Harvey's technicians were listening. Max speed dialled a number. The phone was picked up on the third ring. A nondescript voice answered, "Yes?"

"It's Max. I think the operation will take place next Monday in the afternoon, probably around 15.00 hours. Please advise all stations."

Max hung up. He had been instructed to use telephone communication as little as possible. It was well known that the security services had access to sophisticated listening devices.

He sat looking out seeking inner calm for what lay ahead of him. He decided to visit a few bars and a nightclub tonight. He told himself that nightlife in Pyongyang might not be as good as London, although he'd been promised a special hero's social life.

It was noon. He roused himself and decided to shower, dress and visit the local pub for lunch.

***

Dominic Barns was having a late breakfast, cooked by his latest girlfriend. After leaving the Army and going to work for Major Havers, Dom had initially led a bit of a monastic life, except for a few dalliances with the lovely Samantha, who worked for the major. Not having had a mission for several months, Dominic had re-entered society and had enjoyed a fairly hectic social circle consisting of mainly female companions. None of the women knew how he made his living, and he would keep it that way despite several attempts to discover his secret.

His latest steady girlfriend, Carole, was a nurse. She was in her early thirties, blonde, five foot nine and stunningly good looking. The fact she worked shifts meant Dom could indulge other ladies when Carole was working. He was finishing his toast as Carole, dressed in a warm sweater and jeans, kissed him on the cheek and said she was running late. "I'll call you this evening," she shouted as she went down the stairs that led to Dom's front door. As she exited, she called again. "The post's here, there's a large brown envelope for you."

Dom heard the door closing and the news there was a brown envelope for him meant only one thing. He had his next mission. Having been briefed previously, he knew his target even before he opened the envelope. He remembered the meeting and that the major had been unusually indecisive as he placed Dom on standby. Dom knew that a Squadron Leader Max Ho was his next target and that there was no need for a subtle killing. This man was to be terminated by any means.

With the last mouthful of toast Dom stood and went downstairs to collect the envelope. He decided to shower first and then deal with the contents and do some preparatory work. If he gave himself the weekend, he could carry out the execution on Monday or earlier if an opportunity presented itself.

***

Max Ho made his call at 11.51 a.m. Terry Harvey's senior technician, Andrew, picked up the call and immediately relayed what was said to Bob Class who, seeing the content, contacted the DCI who was on his way to meet Sir Patrick Bond.

"Ho's been on the phone, sir. Looks like he's planning to steal the aircraft on Monday afternoon. He's asked a contact to alert all stations. Looks like he'll nick it around three p.m. on Monday."

"Thanks, Bob. Do we know who he called?"

"Not yet, sir."

"OK. Ask Terry Harvey if he can work his magic and tell us in which area the other phone was used?"

"Will do, sir. I think he called it reverse triangulation."

Steve laughed. "If you say so, Bob. Thanks." Steve hung up just as he approached MI6's headquarters.

Steve entered Sir Patrick's office to find him seated at a large conference table with Timothy Shand. Both men were deep in conversation and Steve noticed there were piles of brown files covering at least half of the table.

"Ah! Steve. Come in and grab a seat." Sir Patrick was welcoming and began to pull the chair from the table that was next to him. "I hope you have good news for us?" Sir Patrick seemed in high spirits.

Steve was suspicious and decided to be circumspect in how the conversation went from now on. Timothy Shand was seated opposite Sir

Patrick. He simply nodded to Steve and returned to reading a file that was open in front of him.

"Steve, I've told Tim here that you are one of the best cops in the Met and that you'll come here today with a waterproof plan." Sir Patrick smiled. "Now don't make me out to be a liar, let's hear your devious plan. Remember, we're not interested in Ho just now, we want this Sky character."

Steve had brought a report of their sketchy plan. Commander Perry Hargreaves had liked it and had given the DCI the green light to present it to MI6. Before he started Steve told the two MI6 officers about his call from Bob. "Seems the hijacking is planned for Monday afternoon, around three. If we haven't picked up Sky by then, and assuming we don't let Ho take off, it's odds-on Sky will be off and smuggled out of the country. They'll know their plot has been discovered. He'd have no reason to hang around."

"What do you think, Tim?" Sir Patrick looked at Timothy Shand.

"We're not concerned with Ho. He can be pulled in at any time. He certainly won't be allowed near the aircraft on Monday despite what he might think. No, Sir Patrick, our focus has to be Sky."

"Quite so. There you have it, Steve. Now, what sort of plan have you dreamt up for us?" Sir Patrick's voice was its usual smooth self. Looking at him Steve thought Patrick Bond looked younger now he was back as head of MI6.

Opening his file, Steve pushed single sheets towards Sir Patrick and Timothy Shand. He took a deep breath. "Right. In front of you is an outline of our plan. From your briefing you are only interested in this Sky. You believe he is North Korea's top man in Europe." Steve paused to look at the other two men trying to gauge a reaction. He got none so continued. "This plan is illegal and is subject to total deniability. I trust this is clear?" The DCI had been instructed to say this by Perry Hargreaves. He thought it made him sound like a civil servant.

Both recipients of Steve's briefing nodded.

"When we lifted Max Ho's phone to insert various high-tech devices, our heads of Technical Resources downloaded Ho's call history for no other reason than he thought we might need them. At the time we decided not to use them for fear of spooking Ho and anyone he was in touch with." Steve paused again and saw his audience were fully attentive. "One of my DS's figured out that Sky would probably be attached to the embassy of a power friendly to North Korea. If we had Sky's real name, I'm sure the Foreign Office would be able to tell us. Unfortunately, we don't have his name. We think he's accredited to either the Russian or Chinese embassy. It's a pretty safe assumption as they are both partners in stealing the aircraft."

Steve examined his notes before continuing. Both Sir Patrick and Timothy Shand appeared to be following but looked puzzled.

"We need a way of knowing which embassy Sky is using." He went on to explain about using the numbers from Ho's call history and seeing if they got a ping from the mast nearest which embassy.

Sir Patrick looked up from his briefing note. "Very clever. Very clever indeed. Carry on, Steve."

"Thank you. Our technical wizard can go one better. If we get a ping for either embassy, we'll have Sky's mobile phone number. With it and with the collusion of the provider we can track Sky everywhere he goes provided his phone is switched on. When he leaves whichever embassy, we'll know. Once he's outside he can be arrested. You'll have your man." Steve sat back.

"Brilliant, Steve, we won't have to concoct a reason for Max Ho to meet Sky. We simply wait for him to step outside whichever embassy he's using?"

"That's about it, Sir Patrick."

Timothy Shand remained staring at his briefing note. From his expression Steve thought he had concerns. "What will you say to the people you call from Max Ho's caller list? Presumably some of them will be in the spy ring and we don't want to alert them we're on to them?"

"Good point. We're writing a script for my DI to use. He'll say he's from the phone company and he's calling because there is a problem with the account. He only needs to keep the line open for our technicians to identify the mast."

"Hm. I see." It was obvious Timothy Shand didn't really see so Steve explained further.

"People get calls from their phone providers all the time. After five seconds, my DI will cut the call as though the signal has been lost. We believe no one who they call will suspect anything."

Timothy Shand leant forward and spoke slowly. "Yes. I see that. What if none of the numbers ping a mast close to either the Russian or Chinese embassies?"

"Then we'll go to plan B."

"Which is?"

"It's a work in progress, but basically, we poison Ho to make him sick. We believe Sky would have to break cover and visit him. He has a date for the hijacking. I'm sure he'll have passed this on to his superiors. If Ho can't fly the plane, he'll have to revise his plans and learn when Ho might be fit again." Steve opened his arms. "As a plan it's a bit rough but we believe it would smoke Sky out. At least we have a fall back if our electronic plan doesn't work."

Sir Patrick looked at Timothy Shand. "I told you, Tim, these people are good." He turned to Steve. "Well done, Steve. Two plans for the price of one. Now…"

The DCI's phone rang. He looked at the screen and saw it was Bob. "Do you mind, gentlemen. I should take this."

Steve stood and walked to the far side of the office. "Yes, Bob?"

"Sorry to disturb you, sir but Inspector Harvey said you'd want to know. He's traced the call that Max Ho made confirming he'd put their plan into operation on Monday."

Steve could feel his excitement level increase. "Yes?"

"Well, sir. Inspector Harvey traced it to Whitehall."

"What!" Steve forgot where he was as he shouted. Realising he now had Sir Patrick's and Timothy Shand's unwanted attention, he spoke more softly. "Is he sure?"

"Yes, sir. The recipient was definitely in Whitehall when he answered the call."

Steve stood with his back to the two MI6 officers. His brain was spinning as he tried to make sense of this latest piece of information. Realising he had to finish the call he simply said, "Well done, Bob. I'll be back shortly."

Returning to his chair, Steve apologised for the interruption. "So, Sir Patrick, you were saying?"

Sir Patrick looked quizzically at Steve obviously expecting an explanation of his phone call. Steve had already decided to keep Bob's information to himself. At least for now. A stony silence descended, and once Patrick Bond realised the DCI had nothing to say, he carried on but was suspicious.

"Well, DCI Burt, as I said this is fine work. You can leave it with us now. We'll take care of everything going forward but rest assured, a glowing letter of thanks will be on its way to the commissioner highlighting your cooperation and input."

For the second time in five minutes, Steve couldn't believe what he was hearing. "You're not suggesting I stand my team down? How will you access the phone numbers and the technology you'd need to trace them?"

"Don't worry about it. Just close everything down. Remove your surveillance teams and close down your electronic monitoring. As I said, leave it all with us." Sir Patrick's voice was less friendly and sounded firmer. He was giving commands.

Steve tried once more. "Look, Patrick, you asked for a plan to smoke out Sky. We've given you a plan that should work, but you need the resources of the Met to make it work. Unless I'm missing something here, you're sabotaging the plan before it's implemented."

Sir Patrick Bond looked angry. His usual reddish complexion had become bright red. He stood up indicating the meeting was over. He drew a deep breath as Steve also stood. Timothy Shand remained seated.

"Steve, there are things going on that unfortunately you cannot be made aware of. You must understand MI6 and MI5 exist for a reason. The fact you were called in on this Ho and Sky thing was unfortunate. I believe Colonel Walters went outside his brief by seeking police help. However, we cannot go back. Walters did what he did, and you became involved. You have performed brilliantly, but now it's time to give it up. Go back to your police work and leave the spying to us. This is now a matter of national security."

The DCI looked fiercely at Sir Patrick. He knew he should simply walk away but he also knew something, was wrong. The call from Bob

Class had inadvertently started a chain reaction that was fuelled by Sir Patrick's comments. The DCI knew someone in the Government was involved with Max Ho. But who?

"Something's not right here, I know it and you know it. You can tell me to walk away but I'll keep a watching brief. Something stinks and I'll find the cause." The DCI spoke in a measured way that almost frightened Sir Patrick.

"Now, Steve." Sir Patrick was back as an old friend. "Don't do anything hasty. There are forces at work here that you need know nothing about. We appreciate everything you've done but please leave it to us."

Steve saw he was getting nowhere. He knew instinctively he'd been set up but didn't know why. "Tell me, Patrick, did you really want that plan?"

"Oh yes, you'll never know how much!" Patrick Bond put his hand on Steve's shoulder and began guiding him towards the office door. "You'll never know how much we needed your plan."

The DCI left feeling he had been let down. He couldn't fathom why, but he suspected he'd just become a patsy in a grander plan. He was determined not to let it go. Something was going on and he'd find out what.

With a new determination, he strode out, walking with purpose back to his office and his team.

***

After Steve left Sir Patrick Bond placed a telephone call. He left Tim Shand sitting at his conference table while he spoke for exactly sixty seconds on the phone.

As he finished his call and returned to the table, Timothy Shand asked, "Well? Do you think he'll cause trouble?"

"Yes. That's why I just made the call. Steve Burt will huff and puff, but ultimately we can use him, provided he's controlled."

"I hope you're right."

"So do I. Now, when do you want to start? We have the plan and it's feasible. You're the expert at misinformation, so I'm leaving this to you Tim. My only stipulation is you start the ball rolling now, before something else happens. Steve Burt won't give up and even if we do control him, there's always a danger he'll latch onto something."

Timothy Shand gave a sly grin. "Don't worry. I'll drop the plan on him first thing Monday morning. We'll give the poor sod a weekend to enjoy himself. If he reacts as we think, we'll have him by Monday evening." Timothy Shand drew a deep breath. "Once we have him, what you do with him is up to you of course, Sir Patrick. My brief is to set the scene. Your brief is to finish it off."

Sir Patrick Bond acknowledged Timothy's remark with a wave of his arm. "Just so Timothy, a brief and a task I relish."

***

It took Steve fifteen minutes to walk back to New Scotland Yard. The walk had helped him clear his head, but he had failed to come up with the reason he felt as though he were a patsy in a grand plan. As he walked into his outer office, Bob Class jumped to his feet. "Sir, you're to go see Commander Hargreaves the instant you got back. He said to tell you it was urgent."

Steve had planned a canteen snack and a coffee but realised such a pleasure would have to wait. With a reluctant acceptance, he thanked Bob and took the lift to the twelfth floor.

As soon as he entered Commander Hargreaves's office Steve knew from the atmosphere, something was wrong. Perry Hargreaves was at his desk in full uniform. There was no evidence of the usual informality the DCI had come to expect. Steve, as was usual, went to take a chair from Perry's conference table.

"Don't bother to sit down, you're not staying long." It was obvious something wasn't right. Perry continued in a formal, crisp voice that left Steve in no doubt that Perry was the boss. "I've had Sir Patrick Bond on the phone. He says he's made it very clear to you that this spy caper with Ho and the North Koreans is now off limits to you. It's over but you apparently wouldn't accept it. Well, mister," the commander's voice rose a few decibels. "Listen to me. You are not to go near Ho or anyone else. Is that clear?"

Steve was shocked that Sir Patrick would have called Perry and instructed him to warn him off the investigation. To Steve's mind this confirmed Patrick Bond as head of MI6 was up to something and it affected Steve personally. He knew he could simply nod, apologise and leave, or share his concerns with Perry, if the commander were prepared to listen. He thought he would try.

"Look, sir. Yes, I may have been a bit high-handed but remember, all along we have been asked to use our resources to aid the security services. When we give them what they want they suddenly tell us to leave everything, walk away and they'll handle it."

Steve was pleasantly surprised Perry had allowed him to sound off like this, so he pushed on. "They asked for a plan to smoke this North Korean called Sky out. I've just presented the plan I told you about earlier. It's a good plan and it should work. When Patrick Bond and that weedy looking Timothy Shand heard it, they agreed and then told me to drop everything. Why?"

Perry Hargreaves was listening. "Then we traced the call that Max Ho made to an unknown number. We have the recording, but in the call, he tells this other person that the mission to steal the aircraft is on for Monday afternoon, and to set things up." Steve was allowing his own fury to surface. "That call Max Ho made was picked up in Whitehall. The same place I've just come from. Now tell me, SIR… is that a coincidence too far?"

Commander Hargreaves sat quietly with his fingers steepled under his chin.

"Sit down, Steve. As you know it was me who thought we should help out Colonel Walters when he came here. The commissioner more or less gave us the green light to help out Sir Patrick and I know they asked for the plan." Perry leant forward. "But why do you think there's some kind of conspiracy and why in hell do you think only you can deal with it?"

The DCI had no immediate answer. He sat in silence appreciating the commander's more reasonable mindset. "I don't know, sir. All I do know is Sir Patrick is a devious old bugger, even the commissioner said so. If Terry Harvey is right, and I'm sure he is, there's someone in Whitehall whose part of this scheme to nick that plane. No one has ever said anything about that. Remember, this started as a simple 'let's put a suspect under surveillance to help out a government extermination team'. They didn't want to kill an innocent man. Apart from the ethics of us as police officers colluding in a murder, we proved Max Ho was probably guilty. That was our initial brief."

"Agreed. You and your team initially thought he was innocent but then when he didn't report his meeting with this master spy calling himself Sky, you changed your mind. It's circumstantial but probably correct. You declared Max Ho was guilty."

Steve sat recalling the events. "Right. It was likely the word would go out to their assassin and Ho would be killed. We hadn't spoken about how to prevent it, but your attitude was these things happen."

Perry fiddled with a plastic ruler. "We have to accept, Steve, that certain things are done that are against the law but need to be done to protect the country."

Steve nodded. "I accept that." He paused, "But moving on. We gave the spooks what they wanted but then they wanted more. They suddenly introduced this Sky person. Why?"

Perry sat in silence. He clearly had no answers.

Steve continued. "They tell us they want a plan to bring Sky out into the open. We give them a plan and suddenly we're warned off. We're told to call everyone off and leave Ho alone despite proving him guilty. Then we learn somebody within the government is involved." Steve paused and spoke in a more conspiratorial tone. "They don't know we know but it's a bit of a coincidence. Sir Patrick is playing a game and whether we like it or not the Metropolitan Police Force are in the middle of it."

"I can see your point but how are we involved?"

"I don't know, sir, but I think we should carry on. Leave MI6 out of the loop. We have our plan. If it works, we could have Sky in the cells within twenty-four hours. We have enough on Ho to arrest him now. We could have both men off the street and in custody. At least they'd be safe and could expect a fair trial."

Perry Hargreaves sat bolt upright. "Hold on, detective chief inspector, that is not going to happen. We have no mandate to investigate this, and besides the security services are there to deal with issues like this. Now here me Steve, loud and clear, do not approach either Ho or this Sky. Do you understand?"

Steve smiled. He knew he would get a fierce reaction from Perry. "Of course not, sir, I was only looking at what we could do. We are police officers charged to uphold the rule of law." Steve was calm as he pleaded his case one last time. "We surely can't condone the murder of innocent people."

Perry Hargreaves became visibly angry. "Listen, Steve don't be so bloody simple. Things happen all the time. It just so happens we've become involved in something we shouldn't. Sir Patrick was very clear." Perry raised his voice another few decibels. "Stay away and shut down the surveillance. Get back to regular police work!"

Steve knew he wasn't going to win. "Yes, sir. So, we call off all surveillance of Max Ho?"

"Yes, with immediate effect."

Chapter Sixteen

Steve returned to his office and closed the door. He sat for fifteen minutes doodling on his A4 pad trying to make sense of his conversation with Perry Hargreaves and work out what Sir Patrick Bond was up to. The fleeting thoughts he had experienced during his meeting with Sir Patrick and Timothy Shand were beginning to crystallize, but they hadn't yet surfaced. The DCI knew from experience this process couldn't be rushed.

He called Matt and Bob in and joined them at his small conference table. During his doodling he'd reached a decision and wasn't sure how to present it to his colleagues. He was about to begin when there was a knock at the door and Si Griffiths pushed his head in.

"Anything going on I should know about, sir?"

Steve smiled to himself. What he was about to do would affect Si, and Si had been helpful in forming the plan. The DCI also knew Si was street smart and devious. Maybe he could have a part to play.

"Come in Si, grab a chair."

Si smiling, closed the door and took a seat. He had an expectant expression on his face. Steve took this as a positive sign.

"I had a meeting over at MI6 at lunchtime. You all know it was to present our plan. I'd expected to be given the go ahead and with luck we'd have this Sky person in custody ready to hand over to the spooks. Unfortunately, I was told to back off and leave everything to MI6."

Matt interrupted. "What! They can't do that. It's our plan and Terry Harvey's technical equipment. I doubt they could implement the plan without our help."

Steve looked at Matt like a schoolmaster might look at a dumb child. "You're right, Matt, but that's the ruling." Steve continued as he surveyed the faces around the table. "When I got back, I was summoned to Commander Hargreaves's office. It seems Sir Patrick and MI6 wanted to be sure we were off the Ho case. He more or less ordered Hargreaves to warn us off. We are to remove all surveillance from Ho with immediate effect and in Hargreaves's words, get back to normal policing."

Steve sat back scanning his colleagues' faces for reactions. The room was silent for what seemed a long time before Matt Conway spoke up. "OK, you've told us what has happened, but I haven't heard you tell us to actually call off anything."

Steve loved working with this small group. Matt in particular had formed a sixth sense. He seemed to be able to second guess Steve's moves.

Looking at his colleagues in general, Steve nodded to Matt. "I'm convinced something is going on and we're in the middle of it. Terry Harvey traced the call Max Ho made to set up the heist of the aircraft for Monday to Whitehall. Someone within the government is involved with Ho. Sir Patrick withheld this piece of information from me, and I didn't tell him we had it."

Si Griffiths sat up. "Bloody hell. This is better than the films. You lot get into all kinds of things." He looked at Steve. "What are we going to do, sir? I presume you're telling us all of this for a reason?"

"Yes, Si." Steve took a deep breath. "I've decided to maintain the surveillance on Max Ho and go ahead with phoning the numbers from Ho's phone."

"Jesus, Steve that's a bit dangerous. You're disobeying a direct order." Matt Conway had a concerned look on his face.

"Yes, Matt. I am and that's why I'm telling you all. This is my call and my call only. If any of you don't want to be involved, I'll totally understand."

Once more the room was silent. Bob Class spoke to break the silence. "Look, sir, I'm the junior here and happy to be guided by the others but to protect everyone, including yourself, it strikes me that if you forgot to tell us to lay off, then no one can be held to account if it all goes wrong." Bob blushed as everyone zeroed in on his remarks.

Steve smiled. "Good point, Bob but unfortunately the Met doesn't work like that, but you are right. If I don't tell you to withdraw the surveillance, then you can't be held responsible." Steve smiled. "You know you are getting more devious by the week, well done, Bob. So as of now, this meeting never happened. You carry on as planned. The surveillance stays and we make the calls. Once we know more, we can decide on our next..." Steve paused, "very unofficial move."

Matt Conway looked at Steve. "Sir. It might be an idea to read Terry Harvey in on this. I know you want to protect him but it's his technical stuff we're relying on. If the brown stuff hits the fan all the illegal technical stuff he's come up with might get him in serious trouble."

Steve sat back. It was true he wanted to protect his friend and Matt was right, Terry was exposed. "Good point, Matt. I'll talk with Terry."

A strained silence descended. "Right. Are we all clear? It's business as usual. This meeting never took place, and we don't tell anyone outside of our group what we are up to. It's my head on the block alone. Clear?"

Si Griffiths stood up. "Well, sir. I've heard some things in my time and worked for a load of senior officers who frankly couldn't tie your shoelaces. You're either very brave or very stupid but either way, I'm hanging around to learn which." Si collected a few papers and nodded to Matt. In his usual insubordinate manner he said, "Come on, sir. We've to plan a telephone campaign. We've got the script, now we need your voice."

In his enthusiasm to brief his team Steve had overlooked the fundamentals. "Matt? What's your thoughts on timings? Telephone companies with account queries won't call at the weekends. Should we wait till Monday morning before we start?"

"Yes. Good point, sir. DS Griffiths and I will finalise the script and have a practice. I've to check up on the watchers anyway and I suppose you should speak with Terry."

"OK. We start the telephone calls on Monday at say nine. We keep the watchers on Ho, and Bob, you'll continue to get the hourly movements updates and the instant voice recordings." Steve once more looked at his team for confirmation. "Right, that's it. Let's all keep in touch over the weekend, and guys." The DCI stood and with a weak smile said, "Thanks."

Steve left to visit Terry Harvey. He didn't want to get the inspector involved but conceded that Matt was probably right. They needed Terry and his technical wizardry. As was usual, Steve saw Terry talking with one of his technicians in the middle of the vast open plan area that was

Technical Support, but seeing Steve enter his domain, Terry signalled they should go to his office.

Steve sat in front of Terry and explained the events of the past few hours. "I'm not happy, Terry. Something's not right and I don't know what but I'm sure we're being used."

With a deep breath the DCI confessed to his friend that he was deliberately disobeying an order and intended to leave everything in place, including the electronic surveillance. He hesitated, waiting to see what reaction he got from the head of Technical Support.

Terry Harvey steepled his fingers in front of his face as he sat back in his chair. "You're taking one hell of a risk, Steve. I don't need to tell you that or that if you're found out, your career is down the river."

"I know. The question is, based on my not having told you anything, can you keep the surveillance going?"

Terry leant forward and with a grin said, "Yes. It's also lucky we got a warrant, and the service providers are on board to allow us access to the data from the masts. That's a bit of luck because if the powers upstairs saw the warrant application now…" Terry looked at Steve. "Chances are they'd not approve it."

Steve laughed. "Well. At least we've got some luck. I've told Matt and Si Griffiths to start making the calls on Monday at nine. How many numbers do you have?"

"There's about fifteen. Shouldn't take too long. The whole exercise should be over by mid-morning."

Steve stood up and once more thanked his friend. "Remember. If things go pear-shaped, I didn't tell you to pull the surveillance, but it might be politic to keep the flow of information to Bob Class under the radar."

With a final goodbye the DCI set off to find Si Griffiths. He remembered Si had something to tell him about the hooded gunman who had killed Poppy's murderer.

***

Dominic Barns parked his Discovery in a public car park in Greenwich and made his way on foot to the address he had for Max Ho. It was approaching three p.m. Dom had opened the envelope and found the different coloured envelopes inside. As usual, each envelope had a purpose which was to prepare Dom for his mission.

The data told him Max Ho was a serving RAF officer and a test pilot. The information pack gave Max's address, photograph and make of car including the registration number.

The envelope that usually suggested the way in which Dom should eliminate his target was unusually slim. It merely said he should use his discretion. There were no limits on how he might carry out his mission.

Dom remembered his conversation with the major who had told him to hold off until he received the envelope authorising the hit. To Dom, it all sounded a bit odd and didn't conform to his earlier jobs, where everything was organised and laid out. Within the executive summary envelope, mention was made of the fact Max Ho was under police surveillance and Dom should proceed with caution. Just as he was parking his car, he'd received a call from Major Havers, telling him the surveillance had been lifted. He now had a clear run.

With this welcome news still uppermost in his mind, Dom approached the high-rise luxury apartment block where Max Ho lived. He walked past a few times looking for CCTV cameras. He spotted four that appeared to cover the area around the building and one that was focused on the main entrance. Dom had taken the precaution of dressing down and was wearing an old overcoat against the harsh February temperature and a cap that was too big but covered his head and most of his face. He was also wearing a pair of cheap and very weak reading glasses that he didn't need but changed the appearance of his face. He walked around for about twenty minutes studying the area and working out a plan. His first problem was knowing if Max Ho was in his flat and if he had the correct address. The briefing notes told Dom that Max was enjoying a week off.

Dom decided on a frontal approach. He walked up to the main entrance to see it was security controlled. He studied the list of names that had been neatly typed against each button that obviously connected visitors to the flats. The system had a camera attached so residents could see who was calling them from the entrance.

Dom found Max Ho's name and pressed the button. He could hear an audible buzz that told him the system was working. After a long ten seconds, the small screen lit up and a slightly distorted voice came through the speaker.

"Yes?"

Dom had prepared himself. "I'm sorry to bother you, sir, but I'm looking for a Thomas Green. I was told he lived here but I can't see his name on the list of residents."

"Sorry, I can't help you."

The connection was broken but Dom now knew Max Ho was in his flat.

***

Unknown to Dom, an unmarked and ancient looking Ford Focus was parked diagonally opposite the entrance to Max Ho's apartment block. Inside were two police officers whose task was to keep Max Ho under surveillance and report his movements on a regular basis. Since their shift had begun at nine a.m. the only excitement they'd had was to follow their target to a local pub and watch him eat. The policemen had also taken the opportunity of eating before following Max back to his apartment.

Neither officer relished this form of duty. It was usually hours of boredom interspersed by panic when the target moved, especially if he were on foot. One of the officers had a powerful pair of binoculars hanging around his neck. The pair were bored and looking forward to being relieved at six p.m. They became more alert when they witnessed a scruffy looking individual walking slowly past the apartment block and spending time examining the front entrance.

"Looks like he's casing the place." the officer sitting in the passenger seat commented as he pointed in the direction of Dom Barns. The pair sat watching as Dom circulated around the building and crossed the street several times, seldom taking his eyes off the building.

The senior officer using the binoculars was a thirty-year veteran. Kenny Johnstone had only ever had one promotion from uniformed constable to detective constable. He'd seen most things in his career and his well-established gut instinct told him this individual was connected to their task at hand. Raising the binoculars, he followed Dom as he wandered apparently aimlessly around. Once Dom walked towards the main entrance of Max Ho's building, both officers were on full alert. Looking through the binoculars Kenny watched Dom press a button that was connected to the fourth floor. He knew this from the position of the button on the panel that contained intercom connection to all the flats. This stranger clearly had a discussion on the intercom system with someone inside the apartment block. The powerful Zeiss lenses gave an excellent view, and the officer knew from the position of the button, that he had just seen the individual speak with their target, Max Ho.

"Who the hell is this guy?" The younger policeman was intrigued as he took several photographs of Dom.

"I don't know but maybe we should find out." The older man handed the binoculars to his colleague. "You stay here and keep your phone handy. I'll just tag along with our mystery man. See where he goes. I'll give it fifteen minutes and if there's no joy, I'll be back. If our boy inside leaves, follow him and call me. Got it?"

"Yes. But don't be too long. If we screw this up, we'll be on point duty for months."

With a grin Kenny left the car and fell in about one hundred yards behind the assassin.

Dom saw no reason to be overly concerned about being seen. He knew Max Ho wasn't under surveillance and that his disguise would stand up to normal scrutiny. He walked straight to his Discovery, and removed his overcoat, spectacles and cap before climbing inside. He sat for several minutes analysing what he'd discovered. He knew it wasn't much, but he now had confirmation Max Ho lived where he'd been told. He knew security on the building was average and was confident he could bypass the intercom system and gain access if he decided he needed to. The CCTV cameras were a worry. He'd prefer to get his target into a situation away from any CCTV, but as of now, Dom didn't have a plan to lure Max away from his flat. He told himself he'd return tomorrow after thinking of a plan overnight. A few beers usually started his brain motoring.

Kenny Johnstone stood at the corner of the car park. He'd followed Dom and stopped at the entrance. He witnessed Dom shed his outer clothing and get into his car. As Dom sat looking straight ahead, Kenny moved between a row of cars in order to view the registration number of his target's car. Standing behind and off to one side he wrote the number in his notebook. Not wishing to be seen, he reversed his route into the car park and set off on the quarter mile walk back to his junior colleague in the old Ford Focus.

Kenny's gut was rumbling. This was a sure sign he was hungry but more importantly it told him he was on to something. His note was timed at 3.12 p.m.

***

Charlie Robb's probation appointment was set for four p.m. After returning to Bushy Park and collecting his Honda he'd driven carefully to his hotel. He remembered he had gunshot residue on his hands and had asked hotel housekeeping for a tub of scouring powder. As suggested by his prison tutors he knew how to cleanse his hands. He'd spent ten minutes scrubbing his hands and then took a long very hot shower.

His mind wasn't settled after the killing, but Charlie was surprised how calm he was. He even felt elated at the thought of revenge. However, he couldn't focus; he put his killing clothes back in the foot of his wardrobe, lay on his bed and once more relived the shootings of Colin Clark and Anthony Maple. He recalled Maple had pleaded with him and even offered him money. Charlie thought about this, and a smile appeared on his face. "Why not?" He shouted into his empty room. "Why shouldn't I take money from them before I kill them? They owe me." Charlie sat up. "Yes. That's it. I'll see how Sebastian De Roy lives. If he's still living high, I'll offer to spare his life if he pays up. Once I've got the money, I'll kill him anyway."

Decked out in his best suit and a new white open neck shirt Charlie set off for the probation office in Hackney. He'd succeeded in putting the murder out of his mind and now thought only about his meeting with Connie O'Sullivan. He'd found himself looking forward to this appointment all week.

Charlie arrived at 3.54 p.m. He'd found a metered parking space and filled the meter. He'd put the maximum two hours on it and hoped that would be enough.

The waiting room was empty. Clearly Friday afternoon appointments were not popular. A different but equally unhelpful and badly dressed middle-aged woman receptionist ordered him to take a seat. "Mrs O'Sullivan will see you when she's ready."

Charlie acknowledged the instruction and took a chair beside the door he knew led to Connie O'Sullivan's office. He sat quietly, visualising what Connie would look like today. His memory of her was a bit hazy but he remembered her smile and her cultured voice.

The receptionist slid the glass pane open and barked out. "You can go through." It was 4.04 p.m. Connie O'Sullivan was standing beside a filing cabinet with an open file in her hand. As Charlie entered, she smiled and invited him to sit. "I won't be a minute. I just need to check something."

As Charlie sat, he admired Connie's poise and grace. She was wearing a pale blue blouse and a tight fairly short skirt that accentuated her shape and persuaded Charlie he really would like to get to know his probation officer better. As she replaced the file and closed the filling cabinet drawer, Connie turned to face her client and Charlie once more noticed her large brown eyes.

Connie opened Charlie's file while she scanned his clothes. "You look a lot better than you did on Monday. How are things with Geoffrey Lockwood Associates?"

"Fine. No problems." Charlie wasn't sure how to play this situation. The old lads in prison had advised that he say as little as possible to his probation officer, but they hadn't met Connie O'Sullivan."

"How are your accommodations?"

Charlie knew he was about to lie. For a few seconds he wasn't sure how to answer. In the end he simply said "Fine."

"No complaints?"

"No."

"I'm not surprised. Since we met on Monday, you haven't been back to your digs. Where have you been staying?"

Again, Charlie was tongue-tied. He rapidly thought of something to say. "I've been staying in a better halfway house."

Connie closed the file and placed her interlinking hands-on top. "Charlie, I need the truth. Not staying at the designated halfway house is a breach of your parole. I learnt about you absconding on Wednesday and I should have reported your absence, so I've done you a favour. Had you not turned up for your appointment today then I would have informed the police." Connie sat back. "So come on, Charlie, you're sitting there dressed in an expensive suit and not staying in your designated accommodation. Tell me!"

Charlie smiled what he hoped Connie would take as a warm, friendly smile. He tried to compose himself and work out exactly how much to confess. He certainly wouldn't mention the killings. He decided to take it slowly.

"OK, I'll tell you, but it has to be in confidence. I'm not living by your rules but I'm no threat to the public and just because I can afford nice clothes and live in a decent hotel doesn't mean I'm about to commit further crimes." Charlie felt himself blush at this last statement. Two murders might count as crimes.

"The system doesn't work like that. Staying in the halfway house is part of your sentence. Remember, you're out on parole. You are not a free man. I really should have you re-arrested." Connie looked angry. Her lovely deep brown eyes were large and staring at Charlie. He felt he could swim inside Connie's eyes.

"Look, it's a long story. Last time I was here you told me all of your clients claimed their innocence at one time or another. Well, I am the exception, I really am innocent." Charlie saw an opportunity. " I'd like to tell you the whole story but not here. How about I take you for a drink and maybe dinner? I'll explain everything then."

Connie put on a theatrical surprised look. Since meeting Charlie Robb, she had thought about him more than she should. His invitation was against all the rules, but she'd already broken the rules by not reporting Charlie's absence from his accommodation. Without knowing why, she agreed. "I want the whole truth, remember. I never see clients outside office hours. This is a first for me."

Charlie smiled. "I've never taken a probation officer for a drink either, so we're both breaking new ground." Charlie hoped a drink would lead to dinner and an invitation to a night cap at Connie's place." His plan was quickly smashed.

"It'll only be one drink. I'll have to catch my train. I live in Bishop's Stortford and the trains are overcrowded and unreliable. If I don't catch the 5.55 pm, I'll have to wait forty-five minutes for the next one."

Charlie quickly recalibrated his options. Without working anything out he said. "I have my car downstairs. Why don't I drive you up to Bishop's Stortford? I'm sure you know a nice pub where we can have a drink and a meal. That'll give me plenty of time to tell you the Charlie Robb story."

Connie was pleased that Charlie had offered and wanted to accept. However, she didn't want to appear too keen.

After a few lame reasons why she couldn't possibly take Charlie so far out of his way, and Charlie countering each objection with a reasonable reply, Connie agreed.

It was 4.57 pm when Charlie's hired Honda CRV left its parking spot in Hackney and headed for the M11 motorway, Bishop Stortford and as yet unknown pleasures.

***

At the very moment Charlie was entering Connie O'Sullivan's office the DCI was entering his. As he passed Si Griffiths sitting at his desk in the outer office, he signalled that Si should join him.

Steve took his seat behind his desk as the still slightly insubordinate detective sergeant walked in and casually pulled up a chair and sat. Steve knew there was no point in taking issue with Si. He was never going to change.

"Right Si. You said earlier you had something for me to do with the mystery hooded gunman?"

"You mean the information that'll see me out of the force with a full pension?"

Steve smiled despite his annoyance with Si. It was almost impossible not to warm to this policeman and his cheeky ways. "Perhaps. What have you got?"

Si had decided not to share his information with Steve. He was trying to see an angle that would be to his benefit. Besides he was having fun working in this unit and wanted to contribute.

"Well. It's not as much as I thought when I spoke to you this morning." Si lied. "I've got a few reliable contacts working on it and one says he knows of a killing that was government sponsored but he doesn't have a name. I've got an appointment tomorrow. Maybe I'll get lucky."

Steve couldn't help himself. "Si? You do know tomorrow is Saturday?"

Si stood indicating to his boss that this meeting was over. "Ha, bloody, ha!" Si left, grinning.

Steve called Matt and Bob in to discuss events.

"There's not much more to do, Steve, if we're not making the calls till Monday morning. I've got the watch teams on station and the weekend roster has been agreed. As a precaution, I've told them not to put in for any overtime, just in case word gets out. I've told them they'll get time off in lieu, but goodness knows how I'll arrange that with their bosses."

"Good thinking, Matt. Bob, anything from you?"

"No, sir. I've arranged to get all the electronic data from Inspector Harvey, and I know to call you if anything looks interesting. The watch teams will also get updates from Ho's phone if we think it'll help them."

Matt Conway spoke. "You're sure about this, Steve? Personally, I don't understand why you just don't stand down. It would be a lot simpler and safer."

Steve looked at Matt seeing the concern on his DI's face. "You're right of course, Matt. That would be the sensible thing to do, but I've got a feeling if we don't follow up whatever is happening, we'll always regret it. Plus, I think we're being used but I don't know how. I suppose it's just my natural copper's curiosity."

Steve gathered up his papers and put them in his briefcase. He knew there was nothing in the papers for him to deal with, it just looked good.

"I'm off. You two get off as well and try and relax over the weekend, but if anything interesting comes in, call me, any time."

Everyone stood, said their collective goodbyes and were gone. Si Griffiths was left behind. He had started plotting his visit to Benny Stockton's car showroom tomorrow and how he would treat the mystery man who arranged murders. He had a wicked grin on his face as he thought about what tomorrow might bring.

***

The drive out of London had been slow. Traffic was heavy and an accident before Redbridge hadn't helped. It took almost two hours to reach the M11 and a further fifty minutes to reach the Bishop's Stortford turn-off.

It was 7.33 p.m. as Charlie drove through the centre of the town. Connie had originally suggested they might go to her place so she could freshen up before they ate but given the length of the journey, she directed Charlie to the Six Bells Bar and Restaurant located just outside the centre.

The place was busy, and they were lucky to find a table. They selected their meal from the extensive menu and ordered a bottle of wine and some water. On the journey from London, Charlie had deliberately kept the conversation light, as had Connie. They discussed their earlier years, football, music and formula one racing. It seemed they both liked the same things. Each time the conversation stalled, and Connie raised Charlie's time in prison, he told her he wasn't comfortable talking about it but promised to tell her more over their dinner.

As they finished their first course Connie decided to take the initiative. "OK, Charlie, you promised me your story." Connie sipped her wine and sat back.

Charlie did likewise and looking around the restaurant, he could see the waiting staff were rushed off their feet. Their main course wasn't arriving any time soon, so he reluctantly started his narrative. He talked in a loud whisper hoping none of the other guests could hear him.

"I was an independent financial advisor. I had a wife and a son. I was doing fine, you know, not making a fortune but making a good enough living. Then a guy called Geoffrey Lockwood appeared one day. He said he had a lot of money to invest and wanted me to invest it for him."

Connie interrupted. "Is this the same Geoffrey Lockwood you're working for now?"

Charlie was embarrassed because he'd lied to Connie. "No, I'll explain later." He still wasn't sure how much to tell this beautiful woman, but he continued.

"As an IFA it wasn't my job to invest clients' funds directly, but Geoffrey insisted this was a condition of him placing his money with me. He said he'd pay me my usual fees and commissions plus a bonus on profits his money made. He told me he'd pick the investments. All I had to do was take his money and buy the shares." Charlie looked down at his empty soup bowl. "I knew it was against the rules but the prospect of a load of money for only bending the rules slightly seemed too much like a good thing, so I agreed."

Connie was looking thoughtful. Her large brown eyes looked sympathetically at Charlie.

"So, you took his money and invested it. What happened next?"

"Nothing. He'd call me, tell me to invest an amount in a company and send a cheque for my fee based on the amount. Once every two months or so, I'd get a separate cheque for what Lockwood called his profits."

"Did you ever sell any shares for him?"

Charlie blushed with embarrassment. "Well, that's the thing. The way Lockwood set the thing up everything was in my name. His money was in my client account, I bought the shares on his behalf and the sale of shares went through my trading account that Lockwood set up."

"Didn't you find that strange?"

"With hindsight, yes, but at the time I didn't think about it. I was greedy and from what I could see I wasn't acting illegally."

Connie took another sip of her wine. "So, what happened next?"

"I was making a load of money, so we moved into a bigger house and Lockwood introduced me to a supposed friend of his, a man called Sebastian De Roy. De Roy said he'd been recommended by Lockwood, and he had a shedload of money to invest but it had to be under the same terms as Geoffrey Lockwood. In fact, he said I should use Lockwood's existing accounts for buying and selling. He told me Lockwood would select the shares to be bought for both of them. The cash I was to handle almost doubled and so did my fees."

"So, life was good. What happened?"

Before Charlie could answer a waiter appeared with their main courses. They smiled warmly at each other as they started to eat in silence. Apart from the odd enquiry as to how was the food, neither of them said very much. Both finished their wine, and a waiter refilled their glasses.

Charlie, not being used to drinking alcohol after his time in prison, felt relaxed and happy. The plates were cleared, and they asked the waiter to give them some time before they ordered their coffee.

Connie was also relaxed and happy. She didn't eat out much, so this was a rare treat and despite the circumstances she found she was enjoying Charlie's company. She was interested in Charlie's story and asked him to continue.

"Right. Well, there I was, handling millions and getting well paid. Then another two people appeared also on the recommendation of Lockwood. They were lower rent than Lockwood and De Roy, but they had a couple of million between them. I set them up in line with Lockwood's instructions and life carried on."

"Until it didn't. Something happened?" Connie was engrossed.

"I got a knock on the door from the city watchdog, the Financial Authority. They asked to see my accounts and told me they suspected me of money laundering and running a Ponzi scheme. I'd no idea what a Ponzi scheme was, never mind run one. They put a freeze on all my accounts and contacted my clients telling them I was under investigation. What I didn't know was that the money I had invested looked like my money but of course it wasn't, so when they closed my accounts there was only my own private money in the account. The four investors had already told me to invest everything and unknown to me had transferred the shares from my name to some mysterious offshore company."

Connie leant forward trying to understand. "So, it looked as though you had bought and sold shares with money you didn't have?"

"No. The money was in my client account but when they investigated the money just seemed to appear. There wasn't a normal paper trail that's supposed to prevent fraud and money laundering. You see, I should have carried out checks, but I didn't."

"So, the only money that was found was your own fees and commissions?"

"Yes, and my personal account was frozen."

Connie puffed out her cheeks. "So, what did you do?"

"I explained everything. Admitted I'd been duped and that I'd been stupid. The police got involved and I was arrested and bailed. I went to see the four investors at Lockwood's offices. They denied they were crooks, claimed it was a misunderstanding and they'd sort it out. A few weeks later I was charged and remanded."

"Did these people help you?"

"No. Lockwood came to see me. He said it was all a big mistake but that the police would not accept his explanation of what I had done. He said if I kept my mouth shut, I'd be looked after together with my family. He let slip that he had been running a Ponzi scheme, but he had a load of money stashed away that no one knew about. He pleaded with me not to say anything and if I did my time, I'd come out a rich man."

Connie couldn't resist a light joke. "By the look of you, you have come out a rich man."

"No, Connie, after the first visit from the authorities I took out an insurance. I gathered a hundred grand in cash and hid it. Those four investors didn't come near me after I'd been convicted. They promised to give evidence at my trial, but they didn't." Charlie suddenly had a tear in his eyes. "While I was on remand, Lockwood sent a heavy to scare my family. But instead of scaring them he went too far and killed them. It was supposed to be a warning to me to keep my mouth shut. I was allowed out for their funeral and that's all."

Connie reached over and took Charlie's hand. "I'm sorry, Charlie. I suppose innocent men do go to prison."

They sat holding hands for several long seconds, and then Charlie ordered the coffee.

Connie was suspicious and thought there was more to come. She gently probed. "So, what now Charlie? I don't believe you are working for Geoffrey Lockwood, so you've no job. You're not living in secure accommodation, and you've admitted to me that you defrauded the authorities out of one hundred thousand pounds. I'm an officer of the court. I should report all three offences, or I could help you get justice."

Charlie was sceptical. Knowing what he had already done he knew he didn't want traditional justice. He wanted revenge but he couldn't admit it to Connie.

"What do you mean?"

"I could report this conversation but leave out the incriminating bits and ask for a judicial review. I know a few lawyers who'd be happy to help. Do you still have the names of the four men?"

Without thinking and forgetting the first thing he was told in prison, he gave Connie the names including his first two victims. "The names are Geoffrey Lockwood, Sebastian De Roy, Anthony Maple and Colin Clark, but I wouldn't bother. I'll sort myself out."

Their coffee arrived with the bill, and before Connie could object, Charlie had put money in the small wooden box.

Charlie drove Connie home to her terraced house on the Stansted Airport side of Bishop's Stortford. Charlie awkwardly escorted Connie to her front door.

They stood looking at each other in silence until Connie said, "It's been a wonderful evening, Charlie. I'm sorry you had to relive your experiences but thank you for sharing. I'll see you next Friday at four and I won't report your bending of the rules nor the money, but please, be careful."

Charlie could hear a quiver in Connie's voice. He leant forward and kissed her lightly on the lips. "Maybe I could take you to lunch on Sunday?"

Connie was pleased. "Yes. That would be good. Pick me up at one. I'll book a nice country inn."

Charlie leant forward again but this time Connie turned her cheek to be kissed. A reluctant Charlie walked back to his car, turned and waved as Connie disappeared inside her house. The drive back to the Mayflower Hotel took no time at all. Charlie felt as though he was flying. His head was in a happy place. All guilt about killing two people had vanished.

Chapter Seventeen

Steve was planning a relaxed weekend, starting this morning, Saturday, February 12. The weather as he looked out of his lounge window looked dry and there were a few signs the day might even be sunny. It was 7.36 a.m. Steve had woken early and showered without disturbing Alison. He'd looked in on Rosie, their daughter who, now aged six, seemed to be able to sleep for Britain in the mornings. As it wasn't a school day, she was allowed to lie in. He could hear Alison in the shower as he poured the boiling water into the teapot and put another two slices of bread into the toaster. He smiled to himself as he remembered Alison telling him that tea, toast and marmalade, didn't constitute a full breakfast but this was as far as his culinary skills went.

He was just setting the breakfast bar when his mobile vibrated on the countertop. He lifted it and saw it was Matt Conway.

"Morning, Matt. You're around early."

"Tell me about it. This surveillance job isn't easy. Anyway, it seems we may have a problem. That's an unofficial problem, as we don't have a surveillance job at the moment."

The DCI could tell by Matt's tone of voice and his choice of language, that something was up.

"Go on."

"One of the teams spotted a character apparently casing Max Ho's apartment block. They saw this figure press the intercom button to Ho's flat and speak with someone they assumed to be Ho. The conversation only lasted less than a minute and the guy walked away."

Steve was interested but knew there was more, otherwise Matt wouldn't have called. "Go on."

"The lads took pictures. We've spent most of the night running facial recognition software but so far, we've no match. I don't suppose that's unusual unless the guy had a record. We're running all the other databases in the hope we get lucky. Terry Harvey's been in all night. I've had his wife on, and I have a message for you."

Steve knew Terry's wife well and had worked with her from the instigation of the Special Resources Unit. He smiled imagining what Mrs Harvey, known to him as Twiggy, had to say.

"What's the message."

"She says to tell you 'Twiggy isn't happy'."

"OK. I'm surprised that's all she said if Terry's been out all night." As he grinned thinking of Twiggy and what else she probably said, Steve instinctively knew there was something else Matt had to tell him. He waited.

Matt continued. "One of the watchers was an old-time cop and had a well-developed sixth sense. He followed the guy to his car and got the registration number."

Steve knew a bombshell was about to drop. "Yes."

"I only got the report this morning and the PNC check came back a few minutes ago. DVLA have the car registered to the government. It's sub-registered to national security, Steve. The prowler at Ho's block of flats works for the government. We've run all Whitehall staff facial recognition and he's not there. Terry ran the security services database but unofficially and the guy isn't there either, but he's driving a security car."

Steve sat looking at the toast that had most recently popped up. "And we've nothing on facial, you're sure?"

"Positive. One of Terry's lads is running all facial databases but like I said, we've nothing so far. What's going on, Steve?"

"I don't know, Matt. Whoever this mystery man is, he is connected. We've been warned off and the powers that be think the surveillance of Ho has been lifted. The kill order was lifted earlier but who knows what that old fox Sir Patrick is cooking up."

"What do you want us to do, Steve?"

"Tell Terry to go home. Mrs Harvey would give me hell if she thought I was abusing our friendship. Make sure he keeps one of his lads on the facial recognition though." With a sigh, Steve continued. "I'll come in. I'll be about an hour. In the meantime, just sit tight. We need to work out what's going on." As he ended the call, he knew his plans for a quiet weekend with his family were in jeopardy. He didn't realise just how disruptive his plans would be.

***

Steve arrived at New Scotland Yard at nine. After visiting the canteen and buying three coffees he headed first to his office where Matt Conway and Bob Class were seated behind their desks in the outer office. Steve handed the coffee out and sat on the edge of the empty desk allocated to Si Griffiths.

"Bob, anything on the electronic surveillance from Ho?"

"Not much, sir. Seems he had a quiet day yesterday although we did pick up his end of that intercom call he got from the bloke the watchers reported. It's faint but you can make it out. The internal intercom phone must be in his lounge."

"You mean otherwise the phone wouldn't have picked up the conversation?"

"Exactly. Unfortunately, it doesn't tell us anything. The guy says he's looking for someone called Thomas Green. Ho says he doesn't know anybody of that name and hangs up."

The DCI had a thought. "I don't suppose the recording's good enough for a voice match?"

"Sorry, sir. Inspector Harvey says it's too weak."

"Mm. Any thoughts on this prowler who drives a government registered car?"

Matt pulled a slim file from the top drawer of his desk. It contained blown-up pictures of the prowler taken by the watchers. It showed a man, with his cap pulled low on his forehead wearing an overcoat. It was impossible to see his face other than to establish he was Caucasian. They could estimate his height but that was all. The photographs were of little use.

"Why would a guy from the government be casing Ho's place if we've been told to step down and had everything in place?" Matt Conway had a habit of asking good questions.

Steve was thinking and as usual, he didn't realise he was talking out loud. "At the meeting in Whitehall with the minister he told Lord

Scotland that his committee was disbanded, so this guy casing Ho's place can't be from the official assassination team. The other bloke, that Major Havers was told by Sir Patrick not to proceed with the kill order but the reason for the meeting in the first place was that the left hand didn't know what the right was doing. They were getting ready to kill Ho when they thought he was acting for the government."

Steve stopped talking and as though he hadn't realised, he'd been talking he suddenly announced, "Suppose this guy's an assassin and someone in the government has gone freelance. Suppose Ho is still on a kill list?"

Bob Class looked up from his laptop. "You mean, we've been stood down and so has everyone else but this guy driving a government car hasn't?"

"It's a possibility." Steve stood away from Si's desk. "Bob, what make of car is this guy driving?"

Bob's fingers flew over his keyboard. "It's an older Land Rover Discovery. Why do you ask?"

"When we're allocating cars for surveillance jobs, we often use unmarked cars or cars we've found in the pounds that are old but serviceable. Cars that don't stand out. I wonder if that's why this bloke is driving the Discovery. Older ones are ten a penny."

Matt looked at his boss. "So, you think Ho's still on the kill list?"

"I wouldn't bet against it." Steve paced the office for a few seconds. "Matt, get word to all the watchers. Tell them to be on the lookout for this bloke but not to approach him. If he is an assassin, he'll be armed. They should call in all sightings and await armed response back up."

"Bloody hell, Steve. For a non-operation, this is getting serious."

"Yes, it is, so keep your heads down." Steve looked down at his seated companions. "I mean it. Remember our briefing yesterday. You two know nothing. You're not aware the operation has been called off."

Both Mat and Bob smiled at each other and in unison said, "Yes, boss."

Steve looked at his watch. It was 9.57 am. "Has Terry Harvey gone home?"

"Yes. About ten minutes before you got here. Andrew is working on the facial recognition job. He'll call Bob if he gets anything."

"Right. I'm off. Don't you two stay too long. Remember, we do have things called phones to keep in touch. You don't have to be chained to your desks. Call me if anything breaks."

With a wave Steve left to continue what he hoped would be a quiet family weekend. How wrong could he have been.

***

Si Griffiths woke early and set about reviewing the plan that he hoped would see him achieve his goal of retirement on full pension. His current girlfriend and probable Mrs Simon Griffiths number five was still asleep. Si had moved out of the section house and into his girlfriend's house after Steve had arranged the five hundred pounds emergency grant and put him on the case of finding the masked gunman who was present when Poppy had been shot. The promise that, if he found the gunman, he could have his early retirement had cheered the future Mrs Griffiths up to the point where she believed he would soon be a civilian. This thought had persuaded her to invite Si back to her house and her bed.

Si had been the last to leave the office last night. He'd called in a few favours from old mates and had his plan ready. All being well, he'd be handing over the masked man by midday. He was happy and smiling as he shaved and dressed.

It was 8.46 a.m. when he left his girlfriend's house and headed for Benny Stockton's car dealership in New Cross.

Traffic was lighter than he had thought, and he arrived just as Steve was heading home, and Benny and his overweight bodyguard were opening up the showroom. They officially opened at ten on a Saturday. The bodyguard on seeing Si approach, started to walk in his direction. His face was angry and full of aggression. Si recalled how easily this brute had gone down when he had had had to use force to get to Benny.

Si held up his right hand and stretched out his arm. "Now don't be silly. You don't want any more." As the big man got closer Si noticed a large bruise on the side of his face, obviously from when Si accidentally kicked him.

The big man kept coming obviously intent on ripping Si's head off. He stopped when Benny Stockton shouted to him. "Don't be daft, Keith.

Leave the copper alone. He'll only give you more and probably arrest you."

"You'd better listen to your boss. Your next move could be your last for some time." Si breathed a sigh of relief when he saw the facial expression on Keith soften as he shrugged his shoulders and turned back towards Benny.

Once the showroom was open Si cornered Benny in his office. "Now here's what we're going to do. I've got a van load of bobbies sitting round the corner. I'll be in my car outside and you'll do whatever it is you do here on a Saturday morning. Once you see your man arrive you call this number." Si handed Benny his private mobile number. "I won't answer. Let it ring twice. Once I get the call I'll be here. Is that clear?"

"I suppose so but what happens after I ring you?"

Si smiled and tapped Benny's check. "Don't you worry about that Benny; you can leave everything to me." Si paused and with as much menace in his voice as he could muster, he continued. "Don't even think of not doing as I say. Remember, I'm your worst enemy, so be good and do as you're told."

Si turned and left. He called the uniformed sergeant in charge of the squad officers he'd arranged the night before and confirmed they were on standby. He reached his car parked in a street opposite the car showroom but giving him a view of Benny Stockton's site.

Now all Si had to do was wait. His days as a police officer were almost over.

***

Dom had had a quiet night. Carole had said she was meeting friends after her shift on Friday night, and they were going for a meal. As her flat was nearer the hospital, she told Dom she'd stay there and see him Saturday late afternoon.

This suited Dom, as following his survey of where Max Ho lived and his instruction that the killing didn't have to be subtle, he'd decided to eliminate Max Ho in his apartment.

As Si Griffiths was parking his car beside Benny Stockton's car emporium, Dom was ringing the bell of the upholstery repair shop in

Brompton Road. This was the headquarters of the firm Dom worked for and was controlled by Major Havers.

The usual lady who fronted the business known as Mother, wasn't on duty. Instead, a pimply youth was sitting on a stool behind the counter as the door was opened and Dom entered.

"I'm here to see the armourer."

The youth shrugged, hit a few keys on a laptop computer in order to confirm Dom's picture and buzzed him through to the back room. The youth was either dumb or just uninterested in his job. He didn't say a word.

Thirty minutes later Dominic Barns exited the upholstery repair shop with a Glock .45 in a shoulder holster tucked under his left shoulder. The magazine was full. The Glock held fifteen rounds.

Dom had devised a simple plan. Because there was no need for subtlety Dom had decided to simply gain entry into Ho's apartment building. He'd either wait for a resident to leave or arrive and enter with them. If no one was around, he'd press a few buttons on the intercom and say he had a parcel for one of the residents. Once inside he'd knock on the door of Max Ho's apartment, number 403 and simply shoot him. He suspected there would not be any CCTV cameras on each individual floor. With the Glock came a silencer that Dom knew he would have to use. However, it was a large cumbersome thing that could only be screwed into the end of the weapon with the weapon out of its holster. This meant he would have to usher Ho into his apartment by threatening him with the unsilenced gun and quickly screw the silencer into place while Ho was in a state of shock. He knew this would work.

It was just before eleven. Dom decided his plan was the best he could come up with, simple and direct. His concern was the CCTV cameras by the front door, but he felt he could largely avoid them by keeping his cap low over his head. The countdown to an assassination had begun. But first, Dom decided to treat himself to lunch. He drove back to his Chelsea apartment, parked and walked to his favourite Italian restaurant. He told himself shooting someone was easier on a full stomach. Unknown to both Dom and Charlie, both killers sat down to eat their lunch at exactly the same time. It was 12.24 p.m.

***

Detective Constable Kenny Johnstone and his associate were back in their preferred parking spot opposite Max Ho's apartment building in Greenwich, still in the old Ford Focus. Their shift had started at ten. It was now 11.15 a.m. and so far, they had nothing to report. Detective Inspector Matt Conway had told them they wouldn't be getting paid overtime for their weekend shift, but he'd arrange time off in lieu. This suited Kenny as he had to pay tax on his overtime payments, and he preferred extra time to spend with his grandchildren. His younger colleague didn't care. He was single and preferred to work even if it was this boring surveillance job.

Kenny Johnstone reminded his partner that they had received the instruction to call in back up if they saw the character from yesterday who was casing Max Ho's building. "He must be important. They don't tell us to call something like this in and then just wait unless there's something serious going on."

"Yeah, I suppose. I hope he doesn't appear during our shift. Think of all the paperwork!"

Kenny laughed. "You're in the wrong job if you think being a copper today isn't all about paperwork."

The two bored officers sat back and took it in turns to watch whilst the other either dozed or read a book. They had each brought a flask of coffee and some sandwiches to keep them going until the end of their shift.

***

Si saw a Jaguar saloon pull up outside Benny's car dealership at exactly 11.15 a.m. Within thirty seconds his personal mobile rang twice. Si knew the operation was on. He called the unmarked police van sitting round the corner. The van held four uniformed constables and the sergeant Si had persuaded to help him this Saturday morning. He put them on standby and exited his car. He was in no hurry to cross the road. He wanted to catch the Jaguar driver with the money he was extorting from Benny.

Si casually entered the car showroom and saw Benny sitting at his desk. A well-dressed large man was standing casually in front of Benny. The pair appeared to be chatting and Si spotted a briefcase sitting open on the desk facing the stranger. Although the stranger had his back to Si, it looked to Si as though the stranger was doing something with his hands. To Si's mind, he was counting money.

Si entered Benny's office through the open door. "Well, well, a bit careless to leave the door open, Benny, anyone could walk in on this illegal transaction. Who's your friend?" Si looked at the briefcase and saw the newcomer had been counting the pile of notes that now sat in the briefcase. There was another stack of notes on the desk, clearly waiting to be counted.

The large man turned to examine Si. He had a sneer on his face that told Si he was being held in contempt by this individual.

"And who might you be?" The voice was cultured and sounded calm.

"Oh! I'm only the guy who's going to burst your little scam wide open. What's your name?"

"Don't threaten me, I presume you're the police. One word from me and you'll be out on your ear. Whatever business we are transacting here is none of your concern. Now kindly leave before I call the commissioner."

Si smiled and leant against the door frame with his arms crossed. "I'm sure you don't want me to add threatening a police officer to the list of charges I intend to bring against you." Si left his statement hanging in the air before adding. "Of course, if you help me, I might be able to help you."

The stranger laughed. Si noted he'd stopped counting the money and had glanced at Benny Stockton more than a few times.

"I doubt you could do me any favours, now please leave. Mr Stockton and I have business to attend to."

The man turned his back on Si and continued to count the money.

"Oh dear, that's a pity. All I want is the name of your hitman. The one who pulled the trigger for Benny here when you arranged to get rid of the leader of the Romanian gang. You see, that makes you an accessory to murder, Mr Smith. Add the fact you're up to your elbows right now in extorted money that I bet HMRC knows nothing about, and you could be going down for a very long time."

Mr Smith stopped counting and turned once more to face Si.

"Look, you little weed, there's nothing you can do to me. I have government protection. Anything you do to me will bounce straight back on you. You have no evidence and if you did, I'd still not 'go down' as you put it. My lawyers would chew your balls off. Now, for the last time, please leave or I will call the commissioner."

Si unfolded his arms. Although this Mr Smith was bulky, he was also flabby. Si knew he would have no problem arresting him if he had to. Both men stood looking at each other. Si decided to make things happen. He called the sergeant in the van.

"It's on, Colin, bring your lads."

The well dressed and arrogant Mr Smith's jaw fell slightly. It was clear he hadn't expected Si to take any action.

"For the record, my name is Detective Sergeant Simon Griffiths. I am arresting you on conspiracy to commit murder, conspiracy to extort money and just for good measure, threatening a police officer in the execution of his duties. I now require you to accompany me to Scotland Yard where you will be informed of your rights and interviewed under caution. You will also be given access to legal representation. It would be better if you gave me your real name at this point."

"You cannot be serious, I'm a member of the government for Christ's sake. I cannot be arrested and certainly not on these trumped-up charges." For the first time the man known as Mr Smith turned to look at Benny. "Have you been telling tales, Benny? If this is your doing you know it won't end well. Whatever you've told this jumped-up policeman you'd better withdraw it, and now, before this goes any further."

As Mr Smith was raging at Benny, Si slipped a pair of handcuffs over his wrists.

"What the hell! Take these things off. This is ridiculous. I am a member of the government. I have immunity." The well-dressed Jaguar driver was now panicking. Saliva was visible at the corners of his mouth, and he had turned a bright shade of red.

Si enjoyed the moment. He let Mr Smith have his say. Colin, the uniformed sergeant, arrived with his four colleagues. Si signalled for them to remain outside the small office. He tried once more to get the name he needed from this pompous overweight so-called government official.

"Mr Smith, all this can end now if you give me the name of the person who killed the Romanian gangmaster. A simple name and a few details and all this will be over. You can even keep the money."

The stranger stood; head bowed. The earlier arrogance was gone although he remained defiant. "I can't tell you what I don't know. You haven't read me my rights so I'm not under arrest and I'm not about to incriminate myself. If by any chance I knew a name I'd tell you off the record, but I don't. I have no idea what you're talking about."

Si let out a high sigh. "OK. Have it your way. I haven't formally arrested you. I'd hoped you'd cooperate and save everyone a lot of trouble. You'll go with these officers and help us with our enquiries. If you change your mind and decide you have a name for me, we won't proceed against you. You have the time it takes from now to arriving at Scotland Yard. I hope you come to your senses."

Si turned to his uniformed colleagues. "Colin, take him away."

The sergeant indicated to two officers to step forward. One of them took Mr Smith's elbow and began to walk him out of the office while the other walked behind.

Mr Smith wriggled as he was escorted out. He turned and shouted, "You can't do this. I'll make sure you'll pay for this. I'll be calling the commissioner."

Colin, the sergeant who had as much service as Si, smiled. "We've heard it all before."

Si nodded and turned towards Benny who had started taking the money from the briefcase.

"Hold on, Benny! We're not finished. That money is evidence. I'll be taking it, but I'll give you a receipt once it's been counted and logged." Benny looked sad as he sat back and allowed Si to place all the money in the briefcase. Si took a roll of blue and white sticky police tape and asking Colin to witness it. He closed the case, wrapped a piece of the tape around the lid and using a pen, signed the tape where the lid met the body of the case.

"There you are, Benny. When we get to the yard no one can say the money isn't all there."

Benny's expression was one of bewilderment. He wasn't sure what part he had played in the events of the past thirty minutes but felt he wasn't out of the woods.

"Right, Benny. I need you to come with me and these officers. We're all going to the Yard."

"Oh! No. I'm not going anywhere Mr Griffiths."

"Yes, you are Benny." Si adopted the voice he might use when talking to a child. "I just need you to tell me on the record what you told me on Thursday, that's all. We'll arrange for you to be back here by early afternoon. Come on, you're wasting time.

A reluctant Benny Stockton knew he had no choice. His only hope was that he really would be back in his car showroom by early afternoon, although from experience, he doubted it.

Chapter Eighteen

Alison was pleased to see her husband back so soon. It was 11.07 a.m.

"Good. You're back early." Looking at their daughter Rosie, Alison continued. "We thought Daddy was to be in his office all day, didn't we, Rosie?"

Rosie was sitting on the sofa playing with her favourite doll. She looked at her mother and then at Steve. "Can we go to the park now and can I see Sophia today?" Sophia was Rosie's new best friend from school. She lived a few streets away in a larger property than Steve and Alison and it had a back garden.

"We'll see, darling, I'll phone Sophia's mother later and ask."

"Can't we go now?"

"Daddy's only just got back. It's almost lunchtime. We'll have our lunch and then go to the park. If you're good and if Sophia's mummy says it's OK, you can go round after we've been to the park."

Alison glanced at Steve who smiled and nodded. He loved these domestic moments and wished he didn't have to go to work. He sat on the sofa beside his daughter and tickled and teased her. Rosie's laugh was infectious and soon all three were laughing.

The meal was as usual a happy affair and Rosie insisted on helping load the dishwasher but on condition her help was rewarded by extra pocket money.

As Steve picked up his coffee, his phone rang. He looked at Alison and saw she wasn't happy. His ringing phone could mean only one thing. Work!

"Yes."

It was Commander Perry Hargreaves. "Steve, you'd better get in here. The brown stuff has hit the fan."

"What! What do you mean?"

"Just get here as quickly as you can. There's one God almighty mess to clean up."

The line went dead. Steve felt a lump gather in his stomach. He had no idea what was wrong but told himself it must have something to do with the Max Ho surveillance job. Feeling nervous, he told Alison he had to go, she should still go to the park with Rosie, but he said he might be late back. Reluctantly, he dressed for outside, kissed Alison lightly on the lips and hugged his daughter who had reappeared dressed in her heavy outdoor coat.

It was 1.33 p.m. For the second time on this Saturday, his planned family weekend had been interrupted. He knew his daughter was disappointed and promised himself to make it up to her. As he drove to the office, he played various scenarios in his head but none of them prepared him for what he'd find awaiting him at New Scotland Yard.

***

Charlie Robb slept late on Saturday morning. He had dreamt of Connie O'Sullivan and how their relationship might develop. While he was happy, he somehow felt a sadness and a guilt. His wife and son had been killed by someone hired by Geoffrey Lockwood. After his time in prison, he could no longer recall his wife's features nor the sound of her voice. The guilt he felt at not avenging her death nor that of his son had started to prey heavily on his mind.

He knew Connie would be a new beginning but wondered if it would be possible to develop a long-term relationship with her now he had become a killer. His plan was to kill the four people responsible for his time in prison and for murdering his wife and son, then to disappear abroad to a far-flung remote location. But he felt his plans were beginning to change. Something his second victim Anthony Maple had said about paying him money had resonated with Charlie. This, plus how to plan for his potential new life with Connie O'Sullivan, was giving Charlie second thoughts.

He lay on his bed looking at the ceiling running various ideas through his head. He knew he had to kill the remaining two investors. He told himself these last two were the main players and more responsible than Clark or Maple. Maple had offered money and Charlie smiled as he consciously adjusted his plan to include receiving a large sum of money from his next victim Sebastian De Roy, and an even larger sum from his main target Geoffrey Lockwood. Something else was sticking in his mind. It was guilt at having feelings for Connie.

Charlie raised himself from his bed and took a bottle of water from his hotel mini-bar. He sat in a large comfortable chair positioned by the tall thin window and once more considered his plan. It now seemed weak and unfinished, then without warning a thought flashed into his mind, and immediately energized him. Suddenly it was simple. Before killing Lockwood, he'd make Lockwood tell him who he had hired to scare his family. Lockwood was to be his last victim and the one Charlie wanted to suffer most.

A grin appeared on Charlie Robb's features. He was satisfied by his change of plan. He'd have more money to keep Connie in luxury and hopefully find closure by not only killing the four people responsible for his change of circumstances, but he'd also get his revenge on the thug who killed his family.

A happier and more contented Charlie rose from his chair and set about preparing himself for the day ahead. By noon he was refreshed and ready to face the world. He'd decided to use this Saturday to start his pursuit of Sebastian De Roy. He had an address and knew from his previous dealings with De Roy that he liked to play golf on a Saturday morning. Charlie recalled De Roy boasting that he had spent a fortune joining Wentworth Golf Club and that he intended one day to purchase a property on the course.

Charlie visited the hotel's dining room and ordered lunch. It was 12.24 p.m. He'd have a leisurely drive to the address in Knightsbridge he had for his next victim and take things from there. As he sat waiting for his meal, he remembered the advice he had been given in prison. One long time inmate called Potter had explained the need for flexible planning. Charlie smiled as he heard old Potter's squeaky voice telling him 'Coppers can't solve nothing if you have a plan, but you need a plan you can change if they gets close to you.'

Charlie's meal arrived and he tucked in realising he was hungry. The search for his third victim would begin on a full stomach.

***

Steve walked into his office not knowing what to expect. Commander Perry Hargreaves had taken up residence in Steve's office. Matt Conway and Bob Class were at their desks in the outer office, both looked sheepish. Si Griffiths, to Steve's surprise, was also sitting at his desk. Unlike the other two detectives Si looked relaxed and was playing with an elastic band. As Steve passed Matt's desk, the DI raised his eyebrows and shrugged.

Sensing the seriousness of whatever had occurred, Steve closed his office door and sat at his conference table. Perry remained in Steve's chair behind his desk.

"What assignment did you give that old fool Griffiths?" Perry was clearly annoyed and in no mood for introductions.

"I'm sorry, sir, I don't follow."

"It's a simple question. What assignment did you give him? What was he working on?"

Steve decided to play for time until it became clear what had brought the commander in on a Saturday afternoon. "Well, sir, I presume you've already asked him."

Perry stood up and surprised the DCI by casually walking to the conference table with a smile on his face. He sat. "Of course, I've asked him, but all the cheeky little man told me was he was working on something for you. He's the most insubordinate copper I think I've ever come across."

Steve saw his opening. "Look, Perry, I don't know what's going on and maybe you'll tell me but as far as Si Griffiths is concerned, you're right. He's a cheeky sod, but underneath all that insubordination, is a good copper who just wants out with his pension."

Steve proceeded to bring the commander up to speed by referring back to the murder of WDC Amelia Copper, known as Poppy, some six months earlier. He reminded Perry that Poppy was Terry Harvey's niece and that a hooded gunman had shot and killed the man who had killed Poppy.

"It's a bit of unfinished business and when Si Griffiths was landed on me, and made it clear he had no intention of fitting in, I gave him the job of finding this gunman on the promise that if he succeeded, I'd sign his early retirement forms."

Perry Hargreaves looked sceptical. "And that's all? Nothing more sinister?"

"No. Now what's going on?"

Perry ignored Steve's question. He stood. "You'd better come with me down to the custody suite and bring Griffiths with you." Perry left and Steve and Si followed. As they walked down the stairs, Steve asked Si what was going on. Before Si could answer Perry called over his shoulder. "Not yet, sergeant."

On arrival in the underground interview suite, Perry opened the door to interview room two. The door he opened allowed entry into the viewing room from which interested parties could watch interviews as they took place through one way glass without being seen.

Steve saw a lone figure sitting behind the table that was screwed to the floor. The figure had no tie and was wearing a casual but expensive suit. Having seen many such figures Steve instinctively knew this man had been processed and was probably awaiting interview. Seated next to him was a dapper grey-haired well-turned-out man dressed in a casual sports jacket who again Steve instinctively knew must be a solicitor.

No one spoke as Steve examined the figure. Slowly the penny dropped as did Steve's jaw. "Bloody hell, Si. Did you bring him in?"

"Yes, sir. He's the link to your hooded shooter."

"Not now, sergeant." Perry spoke with authority in his voice. "Let's go to the conference room. The custody sergeant has laid on tea."

Once all three officers were seated and drinking strong tea, Steve tried again. "Will someone tell me what's going on? Why is Lord Patrick Scotland banged up in interview room two?"

"I had a call from the commissioner, she's livid. It seems your sergeant here has brought his Lordship in on suspicion of conspiracy to murder and conspiracy to extort monies."

Si put his hand up. "Don't forget threatening a police officer."

Perry was not amused. "Enough, sergeant, you're in enough trouble."

Steve didn't understand any of this so in a calm voice he asked Si to explain what had happened. Over the next hour Si told his story starting with Steve's promise to sign his early retirement application if he could find the hooded gunman. He told of how Tom Thumb had put him onto Benny Stockton and why. Then he explained how Benny had implicated someone he knew as Smith who had arranged to have the Romanian gang leader killed and how he claimed it was all government-controlled.

"I knew there was a good chance this guy who was getting kickbacks from Benny was either the killer or he knew who he was. All I intended when I saw him was to put the frighteners on him for a name. The name you want, boss." Si looked cunningly at Steve. "Instead, when I saw him counting all that cash and denying he knew anything, I just thought right pal, you're mine. So, I lifted him and Benny. I didn't know who he was, and I still don't know who Lord Scotland is except he's an overbearing twit."

Both Perry and Steve laughed at Si's description.

"Si, be sure now." Steve was talking softly and slowly. "Are you saying this Benny Stockton told you he spoke to Lord Scotland who arranged to have some Romanian gang boss killed?"

Si explained how Benny had told him Mr Smith had introduced the Romanian gang and demanded a cut of the gains from drugs and prostitution. He told his senior officers how Benny told him about the need to remove the Romanian became critical and how Mr Smith had obliged.

"Have we interviewed Benny yet? Is his statement on the record?"

Perry spoke up. "No. The duty inspector called his boss as soon as Lord Scotland arrived for processing." Looking at Si in a kindly way Perry continued. "It seems your sergeant here arranged for back up off the books, and both Lord Scotland and this Benny Stockton were brought here for processing. The duty inspector's boss pushed it all the way up to the commissioner who phoned me with the good news that we'd lifted a very senior public figure and the officer concerned was a detective sergeant who had obviously overstepped the mark. As soon as I realised this involved your Special Resolutions Unit, I froze everything."

Si held up his hand and in a cheeky low voice said, "Excuse me, sir. His Lordship refused to identify himself and I had Benny's statement about the murder and the extortion. I witnessed the extortion with my own eyes. As a copper what was I supposed to do, turn a blind eye?"

"No, of course not, sergeant, in the circumstances you've done well. I just hope the people in their ivory towers see it the same way," said Perry as he sat back and finished his now cold tea.

Steve sat forward. "To be clear, sir, will we be pursuing Lord Scotland on the charges proposed by DS Griffiths?"

"Let's not run until we can walk." Perry was obviously nervous. Careers had been broken on lesser events than he was about to authorise. "Get Benny Stockton's statement on the record. You and Matt do that, Steve. Once we've got that solidly in the bank we'll interview Lord Scotland under caution, but in the meantime, release him on police bail. He's not going anywhere but seize his passport. We need time to build a case against him before we move forward. Sergeant, you and DC Glass start looking for a body that could be this Romanian. If he had been killed locally within the past six months, a body must have turned up. It's probably filed under unsolved. Look at all unclaimed bodies with gunshot wounds. I'd rather we had a body before we start suggesting a peer of the realm is involved in murder."

Steve stepped in not happy that Perry Hargreaves was giving his team orders. "Si, do as the commander asks." The DCI's voice was harsh and uncompromising. "And can you ask Matt to join me in interview room three in ten minutes?" This was where Benny Stockton awaited his fate, next door to Lord Patrick Scotland.

Si stood sensing the atmosphere between his two senior officers. As Si was leaving, Steve added," And Si, finish your report and get as much detail from your interview with Benny in the file. We'll need it during the interview."

Si stopped and grinned. "Already done, sir. That Bob Glass is a one for his files and procedures." With a wink, Si left.

Steve turned to Perry. "Look sir, this is rubbish. We know Lord Scotland was head of the assassinations committee. If this Benny character is correct, you can surely see how easy it would be for him to bypass the committee and order a killing. You heard Major Havers. He's proud of his record of killing undesirables that could embarrass the government. If you told him to jump, he'd ask how high. Plus, Si

Griffiths caught Scotland with the extorted money. He's guilty and we shouldn't soft pedal just because of who he is."

Perry Hargreaves looked shocked. He knew Steve was right but also knew people like Patrick Scotland had friends in high places. He was determined to make sure everything was done by the book. "I know your feelings on these government-sponsored killings Steve and up to a point I agree with you, but we have to deal with them and not waste resources. If we can prove that Lord Scotland did abuse his position and order the killing of this Romanian, then we'll charge him, but I won't sanction a conspiracy to murder charge on the word of a known criminal and I don't think the CPS would either. If you want him charged, get evidence."

"What about the extortion? We have the evidence in the shape of the money, and an eyewitness who is a policeman."

Perry looked exhausted as though the mental effort of dealing with these events was too much for him. "Same thing, Steve, although it is a stronger case. Get everything you can from Benny Stockton, and we'll see where we go."

Commander Perry Hargreaves stood and left. "Remember, we have a case review meeting at nine on Monday morning. I'm off to bring the commissioner up to speed."

After Perry had gone, Steve sat back. "Political coppers, what a waste of space!"

At exactly 2.29 p.m. Steve and Matt entered interview room three. The suspect in interview room two had already been released on police bail. After learning this, Matt thought to himself it was one law for those with influence and another for the low-life criminal who didn't know anyone in high places. There would be no high-priced lawyer to advise Benny Stockton. Matt thought of the unfairness of the judicial system that favoured money and influence. Benny Stockton hadn't been born into wealth and power but poverty and depravation. He'd turned to crime to survive unlike Lord Scotland who was the complete opposite. Yet here they were. Both connected to the same crimes. Matt determined to make sure his Lordship got the same treatment as Benny no matter how difficult it might prove.

Benny wasn't under arrest but was being interviewed under caution. The twin tape recorder was enabled, the relevant comments made for the tape and the interview began.

The next thirty minutes would go a long way in deciding Lord Scotland's fate.

***

Dom, having eaten his lunch, set off for Greenwich. Over the past day he'd been in two minds how to tackle his latest assignment. Once he'd settled on his direct approach, he thought it best to get it done. He'd decided that if Max Ho wasn't in residence on this Saturday afternoon, then Dom would return on Sunday. As he drove through the Saturday afternoon traffic he thought about his plan and apart from the slight risk posed by the CCTV system he felt comfortable it was viable.

He once more parked in the municipal car park he'd used before and standing outside his Land Rover Discovery, donned his overcoat and cap. The weather had turned grey and threatened rain. As he locked his car, he noted it was 2.37 p.m.

Steve and Matt had been interviewing Benny for eight minutes.

Dom decided to carry out another brief surveillance of the apartment block and walked briskly past the front entrance before rounding the corner and surveying the side where the entrance and exit to the underground car park appeared as a great gap under the building. He considered entering the building from the garage but concluded residents parking their cars might be too suspicious of a stranger on foot asking them to let him in.

Satisfied nothing was amiss, Dom walked back to the front entrance. He took up position in a convenient bus shelter that was located opposite the entrance and only about fifty yards further on and waited. He hoped a resident would appear and he could gain access with them. Alternatively, if he saw someone leaving, he would dash across the road and hope to catch the door before it finally closed shut.

After ten minutes Dom was beginning to think he would have to use his plan B. He would press a few buttons on the intercom keypad and pretend he needed access to deliver a parcel. He knew this was more dangerous as people might remember his face, but he thought it a chance worth taking.

Just as he was about to implement plan B, he saw a young woman wheeling a pram approach the building and was obviously intent on going in. Dom looked at his watch. It was 3.04 p.m. He immediately walked across the road timing his arrival to coincide with the woman pressing the four-digit entry code and the door clicking open. Without saying anything, Dom reached behind the woman who was struggling to get the pram through the door and held it open for her. She was young, probably in her early twenties and quite pretty. There was a young baby in the pram.

"Thank you." She looked sweetly at Dom and hurried inside. Dom noticed the common entrance hall was large and the woman had positioned herself in front of one of the two elevators that obviously served the upper floors of the building. He noted number seven was illuminated. Dom saw the sign for the stairs and walked in that direction.

He climbed to the fourth floor and quickly established there were four flats on each floor. Number 402 was in the left-hand corner opposite the exit from the stairs. Dom's adrenaline level was up as it always was when he was about to kill. He stood outside Max Ho's front door hoping his target was home. He listened for any sound either coming from inside Max's flat or from anywhere else in the building. The place was deadly quiet. Dom supposed the thick carpeting in the common areas must act as a good sound insulator. He made a mental note.

There was no bell on the door, so Dom tapped lightly but loud enough for anyone inside to hear. To his relief, Dom heard movement on the other side of the door before it was opened. Max Ho stood appraising the stranger who was disturbing his Saturday afternoon in front of the television. Max enjoyed watching old Ealing comedy films that were always shown on a re-run channel on Saturday afternoons.

Without disguising his annoyance Max said, "Yes. What do you want?"

"Sorry to disturb you, sir but are you Squadron Leader Max Ho?"

"Yes, I am. Who are you and what do you want?"

Dom produced his unsilenced Glock and pointed it directly at Max. "Please back up inside."

Max was stunned and without realising it, backed away from the weapon and in doing so complied with Dom's request.

"What do you want?" Max quickly regained his composure. As a test pilot he knew how to react in stressful situations. He continued to look at the weapon while his trained brain looked for avenues of escape and any angle the gunman might be vulnerable from.

Dom was comfortable he had the upper hand. His target stood in the middle of the open plan living room. He wanted to wait a few minutes before attaching the silencer. He continued to point the Glock at Max.

"Who are you and who sent you?" Max wanted to engage this killer in conversation as a way of buying time in order to work out an escape plan.

Dom didn't usually talk to his victims, but he realised he needed to attach the silencer before killing this airman. "Let's just say somebody doesn't want you around."

Max started to move very slowly, almost imperceptibly to his right. He realised there was more free floor space on the right of the apartment than on the left. He kept Dom talking.

"Who's the somebody?"

"I don't know. I only obey instructions."

"And you've been given an instruction to kill me?"

Max continued his slow journey to the right. He was positioning an armchair between him and his would-be killer. He also sensed this gunman had something on his mind and wasn't quite one hundred percent focused.

Dom was thinking about the silencer and decided to bring it out into the open. He still pointed the weapon at Max's chest. He knew he would have to lower the gun in order to screw in the silencer, but he was sure Max Ho wouldn't try anything. He just had to get his timing right. Max Ho was about twelve feet away from him and Dom was calculating if Max did dive for the gun, whether he'd have time to fix the silencer to the Glock and shoot Max before the pilot got to him. Dom decided he had time.

What Dom didn't know was Max was physically fit and a master in various martial arts. Seeing Dom relax his grip on the weapon and having positioned himself further to the right-hand side of his apartment, Max Ho readied his muscles to pounce.

As Dom lowered the Glock and began screwing the silencer to the end of the barrel, Max, using the agility that his martial arts skills gave him, and his physical strength, suddenly moved without warning. He appeared to fly through the air with his right foot heading directly for Dom's head. Dom saw it coming and ducked. Max's foot swung by Dom's head followed by the rest of his body. Both men fell onto the floor with Max Ho on top of Dom. Dom still held the Glock and as Max quickly regained the initiative and was about to deliver a fatal martial arts blow, Dom raised his right arm and brought the heavy weapon down on the side of Max's head. The blow stunned Max who for a few seconds blacked out. Dom crawled from underneath Max. During the attack the silencer had been lost. Dom quickly looked for it and saw it lying on the floor beside a coffee table. As he scrambled to retrieve it, he felt an arm wrap itself around his neck. Max had recovered from the blow with the gun and was now pulling Dom to his feet using his arm around his throat. As Dom became vertical, he elbowed Max in the stomach, winding the Oriental and forcing him to release his grasp.

Dom was winded from having his windpipe crushed and found it difficult to focus, plus the noise in his ears was pounding. With his only thought now of survival he saw the figure of Max Ho coming towards him. He raised the unsuppressed weapon and fired. The explosion sounded louder than anything Dom had heard before. To his surprise, Max Ho kept coming and Dom fired again.

In Dom's mind everything went blank and was peaceful. He was drifting down a river on a luxury boat surrounded by beautiful women. His eyes were firmly closed, and he was at peace.

Max Ho, having landed a kick against the side of Dom's head rendering him unconscious, sat gasping for air on the floor next to his would-be killer. The first bullet had missed completely but had shattered the large picture glass window that Max loved sitting beside. The second shot had caught Max in the right shoulder. He sat holding his wound and watching the blood ooze between his fingers. He tried to gather his thoughts and decide what to do. In a state of shock, he pulled the cover off one of his cushions and stuffed it into his wound in an effort to stop the bleeding. He needed a few more minutes to regain his composure.

***

DC Kenny Johnstone and his partner were looking forward to the end of their shift at four p.m. They had been a bit lax earlier on, when Kenny had left the car and gone off in search of a café instructing his colleague to keep an eye out. Kenny returned at 3.03 p.m. with two bacon rolls for himself and his partner to enjoy.

"Anything happened?"

"No. All quiet." What his partner didn't tell him was he'd left the car and visited the local supermarket situated over two hundred yards away for a comfort break. There was no one watching Max Ho's apartment building for almost fifteen minutes. This error had allowed Dom access to Max's flat without the policemen being aware that he was even in the vicinity.

The two watchers were unaware of the drama unfolding in flat 402. Dom and Max had been together for around eighteen minutes both talking and fighting. Kenny Johnstone heard the gun shot and the smashing of glass at exactly 3.21 p.m. From his position in front of the Ford he saw the picture window on the fourth-floor shatter and large pieces fall to the ground. Luckily, no one was walking below the falling glass.

"Bloody hell. Call it in, gunshot fired." As he said this, he heard another loud crack. Kenny changed his order. "Make that gunshots fired in Max Ho's flat, number 402. Tell them we need armed back up. You stay here. I'm going up."

Before Kenny's fellow watcher could object, Kenny was running and wheezing in the direction of the main entrance to Max Ho's building.

His colleague did as he was told and called it in.

***

The interview with Benny Stockton hadn't got off to a good start. At first, he played the part of the experienced gangster who knew his rights. "I'm saying nothing till my lawyer gets here."

Steve reminded Benny he was only helping with inquiries and that in all probability, he didn't have a lawyer.

Benny then said he'd only speak to DS Griffiths. "Me and him have an understanding. He promised if I cooperated, you'd let me go. He said I'd be back in the showroom by this afternoon." Benny looked at his watch. "It's already almost half past three."

Steve could see this would be difficult. He decided to let Matt Conway have a go. Matt ceremoniously opened the file Bob Class had prepared.

"Benny. We don't know anything DS Griffiths might have said but he's written down what you told him on Thursday of this week. That's Thursday the tenth. Do you remember that conversation?"

"Bloody right I do. He almost cost my man his manhood. Kicked him right in the middle, poor bloke thinks he's a girl."

Matt looked at Steve who smiled inwardly. He knew Si would have his methods.

"That's not what I mean, Benny. Do you remember what you told DS Griffiths?"

"Of course I do, I'm not losing my marbles."

"Then for the tape can you please tell us what you told DS Griffiths?"

"Well, see, I could, but if I do, how do I know you'll not stitch me up and put the cuffs on me?"

Steve leant forward. "Benny, just repeat what you told Si Griffiths, and I promise you, you'll be out of here in no time." He knew he was exaggerating. Based on Si's notes Benny could be charged with conspiracy to murder the Romanian and various other drug and prostitution charges.

"You promise?"

"Benny, once you've told us what we need to hear, you can walk through that door." Steve pointed to the blue painted door of the interview suite.

Benny smiled, satisfied he'd struck a deal.

"OK. I told DS Griffiths that some time back a guy approached me and said he knew I was running a few girls and selling a bit of coke. He seemed a bit posh to be dealing at my level, but he said he had contacts and could make life difficult if I didn't cut him in on the earnings and supply him with powder and girls when he wanted them. He told me if I didn't do as he said, I'd have the coppers all over me."

"And you believed him?"

"Yes. He was well dressed and spoke proper like. He also said he worked for the government and had contacts that could help me grow the business."

"What was his name?"

"I don't know his real name, but he called himself Smith."

Matt was taking notes even as the twin tape deck recorded Benny's words. Steve sat back listening.

"Go on. What happened next?"

"Well, nothing for about six months. This Mr Smith came every Saturday morning driving that great Jaguar of his. He'd collect his ten percent of the takings from the other business, you know, the girls and that, and leave. He was regular as clockwork."

"How much did you give him each week?"

"It varied but usually between two and four grand."

This time Steve made a note. "Go on."

Well, about five or six months back on one of his Saturday visits he tells me he knows a Romanian outfit struggling to set up in London. He told me their Columbian was high grade and their girls were better than mine and he'd arranged for us to join forces. He said our businesses would grow and flourish and he'd be taking fifteen percent of the combined take."

Benny paused. He'd been talking for more than twenty minutes and was tired. "Can I have a cup of tea?"

Matt signalled to the constable on duty inside the door. The tea was on its way.

Benny, happy to be taken seriously, continued. "This Mr Smith told me that if I was ever in trouble to call him. He boasted there was nothing he couldn't fix. We started working with this other gang and Mr Smith was right. Their Columbian was high grade, and their girls were younger and more obliging than mine. Business did get better, but these guys were a nightmare, especially their boss. He thought he knew more than me and that he should be in charge. He tried to take over everything and when I challenged him, he said if I didn't do as he said he'd have me taken care of."

Matt interrupted. "And you didn't like that?"

"Bloody right I didn't so I called Mr Smith and told him his fifteen percent was in serious trouble unless he got rid of the Romanian."

The tea arrived and coffee for Steve and Matt.

While Benny was stirring in his sugar Steve asked,

"Those were your exact words to Mr Smith?"

"Yes, as near as I can remember."

Matt thought, the poor sod, he's just confessed to conspiracy to murder.

Steve pressed on. "What did Mr Smith say, exactly."

"First, he said we'd discuss it the next Saturday he picked up his money. I told him what was going on and he said he'd take care of this guy. I wasn't to worry. I'd not see him again?"

"What did you take that to mean?"

Benny looked frightened. "He was going to have him killed, but I knew this Mr Smith wasn't the sort to get his hands dirty. He'd have someone do it for him."

"And you never saw the Romanian again."

"No, like I said, Mr Smith took care of him."

Matt pulled an enlarged photograph of Lord Patrick Scotland from the file. "Is this the man you know as Mr Smith?"

Benny looked at the picture and was about to speak when there was a loud knock on the door and without waiting to be called in, Bob Class appeared obviously out of breath.

"I'm sorry to interrupt, sir but there's been an incident at Max Ho's place. I've just taken a call for DI Conway. Shots fired and armed back up requested."

Steve and Matt looked at each other in amazement. They both knew the lid had been well and truly blown off their continued surveillance of Max Ho.

"You'd better get over there, Matt. I'll tidy up here and join you."

Matt immediately left followed by Bob Class.

Steve turned to Benny. "Mr Stockton, thank you for your cooperation. We will have more questions for you in due course. This officer will take you to a nice comfortable cell and we'll continue this chat tomorrow. Interview terminated at 3.27 p.m."

Benny objected but Steve now had other things on his mind. He needed to be in Greenwich and assess the damage that may have been done to his secret undercover operation.

Chapter Nineteen

While all hell was breaking out in Greenwich, Charlie Robb was taking a leisurely drive through Kensington. He knew the address he had for Sebastian De Roy and hoped he still lived there. Traffic on Saturday afternoon through Kensington was heavy and Charlie decided he would cover more ground on foot. Besides, he reminded himself it was time to return the Honda to the rental car company and rent another make and model.

Parking in Kensington appeared to be by permit only and although there were a few on street parking places, Charlie knew not to risk parking in one and getting a ticket. This could potentially lead to the police identifying the Honda and then Charlie. His prison education had warned him against such a basic error.

Charlie drove further on and found a car park in Chelsea that looked normal and was busy. He parked and wearing his well-used disguise, he set off with his London A to Z to find Sebastian De Roy's home.

It took Charlie a while to orientate himself to the map book but eventually he found 76, St. Julian's Gardens. It was an imposing terraced stone built fronted four storey townhouse. While others roundabout had been converted into flats, number 76 appeared to have been left as the architect originally designed it without the banks on buttons stuck to the walls beside the front doors and remained a single-family home.

Charlie didn't see any obvious CCTV security systems as he walked along the affluent street. Everything looked well-kept and clean. Even the cars looked as though they had just been driven from the showroom.

Just off St. Julian's Gardens was a small side street where a small boutique style café had been set up. Charlie saw there were two outside tables that had obviously been placed to accommodate the café's clients who smoked. Notwithstanding the low temperatures of this Saturday in February, Charlie pulled out a chair and sat. The café was positioned more or less at the end of the lane and afforded a view down St. Julian's Gardens.

A young waitress who was clearly from an Eastern bloc country, took Charlie's order for a black coffee and promptly disappeared inside to the warmth of the café. Charlie knew his plan needed refining and his realisation the feelings for Connie O'Sullivan were only serving to complicate things. He sat with the collar of his coat pulled up and mentally reviewed his plan. He had taken care of his first two victims, but they were more or less collateral damage. The really guilty party was Geoffrey Lockwood, but Charlie was convinced Sebastian De Roy wasn't far behind.

His coffee was delivered with the bill. Charlie held the cup in both hands gaining a bit of warmth from the cup. He sipped the hot liquid carefully.

He stared down St. Julian's Gardens thinking about how he could get to De Roy. He knew he'd changed his plans and now intended to force his victims into giving him money in the hope he'd spare their lives. A wicked grin appeared on Charlie's face as he understood he'd take the cash and their lives. His mission for revenge had not changed. In his mind's eye he saw Connie O'Sullivan and wondered what her reaction would be if she ever learnt of his plans. He was determined not to allow self-pity to take over and told himself his first priority was to avenge his family and find the thug who had actually killed his wife and son. He felt he could achieve everything he wanted without involving Connie and provided he could escape the police, she would never know what he had done. Charlie smiled as he pictured the pair of them on a boat in a sunny climate, enjoying the riches he would extort from his next two victims.

Despite the cold, Charlie Robb sat back and smiled. He finished his coffee, left a five-pound note and walked back into St. Julian's Gardens thinking that coffee in Kensington was expensive. He had no idea how to contact De Roy. As he approached number 76, he saw an elderly woman leaving number 78. A quick glance told Charlie that number 78 had been split into flats so this lady must live in part of it. As with number 76, there was a flight of six steps up to the front door. The elderly lady was obviously not as agile as she may have been in her youth and was struggling to take the steps one at a time. Charlie saw an opportunity.

"Can I help you down?"

"No, no, I'm fine. At my age any movement is difficult, but I can't do stairs." She continued to take the steps one at a time.

Charlie stood waiting, ready to assist if she needed it.

"There, made it." The lady smiled and looked up at Charlie. "It was very kind of you to ask. Not many young men would these days."

Charlie gave an embarrassed shrug before setting of on a totally fabricated story.

"It's nothing really. My family used to live here a long time ago. We lived next door in number 76. I've just returned from Australia and thought I'd walk past the old place."

The lady seemed impressed. "I've lived here for over twenty years, perhaps I knew your family?"

"No, I doubt it. We left for Australia about twenty years ago. I think I remember my mother saying they sold to someone called De Roy. I don't suppose they still live there?"

"Oh no, they did until about five years ago. It's a family from the Middle East who live there now. I didn't have much to do with the De Roys." The elderly lady smiled a wicked smile only someone of her years could. "They were a bit stuck up for my liking."

Charlie was disappointed but asked the obvious question. "I don't suppose you know where they moved to?"

"No, as I said, they were a bit snooty. They didn't talk to many of the neighbours." The lady paused. "Is it important? Did you need to see them?"

Charlie didn't want to labour the point. He didn't want to be remembered. "No. It was just curiosity on my part." He started to walk away and waved goodbye to the elderly lady. Inside he was in a state of shock. He needed to find De Roy. But how? As he walked to his car, he tried to recall everything he knew about Sebastian De Roy. He realised it wasn't much. Realising how far west he was he decided to return his Honda to the car rental desk at Heathrow Airport. As he entered the approach to the M4 motorway he decided he'd have a fancy saloon. It would impress Connie at their lunch date tomorrow. As for Sebastian De Roy, he could wait until Monday."

***

It took Steve almost an hour to get to Greenwich. Traffic was heavy and an accident en route hadn't helped. When he arrived at the building that housed Max Ho's flat, the scene looked chaotic. There were marked police cars parked at odd angles across the street. The street had been cordoned off and there seemed to enough police blue and white plastic tape strung up everywhere to wrap around the world. Various white and black panel vans were also in evidence as was the scene of crime van.

Steve parked his car behind a marked police car and made his way to the front door. He was stopped by a very young-looking uniformed constable who insisted on seeing his ID before noting his name on a list and allowing him to pass.

"Fourth floor sir, Flat 402." Steve thought the lad was trying to be helpful.

Another uniformed officer was posted outside Max Ho's apartment and once more Steve showed his warrant card. After placing blue disposable overshoes over his own, the DCI entered the flat. At first glance it looked chaotic with men and women in white all-in-one paper suits apparently scouring every inch of the flat. Steve spotted Matt Conway talking to an older man in a cheap suit.

"This is DC Kenny Johnstone, sir. He was one of the watchers and called it in."

Steve nodded a greeting. "What happened?"

Kenny explained he'd heard the first shot and the window exploded outwards. He explained about the second shot. "I told my oppo to call it in and I ran up here to see what happening. I found that bloke there," Kenny pointed to a now conscious but groggy Dominic Barns. "Out for the count with a gun in his hand and a Chinese looking bloke, the one we're keeping an eye on, lying over there." Kenny pointed to a spot beside an armchair. The floor was red. "He was lying back against that chair and was bleeding badly. I called an ambulance and the paramedics have taken him to hospital. They said he'd been shot and lost a lot of blood."

"Right. Do we know who this bloke is?" Steve pointed towards Dom.

A sheepish Kenny Johnstone answered. "That's the bloke who was casing this building yesterday."

Matt looked surprised. "You mean the one you were told to report as soon as you saw him and call for back up?"

Kenny was looking at the floor. "Yes, sir, we must have missed him. He must have slipped past us."

Matt wasn't about to accept this. In a raised voice he said, "You mean you'd sloped off for something or fallen asleep."

Before Kenny could answer, Steve put his hand on his arm. Addressing both detectives, he said, "Not now, this will keep."

Matt called over the only woman at the scene who was not wearing a white paper suit. "This is DI Sheila Grogan, sir. She's the SIO from the local substation."

After Matt had made the introductions, the SIO studied the DCI. "I've heard about you, sir. You head a special unit at the Met. Are you taking over as SIO?"

Steve glanced at Matt who shrugged. Steve was embarrassed. Whatever had happened in this flat was nothing to do with him. He had officially been stood down from the Ho investigation, but he knew he couldn't simply walk away. He also knew there would be awkward questions to answer if he hung around.

"If you want to take over, sir, I'm sure my superintendent wouldn't mind."

Steve did some quick thinking. "No, DI Grogan, this is your case. I had an interest in the shooting victim but with this that's now over. Can I ask you to keep me updated on developments?" Steve handed the SIO one of his cards. "All my numbers are on there."

Si Griffiths arrived just as the DCI was finishing with DI Grogan. He was talking with Matt.

"We need to find out what the hell happened here. Who is that guy and why was he shooting at Max Ho?" Steve pointed to Dom who was being tended to by a paramedic.

"What's going on here, boss?"

"Nothing to concern you, Si. It seems our spy was on someone's assassination list after all." As Steve spoke the words everything became clear. He took three paces towards Dom and crouched down beside him.

"Do you work for Major Havers?"

Dom who was still feeling the effects of Max Ho's almost lethal martial arts kick nodded his head. He was still not fully conscious. If he had been he would never have acknowledged his connection to the major.

"What's your name?"

Dom struggled to even answer this simple question. The paramedic who was a rather plump lady with a kindly face stared at Steve giving him a warning look that said 'don't push too hard, he's in no fit state to answer questions'.

Dom was obviously dazed, so Steve tried again. "You work for Major Havers, but I need your name?"

Dom shook his head trying to clear his brain. He looked at Steve with wide unfocused eyes. As the paramedic replaced the cooling towel, she was holding to Dom's head he weakly answered, "Staff Sergeant Eric Stokes." His voice was croaky and very weak.

Steve looked at the kindly paramedic. "Will he be OK?"

"He should be. We need to get him stable before we move him. He's had a terrible blow to the head. He'll have a full scan to see if there's any brain damage but from the looks of him, I'd say he'll recover but he'll have a terrible headache for days."

Looking in the direction of DI Sheila Grogan, Steve nodded. "Can you please tell that officer where you take him and keep her up to date?"

"Sure, no problem."

Steve stood, said goodbye to the SIO and told Matt, Si and Kenny to accompany him outside.

Once back at street level, the DCI turned to Kenny. "This is your patch, Kenny, where can we get a coffee and have a chat?"

Despite feeling guilty that he had sloped off for his bacon roll and missed the arrival of the would-be assassin, Kenny smiled. "Follow me, sir. I know the perfect place."

Under his breath Si Griffiths said, "I bet you do." Si, as an old-time cop, recognised a kindred spirit and had already suspected the DC was not at his post when the gunman arrived.

Once the four officers were seated and served their coffee Steve wanted answers. Fortunately, the café was quiet this late on a Saturday afternoon and there was only one other table occupied.

"Right. I'm not interested in what anybody did that they shouldn't have done. I'm not on a witch-hunt. I just need to know what happened and how."

"Sir. How much do we divulge remembering DC Johnstone isn't up to speed?" Matt was sounding a cautionary note for Steve's benefit.

"Yes, good point, Matt. Right, Kenny, from the top and leave nothing out."

A red-faced Kenny Johnstone told his tale. He explained about the bacon roll but defended himself saying he didn't know his partner would leave the car at the same time. He told Steve about hearing the first shot, then the window being blown out, followed by the second shot. "When I got into the flat, one bloke was out cold. He was the one in the coat holding the gun. The other bloke was propped against a chair holding his shoulder. There was a lot of blood. I called for an ambulance knowing my partner had called in the incident. I kicked the gun away from the bloke in the overcoat and within a few minutes the cavalry arrived. I tried to make the Asian guy comfortable before the paramedics took over and took him to hospital."

"Right. Anything else you can remember?"

"No, that's it, sir. The local people arrived and took over the scene. Then DI Conway arrived and then you. The local SIO just told me to make a statement in the morning."

Steve's heart sank at the thought that DC Kenny Johnstone would be making a statement and that he'd almost certainly have to say he was on a surveillance operation authorised by the Special Resolutions Unit at the Met. The DCI brushed aside his concerns for himself. He'd take what was coming.

"All right, Kenny, going into that flat knowing there was a gunman inside was a brave thing. I'll see you get a mention." Steve indicated that Kenny could go.

As he stood, he looked at the three remaining officers. "Thanks, but I'm sorry we screwed up. If I hadn't gone for that roll, none of this would have happened." A depressed Kenny Johnstone departed leaving Steve's team to order more coffee.

"Kenny has explained what happened here but not why." Steve examined his colleagues' faces for a reaction. Si Griffiths was the first to react. His old copper's instinct was sharper than Matt's.

"What did you ask the guy who was flat out?"

Steve smiled. Si was quick. "It turns out his name is Eric Stokes. He's ex-army but his driving licence says he's Dominic Barns. His other ID was a pass to the British Museum. It says he's employed there as an architectural historian."

Matt Conway chipped in. "Which is he, Eric or Dominic?"

"When he was groggy, he said Eric Stokes. Si, get onto Bob. Ask him to check military records for an Eric Stokes and have Tech Services run our mystery man's picture against that database. I bet our mystery man is one Eric Stokes, aka Dominic Barns."

Si stood and took out his phone. He walked outside to make the call. It was 5.17 p.m. Saturday, February 12. All of Steve's team were working. Bob Class was hunting down unclaimed bodies who had died from gunshots as Si called and passed on the DCI's request. Bob Class got straight on to it.

Si returned and nodded. "Bob's on it."

"Good. Now, when I went with the commander to the meeting I had in Whitehall, the Minister for Security, Edwin Pinter, was there with an army type called Major Havers. A real ramrod backed soldier. He admitted he ran one of the hit squads the government used to eliminate people they wanted silenced. Our Lord Scotland, currently out on police bail, was chairman of the committee that gave the major his orders. If I'm right, our Eric Stokes or Dominic Barns is one of the major's assassins. I asked him if he worked for Major Havers and he said yes. I bet we'll find that Land Rover Discovery parked nearby, the one registered to the government, and we'll find this guy's prints will be all over it."

Steve sat back and waited for comments and observations.

"But you were told to back off, to withdraw the surveillance on Max Ho and to forget about the whole spy thing. I thought Max Ho wasn't on the assassination list and Lord Scotland's committee had been disbanded." Matt was having difficulty remembering the sequence of events but thought he had it correct.

"That's right. So, no committee, no Lord Scotland means no kill order which means Major Havers couldn't have ordered Ho's assassination, and if he didn't, who did?"

Si gave a light cough to attract his two colleagues' attention. "From what little I know, didn't you tell me this whole thing started because one side of the street wasn't talking to the other side? Suppose that's still the case. Suppose this major didn't get an order telling him to hold off killing Ho. Suppose it's happening all over again."

"Mm, good point Si, except I was at the meeting and there could be no doubt, everyone knew what was happening. The committee was disbanded, and Major Havers was warned to stay away from Ho until further notice."

Matt looked slyly at the DCI and in a quiet voice that was almost a whisper said, "Unless someone didn't like the order. I know a DCI who has disobeyed orders recently. Suppose there's another independent minded official out there who has ordered the killing of Ho regardless of orders."

Steve leant forward as Matt's word's struck home. "And the only one who could order Dominic Barns to kill Ho…" All three spoke in unison. "…is Major Havers."

The meeting broke up at 6.03 p.m.

Having told Matt and Si to finish for the night, Matt reminded Steve he'd have to stand down his watchers. Once he'd done that he'd head home. Surprisingly, Si said he'd go back to the Yard and help Bob with the body search and the facial recognition.

As a joke, Matt said to Si, "There's no overtime."

Si pulled a theatrical face. "You know, sometimes I feel I'm not appreciated. I'm going back to make sure the boy finishes at a decent hour. He'd stay there all night if he didn't get a result."

All three walked back to their cars deep in their own thoughts. Each wondering how the Ho incident would play out.

Steve looked at the time and realised, subject to traffic, he'd be home to see his daughter off to bed. She was allowed up later at the weekends and tomorrow was Sunday.

Chapter Twenty

Sunday, February 13 started for the DCI with a shock. It was 8.12 a.m. and he was in a deep satisfying sleep. Alison was beside him and the whole house was eerily quiet. Suddenly his eyes opened with a start. The landline phone beside the bed was ringing. Even in his semi-conscious state, Steve knew this was unusual. Most of his calls came on his mobile. He thrust out an arm and found the receiver. Without sitting up he placed the receiver to his ear and mumbled. "Yes?"

A cheery voice answered. "I hope I didn't disturb you." It was Commander Perry Hargreaves. "You've been summoned. You're to be in Whitehall, room 1122 at noon, best suit. The Minister for Security, Edwin Pinter, wants to be debriefed on the Ho thing. The commissioner herself will be there along with other important people. For some reason, I'm not invited and to be honest, I'm glad, so, high noon, sharp, room 1122 in Whitehall."

Steve was rapidly digesting this news and it sounded as though Perry Hargreaves was about to hang up.

"Hold on! What's this about?"

"Steve, I don't know, but you have been mixing in some exalted company lately. All I do know is I got a call from the commissioner's PA, telling me you were to be at the meeting, and it was to debrief the minister."

Steve rolled onto his back still holding the phone. He let out a great sigh. "Bloody hell, Perry, it's Sunday."

The buzzing in his ear told him the commander had hung up; he was on his own.

Steve got out of bed and spent twenty minutes in the bathroom preparing himself for his meeting. As it was only just after eight thirty, he put the kettle on and sat in the living room in his dressing gown contemplating why he had been invited by no less a person than the commissioner.

At 8.53 a.m. his mobile rang. "Steve Burt."

"Good morning, Steve."

He instantly recognised the smooth tones of Sir Patrick Bond, head of MI6.

"Good morning, Patrick. What can I do for you?" Steve was annoyed at being called by this old warrior and allowed his annoyance to affect the tone of his voice.

"It's what I can do for you. Come along to room 1122 at eleven. I'll brief you on everything. Having knowledge of what we know may just save your career. See you at eleven."

Sir Patrick hung up and a knot formed in Steve's stomach. What did Sir Patrick mean about 'knowledge saving his career?' Not for the first time the DCI became nervous. He knew he'd disobeyed orders over the Max Ho surveillance but that was a police issue, nothing to do with the Minister for Security or MI6. Steve sipped his tea and wondered what lay in store. Being pragmatic as ever, he shrugged and returned to the bedroom, where despite everything, Alison lay sound asleep.

As he left the bedroom his mobile sounded again. It was Matt Conway. "Steve, I'm not sure what's going on, but I've had Si Griffiths on saying he was hauled in by some spooks and questioned about Lord Scotland. They wanted to know how he had come to arrest his Lordship. Si being Si he told them he hadn't arrested him, and he was just being questioned, but I could tell he was rattled." Matt paused. "There's more, Kenny Johnstone was visited at his home last night and questioned over his surveillance and asked why he was first on the scene of the shooting. What's going on, Steve? Are we in trouble?"

The DCI was shocked at this news but tried to sound calm. "No, Matt, everything's fine. I've been called to a meeting later today. I'll call you when it's finished."

Steve hung up. He was both angry and curious. The phrase 'knowledge saving his career' seemed to haunt him.

Steve arrived in room 1122 located on the first floor of an annex off the main Whitehall office complex at exactly 10.57 a.m. He was smartly dressed in his best suit and had taken care over his grooming including an especially slow shave. Sir Patrick Bond, was already there, as was Timothy Shand. Both men were immaculately dressed in what Steve thought of as the Whitehall uniform of dark blue pin striped suit, white shirt and some kind of diagonally striped tie.

Neither man stood as Steve entered. Sir Patrick acknowledged Steve's arrival and invited him to sit. Timothy Shand gave a weak smile and continued to review the file in front of him.

"Right, Steve. I know you've been digging into the Max Ho case…" Before Sir Patrick could continue Steve let his anger show.

"You've been questioning my team behind my back, and I want to know why?" Although the DCI was angry, he put on more of a theatrical performance of anger in order to get Sir Patrick's attention.

Sir Patrick smoothly flicked an imaginary speck from his jacket. He looked up at Steve before continuing. "As I was saying, DCI Burt, you've been digging into the Ho case, and we know you were at the scene of his shooting yesterday. We've put two and two together and spoken to the CID fellow who was first on scene. We know you carried on with the surveillance after you were ordered to stop."

Steve started to say something, but Sir Patrick held up his hand giving a clear message that he should not interrupt.

"As a result of your actions we believe you are in possession of facts that we would not want broadcast. Had you obeyed orders we would not be having this conversation. I need to clear this Ho thing up now and have told the Minister we will finalise everything at noon today." Sir Patrick took a sip of water. Steve noticed Sir Patrick was talking without notes but saw Timothy Shand pass a single sheet of paper to him.

"I'm going to give you the whole story Steve in anticipation that it satisfies your natural copper's curiosity, but when you have all the facts, I want you to immediately forget them. If you do, then this morning will be a happy occasion. I hope you understand?"

"No, I don't Patrick, but I'm sure you're going to explain."

Steve had known Sir Patrick Bond for a number of years. Sir Patrick had even tried to recruit the DCI into MI6. The use of his Christian name without his title was allowed.

"Some time ago we thought we had a mole in Whitehall. There was nothing concrete, just a few whispers. Tim here was tasked with finding out if there was any truth in the rumours. He learnt that Patrick Scotland seemed to be living beyond his means and was meeting people he had no right to meet: Drug dealers, money launderers but most worrying, people from the Chinese Embassy. We felt we not only had a rotten apple but a potential security risk. A few surveillance jobs of our own convinced us the rumours centred around Lord Scotland were true. Unfortunately, we couldn't prove anything, and Tim came up with the idea that Max Ho might be prepared to steal the experimental jet. Max was of course working undercover. We'd dropped the notion of the jet in various documents that Patrick Scotland would have seen and when Ho reported he'd been contacted by some North Korean, we felt we were onto something." Sir Patrick took another sip of water and Tim Shand slid another sheet of paper in his direction.

"Unfortunately, the contact that was made was with an idiot who calls himself Sky. He's North Korean and affiliated to the Chinese Embassy." Sir Patrick broke off his narrative.

"Oh! By the way Steve, your analysis that Sky must be in the Chinese or Russian Embassy and your proposal to find out which was brilliant."

"It wasn't me, Sir Patrick, it was Inspector Harvey, head of our Technical Support who came up with the idea."

"Quite so, a brilliant chap." It was clear Sir Patrick hadn't taken on board Steve's comments. He continued. "We've been feeding Sky rubbish for years. He thinks he's a master spy and his masters must think the same. We knew that if the aircraft heist was to be taken seriously, someone else had to be involved and not a Chinese or a Russian. It had to be one of us and we had Patrick Scotland in the frame, but we lacked proof."

Tim Shand passed another sheet of paper to his boss. "We decided to put out the story that Max Ho was a North Korean sympathiser, and that the aircraft story was real. At first Max played his part but we felt something wasn't right. We arranged for Lord Scotland's assassination committee to put out a kill order, suspecting it was the last thing his Lordship would want if he were somehow involved. As you know, the order was heavily caveated as a way of fudging the order. Colonel Walters exceeded his authority when he approached Scotland Yard as you did when you involved me. I only became aware of all of this when I started asking questions and found that Michael Russell character wasn't up to the job. Luckily, the minister asked me to take over." Sir Patrick sat with his chest out looking pleased with himself.

"You were asked to put Max Ho under surveillance, and you did it admirably." Another sheet of paper was passed between Tim Shand and Sir Patrick.

"You will recall Tim here asked you for a plan to help us catch Sky? In reality we already knew about him, but we needed something believable to drop on his Lordship and prove he was involved in the hi jacking. You were ordered to remove all surveillance from Ho after you proved he was in fact planning to steal the bloody plane and you'd given us your plan."

Sir Patrick studied the last piece of paper handed to him before he continued.

"Everything was set until your DS Simon Griffiths came on the scene and arrested Lord Scotland. We've had words with your DS and have the full story. He only stumbled across his Lordship because he was looking for a hooded gunman that was present when your WDC was killed, a totally unauthorised action." Sir Patrick stared hard at Steve.

"As it turns out the information your DS gathered on Patrick Scotland's other life together with your disregard for a direct order to call off the surveillance has worked out well. Unknown to us Major Havers who worked for Lord Scotland activated the kill order on Max Ho. If your man hadn't been watching goodness knows what would have happened. Overall, what should have been a disaster has worked out well. We've proven the link between Lord Scotland and a foreign power. The call from Ho to Lord Scotland saying he was ready to hijack the plane on Monday proves that. We didn't know Ho had been turned and was prepared to steal the aircraft plus we have evidence Patrick Scotland was involved in the seedier side of crime. He was obviously short of money and would do anything to get it."

Sir Patrick handed the sheets of paper he'd received from Tim Shand back to him.

"Overall, DCI Burt, I'd say you've dodged a bullet. As you will have gathered, we interviewed a few of your people overnight to get the full picture. I intend to praise you and your team's efforts in this affair and not refer to what might have been had things worked out differently." Sir Patrick sat back. "Now, Steve, do you see why you need me to save your career?"

Steve sat having listened intently. He saw how things looked and how, through his actions, things could indeed be looking very different now. He didn't appreciate Patrick Bond's patronising tone and felt the need to defend himself.

"Sir Patrick, if, after Colonel Walters approached us and I called you, you'd been straight with us, none of this cloak and dagger stuff would have been necessary?"

"Ah! That's the question, DCI Burt, and perhaps in hindsight you are correct. The fact remains however, we have a successful outcome to a problem thanks to you. Don't look for issues where none exist. Only the three of us will ever know the whole story. Sit back and accept the accolades that will come your way. All the other stuff is history." Sir Patrick stood and examined his watch. It was 11.53 a.m. He pressed a wall mounted bell. Turning to Steve he smiled. "We'll have our refreshments now, I know you like your coffee."

The DCI knew Sir Patrick was right. He was offering Steve a clean bill of health and on reflection, Steve didn't feel guilty about sitting tight and saying nothing. He ran through the events of the past week and MI6's involvement. With a smile he told himself, 'It's a two-way street Patrick, I've seen your hand and you've seen mine; my memory is as good as yours.'

"OK, Patrick, you've got me, and I appreciate it, but my concern is, what will this cost me going forward?"

Patrick Bond gave a sly smile. "Oh! I'm sure we'll think of something."

***

As Sir Patrick was ordering refreshments, Charlie Robb was heading out of London towards the M11 motorway. He was driving a black Mercedes 'E' class that he'd hired from the Hertz desk at Heathrow Airport yesterday. He'd bought flowers at the hotel's gift shop for Connie and hoped he'd dressed appropriately for his date.

Charlie had spent little time thinking about Sebastian De Roy. He was excited about taking Connie for lunch. He knew he liked this woman and felt she liked him. His guilt at betraying his wife and son with another woman was diminishing. He told himself he had to forge a new life and let the past go. He had thought about their date today, he knew it was fantasy, but he wanted Connie O'Sullivan in his life. His problem was would she want to join him in his new life abroad? He knew Connie was important to him but his need for revenge was still strong.

He turned onto the M11 on his way to Bishop's Stortford and his date. He told himself not to rush things. He'd keep seeing Connie, but he'd finish his task and despatch De Roy and Lockwood. He'd also added the thug who'd killed his family to his list. He had three killings to complete before he could talk seriously to Connie about their future. The thought of how he'd find Sebastian De Roy floated into his mind, but he quickly dismissed it. Today was to be enjoyed.

***

At exactly noon and with coffee and snacks having already been delivered, the door to room 1122 opened and the Minister arrived, followed by the commissioner dressed in her best uniform. Steve was surprised not to see anyone else behind her.

Once everyone had taken their coffee to the conference table, Sir Patrick invited everyone to sit and he opened the meeting.

"Thank you all for coming. I wanted to debrief the Minister on recent events concerning a spy network that has been uncovered and our efforts to contain it. I am aware the Metropolitan Police became involved in this affair when in truth, they should not have been. However, they have been instrumental in assisting MI6 in uncovering the person we were concerned about and have helped bring this sorry event to a speedy close. After this meeting the files will be locked or shredded and no record of recent events will ever be in the public domain."

Sir Patrick wasn't interrupted as he outlined the events as he had to Steve. He referred to Colonel Walters and Major Havers, then about Sky and the turning of Max Ho. He spoke of the DCI's innovative plan and went into greater detail about how they had set the trap for Lord Scotland. Once he was finished an air of anti-climax was evident. No one spoke.

After a few minutes, the commissioner spoke. "Where are the suspects now and how do you intend to prosecute them?"

Sir Patrick gave a pained expression. "Unfortunately, Lord Patrick Scotland suffered a heart attack at his home last night. He's dead." Sir Patrick looked around the table. Seeing blank faces, he continued. "Squadron Leader Ho has been removed from all RAF records and once he is fit to travel, he will be transported to China and no doubt onwards to North Korea. Major Havers has resigned his commission but will receive his full pension. No further action will be taken against either Colonel Walters or the major."

Steve saw the commissioner raise an eyebrow at this statement. For himself, Steve didn't believe Lord Scotland had died of a heart attack but realised there was nothing to be done. He glanced at the commissioner who shook her head. No one said anything.

Sir Patrick continued. "The other man found in Max Ho's apartment has been identified as one Eric Stokes. He was recruited by Major Havers straight from his army career and trained as an assassin. We are reviewing the major's records to identify how many authorised killings this man was involved in. However, the news from Bart's Hospital is that the blow he took to the head has left him in a serious condition. He is presently in a coma and not expected to recover."

Steve thought that was code for if he does recover someone will make sure he doesn't.

Sir Patrick concluded. "Commissioner, I believe we owe a debt of thanks to Detective Sergeant Simon Griffiths and Detective Constable Kenneth Johnstone. Their actions were above and beyond the call of duty. I'm sure the Minister would agree some form of recognition for these two officers should be forthcoming?"

The Minister who had been listening suddenly burst into life. "Yes, of course, I'm sure the commissioner will oblige if she feels it's warranted. I personally would like to thank DCI Burt for his tenacity in this case and for his sensitivity concerning the seriousness of the matter at hand."

The minister stood as did everyone else at the table. "Well done, everyone, I'm glad this matter is now behind us, and Her Majesty's Government has not been embarrassed."

As the minister and the commissioner filed out the commissioner turned to Steve. "Well done, Steve, back to normal policing tomorrow." She smiled as she left.

Sir Patrick and Tim Shand sat. Steve remained standing and was anxious to leave.

"Well, that's that, Steve, all's well that ends well."

Steve looked at Sir Patrick. "You know, Patrick, I really don't like you but I'm glad you're on our side." Without any form of goodbye or acknowledgement, the DCI left. It was 12.56 p.m. He had at least the rest of the day to spend with his family. Monday would see him back at his desk expected to tackle other crimes, the events of the past eight days forgotten about.

***

Charlie rang the doorbell of Connie O'Sullivan's neat, detached house at exactly 12.56 p.m. the same time on this Sunday afternoon that DCI Steve Burt was leaving to go home to enjoy what was left of his weekend.

Charlie stood holding the flowers he'd bought anticipating meeting the woman he thought might become his soulmate. It took several minutes for Connie to appear at the door. She opened it and stood away from it expecting Charlie to follow her into the house. This wasn't the welcome he had envisaged.

Charlie closed the door and followed Connie into her kitchen. He could immediately feel something was wrong. Connie didn't appear able to look in his direction.

"I brought you flowers." Charlie held them out. Connie who had her back to him turned and took the bunch.

"Thank you, I'll put them in the sink for now." Without making eye contact she filled the sink from the tap and dumped, rather than placed the flowers in the water.

Having spent eight years away from women Charlie wasn't sure how to deal with an obviously distraught and angry woman. "Did you make the lunch booking?" was all he could think to say.

Connie still standing by the sink looking out of the window replied in a weak and feeble voice, "Yes."

Charlie stood in the kitchen shuffling his feet as Connie remained glued to her spot opposite the sink. He lamely asked if the restaurant would keep the table if they were late. Connie seemed to shake herself and moved away from the sink. She brushed past Charlie. "I'll just get my coat. I won't be a moment."

As they drove to the restaurant the atmosphere in the car was frosty. Charlie decided to stay silent. Whatever was on her mind must surely come out over lunch although the prospect of a silent lunch didn't appeal to Charlie.

Charlie parked the car in the restaurant's car park, turned to Connie and blurted out, "What's wrong with you? Have I upset you or something?"

This sudden outburst seemed to galvanise Connie into also speaking out. She turned to face Charlie with a sad but defiant expression on her face.

"What happened to Colin Clark?"

Charlie's jaw dropped. His head began to spin as he scrambled for an answer. All his anger disappeared as easily as it had arrived.

"What do you mean?"

Connie had turned a full ninety degrees and was looking Charlie squarely in the eyes. "It was on the news this morning. Police found a body of a man outside a pub off Fleet Street. They said his name was Colin Clark and they're appealing for witnesses."

Charlie tried valiantly not to look guilty. "Why are you telling me?"

"Because Colin Clark was one of the names you told me were responsible for having you put away. Not two days after you told me he finishes up dead."

Connie had started to cry and was clearly distressed. "Did you kill him, Charlie?" Her voice rose to almost hysterical levels. "Did you shoot him? Is this revenge? Are you a common murderer?"

Charlie sat and turned away from Connie. He stared ahead. He had no idea what to say to this woman that a few hours ago he was considering spending the rest of his life with. His secret was out, but he had no idea how to deal with this turn of events.

The couple sat in the car in silence. Charlie had to come up with an answer for Connie otherwise she would hand him into the police. If he were to finish his task, he knew he had to avoid the police at all costs. Charlie saw on the car clock it was 1.26 p.m. The table was booked for one thirty.

Chapter Twenty-One

Monday, February 14 was like the previous Monday, wet and dull. It seemed to match the DCI's mood as he walked to his office. So far, every day this February had been the same.

Steve stopped off at the coffee shop conveniently located on his route to work. He bought four large black coffees to go and arrived carrying the cups in a cardboard tray.

He found Bob, Matt and to his surprise Si, all sitting at their desks apparently working. Steve, pleased he had bought four coffees, handed them out. "Give me a few minutes and then come through, I need to brief you."

With his office door closed Steve sat and thought back to yesterday's meeting with Sir Patrick. He knew the Ho case had been a distraction and wasn't really anything to do with policing. He replayed the events in his head and agreed the whole sorry tale was best forgotten, but... for some reason he couldn't let it go. He knew a Romanian had been murdered on the orders of Lord Scotland, but no one had been charged. The man known as Dominic Barns was an assassin but so far, he had no idea how many people the man had killed. He still didn't know the identity of the masked gunman who almost saved Poppy's life and more importantly, he felt he'd been betrayed by the system. Policemen caught criminals; they didn't collude in covering up crimes.

There was a knock at Steve's door and his three detectives walked in.

"Right. I had a meeting yesterday with no less a person than the commissioner and our Minister for Security. Sir Patrick Head was also there with his sidekick Timothy Shand. You know they are both MI6?"

The listening trio nodded.

"The Max Ho investigation," Steve paused before wearily continuing, "if it ever was an investigation, is now officially over. Our involvement was real but part of a bigger plan to root out a senior Whitehall mandarin who was up to no good. The person involved has been identified," again Steve paused, "but surprise, surprise, has died of a heart attack over the weekend."

The DCI smiled and looked at Si. "I think you know the gentleman, Si, and I am told his arrest had nothing to do with his heart attack."

The sombre mood in the room lifted. With everyone looking at Si he responded. "A heart attack, that's a new one! They can't pin that on me, maybe a good kicking, but not a heart attack."

After the laughter had subsided, Steve brought the meeting to order.

"Bob, can you please bundle up all the hard copies we have on the Max Ho case including how we stole his phone and…"

"Hold on, sir, that's a bit dangerous. Suppose these papers fall into the wrong hands? You told me there would be no record." Si Griffiths, as the instigator of the theft of the phone, felt he may have something to lose.

"Don't worry, Si, all the hard copies are going to the furnace. The men in suits don't want anything to come back on them or us. You're safe."

Si was scowling like a schoolboy as he said under his breath, "Can I get that in writing?"

Steve ignored him. "Bob, get all the computer files downloaded onto usb sticks and send the whole lot over to MI6 for the attention of Timothy Shand."

"Will do, boss. What about the outstanding bits? I'm still looking for a body with a gunshot."

This was an area Steve felt uncomfortable dealing with. He had his orders to shut everything down, but something wouldn't let him give everything up. He made a decision. "Bob, hold back on your search for the body. Keep at it but it's not a high priority. Also, it's unofficial, so go easy, let's give it a few days. If nothing comes up, we'll drop it. OK?"

"Yes. Fine by me."

The DCI looked at his watch. It was 8.51a.m. "I have to be upstairs at a case review meeting at nine. Well done, everybody. You've all performed well throughout this Max Ho thing. I wish I could tell you more, but I just can't. The reputation of Special Resolutions has never been higher."

As Steve stood and his team started to disperse, he heard Si ask Matt, "Does the DCI always deal in crap or am I just lucky to have come in when I did?"

He didn't hear Matt's reply.

***

Charlie hadn't slept well. Monday morning saw him up early. His mind was in turmoil as he fidgeted and paced around his hotel room unable to settle to anything. He'd called room service and had an early breakfast delivered to his room for something to do. He wasn't hungry and had only drunk the coffee. As he paced, he realised he had to get to grips with his situation.

Lunch with Connie hadn't been a great success after she accused him of being a murderer. In the circumstances he was surprised she agreed to continue with the lunch and to give him a chance to explain. His first strategy had been to deny everything, after all Colin Clark was a common enough name. At first Connie seemed to be persuaded but as she questioned him it became clear to her that her suspicions were well founded. The newspaper had given a brief biography of the murder victim and she had remembered what Charlie had told her about the men who were responsible for his prison time. Charlie now realised telling Connie about his background in such detail had been a mistake. He also regretted giving her the names of his four targets. If the press ran a story on the killing of Anthony Maple, Charlie knew he would be in big trouble.

He paced around, sat, stood and paced again. He needed a clear head to think about the best way to keep Connie and also succeed with his mission. Despite it being only 8.14 a.m. Charlie decided that a walk in the fresh air might help. He walked around the area of his hotel, stopping at a coffee shop to have another coffee when he had a thought.

He wondered if he should tell Connie how he really felt about her and how he needed her in his life. If he told her she was the most important person in his life, but he still felt he owed it to his first wife to revenge her death and that of his son. If he told her that he could never settle down with her unless he could release the anger he felt towards these individuals, but as soon as he had completed his task they'd go abroad. They would have enough money to live comfortably in the sun for the rest of their lives and he would promise that he'd never commit another crime.

As he ran these statements through his head, he realised he was smiling. It might just work especially if he told her the police would never catch him and explained what he'd learnt in prison. Charlie with a grin spoke out loudly but to himself. "It might just work!"

He took out his mobile phone and called Connie. After the revelations of yesterday, she'd called in sick. Like Charlie she had needed to clear her head and decide how to react to the fact the man she had fallen for was a killer.

Connie answered on the third ring. Before Charlie could speak, she shouted at him. "How could you, Charlie? I thought we had something but now you've spoiled it. I had dreams involving us as a couple, but you've shattered them. How could I live with a murderer?" Connie was crying and talking quickly for fear Charlie might say something she didn't want to hear.

Charlie, with his plan fresh in his mind and no longer afraid of his feelings for this woman, spoke as Connie drew a breath. His voice was reassuring but decisive. "Connie, I know I've upset you but it's not as bad as you think. Listen, why don't I come up to you? We can have lunch and I'll explain everything." He paused waiting for a reply that never came although the sound of tears had gone. He continued. "You caught me off guard yesterday with your Sherlock Holmes act. Let me explain and if you're not convinced, I'll hand myself in to the police." Charlie lied but felt he had to say something.

There was silence from Connie for a full thirty seconds. "OK. Get here about one." She sniffed as she added. "But no lies Charlie, I want the truth."

A light-hearted Charlie agreed and hung up. If he could persuade Connie not to hand him in, he might yet realise his dream of revenge and future happiness. The next few hours would determine his future.

***

Steve arrived in Commander Perry Hargreaves's office at 8.47 a.m. He knew from experience that the now weekly case review meeting always started with tea, coffee and biscuits and that Perry rarely started on time.

As Steve entered, he saw a gaggle of senior uniformed officers all chatting and drinking their beverage of choice. There were a few plain clothes officers and Steve immediately recognised Superintendent Alister Staples. Ally was head of the most successful murder squad in the Met and was said to be heading for great things. Still in his early forties, Ally was around six foot tall, slim with broad shoulders and a preference for loud multi-coloured ties, today was no exception. Steve helped himself to a coffee and sidled up to him.

"Morning, sir. I haven't seen you for some time."

Both men shook hands and Ally introduced Steve to the other CID officer he was talking to.

"This is Crosby Gunner, Chief Super attached to the new drugs initiative. DCI Steve Burt, the Yard's best detective and the most cavalier about the rules."

All three laughed and discussed various issues to pass the time. The DCI asked Ally if he had anything on that might suit Special Resolutions.

"Oh no, you don't, I'll deal with my own murders thank you. I'm not giving anything away, at least not today."

Steve's unit was infamous for taking on difficult cases that senior officers either didn't want on their books for fear of spoiling their clear up rate, or cases they genuinely couldn't solve. Passing a case to Special Resolutions could be seen internally as an admission of failure especially as Steve's record in solving such cases was almost one hundred percent Despite this, most department heads had been glad of Steve's skills in the past.

Perry arrived later than he had intended. He stopped by the doorway and looked around. He singled out Steve and indicated he needed to talk to him. Steve excused himself to the two senior officers and headed towards the commander who had walked away from the throng of officers and now stood on his own in a far corner.

"I've just come from the commissioner. She's pleased with your performance yesterday and is giving you a citation for efficient policing." Perry looked curiously at the DCI. "Whatever that is."

Steve stood and smiled. He had no idea either.

The commander continued. "Your Sergeant Simon Griffiths is to receive a commendation for his work on the Ho case as is DC Kenny Johnstone, who was seconded to you as a watcher. You can tell them now, but the official announcement won't be made until Wednesday."

Steve was glad his colleagues were being given recognition. All too often the senior ranks were given credit only because their junior officers had done all the work.

Commander Perry Hargreaves called everyone to order and once they were seated around his large conference table, he opened the meeting.

Steve had nothing to contribute, so sat quietly and listened, trying to look interested. He heard all about clear-up rates involving knife crime, hate crimes, auto crimes, domestic abuse statistics, even shoplifting figures. The meeting dragged on discussing drug-related offences, successes against organised crime, murder rate statistics and murder analysis. Deaths from road traffic accidents were discussed when someone brought up thefts of bicycles. By this time Steve was ready to leave. After two hours of sitting at this table surrounded by senior officers, he hadn't uttered a word.

Perry was drawing the meeting to a close when he referred to Steve. "DCI Burt has been off helping out elsewhere for a few weeks. Does anyone have anything they'd like to pass onto Special Resolutions?"

There was a general buzz around the table. No one spoke and everyone shook their heads. Perry opened a file and addressed Alister Staples. "Ally, I note your unit are sitting on seven live murder cases and from your information today, you're not making much headway with any of them."

"Oh. Come on, sir! That's a bit harsh. I told you we weren't expecting to make any arrests in the next few days on any of the current cases. I didn't say we weren't making progress."

"That's true but I see you've got a double murder on your books, two identical shootings and so far, you haven't even registered a case file number, nor appointed an SIO. Looking at the file I think it's an ideal case for Steve and his team. We need to improve our murder clear-up rate."

Superintendent Alister Staples laughed and spread his arms in surrender. "OK, sir, I give in. I know a set up when I see one. I suppose we are a bit overloaded and yes, Steve's input would be useful. I'll get the preliminaries down to you Steve. There's not much… in fact there's bugger all so you'll be starting from scratch."

Perry Hargreaves stood up and addressed the meeting. "Just so everyone knows, Steve has been on secondment for the past couple of weeks working with some very shady characters. His work was secret and that's why he has no caseload at the moment."

Steve felt himself blush slightly as he nodded to Perry and Ally. "Thank you, sir."

Satisfied all his teams were now up to date with each other's cases, Perry closed the meeting, and everyone began to filter out. As Steve was leaving Perry tapped him on the shoulder.

"You have handed everything over to MI6?"

"Yes, sir, Bob Class is on it."

"Good. You have shut everything down? You've got a double murder to deal with and no time to chase after shadows from an old case."

Steve lied. "Don't worry, sir, we will concentrate one hundred percent on this double murder case." If Steve were superstitious, he'd have crossed his fingers behind his back. He was still looking for the Romanian body with the gunshot wounds and he needed to find and speak to Major Havers about the masked gunman.

***

Once back on the eighth floor he called out to Matt Conway to come into his office. "Matt, the DC who was on the surveillance of Max Ho, you know the one who was first on the scene of the shooting?"

"Yes."

"He's getting a commissioner's commendation for his bravery. Will you contact his boss? It might be an idea if you went to see this Kenny

Johnstone and told him yourself. We won't mention his love of bacon rolls, but he did well once he knew the shooter was in Max Ho's flat."

"That's good news. He's an old-style cop. I'm not sure how he'll take it, but his family will surely be pleased."

Steve sat back. "There's more. Our very own Si Griffiths is also getting a commendation for his work with Lord Scotland. Keep it to yourself but Si arresting Lord Scotland was the catalyst that MI6 needed."

Matt laughed. "Bloody hell, Steve, there'll be no living with him."

"And I'll have to sign his retirement papers. He should be a happy man." Steve paused. "Better send him in."

Once Si was seated Steve told him about his award and said he would sign his request for early retirement. The DCI was taken aback by the cheeky officer's response.

"Well, that's something, sir. I've been in the job all these years and never had any form of recognition. Then I get dumped on you and here I am with a commendation. I don't think I'll take retirement, not just now."

The DCI was amazed by Si's attitude. He sounded as though he were debating on some BBC Four intellectual programme. "The truth is, sir, I've had so much fun in the job since working with your lot. If it's OK with you, I'll take the commendation and stay. I can tell you need my skills around here. But one point, if I decide later to go for early retirement, I need to know you'll sign off on it." Si gave a wicked grin and actually winked at Steve.

"Well, Si, I'm surprised by the thickness of your skin but pleased. I have to admit you've livened things up around here since you arrived. So yes, it's OK with me. I'm happy you've decided to stay. As for signing off on your early retirement as a given, let's see how things develop. If you are as needed as you think I may not be able to sign off on your retirement as that would mean losing you."

"Why is it I always come off second best? OK, sir, you've got a deal." Si left a happy man.

Steve went into his outer office and told everyone to grab an early lunch as they had a new case to get a start on. "Meeting, my office, at one."

***

Charlie was early. He arrived at Connie's house in Bishop's Stortford confident he could convince her to give him a chance. He was also conscious that his quest to find Sebastian De Roy had suffered because of his relationship with Connie. Doubt started to set in the nearer he got to the turn off from the M11. He wondered what he would do if she insisted, he give himself up to the police? He knew he couldn't do that. His feelings for Connie were one thing but his hatred of the two investors and their hired killer was eating him alive. Charlie knew until he had finished his killing spree, he would have no peace.

As he parked outside Connie's house, he was full of doubts. He nervously rang the bell. To his amazement the door was thrust open, and Connie sprang into his arms and started to kiss him with an unbridled passion. She continued to hold him. He had never been much of a womaniser and was unsure how to handle this suddenly amorous woman who apparently didn't care what the neighbours thought. Charlie, feeling slightly embarrassed, gently pushed Connie away.

"Wow, that's some welcome."

Without saying anything, Connie turned and retreated into her living room with Charlie following. As soon as the pair were standing opposite each other Connie once more flung her arms around Charlie.

"Slow down, Connie." Charlie once more eased the woman of his dreams away. "What's going on, I thought you hated me?"

Connie sat on her sofa looking meekly at Charlie. "Oh, Charlie, I hate you and I love you. When you admitted to me what you'd done, I was shocked and angry. All my life I've been a good law-abiding citizen. I've had no real excitement in my life but from the first Friday you walked into my office I felt you were special. You've told me you care for me, and I began to realise I care for you. I know you've been to prison, but I understand why, and I believe you. I began to think what if I were you? How would I react, and you know what?" Connie looked up at Charlie who immediately sat beside her and took her hands in his.

Sitting close to Connie Charlie felt alive. "No. What?"

"I don't think I'd have the guts to go after the men responsible. You see I'm weak. I've had no excitement in my life, and suddenly, an ex-con turns up and I fall head over heels for him. You may not know it, Charlie, but you're the most exciting thing I've ever had in my life, and I like it and I don't want to lose it."

Connie looked directly into Charlie's eyes. This time it was Charlie who took the initiative and put his arms around Connie who appeared to melt into him. He spoke to Connie, explaining all the things he'd rehearsed earlier. How they would make a new life abroad in the sun with enough money to live comfortably. He said that he felt an attraction for her he couldn't explain from their first meeting.

"OK, Charlie." Connie was excited like a schoolgirl on her first date. "I understand your need for revenge, but I want you to stop now. You've got away with it so far, but you may not be so lucky next time."

Charlie was upset to hear Connie's words. He explained again about his need for revenge. About his feelings for her, about not being whole while he harboured such anger against the men who ruined his life. "I need you in my life, Connie. We can have a fabulous life together but not while this is still hanging over me. I must see this through otherwise I'd be no good for you."

Connie turned to Charlie. Her expression had softened, and she spoke in a low voice.

"Oh, Charlie. I don't want to start a new life wondering if the next knock on the door will be the police. I thought I was happy until you walked into my office. Now here I am, prepared to accept you have broken the law."

Charlie was ready. He took Connie's hands again. "When I was inside the old lags taught me a lot. Things like never keep the same hire car for more than a few days. You know, telling me what got them caught so I wouldn't. When I'm finished, I promise no more. As soon as I get the last one, we'll fly away the same day and leave everything behind us. The police won't know who to look for and we'll be long gone. There'll be nothing to connect us to the killings. No one will know us, and my mind will be clear. My only thought will be to make you happy." Charlie hoped he wasn't laying the charm on too heavily, but he believed everything he was saying.

Connie once more reached out for him and held him tight. She could see he had a mission but wasn't sure how to react. Deep down she knew whatever this man wanted to do she'd agree to. She hadn't felt so contented or happy for years.

As they sat in each other's arms, Charlie said, "Let's go to lunch and talk about our future."

Connie pulled back slightly and with her eyes on Charlie, said, "No Charlie, take me upstairs."

Charlie stood and with more than a little trepidation took Connie's hands and climbed the stairs. He'd been in prison for eight years and hoped he would not disappoint. He also wondered if she would allow him to complete his mission.

As they entered her bedroom, Connie turned to Charlie. His mind went blank. He instantly knew he would not disappoint.

***

As Connie and Charlie were climbing the stairway to her bedroom, Steve placed a call to Sir Patrick Bond.

"Patrick, how can I get in touch with this Major Havers?"

There was silence at Sir Patrick's end of the line. Steve tried again. "Patrick, are you there?"

"Yes, I'm here. I'm trying to work out what the hell you're up to. You're finished with the Ho thing."

"Yes, I know. I just have an unrelated question for the major."

"Listen, Steve. Keep out of this, it's over. If you're seen to still be involved your career will be over and I won't be able to help you."

"Patrick, I only want to ask one question and I assure you it has nothing to do with Ho." Steve went on to explain about his previous case and the murder of his WDC, Amelia Cooper, also known as Poppy. "I think one of the major's men was there and witnessed what happened. I need to know to get closure both for myself and for her uncle. The major is the only person who knows who the hooded gunman was."

Patrick Bond was silent again. Steve held the silence knowing there was no more he could say. Eventually, Patrick spoke.

"He's retired and left the army. I don't know where he is. He's drawing his military pension so I suppose they may have an address. All I can tell you is he had an office done up to look like a shop. It's been closed down, but you might find something there to help. I think it's somewhere in Brompton Road." Sir Patrick sounded tired as though giving Steve this information had been a great strain. "If anybody asks, you didn't get any of that from me. Now, DCI Burt, I believe that concludes our business. Please do not call me again unless it's a matter of life or death."

Sir Patrick Bond hung up.

***

At one exactly, Steve began his meeting to consider the double murders.

Bob had received the files earlier and was prepared to pass on to the team what they knew. "The first victim was called Colin Clark." Bob wrote the name and using magnets, secured a post-mortem photograph of the deceased below his name. He carried on talking and writing. He was aged fifty-five, divorced, lived in Bromley. He worked as a clerk in a city firm involved in imports and exports and also part-time in a pub called the Cock and Squirrel, just off Fleet Street. He was found by a binman in an alley outside the pub. He'd been shot in the head with a .22 calibre round. There were no signs of robbery." Bob turned to his audience. "Just an unexplained killing of an ordinary bloke."

Steve sat back. "When was he killed?"

Bob looked in the file and wrote Wednesday, February 9, on the board.

"So not even a week ago. What about the post-mortem? Anything there?"

"Not really. It's all a bit lightweight as though no one was too bothered. It just says shot through the head. A bit of liver damage from too much booze over the years but that's it. No meaningful toxicology and no trace evidence. I'll run it through my PM checker. See if anything comes up or wasn't done, but on the surface, it seems an ordinary bloke who was murdered."

Matt Conway spoke up. "Well, Steve, a .22 is the calibre of choice for professional killers and it's highly unlikely an ordinary bloke with nothing to hide would finish up dead with a hole in his head." Matt paused having had a thought. "Where exactly in the head was he shot, Bob?"

Bob Class once more studied the file. "In the forehead more or less between the eyes."

Matt smiled. "There it is. He was facing his killer. I'll bet he knew his killer, and this is a revenge killing, but I don't like the choice of weapon. That suggests a professional hit."

The DCI had been listening. "Good point, Matt. Bob, do your thing with the files. Is there anything from the CSIs?"

"No, sir."

"Let's get to know Mr Clark better. Run a full background, bank accounts, the works. Check out any CCTV in the area. It's off Fleet Street for goodness' sake, the place must be crawling with cameras."

Bob Class was uncomfortable without his laptop. He hated having to refer to paper copy files. With relief he readily agreed. "Will do, sir, no problem, but Inspector Harvey might be useful in dealing with the CCTV."

"Good point, Bob. I'll have a word. Now what about our second victim?"

Bob Class placed his files on Colin Clark on the table and lifted the next set. "His name was Anthony Maple." Once more Bob wrote the name on the board and stuck a post-mortem picture below it. "He was aged fifty-one, married, lived in Bushy Park. No post-mortem results and no background details. It was supposed to be done this morning but when I phoned, they said it would be tomorrow. The path lab assistant said it wasn't urgent, but I did get her to confirm he'd been shot in the head." Looking at Matt Conway, Bob added, "The bullet entered the front lobe between the eyes, same as the first victim although we don't know the calibre of the bullet."

Si Griffiths, the newest and recently decorated member of the team, said, "Are the two connected do you think?"

Steve leant forward. "Well, without the post-mortem on the second victim and not yet having the ballistics information it's difficult to say, but the nature of the murders is very similar so yes, Si, I think our initial working hypothesis is that we are looking for the same killer." The DCI paused. "Bob, when was Maple killed?"

Bob Class once more consulted his hated paper reports. He wrote on the board as he answered. "Last Friday the eleventh. The body was found in a coffee shop toilet in York Road close to Waterloo Station."

Si gave a loud sigh. "We have two bodies, shot in the same manner probably by the same gunman, two days apart. What about forensics?"

"Like I said, nothing in the files."

Steve sat up slightly shocked. "You'd better get onto that, Bob. We need forensics and any search data. I know there was no SIO appointed to either case but who was in charge?"

"Sorry, boss, there's nothing in the files. Looks like we're starting all over again."

Si Griffiths was enjoying himself. "So, what do we do? Two bodies killed the same way, there must be a link."

Steve was patient with his DS, but he didn't want Si on these murder cases just yet.

"Good point, Si. Bob, do a full background on both victims, the works. CCTV from both locations and I'll talk with Terry Harvey. Matt, give me twenty minutes and we'll go and see Colin Clark's next of kin if he has any." Steve paused. "Bob, don't forget the financial checks and chase up forensics. Tell the mortuary we'll attend the PM on Anthony Maple tomorrow morning. Get a time. OK, everybody. That's it. Any questions?"

No one answered.

Steve rose. "I'm off to see Terry Harvey. Si, hang about, I need a word when I get back."

The suspicious detective sergeant went to sit at his desk telling himself if he didn't like what the DCI had to say, he'd put in for early retirement.

***

It had been a long time since Charlie had been with a woman, but he realised his own need was nothing compared to Connie's. She had an insatiable appetite, Charlie thought she could go on forever. Once they were showered and dressed, they sat on Connie's sofa. It took Charlie a few minutes to realise Connie had fallen asleep with her head on his shoulder. This gave him time to think about recent events. He was now certain Connie would not turn him in. He had a feeling she would do anything for him provided he continued to perform well in the bedroom.

He smiled as he recalled an inmate in Whitby prison telling him what he called his Bonnie and Clyde moment. He told Charlie he'd been seen by this woman as he knifed an old enemy. She had screamed revealing her presence. The prisoner basically abducted her to keep her quiet and after a few days together she couldn't get enough of him and finished up assisting him in his life of crime.

As Charlie sat his mind drifted to what he'd said to Connie. He knew he meant most of it but knew he couldn't differentiate between his true feelings for this woman and the rehearsed speech he thought was necessary to convince her not to give him up. He knew he would do anything to achieve his revenge but wondered if the Bonnie and Clyde idea might work. Could he convince Connie to help him? He smiled relaxing and enjoying the thought.

Connie stirred and sat up. "I'm sorry, I must have fallen asleep."

"You did but it was nice having your head on my shoulder." Charlie suggested they should go out and have a late lunch or an early dinner. He was starving.

"I'll just go and tidy up and put some make up on. You can smudge it up when we get back."

This probation officer who only a week ago was so prim and proper was now a sexual predator that Charlie hardly recognised. Her whole attitude seemed different, and she was using words that he didn't think lady probation officers knew. For whatever reason Connie O'Sullivan had changed. She was out of her shell and Charlie using basic prison psychology felt she had been liberated and he was the reason.

Over a simple bar meal at the nearest pub, Charlie tentatively approached the subject of what Connie was going to do. She looked longingly at him and smiled.

"Anything you want, my love. I've come to realise that I need you, regardless of what you've done. You are my life now; I've never felt so liberated. I believe you when you say we'll go abroad once you've had your revenge, but please, don't get caught." A slight tear appeared at the corner of Connie's eye. She stretched out and took Charlie's hand. "I've only just found you. I've really only just found myself. I couldn't bear to lose you so soon."

Charlie smiled inwardly as he told Connie everything she wanted to hear, but while Charlie's thoughts were on his next victim, Connie had been planning their future.

"I'll put my house on the market tomorrow and resign from the probation service. I'm supposed to give a month's notice, but I have over eight weeks accrued holiday, so I won't have to serve my notice." She squeezed Charlie's hand. "We can be together now. I'll be with you every step of your journey. Isn't that wonderful?" Connie was excited like a young schoolgirl might be as she went on her first date.

Charlie was over the moon at this turn of events. He hadn't expected things to develop so quickly nor for Connie to become such a willing partner.

"You mean you'll help me get to the three people I have to take care of?"

"Yes, of course my darling, I'm yours. We're a team from now on. Come on, let's pay the bill and get back home. I need you."

Almost with a groan but also with a smile on his face, Charlie left payment for the meal and followed Connie out of the pub. It wasn't yet 4 p.m. and he knew it would be a long night.

Chapter Twenty-Two

Steve arrived back from visiting Inspector Terry Harvey who, as head of Technical Support, was best placed to examine the CCTV output from both murder scenes. As he walked into his outer office Si Griffiths stood and silently followed his boss into his inner sanctum.

"Right, Si, as you are so good at finding people, I have a little project for you. There's no reward this time, just a little arrangement between you and me."

Si liked these little projects. It gave him independence and made him feel needed.

"Fair enough, sir, fire away." Si sat back and crossed his arms.

"There's a bloke called Major Havers. He's ex-army or at least is now. Up until a few days ago he was involved in the killing of your Romanian, you remember, the one Benny Stockton told you about. I think he worked for the guy you lifted at Benny's showroom, Mr Smith or Lord Scotland as he actually was."

Si interrupted and with a grin said, "Yes. I remember, I enjoyed that little caper."

Steve looked at his DS with a sad smile. "Yes, you know your Mr Smith is dead, supposedly a heart attack, so be careful, Si. These are dangerous men."

"Wow! You don't say?"

"I want you to find this major. You might get an address from army pension records, but I doubt it will be easy. He ran his unit from a shop in Brompton Road. It's closed now but it's only been a few days. There may be someone around who'll know something. That's all I can give you Si. The rest is up to you."

"What was this shop in Brompton Road?"

"I think it was an upholstery repair business."

Si Stood up. "OK. I presume anything I find is off the books and for your ears only?"

Steve smiled. "Got it in one."

***

It was almost four when Steve and Matt arrived at the Victorian terrace where Colin Clark lived with his girlfriend. Unknown to them, the killer they sought was at the same exact moment leaving a pub outside Bishop's Stortford with his girlfriend.

They rang the bell of the front door and almost immediately, an untidy, thin woman wearing a stained tight-fitting black nylon top and a black mini-skirt answered.

"If you're from the insurance you can come in. If you're not you can bugger off."

Steve stood his ground and produced his warrant card as did Matt. "I'm DCI Steve Burt, this is DI Matt Conway. We're looking into the death of Mr Colin Clark. We understand he lived here?"

The woman seemed to soften.

"Oh! I thought you were from the insurance. I filed the claim and some snotty youth phoned earlier saying Colin hadn't kept up his life insurance and the policy had lapsed." The woman was beginning to get into her stride. "I told them. He's paid in for years and…"

As gently as he could, Steve suggested they be invited in. The woman looked shocked at the interruption but agreed. She showed the officers into a neat but poorly furnished living room. Without being invited both detectives sat on the old sofa. The woman stood looking uncomfortable. She held her hands together and eventually she sat opposite the two CID officers, produced a packet of cigarettes from nowhere and lit one. She inhaled deeply and this seemed to calm her. As she visibly relaxed Steve led the interview while Matt made notes.

"We're sorry for your loss Miss…?"

"Rogers, Mary Rogers, I was Colin's partner." The woman seemed to be about to cry and took a paper tissue from a box located on a side table and dabbed her eyes. Steve thought this was a theatrical gesture. The tissue was now black from the mascara.

"Yes. Well, Miss Rogers can you think of anyone who'd want to hurt Colin? Enemies, anyone he's fallen out with recently?"

"No, Colin was a gentleman. I'm not saying he was a saint, but he took good care of me."

Steve was used to such bland answers from grieving relatives. "What can you tell us about Colin? How long had you known him?"

"Oh! Well, I was the other woman you see." Mary Rogers gave a sad smile as she drew more smoke into her lungs. Both Steve and Matt hated being anywhere near someone who smoked but this was Mary's house so they could hardly ask her to stop.

Mary continued, "When I met Colin, he worked in Totters Bank. He was the assistant manager. I got a letter from him one day saying my account was out of funds and could I call in to discuss things with him." Mary seemed to have drifted back to happier times. Her eyes glazed over as she smiled and continued. "He was a nice man and of course we're talking about eleven years ago. I was younger and even if I do say so, I could turn heads. Colin sorted out my account and as a thank you I asked if he ever took his clients to dinner."

Steve felt something had been skipped over so he interrupted Mary's flow.

"You said he sorted your account. How did he do that?"

Mary sniggered like a teenager. "When I went into his office, I could see him looking at me. You can always tell when a certain type of man fancies you. Colin went through the usual questions about income and expenditure and said he'd approve an overdraft to see me through. I was working as a hairdresser, but I was freelance and didn't have many clients."

Steve saw Matt making notes. "Please carry on, Miss Rogers."

"Well, Colin and I went out that night and pretty soon he was spending one night a week with me. He said his marriage was over and he'd leave his wife and move in with me. I still wasn't getting a lot of work, so Colin arranged for two grand a month to be credited to my account at the bank."

Once more, Steve interrupted. "Where did this money come from?"

"Colin never said. He just told me not to worry and no one would ever know."

The DCI looked at Matt who shrugged and carried on with his note taking. "Go on, please."

"When we'd been together a few months, Colin left his wife but didn't try to divorce her, not then. One day he came home early and said he'd had a bit of luck and we were going to be wealthy. He said we could both go away somewhere and live the high life."

Steve suspected this might be something to do with the killing, so he probed deeper. "When was this?"

"Oh, I don't know. We'd been together for about six months, so I suppose just about ten years ago, maybe a little less. Anyway, Colin told me he was going to stay at the bank; the windfall money he'd just invested wouldn't be seen. He told me he'd fiddled a few dormant accounts and that no one would ever find out. He said after a year or so we'd go off and start a new life."

"How much money was involved, Miss Rogers?"

"Colin said it was just over a million."

Steve raised an eyebrow. A million in stolen money could be a motive for murder. As he looked around the house, he realised this was not the living quarters of someone with that kind of money. He said this to Mary Rogers.

"Yeah, well that was Colin. He always had a scheme but this one was supposed to be real, but of course as usual it all fell apart. Not long after he'd set up some investment deal with the money, the bank decided on an audit. Everything came out, my two grand a month and Colin stealing the million."

Steve was almost sympathetic. "Hard luck. What happened?" He already knew Colin Clark didn't have a criminal record.

"There was an investigation and they told Colin if he paid the money back and resigned with no pension, the bank wouldn't press charges."

"I see. How did that work out?"

"I don't know. It took a long time to sort out. I think the company he used to invest the money went bust and the owner went to jail for insider trading, and I think Colin got the money back, but I don't know how." Mary Rogers lit another cigarette. "I suppose he must have managed to get it back because he didn't go to jail."

The DCI sat and pondered this information. Stealing a million pounds was not an everyday occurrence but where did Colin Clark put the money.

"You don't remember Colin ever telling you where he put the money?"

"No. All he said was he gave it to some investment house and the bloke he gave it to would double it. He was acting a bit strange at the time, but I put it down to the excitement of doing something right for once."

Steve was almost finished. Mary Rogers had been open and honest, and he felt he'd not uncover much more, then another question entered his head.

"Has anything unusual happened over the past few weeks?"

Mary sucked in a large amount of smoke from her cigarette before answering. "You mean apart from Colin getting himself killed?" Mary stubbed the remains of her cigarette into an over-filled ashtray.

"No, nothing, although a man came looking for Colin last week but that's not so unusual. Colin was always hiding from people he owed money to."

"Did this man say he was owed money?"

Mary sat back in the old chair. "I can't remember. I think he said he just wanted to meet up with Colin again. You know, like he was an old friend."

"What did this man look like?" Steve wondered if this was important.

"I don't remember. He could have been anybody."

"Did Colin have a study or an office here?"

Mary coughed, a combination of smoking and laughter. "A study, in this place, you must be joking!"

"Did Colin keep any papers in the house?"

Mary reluctantly stood and made her way to a floor standing unit. She scrabbled around in the top drawer for a few minutes and returned with an untidy pile of papers about an inch thick. She placed the pile in front of Steve.

"There, that's all Colin's official stuff as he called it. I found his life insurance policy in with that lot, although a fat lot of good it'll do me."

"Thank you, Mary. Can we take these papers?"

"Help yourself, they're no good to me."

Steve stood, followed by Matt. "And there's nothing else you can tell us?"

"No, but can you tell me how I'm supposed to pay the rent on this place without any money coming in now and how I can get the life insurance money I'm due?"

The DCI made placating noises and suggested social services might help.

After leaving the house both detectives agreed they smelt strongly of smoke. As they stood outside the rundown-looking property, Steve looked around. "No CCTV."

"No, I think she was telling us everything but unless Bob comes up with something we've nothing to go on. I only hope there's something in that pile of papers."

The DCI suggested they walk around the area for a few minutes, but they saw nothing that might help their investigation. Steve saw it was after five pm and knew traffic would be heavy.

"Let's get back and call it a night. We'll do the post-mortem tomorrow and visit both crime scenes and then visit Maple's widow. Maybe she'll be able to tell us more. I'll give these papers to Bob, perhaps he will find something of interest in them." Both detectives left in their pool car.

The investigation into the double murders had begun. Steve drove and dropped Matt off at a tube station for his journey home. He carried on and arrived at New Scotland Yard at just before six p.m. Traffic had been ordinary, for a damp and dark Monday evening in February, and he'd made reasonable time.

As Steve walked in, he saw Bob Class hard at it hitting keys on his beloved laptop.

"Still at it, Bob?"

Bob on seeing his boss, sat back and put his hands behind his head. "Yes, sir, I've got a load of stuff I'm putting onto the file."

"Anything interesting?"

"Well, yes there is. I'm still waiting for the background checks on the second victim, Anthony Maple, but the first guy Colin Clark wasn't what he seemed. He narrowly missed being done on an embezzlement charge about ten years ago. He worked for a bank, but they didn't press charges. Seems they got their money back and Colin was quietly removed, and he's struggled ever since. He was working two minimum wage jobs when he was killed. Apart from that there's not much on him. He had a bank account that ran practically at zero, and a credit card that he paid the minimum off on each month and he didn't own a car. The house he lives in was rented and he's two months behind with the rent. He was working two minimum wage jobs and didn't seem to own any assets." Bob looked up at Steve. "Who'd kill a guy like that, boss?"

Steve knew most of what Bob had told him but didn't admit it. Bob had worked hard and deserved some praise.

"I have no idea, Bob, but that's good work."

"I've got more. I ran the post-mortem report for Colin Clark against my own programme. It's very ordinary. Shot in the frontal lobe and death was instantaneous. He suffered from a bit of kidney and liver damage, but we already knew that. I got the scene of crime report. That was almost blank and there was nothing from the search teams. I'm beginning to think Matt Conway is right. This was a professional hit. The killer left nothing of himself behind, but why have a professional take out a loser like Colin Clark?"

Steve sat on Si Griffiths' desk facing Bob. He didn't have any answers, but an idea popped into his head. He handed Bob the papers he and Matt had acquired from Mary Rogers.

"Have a look through that lot." He explained what the bundle of papers were. "See if you can link the million he stole to anyone or anything. Go back to his bank accounts when he was working for the bank. If he nicked that million, he must have placed it somewhere. His girlfriend said he'd used some bloke who was investing it for him, and he was going to double it for him. The girlfriend said the guy who handled the money had gone bust and had gone to prison."

Bob was making notes and looking energized.

Steve carried on thinking out loud. "Check financial convictions starting say eleven years ago, Bob. It's a long shot but we might get lucky. See if anything catches your attention."

A smiling Bob Class acknowledged the DCI's instruction. "Will do, sir. Now," Bob paused. "I've got something on CCTV from the night of the first murder. It may not be anything but it's worth a look."

Steve was always amazed how many things Bob could keep current at any one time. He moved forward to Bob's desk as Bob swung his laptop towards him.

"This is footage from the traffic cameras slung over Fleet Street. Inspector Harvey processed it for us." Bob allowed the grainy images to click on until he pressed a button to freeze a particular image. "There, sir, it's not too clear but there's a man crossing the road about fifty yards from the alley beside the pub that Colin Clark worked in."

Steve saw the image but thought it could be anyone.

Bob restarted the images. "This is from another traffic camera further up the road nearer the pub alleyway." Once more Bob froze an image. "Look sir, just on the edge. It's the same man and he has crossed the road again, he's either lost or drunk. Now," Bob went through the same procedure of freeze framing and did it six times in all. "This guy walked past the entrance to the alley on both sides of the road three times. There, this is from a CCTV camera positioned on the opposite side of Fleet Street! It's looking at the pavement, but it must have worked a bit loose, there's a peripheral view of the alley." Bob used a pen to point at the screen. "There! I'd swear that's the same bloke we saw on the traffic cameras."

Steve walked back to Si's desk.

"Bob, from what you've seen, what would you say that guy was wearing?"

Without hesitation, Bob replied. "A raincoat and a cap. He kept his face away from the cameras."

"Did you pick him up coming out of the alley?"

"Yes, at exactly 8.44 p.m. The pathologist estimated time of death between eight and nine."

"Could this be our man?"

"It's possible, sir. I've asked Inspector Harvey to try and enhance the images but I'm not hopeful we'll get anything."

Steve pushed himself off Si's desk.

"So, we may be looking at our killer?"

"Could be, Bob. Right, you get packed up. Go home and we'll tackle this fresh tomorrow morning."

Both detectives walked out together. As it was Valentine's Day Steve stopped off to buy some flowers for Alison and went home to enjoy a pleasant evening with his wife and daughter.

***

Charlie, having performed valiantly and thinking of himself as a stud, was sitting in Connie's living room making calls on his mobile and using the internet to send e-mails and search the web. He'd been at it for almost an hour. He chuckled to himself. This was his Connie free time and he admitted to himself he needed a break. Connie O'Sullivan took a lot of looking after. He had left her in bed as he showered and dressed. Now she was in the shower and had promised to keep her hands off him until bedtime. He worried about this relationship. He'd achieved his aim of getting Connie on his side, but her physical demands were beginning to wear him out.

Charlie relaxed thinking of Smudger Royston. He was a forger and a very good one. He told Charlie he'd made a good living forging government and bank documents until he got greedy. He became involved with a gang of counter fitters and lost his independence. The gang were caught when they tried to pass ten thousand pounds in forged notes to purchase a second-hand car. The police were called, and the gang including Smudger were arrested and charged.

Smudger had told him how to obtain false documents. Anything Charlie might need on the outside. Passports, bank statements, driving licences, birth certificates, bank statements, even work records and references, could be had using Smudger's contacts.

Charlie had spent the last hour talking with and e-mailing some of Smudger's associates, lining up what he needed for the next stage of his plan. Originally, he only wanted to take the lives of the four men responsible for his downfall, then he added the fifth man, but once Anthony Maple had offered him money his plans had changed. He now intended to extort money from his last two financial victims. He knew how to deal with the money but needed discreet routes and banks to ensure it couldn't be easily traced. This was where Smudger's contacts had been useful. Charlie now had everything set up to handle the money he expected to be receiving very soon. He hadn't told Connie, but he vowed he would when the time was right. He thought the least she knew the better for her and him.

It was after six pm and Charlie started to think about his next victim, Sebastian De Roy. All he knew so far was that he'd moved, but to where? As he sat trying to work out how to discover Sebastian's address, Connie appeared fully dressed in a very short dress that was anything but suitable for a visit to a local restaurant on a miserable evening in February. Charlie had to admit she looked stunning and if he'd had the energy he might have surrendered to Connie's obvious advances. She was holding two glasses of white wine.

"Well, if you don't want to play, at least we can have a drink. I've booked the table for seven thirty."

Charlie readily accepted the wine as Connie sat beside him.

"Connie, you do know I have to carry on with finding the people who screwed me, don't you?"

Connie sipped her wine. "Well, of course and I'm going to help you. I told you it's just us from now on, you and me. Whatever you decide is fine by me but only until you've finished this mad quest and we leave the UK. You promised there would be no more killings once we go."

"Yes, I did, and I meant it." Charlie drained his wine glass. He wasn't much of a drinker but felt he needed fortifying. "OK, but I don't have a clue where to find Sebastian De Roy."

"I take it he's your next target?"

"Yes, but he's moved from the address I have for him. I've no idea where to find him nor where he works."

Connie leant over and kissed Charlie on the cheek. She rose from the sofa and returned carrying a laptop computer. After a few silent minutes of clicking keys, she turned to Charlie.

"Right. I'm on the probation service's database. We have access to a combination of all UK citizens whereabouts, based mostly on their driving licence, medical records, entries on the electoral roll, that sort of thing. Even people who don't want to be found usually update these records. It's one of the best things about my job, I can always find my clients. It was an initiative a few years back. The service created a super database of citizens and residents. It's all Big Brother and few people know it exists." Connie laughed as she refilled Charlie's glass and topped up her own.

"Right. The guy you're looking for is called Sebastian De Roy. Is that right?"

Charlie was amazed at how efficient this Connie was. It was as if the sex machine Connie and the office Connie were different people.

"Yes." Charlie watched as Connie input the name. He double checked the spelling and told Connie it was fine.

Connie pressed a few keys and the screen changed.

"Luckily, it's not a very common name. There are only two. One has an address in Wales the other lives on Wentworth Golf course in Surrey."

Charlie leant forward and kissed Connie.

"You're brilliant, that's him. I remember he told me once that when everything was sorted and the investments were making heaps of money, he wanted to buy a property on Wentworth. What's the address?"

"Number 12, Birdie Close, Wentworth. That's all I've got."

"My darling, that's more than enough. Tomorrow morning we'll visit Wentworth and see what's what." Charlie once more drained his glass as he looked at his watch. "Come on, for being so clever, I'll buy you the best meal Bishop's Stortford has to offer."

A happy and apparently normal couple left for the restaurant Connie had chosen. They would make plans over dinner and set out for the first time tomorrow as a criminal couple.

Chapter Twenty-Three

Tuesday, February 15, dawned with some promise of a better day. The DCI was getting depressed with the weather. As he looked from his living room window, he was encouraged that at least the weather may be improving.

As it wasn't raining, he decided to walk to his office via the usual Costa shop to buy coffee. He arrived at 7.49 a.m. to find Bob Class sitting at his desk going through the papers Steve had been given by Mary Rogers yesterday.

"I know you left last night, Bob, but did you come back in the small hours?"

"No, sir, I got here about seven-thirty, fairly normal."

Steve nodded and smiled. "Is that the paperwork I gave you last night?"

"Yes. I'm still trying to sort it out, but I have something else.
It's about the missing Romanian body you wanted me to track down, the one that the car dealer Benny Stockton told Si about, who was supposedly knocked off by a government assassin."

Steve remembered exactly and encouraged Bob to continue.

"Well, there's a body sitting in the Kent Force mortuary. It's been there for a few months and was found on the beach beside Ramsgate. The man had been shot in the back of the head with a .45 calibre round. Kent tried to investigate but with a lack of evidence put it down to an illegal immigrant incident and closed the case. The one thing they did find on the body was a receipt that turned out to be written in Romanian. A bright DC contacted the Romanian embassy, sent DNA and fingerprints and got a name back. The guy's called Viktor Lusiasic."

Steve stood up not knowing how this information fitted into the Max Ho case that he'd been ordered to stop looking into. Before he could voice his thoughts, Bob started up again.

"I haven't had a lot of time. I only got this when I got in this morning, but I did a trawl of the immigration database, you know just the superficial stuff. This Viktor arrived at Heathrow on the twenty-first of June last year." Bob looked disappointed. "That's all I've got, boss."

"That's good work, Bob. I'm not sure what it tells us but keep it under your hat. I don't think we're finished with the Max Ho case." Steve left a coffee on Bob's desk and on Matt Conway's and walked into his inner office carrying two cups. He wasn't expecting Si Griffiths to appear but had bought the fourth coffee just in case.

As he sat thinking about the Romanian, his thoughts quickly turned to the double murder.

"Bob. Any news on the post-mortem of Anthony Maple this morning?"

Bob Class shouted back. "Nothing so far, sir, I'll give them a shake."

Just as Bob finished, Matt appeared at Steve's office door holding his coffee. "Cheers, Steve, are we having a debrief?"

"Yes. Give me five minutes to gather my thoughts."

The team settled down, and Bob brought Matt up to speed on what had been discovered concerning Colin Clark's murder. Like Steve, Matt knew most of it already but didn't say. He reacted as though everything Bob said was news to him. Bob was sitting with his laptop in front of him ready to start keying.

"So, what do we know about our first victim, Colin Clark?" Steve held up his left hand and started counting off points. "One: He stole a million quid so he was no fool but that was almost ten years ago. Two: He kept his girlfriend in funds using the bank's money. Three: He was caught out and returned the money to avoid prosecution. Four: Since he was sacked from the bank, he's lived hand to mouth." Steve continued to hold up his four fingers. He stared ahead concentrating on nothing in particular. He lowered his hand. "Who on earth would kill someone like that? And where did he hide the money after he'd stolen it?"

Matt spoke up. "The manner of the killing worries me. A .22 in the forehead is a professional hit but I can't see it. Maybe ten years ago when the victim had the money, but not now. Surely nobody's going to wait ten years before ordering a hit, and who would want this guy dead anyway?"

"I agree and what about the money? The girlfriend said he'd given it to some crooked investment bloke." Steve broke off. "Any joy with the old cases involving bent financial experts that finished up doing time, Bob?"

"I've run a bit of a programme to help but nothing so far, sir."

Just as Bob finished his laptop buzzed telling him he had a message. He quickly opened the file. "The post-mortem on our second victim, Anthony Maple is set for ten. sir."

"Good." Steve looked at his watch. It was 8.31a.m. "Now, anything on the second victim, Bob?"

"I got the background and financial stuff back, but I haven't processed it yet." Bob Class was reading the information for the first time. As he stared at the screen of his laptop he spoke. "Our victim Anthony Maple was killed last Friday the eleventh. The body was found in the toilet of a small café on York Road. Like the first victim he was shot in the forehead and ballistics have come up trumps. They rushed through the bullet profiling and say it's a .22 the same as the Clark murder!" Bob looked up from his computer with a surprised look on his face. "They say the bullets are a match, they came from the same gun."

Matt Conway whistled. "Well, there goes my theory of a professional hit. A professional would have dumped the gun after the first killing."

Steve was rubbing his chin. "Maybe not if it was a rush job. It has been known for professional hits to use the same weapon."

Matt persevered. "Not very often, Steve, that's what makes them professionals."

"Yes, I take your point. What else does the computer tell us, Bob."

"He lives in Bushy Park, married with a grown-up son who doesn't live at home. Works at a boutique investment house where he's a partner. His bank account is healthy; he seems to draw over seven grand a month from the business. He has a second account with over two hundred grand in it, and he uses an Amex platinum card for all his business and personal expenses." Bob looked up again. "That's all I've got for now. The other background and more personal stuff will come in after the post-mortem."

Matt had been making notes. "So, our second victim is a lot wealthier than our first. They live in different worlds so what connects them?"

"I've no idea, Matt, but there must be something. Keep digging, Bob. Matt and I will head off to the mortuary now. Then we'll go see the widow and visit both crime scenes. I suppose Terry Harvey's still working on the CCTV from the second scene?"

"Yes." Bob held up his hand as he studied his laptop screen.

"The reports for both crime scenes have arrived." Bob silently scanned the data. "There's nothing. Neither site produced any DNA, fingerprints or any other useful evidence and no forensics. The search teams also came up empty. Seems our killer is a bit of a phantom."

"Or a professional." Steve grinned at Matt as he stood up.

"Right, let's get going. Bob, keep looking and if Si ever visits the office tell him I expect to hear from him."

Smiling, Bob Class closed his laptop. "He'll be surprised you care, sir."

***

Charlie and Connie, after a very passionate evening, woke early on Tuesday morning and decided they had to become professional if they were to succeed in tracking down Sebastian De Roy. Bedroom antics would have to be rationed. Connie said she didn't see why but agreed they needed to focus on the task Charlie had set himself.

After a quick breakfast and in order to miss most of the early morning commuter traffic, they set off in Charlie's hired Mercedes at six a.m. By the time Steve and Matt Conway were leaving to attend the post-mortem on Charlie's second victim, the pair were slowly driving around the Wentworth estate where Sebastian De Roy was said to live.

They'd discussed everything under the sun on the drive to Wentworth. Connie confirmed she had e-mailed in her notice and had a reply. Her bosses weren't too pleased but could do little about it. She had told Charlie he should continue to attend his Friday afternoon probation meetings and not admit he knew Connie. "I've seen a few offenders being caught because they got sloppy with details. You should keep going until we leave the country. It would be normal." Charlie was happy Connie had taken to her new role as his sidekick. She brought another dimension to the task. As Charlie drove, they agreed Connie would undertake the research. She would find Charlie's number one target, Geoffrey Lockwood, and research his background.

Charlie felt nervous that this woman was giving everything up for him, but he hadn't yet found the opportunity to admit he had bought a new identity from Smudger's contact, nor the new offshore bank accounts he'd set up. He also hadn't mentioned that he was to meet Smudger's contact later that day to collect his fake documents, including his new passport, driving licence and birth certificate.

As Charlie drove, they'd agreed to split up for a few days. Connie would do the research and they would buy burner phones to keep in touch. Charlie would return to his hotel and Connie to her house in Bishop's Stortford. They agreed it would only be for a few days and Charlie told Connie it would all be over by the weekend. They would be flying off to somewhere exotic early next week. Connie could hardly contain herself and her sudden passionate advance on the M25 caused Charlie to swerve into another lane much to the annoyance of the early morning drivers who called the M25 their car park.

Number 12 Birdie Close was a grand mansion. It was similar in size to all the other properties but had a detached four-car garage with living space above it. The main house was a mixture of render and natural stone whilst the front entrance was locked inside a large modern glass box. The house looked fairly new and was obviously expensive.

Charlie and Connie drove past number 12. Charlie was looking for CCTV cameras, both police and private. He'd spotted notices up as he drove through the manned security gate at the entrance saying that the whole estate was patrolled by a private security company. He'd lied his way in saying he and his wife were considering buying a property on the estate and had been told by an upmarket estate agent that on mentioning their name the guard on duty would allow them entrance. It wasn't perfect but was the best Charlie could come up with and it worked but only after Connie appeared to be upset at initially not being allowed in.

Number 12 had a large open-plan garden to the front. There was a team of gardeners working hard at maintaining the immaculate lawn and flower beds. As it was February they were mainly pruning and replanting.

Charlie spotted a small visitor car parking area a short distance from number 12. Arm in arm, Charlie and Connie approached the house. On seeing them arrive the man Charlie took to be the head gardener approached them.

"They're not in. He's at work making the money and she's out spending it. Tuesday's her day in town as she calls it. She meets her other stuck-up pals and spends a fortune. I've heard them having arguments about it."

Charlie had no idea what to do or say. Connie using all her feminine ways walked over to the gardener. His boilersuit was heavily stained, and his thinning grey hair wasn't too well combed. Connie smiled. "That's a shame. We've travelled all the way from Yorkshire to surprise them, well Mrs De Roy actually. The lawyer dealing with the probate asked my husband to deal with Mrs De Roy. A distant relative of hers has died and she's the main beneficiary." Connie gave a small sexy smile. "I don't suppose you know how we might get in touch with Mr De Roy?"

The head gardener was smitten by Connie. Charlie walked towards the pair and stood beside Connie.

"Well, I do have a phone number for him. He gave it to me in case anything happened when I was here."

Connie took on the role of an excited teenager. "Oh! If you could let us have his number that would be wonderful. We could tell him the good news and arrange to meet them both maybe even tonight." Charlie thought her bubbling performance was over the top. Still, one look at the gardener told him it was just right. Charlie was impressed by Connie's performance. She'd taken to her role of Bonnie to Charlie's Clyde better than he could have hoped.

The gardener took a small scruffy notebook from a pocket in his stained overall, fingered his way through it and with a triumphant wave designed to impress Connie he grandly announced, "Got it."

Charlie and Connie were back sitting in the Mercedes. They were both excited but knew bodily contact would have to wait. There was work to do. The pair decided to leave the estate and drive to a pub they'd seen just a few hundred yards before the main entrance to the estate. They knew it was open because a large board was being displayed stating the pub did a full English breakfast. It was 10.07 a.m.

***

Si Griffiths had spent most of yesterday afternoon trying to find Major Havers on army records. He trawled through personal data, payroll data, even pension data but there was no sign anywhere of a Major Simon Havers. Si's copper's instinct kicked in and his gut told him something wasn't right. The DCI had met this major who had been at a high-powered meeting on Sunday. Si knew he was real but where was he?

Tuesday morning had been a slow start for Si. The previous evening he'd told his girlfriend about his commendation, and she'd been delighted. So much so she'd suggested going out for the evening. They'd gone to the local pub and overeaten and drunk too much. Now Si was a hero his girlfriend didn't seem to mind he was a policeman. As the alcohol flowed, she told more and more people in the pub that her boyfriend was a police hero.

Si didn't hold his drink too well and had suffered first thing. His partner on the other hand was fresh and planning who she would phone with Si's news.

Driving with all the windows open and with his mouth feeling like it was made of fur, Si drove to Brompton Road. He arrived at 9. 56 a.m. just as Steve and Matt were entering the mortuary where the post-mortem of Anthony Maple was to take place.

Si had been told the shop that fronted as the major's office had been closed but the order had only been given on Sunday. Today was Tuesday. Si surmised that was not enough time to totally close the operation. Maybe the DCI was right, there could still be people there.

He found the shop and parked on the pavement leaving a 'POLICE ON DUTY' sign on the dashboard. After locking the pool car, he stood back examining the shop. To his amazement it was now a laundrette called, 'WASH AND RINSE'. Two men on ladders were struggling with a sign that was intended to go over the shop.

Seeing no one who looked important, Si entered the now laundrette. It wasn't big, housing just three large washing machines and two smaller tumble dryers. Si knew from his own experience as a many times married man and thus a many times single man how laundrettes worked. He instantly knew this one wasn't for real. It was too small and cramped to make money. He stood and looked around. There were carpenters and electricians working together with two painters who appeared to be painting everything that didn't move.

Si moved further into the shop. He spotted a door that obviously led to a back room but also noted it had a combination lock. Without the combination, no one could enter the back room. Si was about to leave when the door opened, and a large lady appeared holding a mug of hot liquid that Si assumed was tea.

"Yes. Can I help you? We're not open yet."

"So, I see." Si thought he'd push his luck. "I'm here to see Major Havers."

The woman who was dressed in brown tweeds and a high neck blouse, put her cup down on the countertop. "I'm sorry but there is no one here of that name."

"How long have you worked here?" Si produced his warrant card in an attempt to show some authority.

"It's none of your business… e… Sergeant Griffiths but if you must know I've been here two years."

Si knew she was lying. "So why are you converting to a laundrette?"

"The previous business went bankrupt. The premises have been acquired by a chain of laundrettes and they agreed to keep me on." This was the woman Staff Sergeant Eric Knowles, also known as Dominic Barns, knew as Mother.

"So, you don't know a Major Havers?" This lady was beginning to annoy Si.

"As I have already told you, sergeant, there is no such person here."

Si pressed on. "But when you were an upholstery business up until Sunday, a Major Havers worked from here?"

"I don't know where you get your information, but I can assure you, you are very wrong."

Si decided to bring things to a head. He noticed the tradesmen who had been working had suddenly stopped and were listening to every word. Si walked towards the door with the combination lock. "Can you open this door, please?"

"Certainly not. This is private property and unless you have a bona fide search warrant signed by a magistrate you will not be allowed beyond that door."

"For someone who works in a laundrette, missus, you seem to know a lot about the law."

She shrugged and stared Si down.

"I can call now and have half a dozen bobbies down here in five minutes and a search warrant within the hour. You see I know what this place was and if you've been here two years, I know what you are. There are civilians present." Si waved an arm taking in the tradesmen. "You know what's what, so why not save yourself a load of grief and open that door?"

Mother crossed her arms across her not inconsiderable bosom. Pulling herself up to her full height of just under six foot she stared at Si.

"Detective Sergeant Griffiths it'll take more than an ordinary search warrant to allow you to see what's behind that door. Now I'm not interested in your threats. Please leave before I call someone who will physically remove you from these premises."

The tradesmen applauded and Mother blushed. It seemed the people working on the new laundrette weren't fans of the police.

Si had been in this position many times. He knew when to back down gracefully.

"OK, missus, you win but just for my report can I have your name?"

Mother was obviously not expecting to have to give out any information. As she hesitated Si spoke up. "As someone who knows the law, you'll know it's an offence not to give your name when asked by a police officer."

Mother blushed and mumbled. "Bridget Mallory."

Si made a note in his notebook. "Thank you, Bridget, I'm sure we'll meet again." Si walked as slowly as he could from the shop. The two technicians had succeeded in installing the 'WASH AND RINSE' sign and were now testing the illumination. Standing outside the shop Si knew something was wrong. Noting that his car hadn't been towed away and was still free of a parking ticket, he set off to walk the block. The laundrette was in the middle of a row of shops with flats above. As Si walked past the shops, he came to a small narrow road that was no wider than a path, but it appeared to dissect the building giving access to the rear of the properties. He walked down this path past the depth of the building and as he came to the, end he noted a similar path went off at ninety degrees. This second pedestrian path gave access to the rear of the building that fronted Brompton Road. Si walked down this path and stopped at a metal gate built into an imposing high brick wall. He estimated this gate gave access to the back shop of the laundrette and noticed a large extension had been added that took up most of the rear garden space. None of the other shops had such an extension.

Si also noted the CCTV cameras mounted on the wall and the extension. Given what he had been told about this place he wasn't surprised. What did surprise him was the activity that was going on. Realising he wasn't achieving much, the detective sergeant decided to go into the office and talk with Bob Class. He liked young Bob and knew he was full of ideas. It was 10.49 a.m.

***

Steve and Matt arrived at the mortuary at the same moment Si Griffiths was arriving at the shop in Brompton Road. It was 9.56 a.m.

The pathologist was already there together with his technician. After the usual sanitising and dressing, Matt and Steve now suitably gowned up, walked into the vast white tiled space that smelt of formaldehyde and other not very pleasant substances. Steve was glad he was wearing a mask.

The pathologist was a jolly man who introduced himself as John Hardy. He appeared young and still enthusiastic. "Right, gents, let's begin. I hope being hardened police officers I don't have to worry about you being overly squeamish?"

Without waiting for an answer, Doctor Hardy started making the usual 'Y' shaped incision on the chest of Anthony Maple. Steve watched with interest and was amazed at the size of the victim. To Steve's mind this could have been a whale on the cutting table rather than a human being.

Doctor Hardy talked as he worked and often made reference to Maple's size. After about thirty minutes and having valiantly dealt with the layers of fat that appeared to surround every organ, he declared himself satisfied and the post-mortem was complete.

"You'll get my formal report later in the day but there's no doubt your victim died from a gunshot to his frontal lobe. Death would have been instantaneous, and shooting might have done him a favour. His liver and kidneys were about to give up and he had enough fatty tissue around his heart to guarantee an imminent full blown heart attack. Your man was a walking corpse." Doctor Hardy was washing his hands as he added, "I got the bullet out yesterday morning and sent it to ballistics. You should get something back very soon. I know you policemen are always in a hurry."

"Thanks, Doc. We already have the report. Has the body been identified?"

John Hardy looked at his technician. He was a small man of Asian ancestry.

"Yes. His wife was here on Saturday morning."

Satisfied he would learn no more, Steve thanked the pathology team and he and Matt Conway left to visit the newly widowed Mrs Maple.

Chapter Twenty-Four

Charlie and Connie were hungry so ordered a full English breakfast. Connie was still on a high after her adventure at playing her part. As they waited for their food she continued to giggle.

"That was fun, Charlie, I'd no idea being with you would be so exciting and different."

"Yeah, well, we know where he lives but I've no plan worked out to get to him." Charlie wasn't in the mood for Connie's childish actions.

"We've got his number." Seeing her boyfriend had become so serious Connie suggested, "Why not call him? At least find out where he works."

Charlie immediately came out of his fog. He leant across the table and kissed Connie just as their breakfasts arrived. "You're brilliant, why didn't I think of that?"

They ate their breakfasts mostly in silence. Charlie was hatching a plan. Once the table had been cleared the couple were left drinking the remains of their coffee.

"Right, Connie." Charlie took out his burner mobile. "Give me that number."

Connie called out the numbers and Charlie keyed them into his phone. The number was answered after four rings by an upmarket female voice.

"Starling, Bradshaw and De Roy. How may I direct your call?"

Charlie was ready for this. He'd thought it through as he ate his full English.

"Yes. I wonder if you can help. I understand you are an investment house?"

"That is correct. We specialise in helping clients realise the full potential of their wealth."

"Good. I have a modest amount to invest, and I was recommended to speak with your Mr De Roy."

"I see." The cultured voice suddenly became suspicious. "Mr De Roy deals with the top ten percent of clients. I think it unlikely he would be the partner you'd be dealing with." After a slight pause the voice was back. "How much money are you looking to invest?"

From the conversation so far, Charlie had realised he'd have to exaggerate to get onto Sebastian De Roy's radar.

"Well, I was hoping to spread my bets but if I placed everything with you, I'd be investing north of one hundred million."

Charlie looked over at Connie who giggled. She was still having fun.

"Oh, I see." The educated voice suddenly became warm and friendly. "My apologies, I'm sure Mr De Roy would be only too pleased to act as your advisor. May I suggest I arrange a meeting for you? Could we say tomorrow morning?"

"That sounds perfect."

Charlie gave a false name and a fictitious address. The voice told him the firm occupied the entire tenth floor of the Hastings Centre Building just off the Strand. An appointment was made for the next day at nine thirty. As Charlie hung up, he smiled inwardly. Wednesday February 16 would be Sebastian De Roy's last day on Earth.

The couple went to Charlie's hotel to discuss their plans. They bought two burner phones on the way. Connie took the opportunity to tell Charlie she'd miss him over the next few days, and she felt one last afternoon of passion would be good for them.

"Something to hold onto." Connie had struck a provocative pose by the bedroom door.

Charlie, telling himself he was only human, followed this woman he'd met just over a week ago. Things were happening too fast. He needed to slow things down. But how?

***

It was 12.29 p.m. as Steve and Matt Conway rang the doorbell of Anthony Maples' plush residence in Bushy Park. Coincidentally, this was the same time Charlie was having his clothes ripped from his body in his hotel room.

A buxom woman in her mid-fifties answered the door. It was clear she had been crying. The DCI introduced himself and Matt.

"May we come in?"

The woman stood aside and ushered the detectives through the front door into a large hallway. From behind her guests, Mrs Maple called, "It's the second door on the right."

Steve and Matt followed the instructions and entered a large comfortable lounge. At its centre was an ornate fireplace in front of which were three sofas completing the square.

Mrs Maple followed the officers and a little awkwardly suggested they sit.

"We are very sorry for your loss, Mrs Maple." The DCI didn't like these interviews.

"Thank you, inspector, the police have been very kind."

Steve examined this widow. She wasn't dressed in black but was wearing an expensive casual pink coloured trouser suit. Her face was heavily made up while her dyed blonde hair looked as though her hairdresser had just left. The redness around her eyes was the only sign she was in mourning. She sat opposite the detectives and removed a handkerchief from her trouser pocket. She started to fiddle with it and Steve thought this was a sign she was nervous.

"I'm the senior investigating officer looking into the killing of your husband. Please rest assured, we will do everything we can to find his killer." This was the DCI's standard statement.

Mrs Maple nodded and in a weak voice muttered a thank you.

"We know your husband was in finance. Can you tell us anything about his work?"

The widow gave a sad smile. "Tony was always into money making schemes. I think he was good at it, but he worked hard. He was a partner in Holland and Squires. He'd known Frank Holland since university. All I know was he invested other people's money for them."

"Do you know what he invested in and what sums were involved?"

"No. You'd have to ask Frank."

"Yes, we will. What can you tell us about your husband? Did he have any enemies for example?"

Mrs Maple looked shocked. "No, of course not, Tony was well liked. He ate and drank too much. He liked his nights at the pub and being in the pub quiz team, but it was all harmless."

"Is there anything in his past that might cause him to have been killed? You see, Mrs Maple, we don't think this was a random killing."

"Oh! You mean someone singled him out and had a reason to kill him?" The widow sat back on her sofa clearly shocked by this news.

"Yes, so anything you can think of from your husband's past would help."

Mrs Maple sat staring at them in confusion. She seemed to control herself as she searched her memory banks.

"No, there's nothing. I know Tony made a few mistakes earlier on in his career and he once told me once he'd been lucky not to have been investigated for doing deals, he really shouldn't have but that was all in the past. He's been with Holland and Squires for almost nine years now and they are as straight as a die."

"Can you think back to anything specific from his past, anything that was big enough to worry him at the time? Anything you can think of will help."

Mrs Maples considered. She was twisting her handkerchief around her fingers.

"No, nothing, he didn't really discuss his work with me." She sat still; her eyes seemed to lose focus as she thought back. "I suppose there was the incident just before he joined Frank Holland's firm. I know he was worried, but I don't know the details." As Mrs Maples thought back her recollection became clearer.

"Yes, that was it. He said he'd met some high-powered city type who was using a small investment manager to invest in sure things. Tony told me he'd put a lot of his clients' money with this individual but it quickly all went wrong. He was in danger of losing a lot of his clients' money. I don't know the details, but I know he was worried. I think the financial advisor went to jail. That was the time he decided he didn't want to be independent any longer and joined Frank Holland. I remember he told me it was safer. He didn't like the people he'd become mixed up with."

"Did he mention any names?"

"No, but I know he was frightened of the man in the city. I remember he once referred to him as ruthless."

Steve was beginning to see a pattern.

"What about the man who went to jail? Do you remember anything about him?"

"No. Tony said he was a patsy. He felt sorry for him, but he had to look after himself. From the way he spoke this person didn't do much wrong but when the scheme they'd been involved with went wrong, Tony got out."

Matt had been making notes in his notebook and looked up. "Can you remember the date your husband told you this?"

"No. It must have been nine years ago. Probably the first half of the year but I can't be sure. Sorry."

Steve was finished. He'd learnt a bit but was excited by the coincidence that an independent financial advisor had gone to prison around nine years ago. There was a similarity to the Clark case and he wondered if this was what connected both murders.

"Did your husband have a home office here?"

"Yes. He had a study at the rear. Do you want to see it?"

"If we may, Mrs Maple. There may be something in his papers that will tell us something."

Everyone stood up and the widow showed Steve and Matt into her husband's study.

"I've no idea what's in here but you're very welcome to take whatever papers you think might help. I'll be in the lounge. Unless you need me for anything please show yourselves out."

The room wasn't as big as Steve thought it might be. There was an oversized desk against the window wall affording a view over the garden. There were bookshelves crammed with books and a solitary filing cabinet made of metal but designed to look like wood.

"You go through the cabinet, Matt; I'll have a rummage through the desk."

Both detectives set to and after fifteen minutes decided there was nothing of interest. Matt having gone through the filing cabinet said, "Nothing, Steve. Old bank statements, letters, TV licences going back years, he's even got utility bills from ten years ago, but nothing that seems to help us.

"The desk is full of paper but nothing that jumps out." Steve stood from behind the desk.

"Come on. Let's go and look at the crime scenes. Maybe get a feel for our killer. I've got something going on in my head, but I can't make sense of it. We need another briefing but above all else, I need a caffeine boost." Steve and Matt left Mrs Maple at 1.44 p.m. to drive to the two crime scenes.

***

Half an hour later Connie climbed into a taxi that would take her to the train station and then to Bishop's Stortford.

Charlie's meeting with the forger was set for three. He withdrew five thousand pounds from the money he had deposited in the hotel safe, dressed in what he now regarded as his killing uniform and set off for the terraced house in Stratford.

He arrived at exactly three and was shown into a neat but small living space. The forger, who referred to himself as Rex, took Charlie through the house and into a large garden shed located at the bottom of the average sized garden.

Rex was a small, untidy man who smelt heavily of sweat. He stood only about five foot five inches tall and was dressed in a pair of heavily stained corduroy trousers and a long sleeve shirt that had once been white.

"Right, money first." Rex held out his ink-smudged hand. Charlie handed over an envelope containing the money, and after counting it twice, Rex visibly relaxed.

"Now. I've got everything prepared. All I need is a photo for your driving licence and passport."

Rex opened the top drawer of an old and bashed metal cabinet and withdrew an expensive looking Nikon digital camera. He was clearly an expert. In less than five minutes he had produced images of Charlie that he used to complete his driving licence and passport. Rex excused himself for five minutes. "My equipment's in the house. I just need to finish these off."

True to his word, Rex returned with a large brown envelope. He and Charlie sat opposite each other on wooden fold-up chairs.

Rex emptied the contents of the envelope onto his lap. "First: Your birth certificate. Unless anyone checks with Somerset House this will pass any scrutiny. It's a copy of a legitimate certificate. I've changed the name." He held it up to show Charlie and slipped it into the envelope. "Your new name is Edwin Somerset. You're thirty-seven years old and you were born in Birmingham. Second: Your driving licence is not registered at DVLA. I haven't had time to hack their system, so I suggest you drive on your own licence until I get you the final one. Give me a couple of days. Only use this one for identification, don't hand it over to a traffic cop if you're stopped. Got it?" Rex dropped the licence into the envelope.

"Yes."

"Your passport is real. I've changed the name and the photograph but if anyone looks at it, they'll see the real thing. It was lifted a few months back and I've hacked into the passport office database and changed the name and photograph so you should be OK with this." Rex placed the passport into the envelope. "Right. That's you done. I'll only see you once more when you collect your driving licence. Apart from that I'll never see you again unless you want more documents like a National Insurance number, but I charge a lot for that.

Rex stood and showed Charlie out of his shed, through his house and out into the street.

The next part of Charlie's plan was now a reality. After Monday, Charles Robb would no longer exist. Edwin Somerset would be born. He had enough fake documents to set up his new identity.

***

Steve and Matt, having visited both crime scenes, returned to New Scotland Yard at 3.26 p.m. Bob Class was as usual busy on his computer and Steve was surprised to see Si at his desk.

"Bob, find anything?"

"Not really, sir. A few loose ends tied up. The post-mortem report on our second victim is in but you know what it says. The toxicology was negative, and everyone's drawn a blank."

"Thanks, Bob. Would you get the coffees, we'll have a briefing in ten minutes?"

Bob smiled as he set off for the canteen.

Steve turned to Si. "Come on in, Si. I need a word."

Si Griffiths followed his boss into the inner office and closed the door.

"How are you getting on with the major?"

Si took a chair from the conference table and sat opposite the DCI.

"I haven't made a lot of progress. I visited the shop on the Brompton Road, and I tell you something. If that operation has been closed down, I'm a Scotsman. They're refurbishing it as a laundrette, but all the security kit is still in place. I asked to see the back shop, but they refused. There's some fearsome woman in charge but she had officialdom written all over her. If you ask me all they've done is close down on Sunday and are reopening on Tuesday. I think your major is still there and working."

"Bloody hell, Si, do you realise what you're saying?"

"Yes and no." Si didn't see what the DCI saw.

"All the bull we were given when the commissioner and the minister were at that meeting was a load of rubbish. Sir Patrick has clearly lied to everyone." Steve paused and examined his DS. "What do you propose?"

Si's chest expanded. He'd never been asked this question by a senior officer before. He felt important.

"Well, sir. That giant of a woman annoyed me. I'd like to go in mob-handed with a search warrant and tear the place apart. There's no way it can run as a laundrette. Something's going on behind the scenes. If your major is there, we'd be able to round him up and put a stop to whatever activities they're up to."

"Did you try any other way of finding the major?"

"Yes, but they were all dead ends. The MOD told me they'd no record of a Major Simon Havers."

Steve didn't like Si's search warrant plan but thought it the most direct way of smoking out the major and learning what was going on.

A knock on the door stopped the conversation as Bob and Matt entered carrying the coffee.

"Si. Let me think about it. Meantime you'd better sit in on this."

With everyone seated, Steve began. The whiteboard had been updated by Bob.

"Right. We have two murders, both using a .22 calibre pistol and we now know both victims were shot with the same gun. It's not a big jump to assume we're looking for the same killer. Our victims were different. One was living hand to mouth and the other fairly affluent. However, they may be linked by a scam from a few years back."

Steve went on to explain about Colin Clark investing the money he stole and Anthony Maples' sudden need to be employed after he'd got into trouble by investing with what his widow described as a fall guy.

"Something happened around nine years ago that both men may have been part of. They appear to have invested money with an independent advisor who went to jail, and they were lucky to get their money back. Mrs Maples confirmed this earlier today and Colin Clark's girlfriend said the same thing." Turning to Bob, Steve asked, "Any joy with the old fraud cases, Bob?"

Bob looked at his boss with an embarrassing smile. "No. Sorry, sir. You'd be surprised how many financial crimes there are. There must be over a hundred a year that go through the courts. Trying to isolate one in particular is impossible unless we have definite facts."

Steve had an idea. "Bob. Put everything on a disk or a stick. I may know someone who can help."

Bob nodded and made a note.

"Now. Both victims…" Bob Class's laptop pinged indicating he had a message. The DCI was about to continue when Bob held up his hand.

"Sir, Squadron Leader Max Ho is dead. He was being escorted from hospital to Heathrow when he slipped and fell from the hospital fire escape. Seems the officers escorting him were told to use this exit rather than the hospital's main entrance."

Steve sat back not believing a word of it.

"Bloody hell, Steve. What's going on?" Matt Conway looked shocked.

"I'm not sure, Matt. Let's leave that just now and concentrate on our double murder. As you said, a .22 calibre round in the forehead has all the marks of a professional killing, but who'd order a hit on these two?"

"Could it have something to do with this investment scam?" Bob was feeling confident enough to offer an opinion.

"I'm not sure, Bob, but if it is, why wait nine or ten years and who could be behind it? From what we know both victims were independent. One worked for a bank and embezzled a million, the other seems to have invested clients' funds with the same bloke. That's the only connection but we don't know who they invested with. All we know is he was found guilty of some financial crime and was sent down. According to the ladies left behind he was seen as a patsy but who was pulling his strings? From what we know of our victims, it's unlikely to have been either of them."

Matt was doodling in his notebook. "So, you think we're looking for someone further up the tree. Someone who put a fraud together and used this invisible investment bloke as the fall guy when it all went wrong?"

"It has to be a possibility."

The room went quiet while everyone absorbed Steve's and Matt's analysis.

Si, with a wicked grin on his face, spoke up. "It's not my case but from what you've said you're thinking both killings were contracted because of the weapon and the method of shooting. Correct?" Everyone nodded so Si continued.

"Suppose it's not professional, but pure revenge. Suppose it's this patsy getting his own back? After all, if he were set up and did time, he might want his revenge."

Steve saw the signs that Si may be onto something. "Go on."

"Well, if you've been inside, you meet all sort of different crooks. What if our patsy asked about guns and how to get revenge from the people he met inside? The advice he got could look like a professional hit only because that's how he's been told to carry out a hit. Maybe that's why he used the same gun."

Matt volunteered a question. "Where would he get the gun? A .22 pistol isn't your normal street weapon. That's specialist because it's the professional's weapon of choice."

The DCI nodded. "Good point, Matt."

Si came back. "Listen. If you want, I can put some feelers out. I know a few gun dealers who might like to talk to me. If we find the supplier of the gun and he remembers who he sold it to, we'll have our man."

"But only if he's an amateur. If he's a professional we'd have to find who ordered the hit."

Si smiled again. "Look, Bob's been looking at convictions from eight to ten years ago based on the timeline given by the girlfriend and the widow. Is that right, Bob?"

"Er. Yes, sarge."

"How about looking at people released from prison say in the past two months, those that were inside for financial crimes? If this is revenge for what happened all those years ago, chances are our killer has only recently been released and has had an education on how to kill while he was inside."

Steve looked at Bob and instantly knew he'd been wasting Bob's time.

"Good thinking Si. Bob, how soon can you do that?"

"I'll have to apply to the parole board for release data. It should only take a few hours once I get the data. If I sweet talk them, we could be looking at something by tomorrow at this time."

"Good. That's your priority, Bob."

Si Griffiths was feeling pleased with himself. He felt he'd contributed to this inquiry and maybe he would solve it if he found the gun dealer.

Steve finished his coffee. His team were restless and ready to leave before he called them once more to order. He wanted to involve them in the search for the major but suspected it was not a simple search. Steve was afraid Si had uncovered something and knew he would have to follow it up. But involving his team in another unauthorised investigation might not be too helpful for their careers if things went wrong. He debated with himself before making a decision.

"Can you all hold on for a minute? I want to tell you something but if you feel you don't want to be part of anything I'm about to say then I will understand." He looked at his team.. It was obvious they were all ears. "There's something else I think you all need to know. I've always told you everything that's going on when I could. I asked Si and Bob to look into things not related to our murders, but to the old Max Ho case. Now Bob has told us Max Ho has been killed, and I'm not convinced it was an accident, so I asked Si to track down Major Havers. He was the officer in charge of a government assassination squad."

"What! Is that possible?" Si didn't know his target ran an assassination operation.

"Yes, Si, it is. I know you weren't around but during a previous case one of their operatives was present when Poppy was killed."

Si looked confused and Matt explained who Poppy was and the events that led to her killing.

"I want to meet this gunman and learn what he knows of the events on that day. After all, he was there and had to work for the major. That's why I gave Si the job. I want to talk to the major. On Sunday I was at a meeting with MI6, the commissioner and the Minister for National Security. At that meeting I was told Major Havers' unit was to be stood down with immediate effect. I was told he'd resigned his commission but would retain his pension rights, and these units would no longer exist."

Steve paused to survey his audience. Satisfied he had their full attention he continued. "Si visited the major's old office and is convinced it is still in operation. If Si is right, then the Sunday meeting was a whitewash job. We've been lied to." Steve nodded to Si. "Si, would you like to explain?"

Si launched into his story, leaving nothing out. He finished with his thought that a good search of the place would reveal a lot of interesting information.

Matt Conway spoke. "Steve, sir." Steve knew, when Matt called him sir, he had something important to say. "We've been warned off the Max Ho thing, it's closed. Bob has sent all the files over to MI6. If you're seen to still be working on it all hell will break loose."

As always Matt was right. "Yes, Matt, I appreciate that, but we were stood down based on the major retiring and his unit closing down. If Si is right, the unit is still going. It's state sponsored murder and we were duped. I bet no one looks into Max Ho's death and that the major's goons were responsible."

Matt shrugged. "OK. You're the boss. What do we do?"

"I'm not sure. Bob has found the body that started the whole thing. You remember Si found that car dealer, Benny Stockton. It was Benny who said Lord Scotland had arranged to get rid of a Romanian who was giving him trouble."

"Yes. So, we know who was killed and we think the major is still in business. So, what do we do?" It was unlike Matt to show his frustration.

"If we get a search warrant, we'll have to admit we're investigating, so I don't want to go down that route, but I like the idea."

The four detectives sat in silence until Bob Class spoke up.

"There may be a way." He spoke very slowly and deliberately. "I heard that if we apply for search warrants using national security as the reason the whole process is shielded. In other words, we're not required to broadcast the reason because it involves national security."

Steve looked astounded. "But we still need a judge or a magistrate to sign off on it. Don't we?"

"Yes, but there's a special panel. If we ask, we get. No questions asked."

"Bob, you're a genius." Si was smiling and slapped the table. "Bloody brilliant. What do you think, boss, do we go for it?"

Steve sat back thinking. He had no authority to investigate the major. He didn't even know if Si was right, but the killing of Max Ho bothered him.

"Bob. You're sure this is legitimate? Surely someone must know if we apply for a search warrant?"

"Only the person who signs off on it. I suppose eventually it might come out if we make an arrest, but I'm told it's all very secret."

"Si, you are sure about this? The Brompton Road place is still active?"

"As far as I can tell. Yes."

This sounded good to Steve, but he was concerned about what might happen if word got out. He could hardly confide in Perry Hargreaves and his gut told him Sir Patrick Bond was involved. He knew he had to be careful.

"Let's sleep on the warrant issue. We'll discuss it tomorrow. Bob, you've got your jobs. Find out about the recent releases of all men involved in financial crimes and get more info on these search warrants based on national security. It sounds too good."

Bob made notes on his laptop.

"Si, check out the gun dealers you were talking about. See if you can find someone who sold a .22 pistol. We need to get a move on with these murders."

"Will do. What about the major?"

"Leave him for now. Matt, we'll swing by Brompton Road and have a look. Let's call it a day. We'll meet tomorrow at say one to see where we are. Matt and I will visit the offices of Holland, Squires and Maple tomorrow morning first thing. See if his work colleagues can tell us anything."

Chapter Twenty-Five

Wednesday, February 16 was another dull, grey day. Rain threatened as Steve arrived at New Scotland Yard at 8.31 a.m. He cleared his desk of the usual and seemingly endless paperwork that must be important to someone. Matt arrived having booked out a pool car and at 9.11 a.m. the two detectives set out to visit the offices of Holland, Squires and Maple.

***

Just as the detectives left the underground car park at the Yard, Charlie was getting out of a taxi outside the Hastings Centre building located off the Strand. Charlie had not dressed to impress but wore his killing uniform of shabby raincoat and flat cap. Beneath his raincoat he was wearing a new suit bought at a Primark store yesterday evening. Thinking back to the advice he'd received while inside prison, Charlie knew a cheap new suit could be disposed of if he felt he had left any fibres or other material that could allow police forensics to link him to the scene.

After paying off the taxi, Charlie entered the glass-fronted building. To his surprise there was only an information desk manned by an elderly man in a security guard's uniform. There didn't seem to be any check-in procedure. When Charlie asked the elderly guard for Starling, Bradshaw and De Roy, he was directed to the bank of elevators that took up one entire wall of the foyer. "They're on the tenth floor, guv, so take the lift. They have their own reception up there."

Noting the position of the CCTV cameras and the bank of monitors behind the guard, Charlie took extra care to avoid showing his face. He kept his cap firmly pulled over his head.

Charlie did as instructed and exited on the tenth floor to see a hive of activity. People carrying files or on their mobile phones seemed to be dashing everywhere. Charlie walked to the large semi-circular reception desk and told the very attractive receptionist he had a nine thirty appointment with Mr De Roy.

The receptionist looked Charlie up and down. Clearly his dress sense wasn't what she was used to. If asked, Charlie was prepared to say he was an eccentric and didn't believe in dressing up. However, the receptionist quickly gathered her composure, checked he had an appointment and asked the scruffily dressed potential new client to take a seat. "Mr De Roy's personal assistant will be with you shortly."

Charlie sat in a comfortable leather tub chair for a few minutes before an elderly lady appeared.

"Good morning, Mr Canning, I'm Monica, Mr De Roy's PA. Would you like to follow me please?"

Charlie was shown into a plush corner office that was easily four times bigger than his hotel suite. Sebastian De Roy was seated behind an oversized desk speaking on the phone. He smiled at Charlie and waved him to a series of chairs in the far corner of the office. Monica asked if he would like some refreshments. Charlie declined. Fingerprints could be taken from cups. Charlie had been careful not to leave any fingerprint evidence behind even using the tip of a small pencil to press the tenth-floor button in the elevator. He looked around the office and saw no CCTV cameras. Whilst waiting in reception he'd only seen one camera covering the reception area. Charlie had been careful to keep his face turned away from it.

Monica smiled and left. Before Simon De Roy finished his telephone call, Charlie slipped on a pair of skin-toned disposable gloves and removed his cap. He sat waiting.

"Sorry about that, Mr. Canning. The Far East operates in a different time zone. This is the best time to catch my Oriental colleagues." De Roy came bounding over to shake Charlie's hand and was visibly taken aback when he realised Charlie was wearing gloves.

Sebastian De Roy had changed in the intervening years. He almost seemed younger. His athletic body was dressed in an expensive Savile Row suit and his shirt was obviously hand made. His carefully combed hair was cut in a youthful style and any hint of grey was covered by an expensive and natural looking dye. His face was tanned a deep brown leading Charlie to think Sebastian De Roy had recently been on a winter holiday.

"I have a skin condition. It's not serious but it can be infectious. I have to wear these to protect other people." Charlie had practised this lie.

"I see." Sebastian had met all sorts of rich obsessive clients. A skin condition wasn't new to him. "Anyway, Mr. Canning, I understand you want us to look after your wealth. Allow us to grow your money?" Sebastian De Roy said this with an air of arrogance bordering on boasting. "I understand you have a considerable amount to invest with us?"

Charlie had thought about playing along and keeping this man talking but being so close to one of the main people responsible for his present circumstances, anger took over.

"Well, Sebastian." Charlie paused, and De Roy looked slightly taken aback by the use of his Christian name. "I'm not really looking to invest. I'm actually here to make a withdrawal."

De Roy instantly looked confused. "I'm sorry? I was led to believe you were a serious investor, and this is not a bank. There must be some mistake. To the best of my knowledge, we have not done business with you in the past and there is certainly no question of you making a withdrawal."

Sebastian De Roy was clearly disturbed. This untidy individual wasn't what he expected. He continued in what Charlie thought was a very condescending tone.

"Mr Canning, I don't think you understand who we are. I was certainly expecting someone else. Perhaps there is another Mr Canning waiting to see me." De Roy made to stand indicating the meeting was over.

Charlie remained seated and produced his pistol which he pointed at Sebastian De Roy. Sebastian went pale and began to stammer. "Now look here. I don't know what…"

"Be quiet and sit down. You don't recognise me, do you?"

De Roy sat staring at the gun and only casually glanced at Charlie's face. His voice was quivering. "No. No, I don't think we've met."

Once Charlie outlined their previous business relationship Sebastian De Roy now knew exactly who his visitor was. The pair sat in silence, De Roy still staring at the pistol.

In a low trembling voice, he asked, "What do you want? Are you going to harm me?"

Charlie had prepared for this part of their encounter. "If you do as I ask, I'll let you live. But if you try and be clever, I'll shoot you like the dog you are. Understood?"

De Roy nodded and continued to stare at the weapon. He didn't know how to handle this situation, but he knew he had to do something. With sweat forming on his top lip Sebastian De Roy gathered himself together.

"I'm pleased to see you are out of prison, Charles, and believe me when I say I tried everything I could to come to your aid, but it was the others you see. They became frightened for their own skin and their money. I had nothing to do with what happened to you." Sebastian continued to stare at the gun. "Now, unless you put that thing away, I'll have to call security and that could be very unpleasant."

Charlie had expected such a plea but not the apparent composure being shown by his victim.

"Sebastian, I don't believe a word of it." Charlie allowed his anger to show. "You're as corrupt as the others, probably more so. You and your crooked friends have taken everything from me. My life, my family and probably even my sanity. Eight years locked up."

De Roy looked frightened as Charlie continued his tirade.

"Being in prison does things to a man, bad things. Eight years rotting away knowing you're innocent. It's not good and it festers revenge, Sebastian. I need to see you suffer as I have suffered."

De Roy was not so composed now he began to believe his life might be at risk.

"Now, Charles, don't do anything rash. I was your friend. The only one who wanted to help you." The veneer of composure and arrogance was slipping as De Roy pleaded. "Please, Charles, don't shoot me. I'll give you anything you want."

Charlie smiled a cold smile as he allowed his anger to subside. "What would you say was fair compensation for eight years of a man's life?"

Sebastian De Roy didn't answer.

"When I was in prison, I used to wonder how much my life was worth. I calculated a nice round one hundred thousand a year. Do you agree that's a fair sum, Sebastian?"

De Roy mumbled something Charlie couldn't understand.

He tried again but in a louder, firmer voice. "Don't you agree, Sebastian?"

Sebastian was clearly in shock and terrified. "Yes! Yes! Anything. I mean I suppose so."

Charlie was playing the cool and collected injured part. "Good. So, eight years in prison plus my time on remand, that comes to a nice round nine hundred grand." Charlie paused to look at his victim. Sebastian had turned red and was perspiring heavily. He sat still looking at the gun."

"Then there's the compensation for my family. We would have had easily fifty years together, but you took those years away as well. I haven't calculated a figure, but I think a million pounds seems fair. Don't you agree, Sebastian?"

Sebastian De Roy was beginning to see where this was going. He was very frightened and hated guns, but he could see Charlie was after money.

"I suppose it's money you want." Sebastian was losing his fear. He began to believe money would buy his life. He understood the power of money and suddenly his old arrogance returned. He looked at the pistol. "Is that thing even loaded? I remember you from ten years ago when I first came to you. You were weak and greedy. Little people like you don't change. It's all about the money. How much do you really want?"

"Nice of you to assassinate my character, Sebastian, and yes, this gun is loaded and has already been used twice. I will kill you if I have to." Charlie made his voice cold and calculating as he drew the pistol over Sebastian's body, allowing it settle for a few seconds on his more vital organs.

"Now, let's get back to the money." Charlie saw Sebastian's resolve begin to weaken. He'd tried and failed to intimidate Charlie who produced from his raincoat pocket a plastic clear bag from which he took a piece of paper. He pushed it over the coffee table that served this seating area. "On there are bank details. I want you to transfer two million pounds to that account and I want it done now."

Sebastian was thinking furiously. He'd initially been very scared but had recovered and tried to appear brave. He decided that Charles Robb wasn't a killer and all he wanted was the money. Sebastian hatched a plan that satisfied him.

He thought, "Give this madman what he wants and immediately call the police. The money would be returned under new international banking protocols. That would get rid of him, he wouldn't get the money and he, Sebastian, would be safe." Suddenly he felt better. He tried one more time to be brave.

"I don't have the authority for a transfer of this size. I'd have to get it approved by our treasury department."

Charlie saw this bluff coming. He raised the gun. "That's a pity, Sebastian. You see, no money, no life, I'm afraid I'll have to shoot you right here."

Charlie's act convinced De Roy that he was serious. He thought he was close to death and was in a combined state of shock and panic. As a partner he had unfettered access to the business's funds. Knowing he had no choice he reluctantly stood and returned to his desk.

"No funny business, Sebastian. The first hint you've contacted security or the police, I will kill you. Only order up the transfer. Nothing else."

Sebastian, hands shaking, sat in front of his computer and started to hit keys. Three minutes later he walked back to Charlie and handed him back his paper. He knew he had his plan, and that Charles Robb would soon be gone.

"All done. Now will you please leave? Your money is on its way to your bank in the Cayman Islands. I presume our business is over and I will not see you again."

"Not quite, Sebastian." Charlie removed his burner phone. "Until this gives me a message from the Caymans that the money has arrived, we're staying here. I'm told it should be almost instant. If you've tried to con me, I'll know in the next minute."

Sebastian knew he had sent the funds but the tension in the room mounted until Charlie's phone pinged. With a smile Charlie stood.

"Come on, Sebastian, I'll buy you a coffee." From Charlie's actions with the pistol, it was clear this was not a suggestion but a command.

Despite Sebastian's protests that he had work to do and was busy, he knew Charlie had the gun and that gave him the upper hand. With Sebastian leading the way and Charlie following holding the gun in his right hand in his raincoat pocket, the pair exited the upmarket Hastings Centre building.

Sebastian De Roy was angry at this unexpected turn of events.

"Where are we going? You've no right to kidnap me like this. You've got your money."

Charlie, holding the gun, had to nudge De Roy in front of him although he didn't want to attract attention from passers-by. De Roy was clearly upset and angry and talked in his defence the whole time. Charlie knew the power he wielded by having the gun, but so did De Roy and he reluctantly continued walking.

As they approached a slightly seedy hotel situated about half a mile from the Hastings building, Charlie told Sebastian to walk down the ramp to the hotel's underground car park. The whole building was being prepared for renovation. Apart from a few contractors' vehicles the car park was empty, all the tradesmen were upstairs. The renovations and the years of neglect the building has suffered meant there was no CCTV.

Sebastian De Roy was very nervous. As Charlie pushed him deeper into the car park, he turned to face Charlie shaking visibly.

"Please, Charles, you've got your money. I've done everything you've asked of me. Don't do anything to me. I'll get you more money, double, even treble but please don't hurt me."

This man had destroyed everything in his life, Charlie needed revenge. "Do you have any idea what it was like to be in prison knowing you're innocent and knowing your wife and son have been murdered because of greed? You all promised to rally round before the trial but where were you?" Charlie was angry again. A red mist seemed to descend on him. He withdrew the gun.

Sebastian De Roy collapsed to his knees. He held out his arms as he cried floods of tears.

"Please, Charles. I had nothing to do with your family. It was all Geo…"

The bang from the gun echoed around the walls of the garage. As with his first two victims, Charlie had shot Sebastian De Roy squarely between the eyes. Placing the gun back in his pocket he swiftly left the garage using the exit ramp designed for cars. His pulse was quickening, and his ears were ringing from the noise of the shot going off. He didn't stop once he had exited the garage but quickly walked in order to merge with the morning crowds. After five minutes his pulse had returned to normal, and his hearing was almost back. Spying out CCTV cameras, Charlie continued to mingle with the crowds. He knew he would be impossible to pick out from the crowds. He walked for half an hour before hailing a taxi to take him back to his hotel.

On entering the foyer, he had his now folded raincoat over his arm and his cap was in his pocket. All anyone saw was a cheaply dressed guest returning from his morning stroll. Charlie went straight to the hotel's business centre, sat in front of a computer and after logging on, sent an e-mail to his bank in the Cayman Islands instructing them to move his funds to another bank where he also had an account in the name of the new millionaire, Edwin Somerset. It was 10.39 a.m. By 11.07 a.m the two million pounds had moved once more and were sitting in an account in Gibraltar. The links between a two million transfer from Starling, Bradshaw and De Roy, Charlie Robb and Edwin Somerset would be almost impossible to trace.

***

Si Griffiths had spent yesterday afternoon and evening searching his contacts to discover who might have recently sold a .22 pistol. His first port of call was a betting shop in Hackney where he knew his long-term informant, Shorty Weaver, would be. Shorty would bet on anything including how long he would live if some of London's more notorious criminals ever learnt Shorty had sold them out. Si knew Shorty was low rent. He had never come close to big time crime.

Shorty had one thing in his favour. He knew a lot of people who operated on the fringes of society. If anyone knew who might be selling weapons it was Shorty. He was always pleased to meet Si; it meant a few pounds extra to bet. After the usual sparring Si had asked Shorty straight out who he should talk to about .22 pistols.

Shorty, who only stood five foot four inches tall, had pretended not to know. This was part of the game to persuade Si to increase the cash he would hand over.

"Well, Mr Griffiths, you know that kind of gun is in demand by professionals and I'm not putting my head on the block for a few quid."

Shorty looked up at Si. His seven-day beard was turning grey as was his once black hair. Si didn't know how old Shorty was. He could have been anything between fifty and seventy. As always, he was dressed in black tee shirt, black jeans and black trainers.

"I'll make it worth your while. I just need a name."

"Well, I heard there was an Irish bloke asking around about getting a gun. I don't think he was after a specific one, but I know he was sent on to Jimmy Healey. You know, the guy who operates out of the arches beside King's Cross." Shorty looked seriously at Si. "That's all I've got Mr Griffiths. I'm sure it'll be a big help to you in solving the case you're working on. Information like this has got to be gold dust to you."

Si smiled, Shorty never changed, all his information was gold dust. Only in most cases it proved to be painted lead. Si knew Jimmy Healey and didn't think he would be the supplier, but it was a start. He gave Shorty fifty pounds and set off for King's Cross.

Tuesday evening traffic was heavy, and it took Si over an hour to reach Jimmy Healey's workshop in one of the railway arches. Jimmy was well known to the police who allowed him to stay in business as a supposed technician who turned working firearms into safe showpieces. He had been known to have reversed the process for a fee, but the police turned a blind eye to this side of Jimmy's business. They knew he only dealt with small time crooks, but they kept an eye on him.

It was getting late, and Si was tired. Jimmy was sitting at a workbench apparently cleaning the barrel of a shotgun. Si went straight for Jimmy who complained that the DS had no right to accuse him of anything.

"Come on, Jimmy. I know you sold a weapon to an Irishman a few days ago. I can have you on charges for that, now don't be silly. All I want is a name of anyone who might deal in .22 calibre pistols."

Jimmy pretended to be upset at Si's suggestion he was dealing in illegal weapons but saw he wasn't in trouble. All this copper wanted was a name. As luck would have it another illegal firearms dealer had recently brought a .22 calibre pistol to have it reinstated. Jimmy saw an opportunity to perhaps land this competitor in trouble with the law and make a bit of money.

"Well, Mr Griffiths. Say I might know someone you could talk to. What's in it for me?"

Jimmy was a thin man in his mid-forties. Although he was approaching six foot tall, he probably weighed less than one hundred and forty pounds. He would be no match for Si in a punch up.

Si approached Jimmy who still remained seated at his workbench. He casually stood behind him, and in a flash, had gathered lumps of Jimmy's long dark greasy hair in his right hand and pulled hard. Jimmy's head came back, and Si put his left arm around Jimmy's throat.

"I'll tell you what's in it for you. You don't get a good kicking from me, and I don't arrest you for dealing." Si pulled harder on Jimmy's hair. Jimmy was choking as Si tightened the grip his arm had around Jimmy's throat. The gun dealer couldn't make a sound. After a few long seconds Si released his grip and stood back. As Jimmy fought to breathe normally Si patted his shoulder from behind. "There, now I'm sure we understand each other. Just a name will do, and I'll be off for my evening meal."

It took Jimmy five minutes to recover his power of speech. He croaked a name that Si didn't recognise.

"Where do I find him?"

Again, Jimmy croaked a location.

Once more Si patted the arms dealer on his shoulders. "If you're lying to me, I'll be back, and you won't get off so easily."

Si, still the hero, had once more been welcomed home by his girlfriend and had spent a peaceful evening watching television and drinking a few cans of beer.

***

Wednesday, February 16 saw Si on the road just as Steve and Matt were leaving the Yard to visit Starling, Bradshaw and De Roy. It was 9.11 a.m.

All Si had got from Jimmy, the gun technician, was that he sold a .22 pistol he'd brought back to life to one of his competitors called Keith. Despite Si's most persuasive moves, Jimmy had stood by the fact he didn't know Keith's surname, but he drank in The Five Bells off Mile End Road. It wasn't much, but he knew basic police work was all about pounding the pavements following up little bits of information. He wasn't looking forward to his visit to Mile End Road but knew it had to be done. This Keith might be the lead that cracked the case. Si smiled as he allowed himself to daydream about another commendation.

He found the Five Bells pub and knew instantly what the inside would be like. It was 10.51 a.m. as Si parked his pool car and made his way to the pub. After about three minutes of constant banging on the front door, the landlord opened it with an angry expression on his face.

"We're not open yet."

Si gave the man one of his best innocent smiles as he held up his warrant card for the man to see. "Police. I'm here on police business so let's not have any unpleasantness."

The landlord who introduced himself as Spike grudgingly opened the door far enough for his visitor to enter. Si saw what he expected. A one-time traditional London pub that had been neglected by the brewery. The place hadn't had any money spent on it in years. The dark wood panelling was dull whilst the ceiling was dark brown from the time smoking was allowed inside pubs. The wallpaper was peeling in a few places and most of the tables and chairs looked dirty and broken.

Spike offered Si a coffee that he accepted. Once the brew had been poured the pair sat at one of the few tables that still had four legs none of which were held together with string.

"Listen, sergeant, I run a clean pub. I don't allow drugs and no prostitutes in here, so whatever you want I can't help you." Spike had introduced himself as the manager and Si spotted a prison tattoo on his forearm, so Spike had form. Si made a note of Spike's formal name in his notebook. As Spike was an old lag, Si knew how to handle this interview.

"I believe you, Spike." Si was being friendly. "Too many pubs have been ruined and their managers locked up for letting in the wrong type of customer." Si almost laughed out loud at this. He couldn't believe that Spike was dumb enough to believe this apparently sympathetic cop, but he was seriously nodding in agreement. Si continued. "Are you paying much protection money, Spike?"

This change of tack caught Spike off guard. "Er! Well, you know, just the usual business overhead."

Si drank his coffee. "The things we have to do to make an honest living, eh Spike?" Si looked squarely at the manager, his voice low and full of menace. "Here you are running an above-board business and some of your customers are conspiring to put you back inside."

"Now, just a minute copper, like I said I'm clean. I run a respectable pub."

Si nodded in agreement. Spike visibly relaxed thinking he'd made his point.

"So, who's selling guns in here Spike?"

Spike pretended total indignation. "Shooters! Now that's enough. You're not fitting me up for anything to do with shooters. Like I said I run…" Si interrupted.

"I know, you run a clean pub. Thing is I have information a gun was sold here a few days ago. What do you know about it?"

Spike stuck to his story of running a clean pub and told Si he didn't know what deals his customers did while they were drinking. Si finished his coffee. He sat back and let Spike suffer by not knowing what Si knew.

"You have a customer called Keith?"

"Yes." Spike was showing signs of suspicion. "What about him?"

"I need a chat, that's all. Does Keith deal in guns?"

Si could see Spike was frightened. His faraway stare told Si the manager was considering his answer, so he added, "Remember, Spike, lying to me now isn't a good idea."

Spike sat thinking for what seemed a long time.

"I think maybe he sells the odd shooter but it's nothing to do with me. I run a clean pub remember."

Si laughed. "Yes, I know Spike, a clean pub where complete strangers can buy guns." Si was no longer laughing and the sudden hard edge to Si's voice disturbed him. "Now, when will Keith be in?"

A noticeably frightened pub manager stammered, "He comes in most days around twelve for a pint and a sandwich in the lounge bar."

Si looked at his watch. It was 11.32 a.m. "Good. Now just so we're clear, I'm going to sit in the lounge bar and when Keith comes in, you're going to let me know. Understood?"

"Yes."

"Also, you're not to use a phone to tip Keith off as to who I am. Understood?"

"Yes."

"Good. Now I'm off to the other bar and you can bring me a half pint and a packet of plain crisps." Si smiled at Spike. "On the house of course."

***

Steve and Matt walked into the reception area of Holland, Squires and Maple at 10.05 a.m. Bob Class had made an appointment for them to meet Frank Holland at ten.

On being shown into Frank Holland's office the DCI apologised for being late. "I'm afraid the traffic doesn't get any easier, sir."

Frank Holland was a jolly looking man dressed in the city uniform of dark suit, white shirt and meaningless tie. He ushered his guests to a set of four tub chairs set off to one side of his desk that was full of paper and looked disorganised. He offered coffee and the three men sat and spoke in general terms about Anthony Maple while Frank Holland's secretary organised the coffee.

"Can you tell us anything about Mr Maple that might help us better understand the man?" Steve needed to move the inquiry on.

Frank seemed to think for a few seconds. "No, nothing really. He was married and he lived in Bushy Park." Frank Holland broke off. "I know he was very proud of living there, he thought it gave him status."

"What did he do here?"

"He was our investments partner. This is, in the jargon, 'a boutique investment house', it just means we do things for our clients other firms wouldn't."

Matt spoke up. "Does that mean you take more risks with your clients' money, sir?"

Frank Holland blushed at the DI's bluntness. "No. We weigh risk to reward and if our client understands the risk in return for a higher reward then we'll act for him."

Steve knew the answer but asked, "How long had he worked here?"

"I'd have to check exactly but I'd say more or less ten years." Frank Holland was about to continue when the coffee arrived. Once everyone had settled down the DCI carried on with his questioning.

"How did he come to work here, sir?"

"Oh! I see, well it's no secret, Tony got himself into a bit of bother. He wasn't a strong character and fell under the spell of a city grandee who sold him on the idea of doubling his clients' money in two years. Before he joined us Tony ran his own investment house. He was doing pretty well, and a doubling of clients' portfolios would have meant handsome commissions for him. I don't know the whole story, but it seemed a small-time independent advisor was hoodwinked into investing into several Ponzi-type schemes this city gent set up for his own benefit. He needed investors to make it work and persuaded Tony to invest the lot with this small-time advisor."

Steve had heard something similar but not in any detail. His gut told him this could be the motive for the murders.

"Do you know what happened?"

"Well, the whole thing went tits up with the financial crash, but the group Tony was involved with saw it coming and took their money out. I'm not sure but I think this independent guy took the fall when the FSA and the police came calling. A lot of people lost a lot of money. The actual scheme was very clever, and the main investors got out cleanly."

"And this advisor, he was prosecuted for what exactly?"

"As I recall it was insider trading and corrupt practices against the FSA rules. I believe he got quite a long sentence."

"Did Mr Maple ever say who he was?"

"No, but I heard his family might have been murdered while he was awaiting trial."

Matt Conway was all ears and making notes.

Frank Holland continued. "Tony came to see me. He was a bit shaken up having had to deal with the police. He said he'd had enough of being independent and asked if I could use him here. I'd known him from university and knew his reputation within the city. We had a vacancy, so I agreed. Three years later he made partner."

The DCI sat back running through what he'd just learnt.

"So, Mr Maple joined you around ten years ago having narrowly missed police charges for corrupt practices because he had invested his clients' money in some kind of hooky get-rich-quick scheme?"

"I wouldn't put it like that but in essence you're correct."

"And having had this scare he wanted the comfort of a larger corporation around him and joined your firm?"

"Again, correct."

Did he ever mention the name of this city gent who set the deal up?"

"No. I got an impression he was afraid of the man."

"What about the fall guy? The small-time operator? Did he ever tell you his name?"

Frank Holland thought for a time. "No, I'm sure he didn't mention it. Apart from the basic story he never went into details of his past life."

Steve looked at Matt who shrugged. He had no questions. The DCI gave Frank Holland his business card and asked him to contact him if he remembered anything else.

Steve and Matt left Holland, Squires and Maple and arrived back at New Scotland Yard just as Detective Sergeant Si Griffiths was making his way to the lounge bar of The Five Bells and his complimentary half pint and crisps.

Chapter Twenty-Six

Charlie, having moved his money, went to his room and lay on his bed. He found he was exhausted and despite his newfound bravado he was drained. His nervous energy level had spiked and now he felt sick at what he had done. He told himself what he was doing was justified.

As he lay his thoughts turned to his last victim, Geoffrey Lockwood. He knew Connie was searching for him, but Charlie knew he also had to find the man who had killed his family before he killed Lockwood. This would mean meeting Lockwood more than once. He was the only one who knew the identity of the man he'd hired to frighten Charlie and his family. He remembered the police bumbling around getting nowhere. They hadn't found the killer and the case was still open.

Charlie's plan was to meet Lockwood and force him to tell him the name and details of the thug he'd hired. Charlie wanted Lockwood to suffer. He wanted him to know Charlie was after him and the best way of achieving this was to let him know that the thug was dead, and Geoffrey Lockwood was next. As Charlie lay planning, his mind returned to prison and a conversation he'd had with a long-term inmate called Sniffer. Sniffer was named because he had a major sinus problem.

Sniffer had discussed with Charlie how he had been caught. After murdering a business rival, and getting away with it, he'd gone back to the scene and tied his victim to a chair in order to confuse the police. Unknown to Sniffer, a neighbour had called knowing the victim was at home and should have answered. The neighbour called the police who walked in on Sniffer as he was tying his last knot. Sniffer's advice was never to return.

As Charlie thought about this, he realised his plan was flawed. Never go back. He'd have to think about how to deal with Geoffrey Lockwood. He dozed as he considered his options. He was startled when he realised he'd fallen asleep and the burner phone he'd bought was pulsating, telling him he had a call. It was 11.54 a.m. and he had been sleeping for almost an hour.

"Hello, Connie."

"That's not a very romantic greeting. You sound as though you've been asleep."

"I have. I'm exhausted but I did the deed this morning. Sebastian De Roy won't be robbing anyone else of their liberty."

Connie could tell Charlie was not his usual self. "Do you want me to come down? I could be there in a couple of hours."

"No, let's stick to the plan. I suppose it's some kind of post-traumatic stress thing. I'll be fine. Did you get anything on Geoffrey Lockwood?"

Connie didn't like this version of Charlie. He sounded cold and somehow aloof. She realised he wasn't a born killer and that what he was doing wasn't easy for him, but she felt let down. After all, she'd given up her career and made herself an accessory to murder. She decided that this was a temporary glitch in their relationship, and they would soon be together on a warm, sandy beach.

"Yes, he was easy to find. His company is called Lockwood and Marr. Their office is shown as being in the city, in Pudding Lane." Connie giggled at the address.

"Are you sure? Pudding Lane's not exactly high-rise buildings and glass fronts. It's a bit narrow and none of the offices are very big."

"Well, that's what I've got, Charlie. I did a search still using my access to the probation database and he's shown as living in Chigwell in Essex."

Connie gave Charlie both addresses and waited. Silence was her reward as Charlie wrote down the information.

"Thanks, Connie, that's great. I'll have a look later today."

Connie was worried. She'd hoped giving Charlie this news would cheer him up, but he seemed more formal and more distant. She tried again.

"Look. I'll come down, we'll have dinner and spend the night in that lovely big bed you have. I've missed you and what you do to me." Connie had allowed her voice to take on a seductive quality that she knew Charlie couldn't resist. She continued talking and verbally exploring Charlie's and her own body telling Charlie what they would do to each other in a few days' time. Charlie liked hearing this and was lulled into a daydream, allowing his mind to imagine what Connie was offering. He suddenly snapped back to the present.

"Please, Connie, not now. I've got things to do. I'll call you this evening." He hung up quickly. His brain wasn't settled so he got up, stripped off and took a long hot shower, then decided to visit Pudding Lane after he'd had lunch in the hotel's dining room. He told himself he hadn't eaten much and maybe it was lack of food that was the cause of his melancholy. His killing clothes were in the bottom of his wardrobe and the pistol in the boot of his rented Mercedes. He'd devise a plan over lunch but there would be no further killing today.

Charlie also decided it was time to introduce Edwin Somerset to the world. He called the Albion Hotel and Spa beside Heathrow Airport and made a reservation for Edwin Somerset and thought he would also change his car.

***

Si was enjoying his beer and crisps. The pub manager looked nervous as he busied himself wiping tables and cleaning glasses. A few regulars had started to drift in, but they all went into the public bar. At 12.08 p.m. a badly dressed man entered the area of the pub occupied by Si. He gruffly ordered a pint of best and two rounds of ham sandwiches. As Spike made conversation with the newcomer he nervously nodded to Si. Keith the gun dealer had arrived.

Si let him wander to his table of choice and settle down to drink his beer and enjoy his food before he rose and ambled over to Keith's table. Without being invited he sat opposite Keith. He realised Keith was a big man. His undersized tee shirt exaggerated his muscles and chest measurement. He'd removed his jacket when he'd arrived, and it was now hanging over the back of his chair. Si studied his quarry before speaking.

"How's the sandwich?"

Keith looked blankly at Si and said nothing.

"A pint and a sandwich for lunch. You know I admire you low life characters. Nothing to do and all day to do it. I suppose you get a bit bored though. Once the horseracing's over and you've had your beer, what else is there to do?"

Keith remained silent and took a bite from one of his sandwiches.

"I suppose you just go home to the little woman. Isn't that what you do, Keith?"

The use of his Christian name caused Keith to stop chewing his sandwich. His eyes narrowed as he studied Si. With his mouth full, Keith spat out. "You a cop?"

Si smiled and sat back. He nodded but said nothing. He knew curiosity would drive Keith to start asking questions.

"What do you want?"

"Only a chat, Keith. At least for now."

"A chat about what?"

Keith lifted his beer and swallowed half of the remaining liquid and took a further bite of his sandwich.

"Oh, life in general. How you make your living? Who you recently sold a .22 calibre pistol to? You know, things like that." Si retained a friendly smile and kept his voice low. At this stage he was Keith's new best friend.

Keith was an old hand. He thought this policeman might know something about his activities but not enough to charge him. He was fishing.

"No idea what you're talking about."

"Of course you don't." Si was smiling more broadly and keeping his voice friendly. "Trader like you wouldn't know anything about illegal guns." He leant forward. "You see, Keith, I know you had a .22 pistol reactivated and that that pistol has been used to kill two people." Si knew this was a leap. He had no evidence of this, but Keith didn't know that. "Now, here's the thing. If you help me, I'll forget about your trade in firearms at least for now." Si touched the side of his nose in a gesture that said, 'I know.' "Give you time to tidy up before the heavies arrive."

"I don't know nothing. What's your name, copper?"

Si gave a huge theatrical sigh. He gave Keith his name and sat back.

"Thing is, Keith. All I want from you is the name of the bloke you sold the gun to. I'll give you five days to tidy up your operation before reporting your firearms trade. If you're smart it'll be a walk but of course, you'd owe me." Si was experienced enough not to be seen to let criminals think they have the upper hand. Keith would become one of Si's unofficial informants.

Keith could see how this was unfolding. Say nothing and probably be arrested on the spot or give a name and buy five days to hide his weapons for sale.

"OK, Mr Griffiths, I'll tell you what I can, but it isn't much."

Si said nothing but opened his arms in a welcoming gesture.

"This guy comes to me in the betting office around the corner. He says Big Jimbo told him I could get him a shooter."

Si didn't interrupt but made notes.

"He'd been inside. I can always tell, and I know Big Jimbo's doing life without parole up in Whitby."

Si interrupted. "How long do you think this bloke had been out?"

"Not long. He still had that pale washed-out look we all have when we first get out."

Si nodded and Keith continued.

"That's it, I don't know his name. I sold him a .22. Seems he wanted up close and personal like and I told him that was the best weapon."

"Can you describe this man?"

"Not really. He was quite tall, probably about six foot. I remember his hair. It was that funny colour; you know when men are turning grey but haven't got there yet."

"You mean salt and pepper?"

"Yeah! That's it. I'd say he was early forties but that's a guess. That's all I can tell you."

Si took an old and very dog-eared business card from his jacket pocket and handed it to Keith.

"I want you at New Scotland Yard at three this afternoon. I want you to work with one of our identikit technicians and see if you can put a face together for this guy. If you do that, I'll hold off reporting your activities until next Monday morning. Are we clear?"

A depressed Keith finished his beer and nodded.

Si stood and leant over the table until he was in Keith's face.

"Don't screw me. You're mine now and don't forget it. I'll pop by from time to time. Keep the card, it's got my mobile on it. You hear anything you think I should know, you call. Understand?"

"Yes." A dejected Keith looked at his empty glass. As Si left, he called to Spike for another beer. He told himself he'd deal with Spike later.

Si headed for the Yard. He had a job for Bob Class that might just solve the case.

***

Steve and Matt arrived back at the office to find Bob keying away furiously on his laptop.

"I got the prison release records, sir but it's not easy. Data protection says I can't follow an individual prisoner's records." Bob looked slyly at his two senior officers. "But I've found a way. The problem is there have been over fifty prisoners released in the last few weeks who did time for some form of financial fraud and I've no idea which prison to look at first. I've no idea what I'm looking for."

"OK, Bob, take a break. Come on through. Let's see what we have."

With everyone seated Steve looked at Bob. "How did you get on confirming if this security angle on a search warrant is valid?"

"It's kosher. We don't have to divulge the reason for requesting the warrant if we say it's to do with national security. The problem is we only have seventy-two hours to do the search and bring charges. If we don't bring charges, we have to explain why we wanted the warrant. It's to stop fishing trips."

Steve was quiet as he analysed Bob's comments.

"Mm. That's not good. All Si wanted was to get into the back room. If we go with a warrant, we'll get in, but I'm not sure we can prove any terrorist activity. After all, I only want to speak with the major."

Matt held his hand up and with a smile said, "Except we believe it's a hot bed for state-sponsored killing."

"Yes, there is that. If we go for it, it's certain MI6 will get involved, and I don't want that." Steve looked at his colleagues. "On balance, let's not go for a warrant. Matt, from what we saw of the place last night I think we'll go in together. It's not Fort Knox. Two of us will have more…"

Si Griffiths arrived. He looked flustered and without acknowledging Steve looked straight at Bob. "Bob, I need you. Bring your laptop." Si turned ready to leave expecting Bob to follow.

"Hang on, Si. Not only are we in the middle of a meeting but what the hell are you playing at?"

Si realised he'd overstepped the mark. He held his hands up in surrender. "Sorry, boss but if I can have Bob for five minutes, I think we'll have something."

Steve looked at Matt who shrugged as if saying, *'that's Si.'*

Steve nodded to Bob. "You'd better have something, detective sergeant, or I'll have your hide."

Si gave a cheeky smile and left, closely followed by Bob Class and his trusty laptop.

"He's a cheeky sod, Steve, but he has been useful."

"I know but I can see why he's stayed a DS all these years."

The pair settled down to review what they knew of the two murders and debate if the killings were professional or not.

"We know both victims were tied up with a crooked financial advisor and it all seemed to happen around nine to ten years ago. There must be a connection and surely we can find out who this advisor was." Steve was sounding frustrated. Before the two could continue their debate, Si and Bob walked back in. Both had satisfied grins on their faces. Si took a chair at the opposite of the end of the table, opposite Steve.

"OK, Si. The floor's yours but it better be good." Steve sat back.

"Right you are, boss. I found the guy who sold a .22 pistol last week to an ex-con."

Steve immediately sat forward. Before he could speak Si held up his hands.

"Sorry, but he doesn't have a name for the buyer. When I asked him how someone off the street knew he sold illegal guns he told me it was a recommendation from a lifer serving time in HMP Whitby, a bloke called Big Jimbo. Bob has just searched the records for recent releases from Whitby and bingo! Go on, Bob, tell the boss."

Bob Class grinned. "Well, from the prisoner release data there was only one prisoner who had served time for financial crimes, a bloke called Charles Robb. I looked him up; he got sixteen years for money laundering, fraud and perverting the course of justice. He was released on parole twelve days ago. And get this, his wife and son were murdered just before he was arrested. I think this could be our man, sir."

Steve was thinking hard. It sounded possible but he couldn't yet fit all the pieces together. Suddenly Commander Perry Hargreaves walked into the office.

"I'm glad you're all here." He looked worried and didn't stand on ceremony. "There's been another shooting, same MO. A bloke called Sebastian De Roy. It was called in by some workers renovating an old hotel. You'd better get over there. The local boys have secured the scene and the full forensic and search squads have been called. I don't know what's going on, but it looks like we have a serial killer on our hands. The press will be all over this. Get it cleaned up, Steve. It's what you're good at." Perry threw a slim file onto the table.

"What we have is in there. Good luck," the commander said as he left.

Silence filled Steve's office. No one believed a third shooting was possible.

"What now, boss?" Matt Conway looked concerned.

"Well, we need to find this Charles Robb. Si, you and Bob work on finding him. He's on parole so start with his parole officer. He should be in a halfway house so you should find him easily enough. Also get one of the local lads up in Whitby to visit this Big Jimbo, see what he knows about this Robb."

Steve sat thinking while the rest of the team were anxious to get on.

"We've got a lead on this Charles Robb thanks to Si but it's not solid. We can't actually tie him to the gun that Si's contact sold."

Si interrupted. "I've got my contact, that's Keith, coming in at three to make up an identikit. I've still to arrange it but hopefully we'll see this Charles Robb."

Steve smiled. "Good. We know Robb was released twelve days ago and he went down… when Bob?"

"Just over eight years ago, sir. He served half of his sentence."

"And we know our first two victims had financial issues about the same time. It's not conclusive but what are the chances of a criminal being sent down for fraud at the same time our victims are in financial trouble? More than once is too much of a coincidence."

Matt raised his hand. "But they got their money back remember. One of our witnesses described the independent advisor as a patsy, not a real criminal."

"Good point, Matt."

Steve, happy in his own mind that they were on the right track, set about ticking off the items for his team to follow up on.

"Matt, we'll go to the latest crime scene. Si, try to locate Charles Robb and set up the identikit technician. Terry Harvey should help with that. Bob help Si, but also start digging into our latest victim. See if he had any financial problems nine years or so ago, and if there's a link to Charles Robb and our first two victims. Also find out how Robb made his living before he went inside." Steve was finished but had another task for Bob. "Oh! And Bob, get a picture of Charles Robb from his charge sheet. OK, everyone, let's get to it."

Bob Class picked up the slim file and photocopied the one page before handing it to Steve.

"There you are, sir. The body is in the underground garage of the old Miles Hotel. I'll get what I can and update you if anything comes in."

Steve and Matt Conway left. It was 3.05 p.m.

***

Charlie had arranged a late check in as Edwin Somerset at the Albion Hotel. Connie's phone call was playing on his mind. He told himself her information must be wrong. Geoffrey Lockwood couldn't have his office in Pudding Lane. It didn't make sense based on Charlie's knowledge of the man.

Curiosity got the better of him and he decided to visit Pudding Lane to see for himself. He had no plan to meet Geoffrey Lockwood. He only wanted to confirm the address. He checked out of the Mayflower Hotel after he'd eaten and arranged for his car to be left in their garage until five…

As Steve and Matt were driving out of the Yard's car park at 3.05 p.m. Charlie was walking towards Pudding Lane.

It was exactly as Charlie remembered, narrow with cobbles on the road and a series of terraced building lining either side. The whole lane was in permanent shadow. There were several wooden doors that opened onto it and one enterprising individual had opened a wine bar in the cellar of one of the buildings. From the outside despite the high property prices in this part of London, the whole place felt seedy to Charlie as he looked for number twenty-seven.

There were few people around and Charlie saw no CCTV cameras. He stood outside number 27 and examined the names on the multi-keyed entry system. He saw that LOCKWOOD AND MARR FINANCIAL CONSULTANTS were on the first floor. Standing outside this door told Charlie nothing. He decided on an immediate plan of action.

The writing beside the intercom button for the second floor read LONDON CLEANING EXECUTIVES. Charlie pressed this button. After a few attempts a gruff sounding man answered asking what the caller wanted.

"I'd like to hire you for a big cleaning job. Can I come up?" Charlie lied.

A buzzer sounded and the door sprung open. Charlie was in. The entrance was narrow almost the width of the stairs that rose in front of Charlie. A soiled carpet that had once been multi-coloured covered the floor and stairs and stank of something not very pleasant. The walls were covered in embossed wallpaper and had been overpainted with cream gloss paint. The colour had changed over the years, and it was now yellow as was the woodwork on the painted handrail.

Charlie gamely walked to the first floor. He'd rapidly devised a story that wouldn't keep him long in the cleaning office and therefore less easily remembered should the police ask. He knocked on a dirty looking door that proudly declared these were the offices of the LONDON CLEANING EXECUTIVES.

"Hello, I'm looking for someone in charge?" Charlie was wearing one of his best suits. He hadn't planned on visiting these offices, but simply to check out the area.

"I'm the only one here, guv. Cleaners all go out in the mornings see. On the job before five and finished before nine. I'm just here checking on stock. If you want to see one of the bosses, you'll have to come back tomorrow before noon." The man continued his task of moving boxes from one position to another.

This response suited Charlie but while he had an obvious chatter box, he thought he might try a few questions.

"Not much of an office for a large company like yours?"

"Ha! Large, my foot. All the businesses here are struggling, even the posh bloke upstairs. You don't think a proper company would work from a flea pit like this, do you? We'll be lucky to still be here next week."

Charlie, not wanting to be remembered, mumbled a thank you and left. Taking care to fully pull the office door closed, he made his way up to the second floor where an equally imposing sign read LOCKWOOD & MARR FINANCIAL CONSULTANTS.

Charlie stood outside this door that was as grubby as the one below. He could not believe Geoffrey Lockwood had fallen so far. He knew the only way to discover if this was the same Geoffrey Lockwood was to enter. He knocked loudly, turned the dirty handle and pushed the door.

He entered a small foyer surrounded on all sides by a four-foot-high purpose-built counter. Charlie noted the carpet was similar to that on the stairs and the open plan office behind the counter was empty of people although there seemed to be around six desks. There were filing cabinets dotted around and the windows that looked into the lane were bare.

A young woman with pink hair sat on a high chair behind the counter. Charlie noted she had an old-style computer beside her and that the computers sitting on the desks behind her were of a similar vintage. Charlie put the girl in her mid-twenties and apart from her pink hair she sported a large snake tattoo that seemed to spiral from her neck.

"How did you get in? I didn't buzz you."

As she spoke Charlie saw her nail colour matched her hair. Not seeing any doors off the one-roomed open plan office Charlie was sure this was the only person here. He thought he was safe to just ask.

"I'm looking for Geoffrey Lockwood."

"Mr Lockwood don't work from here, nobody does. My boyfriend says it's a scam. I comes in every morning at nine and leaves at five with an hour for my lunch. I don't see a bleeding soul and the phone never rings."

This didn't help Charlie, so he asked, "If nobody comes here how do the employees get their mail and so on?"

"Oh! I gets the mail, but I'm not allowed to open it. I put everything in a big envelope and post it." The girl reached under the counter and produced a large brown envelope securely bound by brown tape and laid it on top of the counter. "I've to go all the way to the main post office with that and pay the bleeding postage out of my own money. That Mr Lockwood's a tight git and no mistake. He adds the postage money to my cheque amount each month, but I have to send him the amount and the dates first."

Charlie didn't understand so he tried again.

"All those desks behind you. Are you saying no one works at them? You're the only employee?"

"That's right, weird, ain't it?"

Charlie saw an opportunity. "I'm going to the central post office now. I could post that envelope for you if you want?"

The girl visibly brightened up. "Great, save me a trip, thanks, mister."

Charlie lifted the envelope, turned and left mumbling a *'no problem'* to the girl.

Once outside Charlie looked at the address. It read GEOFFREY LOCKWOOD, THE GLADES, CHIGWELL. ESSEX. This was the address Connie had given him, but he still didn't think this Geoffrey Lockwood was the one he was searching for. Charlie decided to visit Mr Lockwood in the morning and hand deliver his mail. He decided that he'd take his gun just in case this was his target although he doubted it.

Charlie, in the guise of Edwin Somerset, walked back to the Mayflower Hotel's car park and collected his hired Mercedes. He set out to drive to Heathrow Airport and hand back this hire car as Charles Robb, replacing it with another from a different rental company but still as Charlie Robb, not as Edwin Somerset. The forger warned him not to use his driving licence for anything other than identification. Renting his next and last hire car would be Charles Robb's last outing.

Apart from the necessity of remaining Charlie Robb to hire his car, he would start his new life as Edwin Somerset in a suite at the Albion Hotel and Spa. No one would ever see Charlie Robb again, maybe not even Connie. It was 3.51 p.m. on Wednesday, February 16.

***

As Charlie, strode off towards the Mayflower Hotel to collect his hire car, Steve and Matt were pulling up outside the old Miles Hotel.

The scene was manic with police blue and white crime tape everywhere. Police cars, white unmarked forensic vans and even the black mortuary van were parked at odd angles across the road.

As the two detectives walked down the car ramp to the scene a uniformed inspector was coming the other way.

"You the SIO, sir?"

"Yes, name's Burt. This is DI Conway. What have we got?"

"It's like a circus down there. An ACC from the Met was here a few minutes ago. She came to have a look and said you'd be along. Is it correct this is the third one, sir?"

"I don't know but it could be. Let's have a look."

The three officers descended into the bowels of the garage.

The pathologist was working on the body while the search and forensic teams were looking for any evidence or trace evidence the killer may have left behind. Steve nodded to the doctor.

"Anything, doc?"

"Killed by a single shot to the front lobe, instant and expertly done. I worked on the other two and I'd speculate it's the same killer. Certainly looks like a .22 calibre. Until I get him on the table, I can't tell you much except the poor fellow wet himself before he died. I suppose he knew it was the end and he was literally frightened for his life. I'd say your man enjoyed this one."

Steve looked at Matt. This was a new take on things.

"Thanks, doc. Any ID?"

The pathologist pointed to a plastic evidence bag laid out on a blue plastic sheet. "Over there; wallet etc., the name is Sebastian De Roy. The business card says he has an office in the Hastings Centre building, not far from here. Anyway, the post-mortem will be tomorrow at ten, gentlemen."

Steve thanked the pathologist and the uniformed inspector.

"Come on, Matt. Let's go and check out Stanley, Bradshaw and De Roy." As they walked Steve spotted several CCTV cameras. "Get Bob to check those out. We might get lucky."

After going through the same checks as Charlie had earlier in the day, the two detectives were greeted by Monica, Sebastian De Roy's personal assistant. Standing in the same seating area where Charlie had pointed his gun at De Roy, Monica expressed concern that Mr De Roy had left earlier in the morning with a client but had not returned.

"It is most unlike him."

"Quite. Monica, are the other partners in at the moment and could you ask them to join us please?"

Monica stood and suddenly realised why two police officers were here. "Something's happened to Mr. De Roy? Oh dear!" Monica was obviously a loyal employee. Her reaction of grief was understandable and normal. She held her right hand to her mouth unable to speak.

"Can you please ask the partners to join us?"

As Monica scurried away Steve and Matt looked around Sebastian's office. It was big and well furnished.

"Do you think this client's our man, Steve?"

"Could be. Get Bob to send the mug shot of Charles Robb to your phone and show Monica. She might recognise him."

Monica returned a few minutes later with two tall and distinguished looking city gents. They introduced themselves individually as Mr Starling and Mr Bradshaw. Both were dressed in the uniform of city gents with dark suits, white shirts and ties.

"Before we begin, can I ask you, Monica? The visitor Mr De Roy had this morning, did he sit in any of these chairs?"

Steve pointed to the collection of seating around a low coffee table.

"Well, yes, Mr De Roy is a very thoughtful gentleman. All clients are offered a seat and a drink. This morning was no exception."

Matt looked excitedly at Steve as he asked. "Monica, did the gentleman this morning take a drink?" Steve realised Matt was hoping for DNA from the cup if it could be identified.

"No, he declined."

Matt felt deflated and continued to hold his notebook at the ready.

"Can I ask you please not to touch or go near that area. I'm afraid Mr Sebastian De Roy was killed sometime earlier today, and we are treating his death as suspicious. I'll have a forensics team dust down that area in case there is any trace evidence."

Mr Bradshaw, the older of the two city gents, staggered slightly and took a seat behind De Roy's desk. "How did it happen? You are sure it's Sebastian?"

"We found his wallet with his driving licence. We don't have a formal identification yet but we're pretty sure it's your colleague. I can also tell you he was shot."

Mr Bradshaw gasped. Monica leant on the edge of the desk for support in case she fainted. Mr Starling continued to stand with his hands in his pockets clearly digesting the news. Starling had a more military bearing and Steve thought he might be handling the news of a sudden death better than his partner.

"Can anyone think who might want to harm Mr De Roy?"

Before anyone could answer, Matt's phone pinged. It was the mug shot for Charles Robb.

Matt nodded to Steve who waved Matt forward. Before Matt could ask Monica, she held his phone and nodded. "That's the man Mr. De Roy saw this morning."

Steve allowed himself a small smile. He waited for any answers to his question.

"No. Sebastian didn't have an enemy in the world and his work here was with our high-end investors. He took good care of them; he was very successful." Mr Bradshaw had assumed the role of spokesperson for the firm.

Steve suspected he already knew the answer when he asked, "When did Mr De Roy join your firm?"

Bradshaw put on an act of calculating back before answering. "It must have been just over eight years ago. He came initially as a trader. I think he'd been involved in some get-rich-quick scheme that had gone wrong. I believe he told us he was lucky to get out with his capital intact."

Steve saw the pattern beginning to appear. He knew they now had a suspect and that these people couldn't add anything more. "I'll have our forensics team here tomorrow morning. They'll need to go over this office and examine any papers Mr De Roy was working on. We'll also need to see your CCTV images and unfortunately we'll have to take your fingerprints for elimination purposes."

The two detectives thanked the partners and Monica for their time. As they walked towards the door Matt asked, "Did anything unusual occur today, Monica, apart from your boss's visitor?"

Monica canted her head to one side. "Well. The visitor was very scruffy, almost like a tramp, but no, nothing… except Mr De Roy made a transfer of two million pounds to a bank in the Cayman Islands while the tramp person was still here."

Steve turned towards Monica. "Do you have a copy of the transfer?"

Monica went to De Roy's desk and lifted a flimsy piece of paper. She handed it to Steve who placed it in a clear plastic evidence bag.

Outside, Steve and Matt smiled at each other.

"We've confirmation Charles Robb was here. He was dressed in an old coat just like the image we got from the CCTV at the first scene. If Si's arms dealer can put together a reasonable likeness, I think we've got enough."

"Agreed, and all the victims are linked to some fraud around eight to ten years ago. That has to be the link to Robb. If Bob finds he was involved in finance, it's game over."

A happy pair of detectives headed back to their office in Scotland Yard at 4.41 p.m.

The news they would receive would change their happy state and drive them into a dark gloom.

Chapter Twenty-Seven

After his two senior colleagues left, Si went to see if Keith, the arms dealer, had arrived. Reception told him he was in the technical area with one of Inspector Harvey's identikit technicians. Si wandered into the area and saw Keith and a very young man sitting in front of a larger than usual computer screen.

Terry Harvey recognised Si as one of the DCI's team and walked over to him.

"If you're chasing the image, sergeant, it'll take a while. I'll get it over to you when it's done."

"Thank you, sir."

"Do you need to see your man, Keith, when he's finished?"

Si gave a wicked grin the significance of which was not lost on Terry. "No, I know where to find him." Si thanked Terry and returned to his office.

On his return Si asked Bob to call up Charlie Robb's prison record. Bob immediately e-mailed it to Si's computer. Si found what he was looking for. He dialled the number for the Hackney office of the probation service.

The phone was answered on the fifth ring by a female who sounded harassed.

"Yes, Hackney. What can I do for you?"

"This is DS Si Griffiths from Scotland Yard. Can you put me through to your manager?"

Si was being polite although he didn't like this woman's initial attitude.

"If we had a manager I might but you're out of luck, chum. No one here of that name."

"This is serious police business, madam." Si became very formal. "If there's no manager then you'll have to assist me. I'm looking for the probation officer who is looking after an ex-prisoner, name of Robb, Charles Robb."

"The name rings a bell but we're dealing with hundreds of ex-cons. I don't remember all of them."

"Can you just get into your computer and tell me who his probation officer is and where I'll find him?"

The woman gave a deep sigh and remained silent. Si heard computer keys being punched and assumed this supposedly over-worked woman was accessing Robb's records. After what seemed a long silence, the woman was back.

"You're out of luck. His probation officer was Mrs O'Sullivan. She resigned over the weekend, just out of the blue. She said she had enough accumulated leave to cover her notice period, and that was that. She's gone and I can tell you she's left a right mess behind her. All her cases have had to be spread around. We won't get a replacement for months." Si thought that no matter the issue this woman would be the first to moan. Si wasn't very sympathetic to the staffing arrangements in a probation service office.

"Can you send a copy of Charles Robb's file over to me?" Si gave the woman Bob Class's e-mail address. As a parting gesture and without meaning to sound sarcastic Si said, "You've been very helpful."

"Yeah! Right. Hold on!" A few seconds later the woman was back. "It's gone. If you find anything do me a favour. Keep it to yourself. We're busy enough."

The line went dead leaving Si holding a phone that was buzzing in his ear.

Bob saw the file arriving and printed it for Si. He knew the DS didn't like technical things. He preferred old fashioned paper.

Si sat at his desk reading about Charles Robb. He found the details of the halfway house in Stratford that Charlie had been assigned to. Connie O'Sullivan had conveniently added the phone number. Once more Si lifted his phone.

He explained who he was. "I'm looking for a Charles Robb, I understand he's staying there?"

"Not any more, copper. He only stayed two nights and disappeared. I've no idea where he is."

Si was confused. "Did you report he'd absconded?"

"No point, nobody cares. This place is full, so an empty room is always welcome."

"Did you tell his probation officer?"

"No need. I think she called a couple of days after he'd done his bunk. I told her then, but that's it. These people come and go all the time."

Si had no idea what conditions were like at Mr Collins' halfway house, but he thanked him and hung up. Si scanned the file and found no reference to Mrs O'Sullivan knowing her client had absconded although Si noted, Charlie Robb had attended his initial Monday seventh February meeting and his Friday eleventh February meeting with his probation officer. As Si read the thin file, he realised Robb was off the radar. He called over to Bob.

"Bob, can you track down a retired probation officer called Mrs Connie O'Sullivan? She only resigned at the weekend."

"You don't ask much Si; I've got a mountain of work here."

Si gave Bob a lop-sided smile that said 'please'. Si knew Bob would do it, he just needed to be asked nicely.

"Oh! I suppose but what do you know about her?"

"Nothing."

"Look, Si, get back onto that woman who sent the file. See if she knows where this woman lives, that would be a start. Get everything you can, then I'll see what I can do."

Si, mimicking Bob, looked across his desk. "You don't ask much, Bob." Both men smiled as Si once more phoned the Hackney probation office.

The woman initially wouldn't tell Si anything about Mrs O'Sullivan's private life but on hearing Si was involved in a murder enquiry she became more cooperative.

"She lives somewhere in Bishop's Stortford in Essex. We're not close, only working colleagues but I've often heard her complain about the train to Stortford."

"Thank you again. You've been very helpful." This time Si meant it.

Si pushed Bob to drop what he was doing and focus on finding Connie O'Sullivan.

"It's not that easy, Si. Hold on, I'll run the Stortford area census. She might be on that." Bob keyed away while Si sat on the edge of his desk anticipating good news from Bob.

After five minutes or so Bob looked up and smiled. "I think that's her, only she's not a missus. She's a Miss, Miss Constance O'Sullivan, aged thirty five, single, owns her property on a mortgage, says she's a civil servant. That's it."

"Any phone number?"

"No, hold on, let me see." Bob once more started hitting keys at lightning speed. "She's got a landline." Bob printed off Connie's address and phone number.

Si accepted it, sat behind his desk and dialled Connie O'Sullivan's landline phone number. She answered immediately.

"Yes. This is Connie."

"Miss O'Sullivan?"

A suspicious voice replied. "Yes. Who's calling?"

"This is Detective Sergeant Si Griffiths of the Metropolitan Police. I'd like to ask you a few questions about an ex-prisoner who was one of your cases before you resigned, a Charles Robb."

Si's old police gut instinct told him something was wrong. The woman's reaction wasn't correct. Instead of asking how she could help, Connie asked, "Nothing's happened to him, has it?"

A suspicious Si followed up. "Why would something have happened to him, Miss O'Sullivan?"

The silence on the other end of the phone added to Si's suspicions. It was obvious the woman was thinking of a reply.

"It's just, you know, sergeant, ex-prisoners aren't angels and things do happen to them."

Si thought this was a weak response, but he passed over it, making a mental note to raise his suspicions with the DCI.

"We're trying to trace Mr Robb but he's not at his accommodation. As his probation officer I wondered if you might have an address for him?"

Too quickly, Connie replied. "Oh! No, I don't know where he is. Why should I?"

Si again passed over this response. "Do you know if he's working? Is there anything you can tell me that might help us locate him?"

Once more Si felt Connie was too forceful and quick with her answer. "No, nothing. Anyway, I've resigned so I have no current knowledge about any of my previous charges."

Si, now even more suspicious, thanked Connie for her help and hung up. He sat back and analysed the conversation. The probation officer didn't ask once why the police were looking for Charles Robb. He told himself she knew. Si became excited about this detail. Out loud he declared, "That's it. She's in on it with him."

Bob Class looked across at his colleague. Si winked and asked, "When's the boss back? He'll love this."

***

Connie sat in her living room, shaking. The call from Si had unnerved her. Her big adventure with Charlie was spiralling out of control. The police must be on to him. Her mind was in turmoil. What had been exciting and had shown her another side to her drab existence was now turning into a nightmare. The more she thought, the more frightened she became. Like all basically honest people she immediately thought the worst. She saw herself in prison. She saw a small cell and knew she couldn't serve time. Her clients had over the years painted a horrible picture of life in a female prison.

Her mind turned to how to save herself, to consider what her options were. She began to think how to extricate herself from what could become a real-life drama. She visualised seeing herself being taken into a police station with a coat over her head. Her mind was not focused. She was panicking. She took the burner phone from her handbag and called Charlie. She told herself he'd have a plan. Maybe they could fly off this evening before the police could act.

Connie paced her floor waiting for Charlie to answer. He didn't. Her world became a living hell. What could she do? She called Charlie again and again but still he didn't answer. She poured herself a large brandy and sat on her sofa with her feet pulled under her. She'd call Charlie later after she'd had time to think.

***

Steve and Matt arrived back in the office at New Scotland Yard just after five. .As soon as they walked in, they both sensed something was wrong. Steve realised he hadn't eaten all day and neither had Matt.

"You'd better all come in. Let's see where we are. I'm starving and tired. I need food and sleep so let's get on with it." Once everyone was seated Steve opened the meeting.

"Right. I can tell something's up but let's deal with what we know. Our third victim is called Sebastian De Roy. The pathologist says it's the same MO. Probably the same shooter except he told us he thinks our killer enjoyed this one, but that's speculation. If it's true we may have more murders to come." The mood around the table became more sombre at this news.

He continued. "Our victim worked for a finance house and was in a bit of financial trouble around nine years ago, the same as the other two victims. But this time our killer seems to have extorted a couple of million pounds from Mr De Roy."

Steve rose and wrote these facts on the board. Turning to the table he looked at Si. "Any joy finding this Robb bloke?"

Si slowly opened his notebook. "No, sir, he's vanished. I checked his halfway house, but he hasn't been there for well over a week. He hasn't signed on for unemployment benefit and his probation officer says she doesn't know where he is."

Si paused allowing Steve to absorb this bad news before continuing. "But here's the thing, sir. His probation officer resigned suddenly over the weekend. I discovered she knew he'd skipped his digs but there's nothing in his file, plus I have a feeling she's involved."

"What do you base that on, Si?"

Si grinned. "My gut. She didn't ask what we wanted to talk to Robb about. I think she knows he's going around killing people. I don't have a clue why she'd be involved, but I'm certain she is."

"Mm. That's a leap, Si, but your hunches have been right in the past. Get up to Essex tomorrow morning and invite the lady to visit us here, but ask nicely, she could be innocent." Steve resumed his seat. "Well done, Si."

Steve was looking at a sheet of notes he'd written when Inspector Terry Harvey head of the Yard's Technical Services and a good friend of the DCI arrived. He only said a cursory, "Sorry," and handed the file he was holding to Si. Addressing Steve and by way of an explanation Terry said, "It's the artist's sketch based on Si's gun contact."

All eyes were on Si. He handed the file to Bob who hit a few keys on his laptop before stating, "It's a match. The guy who bought the gun is definitely Charles Robb."

Terry stood in the doorway ready to leave when Steve had an idea. "Can you hold on, Terry?"

The head of Technical Support Services took a seat.

"Right. We believe we now have our killer but let's not stop gathering evidence. Bob, do you have anything on De Roy or the other victims' backgrounds?"

"Not a lot but I dug up some old bank records from nine and ten years ago for Charles Robb."

Steve sat back. "Did you indeed, you must be a mind reader. Well done, Bob, let's hear it."

"Well, I'm not an expert…"

Terry Harvey said under his breath but loud enough for everyone to hear. "No, but we know someone who is." He was referring to his wife Florance, known to Steve as Twiggy. Terry and Florance were married, and Flo was a senior forensic financial analyst seconded from the Treasury to Scotland Yard's Serious Financial Crimes Section.

Steve smiled and nodded to Bob to continue. "Well, as I said, I'm no expert, but large sums of money from various accounts were paid into Robb's personal account over a period of about four months. He then seems to have transferred this money into his business account. Just before he was arrested the money disappeared, transferred out."

"Is there any link between the money being paid in and our victims?"

"I'm not there yet, sir. As I said I'm no expert."

Steve smiled at Terry and fed his own words back to him. "No, but we know someone who is. Bob, put all the financial stuff you have into a file." Steve reached into the inside pocket of his jacket and slid the clear plastic evidence bag over the table towards Bob. "That's a transfer for two million pounds, add it to the file. I'll go up and see our expert first thing in the morning."

"OK. You're roping in the whole family again, so what bit of magic do you want from me?" Terry addressed Steve as he sat back with his arms crossed over his chest.

"Mm, I'm not sure, Terry. Si has confirmed our suspect is in the wind. He thinks he's had help from his probation officer." Steve went into one of his thinking spells. It only lasted a few seconds. "If you were just out of prison, you'd need money if you were to beat the system of halfway houses and minimum wage jobs. Agreed?"

Everyone agreed.

"And who would know the best place to hide a few quid for the day he came out." Steve didn't wait for an answer. "A corrupt money man. I bet he stashed a bit away before they caught up with him."

He turned to his admin assistant. "Bob, what happened to our suspect's house after he went to prison? You said his wife and child had been murdered before he went down."

Bob Class once more set to thumping keys on his laptop keyboard. Everyone waited until he was finished.

"It says here his assets were seized including his house and sold at auction."

"So, he has nowhere else to stay. Let's assume this probation officer isn't stupid enough to harbour a murderer, where else would someone with money stay?"

Si grinned. "A bloody hotel."

"Exactly, and if he were a man of substance before his arrest, what's the odds he's doing himself proud in a five-star place."

Matt Conway who had been listening and admiring how Steve ran these sessions agreed.

"But how do we find him among all the hotels in London? It's not like Europe where each hotel guest is registered with the police."

Steve had a contented grin on his face as he looked at Terry. "I'm sure Inspector Harvey has yet another new toy that might help."

Terry smiled back and shook his head. "Not this time, Steve. I can't think how we would legally get into the databases of every hotel's guest list."

"But it could be done. You could hack into their reservations system?" Steve left the question hanging.

Terry initially failed to follow Steve's thought process as he continued to look for a solution. "Of course, with central booking these days we'd only need to get into three systems at the most. We could design an in and out fix that should leave no trace. These sites are so busy with current bookings and are running so many artificial intelligence protocols, I doubt anyone would be interested in some outside source looking at a previous booking." Terry was talking out loud to himself as he worked out a way of helping his friend. "If we got the right hook we'd be in and out in seconds."

Terry arrived back in the conscious world. "We are only looking for one name, this Charles Robb. Is that right?"

Steve was beaming. "That's right."

"And this is important. It's not just one of your fishing trips?"

"No, Terry, this guy has killed three times and we believe he may do again. We've definitely identified him. All we need is your help to find him."

Terry stood motionless. "I'm glad my wife is on a good salary and pension. One of these days, DCI Burt, you'll talk me into doing something that'll see me directing traffic."

Terry turned to go. "Leave it with me. I'll get you something for tomorrow morning." With a wave, Terry was gone.

Si Griffiths stood to leave. "You know, this is great. You guys just get the job done without all the red tape; I love it." As he walked towards the office door he added. "Must go, sir. It's after five and I'm not on overtime, I'll see everyone in the morning."

The three remaining officers laughed as Matt said, "That Si, he's something else."

Steve added. "But he's a bloody good detective. I've a feeling tomorrow might be a busy day."

Chapter Twenty-Eight

Thursday February 17 was the first morning that held at least the hint of warmth. Steve had arrived home after seven the previous evening to find his daughter finishing off her school homework and excited to tell him about her day. Alison, Steve's wife, allowed their daughter Rosie an extra ten minutes to chat to her daddy before ushering her to bed with the usual pouting lip and a series of, "*It's not fair. Some of my friends are allowed to stay up till after eight.*"

As a reluctant Rosie was frogmarched to bed Steve knew she'd be sound asleep within five minutes. He sat and smiled; he knew his daughter could sleep for England.

After a quick shower and something to eat he had spent an hour with Alison watching television and then had had an early night. He had admitted he was very tired, bordering on exhaustion. Alison reminded him of his promise to take a holiday on his birthday. Steve had realised this sounded an even better idea than when he'd originally agreed to it.

He rose early while Alison and Rosie slept. Over his second cup of coffee of the day he sat and reviewed the case in his head, but instead of the triple murders he saw Poppy, lying in a pool of blood. Steve knew he would never forget the bubbly detective constable and the thought once more spurred him on to see what was happening at Brompton Road. He knew Sir Patrick Bond of MI6 had sold him a story, but he didn't know why. Also, he knew the major was probably still located at Brompton Road and Steve was sure he held the key to the masked gunman who had tried to save Poppy's life.

Shaking himself awake and hearing Alison moving around their bedroom, he said his goodbyes and left for his office. It was 7.38 a.m.

***

As Steve left his house, Charlie, now known as Edwin Somerset, was lying in his oversized bed. He'd had a restless night's sleep thinking about Connie. He'd seen she'd called his burner phone six times in under an hour. When he'd taken her call, she was in a state of panic. She'd explained the police had called her asking what her relationship with Charlie was. As usual Charlie had to soft-soap her, telling her everything was all right and she shouldn't worry but it was clear she was beginning to fall apart. Charlie felt Connie might be a liability. He'd played back in his mind each murder and knew he'd been careful. He'd remembered being told that the police were good at fitting innocent people up, and circumstantial evidence wasn't real evidence. All the jailhouse lawyers he'd spoken with in prison were clear, circumstantial evidence didn't count.

Edwin, as he now was, went over everything again. He realised Connie had panicked. After all, she wasn't used to seeing how the law was applied when it was against her. He'd spoken with her for over half an hour last night, calming her down and reassuring her everything would be all right. The police had nothing on them. He knew he'd failed to convince her and was glad he'd kept his new identity and his new location secret from her. She knew about the money but not where it was. He arrived at a decision. Connie O'Sullivan would no longer be part of his life. He'd miss her gymnastics in the bedroom but knew there were other ladies in the world who could substitute for Connie.

Edwin stretched out. He knew he was safe, his mind was calm. Connie didn't know enough to hurt him. He sprang out of bed, showered, dressed and went down to the dining room for a hearty English breakfast. After that he'd drive his newly acquired latest model Jaguar to Chigwell to the address shown on the envelope the girl had given him yesterday. Something wasn't right in the life of Geoffrey Lockwood. Edwin couldn't work out what it was, but he would know by lunchtime today.

***

Steve walked into his office to find Terry Harvey, Matt Conway and Bob Class all drinking coffee and talking excitedly.

"There's a coffee on your desk, Steve, and our illegal hacker here has some news." Matt raised his cardboard cup to Terry.

Everyone moved into the DCI's inner office and sat at his overused conference table. Terry Harvey had the floor.

"We ran an overview programme overnight, using our own version of a standard software bundle. As I said with central booking in hotels these days we didn't have to look far. We got in and out quickly. Even if any of their security people look, I'm sure they won't see anything. I think we're clean and my pension's safe." Everyone smiled as Terry continued.

"We found six Charles Robbs staying in London hotels over the past few weeks. With one exception they only stayed one night. The one that stands out is still at the Mayflower Hotel."

"Great work, Terry. Matt, I want to follow up on the financial stuff this morning with Mrs Harvey." Steve had a sudden thought. "You and Bob get over to the Mayflower and lift our suspect. You don't have to be too subtle."

Steve saw Bob's jaw fall but he recovered and tried to look experienced as though arresting serial murderers was all in a day's work for him. Matt left followed by an excited Bob Class.

Terry was still sitting. "That was a nice move, Steve, the lad's better than a pen pusher."

"Yes, I know. I'm afraid he'll be off soon, and I'll have to break in another admin assistant." Steve stood up. He saw a file on his desk he knew was the financial data Bob had gathered together with the bank transfer slip for the two million pounds.

"I'm off to see Twiggy. I won't tell her you broke the law to help us solve this case."

Terry stood. "No, best not. Let's keep things like that between us."

***

Steve arrived at the vast open plan space that was Financial Crimes at 9.07 a.m. He knew where Florance Harvey's desk was. Being a section leader and a senior analyst, she had an area that was partitioned off by the use of portable free-standing screens. Each screen was about five foot high and afforded a degree of privacy.

Steve stuck his head around one of the screens and made a knocking sound as though he were tapping on a door. "Anyone in?"

Florance was busy looking through a large well-thumbed file as she looked up to see who her visitor was. "Steve, come in." She made an exaggerated show with her arms wide open as though she were inviting the DCI into a large office.

For a few seconds Steve recalled those early days when they worked together and how different Florance was now. She'd slimmed down although she would never be called thin and had forged a new career for herself as a forensic financial analyst. Steve shook himself out of his daydream.

"I've got a case that could benefit from your expertise." Without waiting for confirmation that Flo would look at the file he handed it to her and went on to explain about Charles Robb and the three murders. "You see, all three victims must have some connection to Robb going back up to ten years ago. Bob Class got some financial stuff that showed large sums going into Robb's personal account and then being transferred into his business account but that's as far as he got."

Steve knew she couldn't resist a challenge. She took the file and started to look at it.

"What has this bank transfer have to do with it?"

"Victim number three, Sebastian De Roy, made that transfer while our suspect was in his office. We think it's some kind of extortion money."

Flo nodded and continued to scan the file. "So, you're saying this Robb was funded by your three murder victims ten years ago and now he's out of prison and killing them. But why Steve? It doesn't make a lot of sense. Surely if he were scamming them, it would be them out to get him?"

"You see why I came to you?" Steve grinned. "From what we know the three victims got their money back when whatever financial scheme went belly up."

"Well, that's unusual in itself. Most financial schemes that go under do so leaving the investors to suffer the loss."

"I must admit it sounded a bit odd. Also, it's been suggested this Robb bloke was a bit of a patsy and was set up to take the fall."

Twiggy flicked pages in the file. "Intriguing! I must say Steve you know how to keep a girl interested."

The DCI stood up. "Thanks for the compliment, but seriously, if you can make time. I think we have our man, but we need evidence and motive. Like you said, everything seems the wrong way round. The villain's killing his investors. Have a look, please, I'm sure there's something there and if you could track down the two million transfer that would help."

"Only for you. Now go and have a cup of coffee and leave me to get on with this. I'll call you when I have something."

A satisfied DCI left to return to his office. It was only 9.28 a.m. and he felt his day was going well.

***

Despite Si's thinly veiled reference to his lack of overtime payments yesterday, he had left his girlfriend's house early enough to miss most of the rush hour traffic and pulled up outside Connie O'Sullivan's neat little house just as Steve was leaving Mrs Harvey to begin investigating the financial dealings of both his victims and suspect.

Si rang the bell and waited. At first, he thought no one was in but through the frosted glass section of the front door he saw a figure approach and open the door.

Connie saw a ragged looking badly dressed and tough-looking individual, who reached inside his jacket and opened a leather case containing a Metropolitan Police warrant card when she opened the door.

"I'm DS Griffiths. I believe we spoke yesterday on the phone. It is Miss O'Sullivan, isn't it?"

Si saw the look of shock pass over Connie's face as she weakly nodded that she was Miss O'Sullivan.

"Can I come in, please? I have a few questions."

Connie said nothing but dumbly held the door wide open and ushered the detective into her lounge. She invited Si to sit down and took a chair opposite.

Si studied Connie and saw a mid-thirties, good-looking, but tired, woman. Si didn't bother with small talk. He started straight in without any preamble. "Miss O'Sullivan, can I ask you what your relationship is with Charles Robb?"

Connie sat and stared at Si. She'd called Charlie ten times since they last spoke, and he hadn't answered. She felt abandoned but had no idea what to do. At first Si thought she hadn't heard the question. He was about to repeat the question when Connie spoke.

"I don't understand, I was his probation officer."

"We know that Miss O'Sullivan but what about your other relationship?" Si knew he was fishing.

"I don't follow." Connie couldn't look Si in the eye, and she was fidgeting with a handkerchief, rolling it between her fingers.

"When I phoned yesterday you didn't ask why we wanted to talk to Mr Robb. As a probation officer, even a retired one, I would have expected you to be a bit more curious. Why didn't you ask why we wanted to talk to him? Is it because you already know what he's doing?"

Connie suddenly gasped for air and put her hand to her mouth. A small tear formed at the corner of her left eye. She sat in silence. Si let the atmosphere build. He knew he wasn't dealing with a master criminal. It was clear Connie O'Sullivan had something to hide but Si needed to hear her tell him. He tried once more.

"Look, Connie, you're an intelligent woman. You've dealt with ex-convicts like Robb most of your working life. You must know that now we're on to him it can only be a matter of time before we wrap him up together with any accomplices he has. Do yourself a favour and tell us where he is and what your part has been in these murders."

This was the first time Si had referred to the reason they wanted to talk to Charlie Robb. Si didn't know that Terry had found Charlie Robb and that Matt and Bob were on their way to arrest him at the Mayflower Hotel. He'd deliberately mentioned murders hoping she'd slip up and admit she knew Charlie Robb was killing people.

Connie was obviously in some form of mild shock as Si pressed on. He wanted something to take to the DCI. He thought a full confession might get him another commendation. Into the silence Si heard a small whimper. It was Connie beginning to cry. She dabbed her eyes with her handkerchief and looked into Si's eyes for the first time.

"Have you ever been in love, sergeant?"

Si smiled as he replied, "Every time I got married."

Connie smiled weakly at this answer. She remembered Charlie's words from last night that the police had nothing but circumstantial evidence. She knew deep down Charlie had abandoned her, yet she still felt a strong tie to him. As she pulled herself together, she became stronger. The initial shock of finding this rough-looking policeman at her door was wearing off.

"I don't think I can tell you anything, sergeant, without a lawyer."

A disappointed Si stood. "Then I'll have to ask you to come with me, Miss. It's a pity because I was trying to avoid this." Si lied. "Can you please get your coat?"

***

Steve was in his office enjoying the peace that came from not having an outer office full of detectives. Everyone was out and he had time to savour his coffee knowing events were taking place while he sat and sipped his strong brew.

His mind continually drifted back to the major and his desire to find and talk to him. He couldn't explain it but his need for closure was becoming obsessional. He had to speak with the hooded gunman and learn first-hand what had happened when Poppy was killed. He resolved that no matter what, he would visit the Brompton Road shop today.

Giving himself a shake Steve reached for one of the many files that were on his desk demanding his attention. As he opened the file his phone rang. It was Matt Conway.

"Steve. Bad news. Our Mr Robb has flown. He checked out yesterday with no forwarding address. We've been over the room he had but it's clean. He paid cash for everything so we've no credit card info. I've got the hotel CCTV discs. Terry might get something, but bottom line is he's gone. The hotel manager says they only update records each morning so the data Terry was using must have been out of date."

Steve was more than disappointed. "OK, Matt, you and Bob get back here. We'll have to think again." Steve closed his mobile thinking; there was something, a way forward that he knew was staring him in the face. But what? He knew it would surface but hoped it would be soon. Their main suspect was in the wind and so far, they'd no way of tracing him. The clock on Steve's office wall showed 10.07 a.m.

***

Charlie Robb as Edwin Somerset was enjoying driving his hired Jaguar. He'd left his new hotel just before nine in order to drive to Chigwell. As he drove, he called the forger and agreed to pay for the items he needed. He was surprised by the size of the fee the forger demanded for a quick job. Edwin had agreed to pay if the documents he needed were ready on time. He was assured they would be and of the highest quality.

"They'll fool anybody."

His navigation system told him the journey would take fifty-one minutes but as Edwin arrived in Chigwell, he'd been on the road for more than an hour. It was 10.08 a.m. and Steve had just found out that Charlie Robb was missing. The moving map in the Jaguar took Edwin straight to The Glades, the home of Geoffrey Lockwood, his next victim.

Edwin drove slowly past the huge property that had been designed to look like a castle. It was way over the top in its design and could never be regarded as being tasteful. With its rounded turrets in each corner and small windows to the front, it certainly had a medieval appearance. The dark natural stone helped to create the effect. Detached from the castle was a modern block of garages with what looked like accommodation or offices above. The house stood in a large, enclosed plot. Edwin was surprised that there were no gates to the front to stop unwanted cars arriving. The street was occupied by similar houses that were not traditional in their architecture. Edwin thought this whole area said brash new money.

On his second pass of The Glades Edwin spotted a CCTV camera located inside the boundary fence of the property. It seemed to point towards the front door of the main house. This wasn't a real problem for him, but he decided to park his hire car a few hundred yards beyond the entrance, and dressed in his killing uniform of old coat and flat cap, he approached the front door. His .22 pistol was in his right-hand pocket. The entrance consisted of a pair of double doors made of heavy timber and aged to look medieval with black surface mounted hinges and a large black knocker depicting a lion's head. Edwin assumed this was to maintain the medieval effect.

He rapped the lion's head and waited. He carried the envelope from yesterday but had no plan. He wasn't even sure if this was the residence of the same Geoffrey Lockwood. Edwin stood for several minutes and was about to knock again when a well-dressed man wearing a short white coat usually worn by nurses or doctors appeared behind him

"Can I help you?"

The man was in his early fifties, with a full head of dark hair, but it was not Geoffrey Lockwood.

"Yes, I'm here to see Geoffrey Lockwood."

The man looked sceptical. "Do you have an appointment Mr…?"

"Name's Stevens and no, I don't have an appointment, but I have something for Mr. Lockwood."

The man eyed the envelope. "I'm Mr Lockwood's confidant and chief nurse, I'll see he gets the envelope."

Edwin had to think fast. "I'm sorry, my instructions are to place this into Mr Lockwood's hands. I can't give it to anyone else."

"Mr Lockwood is very busy and doesn't see people without an appointment. I think I really must insist you give me the envelope."

Edwin saw this well-dressed lacky was beginning to look menacing. He thought he'd try a different approach but was confused by this man's appearance.

"I suppose I could give it to you if I was sure it was going to the correct Geoffrey Lockwood."

"I assure you it will." The confidential secretary was looking confused.

"The Geoffrey Lockwood this is intended for used to run his own financial investment house ten years ago. He'd be about fifty-nine now." Edwin stood his ground.

"That sounds like my employer although his health has deteriorated in the past few years. I think you can give me the envelope now."

Edwin made one last show of defiance. "I will but does Mr Lockwood live here permanently. I was in his London office yesterday and his staff told me he never visits."

"Mr Lockwood does not leave these premises. His partner, Mr Marr, looks after the business." The well-dressed nurse was clearly becoming annoyed and looking even more menacing. Edwin handed over the envelope.

"Are you Mr Lockwood's carer then?" Edwin tried to sound flippant.

"I am employed by Mr Lockwood. Now if you don't mind, I have work to do."

With his cap firmly pulled over his head Edwin walked back down the drive towards the CCTV camera.

Sitting in his car he tried to understand what had just happened. The man had said Geoffrey Lockwood was ill and didn't leave the house. That might explain the London office. A sudden thought struck him. If Lockwood were ill enough to need a full-time nurse he might be living above the garage. The castle-like house didn't look very inviting. The garage block was modern and would be more suitable if he needed round-the-clock care. As the block looked new, Edwin wondered if it had been built specifically to care for Geoffrey Lockwood.

Edwin eased his car back towards The Glades. The road was wide, and he found a spot that gave a view of the garages. Edwin surmised that if this building were doubling up as a hospital then it would be obvious the longer he watched. He settled down to a boring day. It was 10.39 a.m.

***

Si arrived with Connie at New Scotland Yard as Edwin Somerset settled down to keep watch. He showed her into an interview suite normally used to interview victims rather than suspects. The starker surroundings of the interview rooms below ground were depressing and Si thought Connie might open up easier in nicer surroundings. He offered her a cup of tea which she accepted.

Si had tried to get her to open up on the journey south, but Connie didn't talk. She just sat sniffing back tears.

Si left her in the company of a WPC and went to his office to report in. As he arrived, he could feel there was an atmosphere that he didn't like. Something was wrong.

Steve called everyone in and confirmed with Si that he had delivered Connie.

"She's in the posh suite but she's not saying anything. I'm sure she's involved but I'm not sure how deeply. She seems a bit fragile but when she was processed, she had a mobile that isn't registered. If we could get hold of it, we might get a link to the boyfriend."

"We'd have to officially arrest her first. I presume she's being interviewed under caution?"

"Yes, she will be but I'm not sure she knows it. Everything's gone over her head. All she did say was that she wanted a solicitor, but I didn't hear her, so I've done nothing about it." Si chuckled to himself at this obvious breach of procedure. The DCI nodded his understanding. There were no witnesses to her request, and legal representation often got in the way of discovering the real truth. Steve considered. "Si, get her the duty solicitor. She might tell him things not knowing he might be bound to tell us. If she's only a pawn he might persuade her to cooperate."

Si made a call.

Once everyone was settled, Steve began.

"Matt and Bob went to the Mayflower Hotel, but Charles Robb had checked out. He paid everything by cash and the hotel have no idea where he went." Steve puffed out his cheeks. "Any ideas?"

"Our lady downstairs might know if we can get her talking." Si didn't sound convinced.

"Mm. Si, you and I will interview her when we're finished here."

The room was silent as everyone thought. Bob was keying away on his trusted laptop. He looked up at his boss. "There's nothing coming through from any of the CCTV cameras and the pathologist sent an e-mail. He's not happy no one turned up for the post-mortem this morning." Bob was reading as he spoke.

"He says it's a breach of protocol but fortunately the post mortem was straight forward. A .22 calibre was found in the forehead. The bullet has been sent to ballistics but he's fairly certain it'll be a match to the other two. His wife's doing the identification this morning, but the doc says it's a formality and if you're busy he'll record it." Bob finished reading and smiled. "He says you owe him a beer."

"Right. So, we're sure our man Robb has killed three times. Mrs Harvey is looking into the financial records, but she thinks it looks odd. She says it's unusual for the perpetrator to go after the victims. She said she'd explain." The DCI rubbed his hands. "Come on folks, ideas. Where the hell is Charlie Robb?"

"We should put out an all ports in case he's skipping the country." Matt Conway looked around the nodding heads. "We should declare him armed and dangerous."

"Good point, Matt. Bob, can you get onto it?"

Bob Class was already keying away.

Si spoke. "If our boy was staying in one hotel, what's to say he's not just moved to another. Maybe we need Inspector Harvey to work his magic again."

"Right. Matt talk to Terry, ask him for another trawl of hotel bookings for last night."

Matt leapt from his chair and dashed off to see Terry.

As Steve sat his brain kicked into gear and he suddenly recalled the thing that had flashed his brain previously. "He must have wheels; you know a car. The easiest way to get a car is to hire one. We should look for our boy on hire car company records."

"Bloody hell, you're right, boss, I should have thought of that." Si was becoming a team player.

Steve spoke to his admin assistant. "Bob, can you search hire car records?"

"I think so. What am I looking for?"

"Charles Robb must have hired a car from say the day after he was released, start there. Search from Sunday the sixth."

"It'll take a while, sir."

"Do your best Bob. We need to catch this bloke."

Steve and Si left to interview Connie O'Sullivan. It was 11.23 a.m.

***

Mrs Harvey arrived just as Steve and Si were leaving. "Don't go, I've got what you wanted." She looked excited, and the DCI knew she had something.

Steve ushered her into his office. Matt had just returned and said Terry Harvey would run his programme again. Steve asked Matt and Si to join him to hear what Flo had to say.

With everyone seated around Steve's conference table she began. With an inward smile, Steve recalled his early days of working with her and how she loved being centre stage.

As always, she had a thick file with her which now sat on the table in front of her. She opened it but didn't initially refer to it.

"This is a bit complicated, so I'll go slowly. Even I have had trouble understanding what's gone on. First, your suspect Charles Robb is an idiot, at least financially. He signed up to something no right-minded finance guy would. I checked where the large amounts that were paid into his personal account came from. It started with a Geoffrey Lockwood, then a Sebastian De Roy, then an Anthony Maple and the last amount for a million came from a Colin Clark. Strangely, the first investors put in the most."

She paused to make sure everyone was following. It seemed they were.

"OK. Each time Robb received these sums into his account he transferred it into his business account making it look as though he were investing in his own business and selecting his own stocks. Only a fool or a chump would do that. I checked with his bank, and it gets worse. Each of these four investors had a power of attorney over Robb's business account and this Geoffrey Lockwood had full authority over the account. In other words, your man Robb wasn't fully in control of his own destiny. Everything ran through Geoffrey Lockwood."

Twiggy paused once more to examine the faces of her audience. They looked blank but she carried on.

"From the records it seems Robb invested in start-up businesses that frankly no one else would touch. However, they all seemed to flourish and as an investor Robb made a lot of money. Lockwood seems to have transferred the profits to his own account in the Caymans. I had a tough job getting details but eventually I got what I wanted. I was able to complete the trail. Each month Robb's investments appeared to make a profit. Ten percent was left in Robb's account and the remainder was transferred from Robb's business account under Lockwood's signature to his own account in the Caymans. From there it seems it was split and transferred in smaller amounts to the UK accounts of De Roy, Maple and Clark. All this was before we had tight money laundering laws and international cooperation. Ten years or so ago this would have been almost impossible to spot. Also, Lockwood was the signatory on the accounts and the audit. He had control of everything. I doubt your man Robb had a clue. Everything Lockwood did was hidden from the authorities at the time. He used shell companies and overseas nominees. I doubt if even now we'd really get to the bottom of it."

Once more Florance paused. Her audience appeared restless still awaiting the punchline if there was one.

"The reason all Robb's investments made money was he was the figurehead for a scheme I believe was being run by Geoffrey Lockwood. Robb's business was seen as successful, so he had no problem attracting small investors with promises of high returns. From what I can see however I don't believe he knew anything about it. Again, Lockwood fed funds into Robb's business account that came from small investors. Because he had control, these funds were declared as profits, not investments. The monthly newly invested money was taken as profit and never invested. The investment period was two to four years. I found investment statements that were sent to these small investors. They were signed by Charles Robb as the sole investment manager, Lockwood's name was nowhere."

The DCI had heard enough but needed clarification.

Steve paused as he ticked off points he'd made on his pad. He continued, "You're saying this Lockwood using Robb as a front raised money from small investors that Robb knew nothing about and declared this as profits and effectively stole these funds that were never invested? So, what happened?"

"As with all such schemes investors expected to see a return. From what I've discovered a few got something in the beginning but as more and more promissory notes become due it would have been clear the funds weren't there. I can't be certain, but I don't think Robb knew much about this. He was an idiot, totally exposed. It appears the initial millions from the four investors were never invested. Lockwood transferred these funds to another account. He probably spun Robb a tale about secrecy or such nonsense. Anyway, Lockwood cleaned out the initial funding so all four got their money back and of course the so-called monthly profits for about three years."

Steve looked up from his notes.

"How much money are talking about being scammed?"

"I'd have to dig deeper and that'll take time, but I'd say at least seventy-five million."

"And Robb would have received his share, not asked too many questions but was the fall guy when it all went wrong?" Steve sat back and threw his pencil onto his notepad.

Florance who hadn't looked at the file in front of her nodded. "Looks that way. Like I told you when you brought this to me. If it's revenge, then it's unusual for the crook to seek revenge on his victims unless the crook was the victim.

"Anyway, the other thing is I was able to trace that two million you had the transfer slip for. I don't have much except it went to an account in the Caymans. The name on the account was Charles Robb. From there it was immediately transferred again to another Cayman bank, but I can't find any record of it leaving the Caymans. This second bank is a known money launderer and if your man was prepared to pay their fees it could be anywhere under any name."

Silence filled the room until Matt said, "So, he's got money, but do we think he's going after the people who set him up? Do we think Geoffrey Lockwood's next on his list?"

"Mm, it's possible." The DCI needed thinking time.

Steve thanked Twiggy for her help and made the usual joke about a family affair. Florance ordered Steve not to keep her husband working late. Despite the news Florance had brought, the meeting broke up on a jovial note.

Steve turned to Matt. "What do you think, Matt? Is our boy going after these four investors?"

"I'd say so. Sounds like he might have cause and if he's killed them starting with Clark and working up, he's saved the biggest crook till last if Lockwood is in fact his next victim."

"Get Bob to sort out contact details for Lockwood. Shouldn't be too hard. He must be London based and still working in finance. A trawl of financial firms should find him." Steve looked at his watch. "It's 12.25 p.m. He's probably in his office so start there. Get a uniform and go see him. Tell him our concerns and offer him protection until we lift Robb."

Matt left and Steve heard him ask Bob Class for the address details of Geoffrey Lockwood.

Steve phoned the interview suite to be told the duty solicitor was with his suspect. "Get them both a hot drink and tell the solicitor we'll be there in about half an hour. Give him some time with his client."

Steve patted Si on the shoulder. "Come on, I'll buy you a coffee before we get started."

Chapter Twenty-Nine

Edwin had sat for almost two hours seeing little activity in and around the garage. A small white van had arrived and delivered something, but he didn't know what it was. At 12.25 p.m. a Range Rover driven by Geoffrey Lockwood's head nurse and accompanied by two other people in similar white coats left through the entrance.

Edwin considered his options. There were no cars parked beside the garage now the Range Rover had gone. He agonised over what to do but maybe no one was around and now would be a good time to visit the area above the garages. Even if Lockwood wasn't there it would give him more information.

He exited his car and walked smartly up the drive keeping to the right-hand side. As the drive swept to the right and the CCTV camera was pointing at the front door, which was off to the left of the drive, Edwin thought he was safe. He still wore his killing uniform, and his cap was pulled over his eyes.

There was an external staircase leading to a door that obviously gave access to the area above the garages. There was a door at ground level by the foot of this staircase. Edwin slowly opened this door. As he peered inside, he saw another Range Rover. There was nothing else in the great space that could hold up to four cars.

Closing this door, he made his way upstairs. He was surprised that this door at the top of the stairs wasn't locked, and a gentle pull saw Edwin step inside. He was met with a smell he associated with hospitals. He was in a small area measuring no more than twelve square feet. Everything was painted white. A set of two doors led off this area. Edwin opened one and found he was looking into an office. It looked like any other office except the desk was clear. There was no evidence of a computer and no filing cabinets. Just a desk and a series of comfortable looking chairs. Again, the walls were painted white, and the floor was covered in some form of highly polished grey linoleum.

Edwin backed out of this room and stood listening for any sounds. He heard none so proceeded to open the other door. As he stepped inside, he saw what might have been a hospital ward despite having only one hospital-style bed. The room was large with natural light coming in through several large Velux-style roof lights. Like the other room everything was white, and the same sterile looking highly polished grey linoleum covered the floor.

Closing the door behind him Edwin saw a man sitting in a wheelchair reading some papers. He didn't look up as Edwin slowly moved towards him.

"I'm not ready for my next infusion." The voice was weak but still held an air of authority. The man still didn't look up.

"Good, because I'm not here to give it to you."

The man looked up and tried to spin his wheelchair to face Edwin.

"Who the hell are you and how did you get in here?"

Edwin immediately recognised Geoffrey Lockwood although he was much thinner. He'd also lost most of his hair and Edwin saw his hands were shaking.

"Geoffrey, I'm your worst nightmare."

Lockwood had a tray positioned on his wheelchair. He put his papers down and changed his glasses. He stared at Edwin for a long time. Edwin let the silence hang between them.

"Good God, it's you. I thought you'd die in prison."

"Sorry to disappoint you. As you can see, I'm here, alive and well and looking better than you."

"What do you want?"

"Well, the first thing is I want four million pounds." Edwin threw down the same piece of paper containing the Cayman Islands Bank account details, that he had had in Sebastian de Roy's office.

Lockwood grabbed it and placed it on his tray without glancing at it.

"You must be mad. Why would I give you four million?"

Edwin repeated the calculation he'd made with Sebastian De Roy only he doubled the amounts. After stating his calculations, Edwin stood back looking at his next victim.

"I wouldn't disagree with your calculations but I'm not about to pay you a penny."

Edwin produced his pistol. After an initial shock at seeing the gun Lockwood recovered his composure.

"What's this? Are you going to shoot me? Look at me, I'm dying. You can't do anything to me. Killing me now would be a blessing. You see I know what's ahead of me, so go on, pull the trigger. I'm almost begging you."

As Lockwood finished talking, he entered into a coughing fit that shook his whole body. He pointed to a cabinet beside his bed and croaked, "Water."

As he continued to struggle for air Edwin smiled a wicked smile. He enjoyed seeing this man suffer and considered how he could prolong his suffering. He didn't move and Lockwood continued to struggle. Eventually and without water, Lockwood reached for an oxygen mask that was connected to an oxygen bottle located under his wheelchair.

It took several minutes for Lockwood to recover. He looked viciously at Edwin.

"Get out! There's nothing here for you."

Edwin moved closer to his victim and put the plastic bag containing the bank details in his hand. "I enjoyed seeing you suffer just now. I came here to kill you but seeing you like this has given me an idea. Unless you make that transfer, I'm going to shoot you in places that won't kill you but will be very painful. I've got ten bullets. I wonder at which number between one to ten you'll crack."

"You're bluffing." A seriously weakened Geoffrey Lockwood didn't sound so confident.

Edwin roughly removed the oxygen mask. This action created a large red weal on Lockwood's cheek.

"Now." Edwin placed the gun on Lockwood's knee. "I'm told the pain from having your kneecap shattered is excruciating. I'll count to three. If you say yes before I get to three then I won't fire."

Edwin could see the terror in Lockwood's eyes. He was a dying man who was obviously in pain, but the thought of further pain was too much for him. Lockwood immediately cried out, "OK. I'll do it. Don't shoot."

It took Edwin and Lockwood several minutes to key in the transfer details into Lockwood's laptop which was located on a cabinet by his desk. Once it was done, Edwin retrieved his bank details. Lockwood looked exhausted.

"Can you please give me my oxygen mask?" His breath was coming in short bursts.

Edwin did as he was requested. Once Lockwood appeared more stable, Edwin addressed the other issue he'd come for.

"The heavy you sent to scare my family killed them. Where will I find him?"

All the fight and arrogance had left Lockwood. He was a broken man but as Edwin asked about the killer, he felt his anger rise.

"His name is Nick Ralph. I don't know where he lives but his sister lives in Tower Hamlets. One of my staff at the time found him. That's all I know."

"Come on, Lockwood. You don't send someone on an errand like that without at least having a phone number."

Lockwood looked at the anger on Edwin's face and feared he might just shoot his kneecap. "All right, my phone's by the bed. There's an old number in there for him but I haven't used it in years."

As Edwin walked to the side of the bed his mobile rang confirming four million pounds had been credited to his Cayman account as Charles Robb."

Having scrolled through the numbers, Edwin found the number for Nick Ralph. He made a note.

"Now, Geoffrey, it's time to say goodbye."

Edwin wearing his latex gloves shot Geoffrey Lockwood between the eyes. He found that with each killing it got easier. His initial panic had gone. His heart rate, although increased, was under control and he was calm. He walked from the hospital room, descended the stairs, and staying on the blind side of the drive to avoid the CCTV, left his fourth victim behind. He almost joked with himself that he'd saved the family a fortune in medical bills.

Edwin slid into the driver's seat of his Jaguar and keyed the postcode of the forger, Rex, into the satnav. It was 1.26 p.m. It had taken less than fifty minutes to get revenge on the man mainly responsible for his time in prison.

As Edwin drove towards the forger's small semi-detached property to collect his more legitimate driver's licence, he dialled the number Lockwood gave him for Nick Ralph. To his surprise it was answered by what sounded like a little girl.

Not knowing what to say Edwin blurted out, "Is your daddy there?"

"No. He's at work and I'm off school with the mumps. My granny's here."

"Can I speak with her, please and I hope you get better soon?"

The phone was obviously swinging on its cord and banging against a wall. A rough north London voice came on the line.

"Yes. Who is this?"

Not wishing to give anything away, Edwin answered, "I'm looking for Nick Ralph. I'm an old friend of his."

"Oh, yeah. How old a friend?" The voice was suspicious.

"We did a bit of business about ten years ago. I've been away and might have a bit of work for Nick."

"What's your name?"

"Geoffrey Lockwood." Edwin smiled at his answer.

"Nick's not in. He's helping our son, young Nick with a removal. Call back tonight after six."

"Right. I'll do that. Are you still in Tower Hamlets?"

"Yeah. The council won't rehouse us, says we're not a priority."

The line went dead. Edwin was close to finishing his mission and becoming a new man.

***

Steve and Si walked into the interview suite at almost the same time Edwin was driving away from The Glades to visit his forger. After the usual formalities and introductions, Steve explained that the interview was being recorded.

Steve began. "Miss O'Sullivan. We understand you know a man called Charles Robb?"

As Connie looked tearfully at Steve, the duty solicitor, a young woman neatly dressed in dark a business suit spoke.

"Detective Chief Inspector, my client is prepared to make a statement but will not answer any questions. She has explained the circumstances she believes have led to her being here and wishes to claim complete innocence in any events leading up to this interview. I trust this is clear."

This was not what Steve wanted but he decided to play along. Clearly this young duty solicitor was no fool.

Steve sat back, nodded and crossed his arms over his chest, waiting.

It took Connie a few minutes to compose herself.

"I first met Charlie Robb on the seventh of February this year. He was newly released from HMP Whitby having served half his sentence. He was released on parole, and I was assigned his probation officer. Right from the start I was attracted to him and allowed him to take me to dinner a few times. On one occasion he told me his story and I felt sorry for him but found I was drawn more to him because of what certain people had done to him. He told me the names of the people who'd robbed him of everything he had and were responsible for killing his wife and son. I felt sorry for him and saw a man I could care for." Connie was struggling to maintain her composure and Steve noted someone had already given her a glass of water. The duty solicitor tapped her gently on the shoulder as an encouragement to carry on.

"I read in the paper that a man called Colin Clark had been murdered and remembered this was one of the names Charlie had given me. I confronted him and asked if he were the killer. He initially denied it but later confessed he had killed Colin Clark. I told him as an officer of the court I'd have to report him, but he persuaded me not to do it.

"I don't know how or why but I suddenly became enthralled with the excitement of what Charlie was doing. He said he'd served his time and now he was out for revenge. He said the legal system had let him down and that he was innocent of the crimes he had served time for. He assured me he was only seeking revenge and convinced me that we had a future together and promised there would be no further killings once he'd taken care of the people who set him up." Connie sipped her water.

Steve sat quietly listening to what he now understood was a very naïve woman.

"You have to understand I have never been married, had few boyfriends and I suppose I needed a release. I needed more from life than I was getting and here was Charlie. A damaged individual with a purpose to his life. Suddenly I could be part of the excitement. I knew I was being silly, but I believed it when he told me we'd be together on a sandy beach somewhere warm, and we'd never return to the UK."

Connie wiped away a tear and sipped more of her water. "I know I've been silly, and I admit I knew what Charlie was doing but I turned a blind eye. I helped him locate some of the people he was after but at no time did I assist or in any way help with the killings."

Connie sat still as the silence filled the air.

"That is all my client wishes to say at this time." The duty solicitor made to stand. The DCI held up his hand.

"Just a moment. Miss O'Sullivan, are you confirming that Charles Robb told you he had killed Colin Clark and that he intended to kill Anthony Maple, Sebastian De Roy and Geoffrey Lockwood?"

Connie nodded.

"Can you please answer for the tape?"

"Yes. He told me."

"Are you aware Anthony Maple and Sebastian De Roy have been murdered?"

"Not De Roy. I haven't heard from Charlie. To be truthful I think he's cut me off. He's abandoned me."

Steve looked at the duty solicitor who smiled back and shook her head. She had allowed her client to incriminate herself.

"DCI Burt, my client has given her statement freely. I have advised her to say no more until you can confirm your intentions regarding charges you may wish to bring. Miss O'Sullivan admits to being a willing partner in the shall we say organisation of three of these murders but denies involvement in their execution."

Steve acknowledged the duty solicitor's comments.

"Miss O'Sullivan, I intend to arrest you as an accomplice to murder. Another officer will go through the formalities that I am sure your solicitor will insist on. I believe you have been foolish and are not responsible for the actions of Charles Robb. If you agree to be a witness for the crown at his trial, I will attempt to let the court know my views as to your involvement. I cannot promise but it may help with your sentencing. Now, we need you to give a full statement. Someone will be in shortly."

Steve and Si stood. Si closed down the twin recording machine and removed the tapes. He gave one to the solicitor and kept the other one. Outside the interview suite the two detectives stood looking at each other.

"Well done, Si, your gut was correct. We've got our witness. She'll come across as credible. Now all we need is to arrest our suspect."

The pair headed back to the office where Steve asked Bob to arrange for someone to take Connie's statement and then to formally arrest and charge her with conspiracy to murder.

***

Matt, accompanied by two uniformed constables, visited the offices of Lockwood and Marr to be told the same thing Edwin had been told earlier.

"Mr Lockwood works from home."

Armed with Geoffrey Lockwood's address in Chigwell the officers set out for The Glades. It was 1.51 p.m. as the marked police car drove up the drive of The Glades and parked outside the house. It was less than thirty minutes since Edwin had driven away.

Matt used the old-style door knocker to tell whoever was inside that he was at the front door. As he waited, the Range Rover with the same three occupants that Edwin had seen leave, returned. The Range Rover stopped short of the garages and all three exited the car. Geoffrey Lockwood's personal assistant walked briskly towards the police officers.

Matt held out his warrant card and introduced himself.

"Mr Lockwood will be in his room above the garage. Is there anything wrong, inspector?"

"Not at this stage, sir." Matt didn't want to alert the man in the white coat. "Purely routine at this stage. We just need a word."

The three policemen and the chief nurse climbed the stairs to the hospital-style rooms. On entering the main bedroom Matt immediately saw that Geoffrey Lockwood was dead.

He held out his arms. "Everyone out, please move back down the stairs."

Everyone did, including Matt, as he reached for his phone. "Steve, Geoffrey Lockwood's been murdered. I didn't go into the room, but it looks like a bullet to the centre of his skull."

With this news the DCI set the wheels in motion. The circus was activated and within twenty minutes The Glades looked like a scene out of a disaster movie. Police cars were parked at odd angles, White, unmarked vans seemed to be everywhere, and a larger black Ford Transit pulled in beside the garages. The scene was secured with blue and white tape everywhere.

The same pathologist arrived and was examining the body as scene of crime officers dressed in disposable white suits with hoods pulled up to examine every inch of the building. Steve arrived at 2.20 p.m. Matt was standing at the foot of the stairs that led to the hospital room.

"What have we got, Matt?"

"Pathologist says death was within the last hour. Cause of death a bullet to the forehead probably a .22 again. Looks like our boy, Robb."

"Let's have a look."

The detectives suitably dressed in blue plastic overshoes and gloves entered the room.

"Nothing much here. It looks like a hospital ward." Steve was taken aback as he saw the victim was seated in a wheelchair.

The pathologist looked up as he saw the DCI.

"Poor sod, only had months to live. Judging by the medication I'd say terminal cancer. Maybe your killer did him a favour. I'll get the body removed and do the PM tomorrow. Please turn up this time, gentlemen, I can't cover for you indefinitely."

Back at ground level Steve was introduced to Lockwood's private nurse.

"This is Mr Steel, sir."

"Did you see anything, Mr Steel?"

"No. Myself and my two colleagues left to collect medical supplies at around twelve thirty. Mr Lockwood was alive then. I left him his medication and some business papers Mr Marr wanted his opinion on. When I returned your officers were here and we discovered poor Mr Lockwood."

"Have you had any visitors recently?"

"We don't encourage visitors, but we had a horrible looking man here earlier today. He brought the daily envelope for Mr Lockwood from his office. He seemed very interested in whether Mr Lockwood was in residence."

Steve glanced around and saw the CCTV camera.

"Would this man be on your CCTV system?"

"It's possible. I can get the disk for you if you want."

"Please. Just one more thing, was this man wearing an old brown coloured raincoat and did he have a flat cap?"

"Well, yes, he did."

Steve and Matt exchanged glances.

"Do you have the envelope this man delivered?"

The chief nurse looked pleased with himself.

"Yes. It's unopened but if you'll excuse me inspector, you won't get any fingerprints. I noticed the man was wearing skin coloured latex gloves, but I'll get the envelope anyway."

Matt scratched his head.

"Who is this guy? He seems to be one step ahead of us all the time." With more than a little frustration Matt kicked at the gravel drive. "Christ. We know who he is, we know what he looks like, but we haven't even had a sniff of a sighting."

Steve considered Matt's outburst. "You're right, this isn't some innocent financial mug. This is a clever and ruthless murderer; he's had an education." Steve brightened up. "Never mind, Matt, we'll catch him. He'll make a mistake, they all do. You stay here and finish things off. I'll see you back at the ranch."

***

Edwin had visited the forger and now had a driving licence that would pass any scrutiny. He returned to the Albion Hotel and arranged for his money to move one more time. He remembered the advice he'd received about making money disappear. With his financial background he knew some of the ways, but his inmate colleagues had told him about more creative ways of ensuring money could not be traced.

Six million pounds was enough to appear on most governments' banking radar. The trick was not to hide it but to make it seem legitimate. Rather than use a fence who would charge a fifty percent fee to clean the money, one of Edwin's teachers inside had offered a selection of more devious and safer ways of cleaning cash.

Edwin had contacted a real estate agent in Edinburgh and had enquired about buying a small Scottish estate for just under two million pounds. The agent had naturally agreed to help with all the details including recommending a solicitor who was part of the same firm. Edwin had contacted the agent the week previously and had agreed to transfer money into the solicitor's client account in order to complete the purchase. Edwin had no intention of completing such a purchase and after a suitable time would withdraw from the transaction and have his funds returned to his new UK bank account.

Edwin had made three such calls and his money in tranches of two million pounds each was now sitting in solicitor's client's accounts in Edinburgh, Glasgow and Inverness. Edwin's teacher, a corrupt Scottish solicitor, had told him in Scotland it was normal for estate agents to also be solicitors so they could accept cash into their client's accounts when a property transaction was being negotiated. The teacher emphasised that everything to do with money laundering and source of funds was a tick box exercise. If the person transferring the funds had a good and believable story, and provided they signed the declaration stating they understood the penalties for lying, then the agent would accept the funds as legitimate. In Edwin's case he'd declared to each solicitor independently that the two million came from the sale of a property in the USA. He knew the forger could supply suitable documents if required. They were not. The teacher told Edwin that if money was transferred from a solicitor's client account into a regular bank account, no one would question the source of the funds. The money would be clean.

Using the hotel's travel desk, Edwin Somerset booked a first-class seat on tomorrow afternoon's BA flight to New York together with a reservation for seven nights in the Waldorf Astoria in New York. It was time to get away and put some clear water between himself and his killings. He still had enough money left from his initial hundred thousand. He told himself it was time for him to relax and recharge his batteries.

It was 5.07 p.m. when Edwin now feeling everything was falling into place left his hotel and drove to Tower Hamlets. His plan was simple. He would park up in a central spot, call Nick Ralph at six and arrange to meet him. By being close by he should meet his victim early. With any luck he'd be in the dining room of the Albion Hotel and Spa eating a delicious dinner before eight p.m.

***

Steve Burt called his team together for a final debrief before sending them home. It was 5.49 p.m. minutes before Edwin put the final part of his plan into action.

"Right, folks. Let's see where we are. Bob, what have you got?"

"I'm sorry, sir, but not a lot. Ballistics have come back. The bullet that killed De Roy is a match to the other two."

"Right. So, we find the gun we find the killer. Si's contact sold a .22 calibre to Charlie Robb and we're assuming that's the gun he's using. When we find Robb, we can hopefully link him to the gun. Anything else Bob?"

"I've been through the CCTV from today's killing. There was only one camera, so it didn't take long. The guy who delivered the envelope knew the camera was there. He seemed to deliberately walk on the side of the drive that wasn't fully covered by the camera. I asked Inspector Harvey to run comparisons between the figure from today against the other images we have from the other shootings. He says it's a match. It's the same bloke in the old raincoat and cap but we've no facial images. I examined the footage from the afternoon, it's the same thing. We see him going in and coming out but no facial recognition. All we do have is the timeline. The pathologist's provisional time of death for today's victim coincides with this mystery character leaving the premises."

"Good. Bob, how about the hire car companies?"

"It's not so easy because they all run worldwide booking programmes. Do you know if you phone to book a car, you could be talking to someone in Canada? It's a bit of a nightmare to be honest, sir, but so far I'm not getting anywhere."

"Have you spoken to Terry Harvey?"

"Yes. He's given me another piece of software that he says will help but he says it's a time thing. It can be done but there's no quick fix."

"Mm. Keep at it, Bob and good work."

"Thank you, sir. There's nothing from the all ports, so our boy should still be in the country."

Si spoke up. "Or he's got a new identity. Remember he got two million from De Roy. If he's changed his name, we may never catch him."

Matt raised a hand. "It gets worse. I spoke with Lockwood's partner, Marr. He told me four million was transferred to a bank in the Caymans today. He's sending over a copy of the transfer, but it hasn't come in yet. What's the bet, our boy Robb is now sitting on six million?"

Steve didn't like what he was hearing. He looked around the table.

"Any other cheerful news anyone would like to share?"

"Connie O'Sullivan has made her statement and added a few more things but fundamentally she knows nothing." Si looked dejected for the first time since joining the team.

Steve tried to lighten things.

"OK. We know who we're looking for. Every beat bobby has a picture of Robb. If he hasn't changed his name then he's still here, it's only a matter of time. You've all done great work. We've built our case. When we get Robb it's a slam dunk." The DCI smiled and laughed. "Now go home and have a late start tomorrow."

Bob raised his hand. "I've had an e-mail reminding us about the post-mortem tomorrow. Ten sharp."

Steve knew his team were dispirited at the lack of progress but could do nothing about it.

"Matt, you and I will do that. Now off you all go and have a good night's sleep."

It was 6.39 p.m. when the meeting broke up.

Chapter Thirty

Edwin called Nick Ralph at 6.09 p.m. He sounded out of sorts and wasn't pleased to get the call. His mother had only relayed part of Edwin's message. Once he explained, posing as Geoffrey Lockwood, that he had a job for Ralph, the murderer became more cheerful and less distant.

Nick Ralph, on hearing that the matter was urgent, and he could earn a significant sum, suggested they should meet in the Golden Goose pub in half an hour. Ralph gave Edwin directions to the pub, and they agreed to meet.

Edwin, now posing as Geoffrey, sat in the prescribed spot nursing a half pint of bitter. A huge man entered through the door, standing well over six foot. He wore a black vest that showed off his massive arms and the training pants he wore looked as though they had been painted onto his legs. This was a very large man. His head was shaven, and his nose was bent indicating it had been broken probably more than once and had never been professionally set.

Carrying a pint of best, he approached the person he thought was Geoffrey Lockwood. Edwin was wearing his killing uniform and had the pistol in the right-hand pocket of his raincoat. Nick Ralph sat down and stared at Edwin.

"I don't remember you. What's going on?"

Edwin was immediately intimidated by this monster of a man. He wondered if his little gun was powerful enough to drive a bullet into his skull. Nick Ralph's voice was croaky from smoking too many cigarettes and Edwin had difficulty in understanding him.

"Yes. I'm sorry but if I had told you who I really am you wouldn't have come."

"Oh, yeah, and who are you then?"

Edwin knew he was entering a dangerous area. When he'd devised his plan, he had no idea the killer of his family would be so large but he was determined to see it through. He told himself he had the gun.

"I'm the husband of the woman you butchered nine years ago and the father of the little boy you knifed to death."

Edwin let this statement hang in the air. He saw the expression on Nick Ralph's face change from one of arrogance to surprise.

"How did you find me?"

"Geoffrey Lockwood gave me your details before I killed him."

Nick Ralph drank down his beer in one swallow and laughed.

"Well, good for you. That sniffling little toad refused to pay me because I'd used too much force. So, what do you want? Are you going to kill me too?"

"That's the plan."

"Well, I admire your balls but it's not going to happen. Are you going to shoot me here because a bullet is the only way you'll get me?"

Nick Ralph seemed too calm. It was almost as though he didn't believe Edwin would go through with it. Edwin produced the gun and because there were no other customers in the snug, he was able to lift it above the table and quickly point it at Ralph. Nick Ralph continued to look calm.

"Very good. So, you think you're going to just shoot me with that pea shooter? Listen, I was a wrestler and back in the day punks like you tried all sorts of ways to get me to throw a fight not realising they was all fixed anyway." Nick laughed at his own story. "You're not going to shoot me here. Better do it outside." He stood up and walked towards the door. "Come on, if you're coming."

The big man filled the door and even had to bend down so as not to bang his head. Edwin followed keeping his right hand on his gun.

There were a few people outside and Edwin saw Nick Ralph amble towards an opening that ran down the side of the pub. He turned into this opening and Edwin followed.

As soon as he turned the corner, he saw stars. Nick had swung a punch that although it failed to connect with Edwin's jaw, still rendered him immobile and he fell against the wall wondering what had just happened. Nick stood over him with his hands on his oversized hips. He stared and said nothing.

After a few minutes Edwin's head began to clear and he realised he'd been stupid and had walked into a trap. His mind hadn't fully focused when he remembered the gun. This brute had the upper hand, but Edwin had the gun. He struggled with his right hand grasping for the gun as he pulled his arm from his raincoat pocket. As he got it out his hand was suddenly on fire. Nick Ralph knowing what Edwin would try kicked the weapon from Edwin's grasp.

"Not very good at this are you?"

Nick took two paces and picked up the gun.

"Now listen. I'm sorry about your wife and kid. I really didn't mean to kill them, but your wife came at me with a kitchen knife and your boy got between us. Stabbing your wife was an accident but I confess, I had to do your son in case he could identify me. Believe me, that has lived with me since then. I know you're out for revenge, but this isn't the way. If you've already killed Lockwood, then that's enough. He was an evil man."

Edwin's head was clearing as he sat on the ground with his back against the wall. "Just tell me. Did they suffer?"

"No. I'm not proud of what I did and it's the only killing I've ever done. You have to believe me."

Edwin looked at this goliath who had ruined his life. "What happens now? I came here to kill you."

"You did and it was a stupid move. I'll keep the gun and you can go back to wherever you've come from. I'm not a killer but you have something on me. If I ever see you around here again, I will kill you. No ifs no buts, understand?"

Edwin rose slowly and nodded. He knew this giant could probably kill him with one hand. He felt relieved but still wished to have his revenge on this man. As his head cleared from the blow his thought process hadn't caught up. He needed to think. The giant was walking away.

Edwin felt low. This was not what he'd planned. As he slowly walked back to his car his mind began to work. He thought things through. He realised he'd lost the gun. This wasn't planned but maybe it was for the best. He'd taken his revenge on the four men who set him up. He knew his killing days were over. He suddenly thought that he might anonymously report Nick Ralph to the police as the killer of his wife and son. As he walked, he smiled. He remembered another inmate telling him that if you could get the police to do your dirty work you would never be caught. With a fresh purpose to his stride, Edwin approached his hired Jaguar. He realised the loss of the gun was a bonus. He'd have to get rid of it anyway. This way Nick Ralph had it and if any questions were asked, Nick Ralph would have to answer them. Edwin spotted a large green wheelie bin parked on the opposite side of the road from his car. He stripped off his raincoat, removed his cap and threw them into the bin followed by the pair of latex gloves he'd been wearing.

Before starting the Jaguar Edwin took a few minutes to compose himself. He felt contented. His mission was over. Once he'd reported Nick Ralph everything would be done. He could relax. He pushed the start button on the car and set off to his hotel. He would enjoy the evening meal he'd promised himself even though Ralph was still alive, but he had a solution to that problem. All was well with the world.

His mind once more turned to Connie. He regretted having to shut her out and considered calling her. He thought one more romp for old times would be the icing on the cake. He considered this for some time as he drove but eventually dismissed the idea no matter how appealing it might be. Connie was in the past. A new bright future awaited him.

***

Friday, February 18 was the start of Edwin Somerset's new life. He lay in his hotel bed totally relaxed. He'd drunk more last night than he intended but told himself it was allowed as a celebration. He had finished his mission and followed the advice he'd received from his fellow prisoners. He'd killed four people and had escaped the police. He had a plan to allow the police to take care of the fifth person he'd hoped to kill. His money was safely being legitimised by the Scottish legal system and he was about to have a week in New York before returning to take up his place in society as Edwin Somerset.

His flight to New York was at two p.m. and he looked at the bedside clock. Because of his excessive alcohol last night, he'd slept in. The clock showed 9.28 a.m. Edwin smiled. He didn't feel hung over. He felt good and relaxed. He'd have a late breakfast, pack, take his hire car back and enjoy the promised champagne in the Concord Lounge at Heathrow Airport. He decided to leave the hotel at eleven after he had checked out and paid his bill by cash. He had the balance of the hundred thousand he'd started with in his newly bought briefcase. It totalled sixty-four thousand pounds.

The drive to the airport took only ten minutes. Edwin followed the return hire car signs and drove into the compound to be met by an Avis employee. Edwin got out of the vehicle and handed over the rental documents. The employee took the documents and scanned the bar code using a portable scanner.

"That's fine, sir. I've just got to log you back in and then I'll get you your bill. I understand you're paying cash?"

"That's right. I think I've got money to come back but please keep it and put it to a charity."

The attendant looked shocked. "I'll have to ask my manager, sir. Please hold on, I'll only be a minute."

Edwin removed his suitcase from the boot and waited. He didn't realise the compound was empty of all Avis employees. As he stood with his back to the car, he heard a shout.

"Armed police. Turn round and put your hands on top of the car."

Edwin was stunned but did as instructed. Two police officers wearing bullet proof vests approached, searched him obviously looking for the gun, pulled his arms behind his back and spun him round so his back was once more to the car. Edwin's initial shock soon wore off. He remembered another inmate, a Scot called Tommy Boyd, telling him how he had talked his way into his first two prison sentences by talking too much in an effort to prove his innocence.

"Say nothing, I learnt the hard way, laddie. Let the cops prove your guilty, you don't have to help them."

As Edwin stood, resolved to say nothing, a tall well-dressed figure appeared in front of him.

"Hello Charlie. We've been looking for you and Connie will be delighted we've caught up with you at last."

Abiding by his strategy of silence Edwin, now once more known as Charlie Robb, said nothing.

Steve nodded to Matt Conway who read Charlie his rights and had him removed to the interview suite at New Scotland Yard.

***

It was two p.m. before the excitement level within Special Resolutions subsided. Steve promised to stand his hand at the local pub to celebrate catching Charlie Robb. Commander Perry Hargreaves arrived to congratulate the team.

The team were in the outer office as Perry arrived and politely made room for the senior officer to find a seat while they mostly stood except Si, who somehow always found something to sit on. In this instance he was behind his own desk.

"Well done all of you. A great result and I'll see you all get the credit. Four murders off our books in less than two weeks, magnificent!" The commander was clearly elated by the team's success and Steve thought he would waste no time boasting to other senior officers about how his team had cracked the case.

"Thank you, sir. He's been arrested and charged. He's being processed now. We'll start to interview him later today."

Perry gave a broad grin. "Bloody well done all of you. Now, fill me in. How did you get him?"

Steve who was standing by his own office door, nodded in the direction of Bob Class who was leaning against his desk.

"It was all down to Bob, sir. Go on Bob, tell the commander."

A hesitant DC Robert Class looked around the room and his gaze settled on Perry Hargreaves.

"Well, sir. We were fairly certain Charlie Robb was our man. We thought he must be staying in hotels, and we got a lead. Unfortunately, by the time we got there he'd checked out. The DCI thought he must also be renting a car, so we started trawling rental car companies, but it was really difficult because they operate a worldwide reservation system."

Bob paused to see if the commander was following. Satisfied, he carried on. "We agreed to call it a night last night, but I came back at eight as I had an idea." Bob was warming to his tale and was becoming more impressive.

"We had the suspect's driving licence number from DVLA but because of the hire companies' data base system we couldn't simply call up the licence. I remembered that some time ago anyone renting a car on a UK licence had to have a unique number issued by DVLA confirming their licence was valid. I put Robb's licence number into the DVLA historic data base and saw he'd been given one of these numbers. After that it was simple. I inputted the licence and DVLA reference and bingo, the uniqueness of the two gave me the information that Robb had hired a car from Avis, but unfortunately, he'd already returned it. I tried again and got another hire reference, this time for Hertz, but again the rental had been returned. I did it a third time, but again the car had been returned."

The commander, in order to be seen to be part of this group, raised a question.

"So obviously our man was changing cars every few days?"

Bob replied, "Yes, sir, DS Griffiths told me it's an old gangster's trick to try to stay ahead of us."

Perry Hargreaves nodded, and Bob carried on.

"So, for the fourth time I inputted the data and got another hit. This time he'd hired a Jaguar from Avis at Heathrow, but the rental was still open. I called the DCI and told him." Bob looked in Steve's direction.

"It was around four a.m. when Bob called. We discussed the implications and decided if we staked out the place then we'd get him when he returned the car, so I called the lads in and alerted firearms. After all, we knew he had a gun."

Si, sitting at his desk, mumbled under his breath but loud enough for everyone to hear.

"At bloody five a.m. and no overtime that I'm entitled to. My lady friend wasn't impressed."

The commander gave Steve a quizzical look. The DCI shrugged; Si was being Si.

"OK, so you staked out the rental car company?"

"Yes, sir. The rental still had a week to run but we got lucky. We briefed the Avis staff and waited. The rest as they say is history."

"Bloody great. All of you, really well done. I'll put something behind the bar tonight. No doubt a celebration is in order?"

"Thank you, sir." His money behind the bar later tonight would be welcomed.

Perry Hargreaves stood, smiled all round and taking Steve's arm ushered him into his office.

"This case is solid, isn't it Steve? You've got the evidence for the CPS?"

"We've got some, sir. A mixture of statements and circumstantial, you know, the way it always is. We'll sweat him a bit for the rest, but I'd say if we went to the CPS now, they'd give us the green light."

A beaming smile appeared on the commander's face. He slapped the DCI on the back.

"Good man, Steve. The commissioner will be delighted, keep me posted." Commander Perry Hargreaves left to seek an interview with the commissioner of the Metropolitan Police to give her the news that one of his units had solved a quadruple murder in record time. The DCI smiled. Some things never changed.

Steve returned to the outer office. Matt Conway could tell he had something on his mind and knew not to enquire. The DCI looked far away.

"Matt, let's go over to Brompton Road. I want to meet Major Havers, I've put it off too long. Si, you stay here and give Bob a hand with the reports. Matt and I will start interviewing Robb when we get back."

Si stared back at his boss. "What about my overtime? As a sergeant I'm entitled but the big bosses have cancelled all overtime payments. All I get is time off in lieu. I can't spend time in lieu you know. Me and my lady need cash."

Steve had realised that with Si, he never knew if the sergeant was being serious or simply stirring for effect. However, he conceded Si had a point. A weary smiled appeared on Steve's face as he looked at his insubordinate detective sergeant. "I'll see what I can do, Si. After all, the Met wouldn't want to lose an officer of your standing over a bit of overtime."

As Steve and Matt left the outer office Steve heard Si say, "I'll hold you to that, sir!"

***

Steve had been quiet on the drive to the Brompton Road headquarters of the government's secret killing squad. As they approached the DCI turned to Matt who was driving.

"You know, Matt, I have no idea what I'm doing. I know I want to talk to the bloke in the black balaclava who was there when Poppy was killed." Steve paused. "I can't get her out of my mind, Matt, if only I'd listened. If I'd given her more backup she would still be here."

DI Matt Conway knew better than to say anything. He just drove waiting for the best detective he'd ever worked with clear this demon from his soul.

Steve continued, "I'm hoping Major Havers can introduce me to his agent. Maybe if I hear directly from him, I can get a sense of closure." Steve deliberately brightened up. He knew he was using Matt as a sounding board and that the DI didn't deserve it.

"Anyway, let's hope the old bugger is in."

The remainder of the journey was silent. Matt parked on the pavement, left the 'POLICE ON DUTY' sign on the dashboard and the pair entered what was now a laundrette at 166, Brompton Road.

They were greeted by the lady known as 'Mother'. Si had described her but both officers were impressed by how big she was. Before Steve could say anything or present his warrant card, Mother stood but didn't move.

"I take it you're the police. The major said if you came back, I was to let you in."

Mother keyed in a code to the door that led to the rear. Without speaking, both officers entered, and Mother closed the door behind them. It was 2.55 p.m.

The major was in his small office. He instantly recognised the DCI from the last conference in Whitehall. He stood and awaited the arrival of the two police officers.

"DCI Burt, nice to see you again." He extended his hand for Steve to shake and after Steve had introduced Matt, all three sat down.

It was only a few days since Steve had met the major, but he looked older, more drawn. If Steve didn't know better, he would have thought he was ill.

After a few trivial comments Steve got to the point. He explained he knew one of the major's assassins had been at the home of Judge Plough-Henderson when DC Amelia Cooper had been shot.

"All I want to do, major, is to talk to him. To hear first-hand what took place. I'm not interested now in who he has killed or your part in these government-sponsored killings. I just want to hear about Poppy."

Major Havers leant back and put his hands behind his head. He stared at a spot above the DCI's head for a long time without talking. He eventually produced a bottle of whisky and poured himself a generous measure. He offered his guests a tot, but they refused. Major Havers took a large slug of the liquid.

"It's all over, Steve. The crap you were fed at that meeting was all smoke and mirrors designed to make you go away. Sir Patrick Bond was scared you'd dig into my cases and bring murder charges against me and my operatives, maybe even him."

He opened his top drawer and produced a piece of buff coloured A4 sized paper. He slid it across his desk towards Steve.

"That's the last straw. The one that broke the camel's back you might say. It's a kill order on you, DCI Steven Burt, to be executed on word from the head of MI6, Sir Patrick Bond."

The major's hand was shaking slightly as he drank more whisky and continued. "I've been a soldier all my life, inspector, and have never disobeyed an order until now." The major nodded at the paper. "That's one order I cannot obey. You were given all the guff about this unit being disbanded, that Max Ho was to be the last authorised killing and that I had resigned my commission. All rubbish for your benefit." Major Havers finished his whisky and poured another.

Steve was in a state of shock. He never imagined he would be a target for a professional killer, plus Patrick Bond had at one time claimed to be a friend. His mind was spinning but he told himself he'd deal with this issue later. The major continued, "Well, it happened just as you were told. I resigned this morning and have shredded all my files on our work here, the cases we carried out on behalf of the government, the identities of my operatives, everything." The major was a bit drunk as he swung his arm in a grand gesture around his office. A wicked conspiratorial grin appeared on his face. In what was almost a theatrical performance of a drunk, the major leant over his desk.

In a loud whisper he said, "But I copied everything onto a memory stick before I shredded the hard copies. It's insurance you see." Major Havers pulled a small envelope from his jacket pocket and slid it across the table towards Steve who lifted it.

"That's the evidence. If anything happens to me, promise me you'll use what's on that stick? I know these people. If you let it be known you have that information, you'll be safe. In fact, we'll both be untouchable. Promise me?" The major was almost pleading.

Steve knew a little about the major's operation and some of the killings it had carried out. He felt if what the major had told him was true, then this memory stick was a danger to a lot of influential people. The DCI saw this needed clear thought and put the envelope in his own jacket pocket. He stole a glance at Matt who looked confused.

"Major, I appreciate your honesty especially the kill order on me." Steve gave a small smile although he didn't feel like smiling. "I promise you we will consider how best to use this information. You've obviously had a traumatic few days but as I said, I'm only here at this time to meet the operative who was present when my colleague was shot."

The major took a smaller sip of the amber liquid and leant on his desk; a tear appeared in the corners of his eyes.

"Ah! Yes, Eric Stokes, ex-staff sergeant Parachute Regiment. The best I ever had. A good operative but above all else, a good man. You've already met him. He was in Max Ho's apartment when you and your team were there. Poor Eric, he allowed a black belt in martial arts to kick him in the head. You must have seen him. He was in a coma for two weeks and I had to agree to switch off his life support. He had no family except the army. I'm afraid Eric Stokes is dead, chief inspector, whatever he saw died with him."

Steve and Matt left the major to his retirement and his whisky. As they walked past Mother, Steve looked at her. "Take care of him, see he gets home OK." He gave Mother one of his business cards. "If you or the major ever need me, call any one of these numbers."

The detectives were lost in their own thoughts during the drive back to New Scotland Yard.

Epilogue

It took several weeks for the case against Charlie Robb for the four murders to be accepted by the Crown Prosecution Service. Steve, Matt and Si all tried to break down Charlie's 'no comment' defence. The CPS were initially unwilling to take the case forward as in their words, "the evidence is largely circumstantial."

The team worked at putting all the evidence together. They had Keith, the gun dealer, ready to swear he sold a .22 pistol to Charlie, and it had been .22 rounds that had killed each victim. The problem was they couldn't put that weapon in Charlie's hand. This was circumstantial.

They had Colin Clark's girlfriend's positive identification of Charlie as the man who had called looking for Colin on the day he was killed. Again circumstantial.

They had Connie O'Sullivan's statement confirming that Charlie had admitted the killings to her but again, without witnesses to the conversation it was circumstantial.

Charlie Robb had been well tutored in prison. He knew how to play the game but like all would be master criminals he eventually slipped up. He was so keen to see Nick Ralph pay for killing his wife and son that he gave the DCI Ralph's address and said he was the killer. This was the only time Charlie spoke during his interviews other than to say, 'no comment.'

Steve wasn't really interested in an old unsolved murder, but his copper's code wouldn't allow him to ignore the information, so a week after Charlie Robb was arrested, Matt and Si visited Nick Ralph at his flat in Tower Hamlets. Ralph wasn't too happy at being arrested and produced a .22 pistol to try and make good his escape. Si Griffiths had dealt with men like Ralph most of his CID career and thought it unlikely the big man would shoot. Si was right and after a tense five-minute stand-off, Nick Ralph surrendered to Si, together with the .22 gun. This was the weapon he had taken from Charlie a few weeks previously.

Nick Ralph talked freely and identified Charlie as the person that had threatened him with the pistol. The team at last had the concrete evidence linking Charlie Robb to the murder weapon that they had been missing. Everything fell into place when ballistics confirmed that the .22 calibre weapon was the murder weapon.

Once Charlie was confronted with this evidence he gave in and confessed to the four shootings. He explained to the detectives his motive for shooting these individuals and swore Connie knew nothing about it. Steve thought this gesture might help at Connie's trial and felt it showed Charlie Robb was a decent man failed by the system.

The case was finally wrapped up and the CPS were at last happy to go to court. No trial date has yet been set and Charlie Robb is on remand.

Bob Class, having prepared all the documents for the trial, has as predicted been transferred to a regional crime unit. His replacement has still to be appointed.

Si Griffiths received another commendation for his part in disarming Nick Ralph but is still awaiting any overtime payments. His girlfriend is happy he is still a policeman and to be living with a hero.

Matt Conway continues as Steve's second in command and was also given a commendation for his part in the arrest of Nick Ralph.

Major Simon Havers resigned from the army and retired to Cornwall safe in the knowledge that his copy of the memory stick was safely lodged with his solicitor. His unit was disbanded, the laundrette closed, and the shop is currently empty awaiting a new tenant. A search carried out by Bob Class showed that the owner of the building is the government.

Steve Burt, having closed the case, finally realised the guilt he felt over the death of Poppy was unrealistic. The meeting with Major Havers had helped him find the closure he sought.

He had the memory stick he'd received from the major and with Inspector Terry Harvey's help had printed out the contents. It recorded each authorised killing over the past three years. There were many more than Steve expected. Terry Harvey copied the stick and locked it in his safe.

The DCI had an uncomfortable meeting with Sir Patrick Bond, the head of MI6, about the kill order Sir Patrick had raised on him. The major had been correct when he said the memory stick was the DCI's insurance policy. Sir Patrick was taken aback by its existence. Steve was safe from future kill orders and was glad to be rid of Sir Patrick and his sleazy secret world of spies and dirty tricks. There would be no more Max Ho type cases.

He and Alison with their daughter Rosie's help had worked their way through a mass of holiday brochures and Alison convinced her husband that a ten-day break in Disney Orlando would be the perfect family holiday. His fiftieth birthday break was still to come.

The DCI is now sunning himself in Florida, recharging his inner self ready for his next case. Alison and Rosie are at Epcot leaving Steve to relax for the day.

DCI Steve Burt is due back behind his desk in less than five days.

THE END

Thank you for choosing this book. If you have enjoyed it could I please ask you to post a review online from wherever you bought it. Every review on social media or a book review platform is much appreciated and helps others to find their next book.

The previous books in this series are available at amazon.co.uk and all good bookshops.

John Reid is the author of the DCI Steve Burt series of mystery murders and a complete list of the series can be found at
www.dci-steveburt.com.

Facebook page – John Reid Author or Instagram – johnreidauthor - where details of upcoming books and new series will be available.